~

Praise for *East of T ... of Hell*

"In *East of Texas, West of Hell*, Rod Davis crafts a story that begs you to look away but keeps you glued fast to the page with machete-sharp prose. Fans of *South, America* will relish the return of Davis's workmanlike, capable storytelling, while new readers will go clamoring for his every published word. Easily the best page-turner of the year." — **ERYK PRUITT, author of** *What We Reckon*

"Jack Prine is on the road again, which is bad news for the bad guys he's hunting. Rod Davis's riveting new novel would best be read with Warren Zevon turned up loud. Send lawyers, guns, and money—and maybe a voodoo priest and a coroner. *East of Texas, West of Hell* should come wrapped in crime-scene tape, or its own body bag." — **MARK MCDONALD, award-winning journalist and author of** *Off the X*

"Rod Davis is the real deal, a storyteller of immense talent. *East of Texas, West of Hell* has it all: gripping characters, a page-turning plot, and a whole lot more. Don't miss this book." — **HARRY HUNSICKER, author of** *The Devil's Country* **and the former executive vice president of the Mystery Writers of America**

"Attention lovers of Southern noir, Grit Lit, or simply the pulse-pounding, twist-a-minute thriller: a master of the form is back with an edge-of-your-seat read. Rod Davis's *East of Texas, West of Hell* starts at full speed and never slows down. With a plot as complex and ultimately illuminating as the existential mysteries that Davis explores, *East of Texas, West of Hell* delivers not just a gripping story peopled with jump-off-the-page characters, but a heartfelt meditation on life, justice, and the murky areas in between." — **SARAH BIRD, award-winning author of** *Daughter of a Daughter of a Queen*

"Rod Davis's lead character Jack Prine takes us on a wild ride across the South from Savannah to the ranches of West Texas, following the blood-splattered trails of criminals, con men, lowlifes, fascists, and other troublemakers to save lives and right wrongs. A telling so fiery you can see the steam rising from the pages." — **JOE NICK PATOSKI, author of** *Willie Nelson: An Epic Life* **and** *Austin to ATX*

"In *East of Texas, West of Hell*, Rod Davis goes assuredly into a landscape of crime fiction mapped by writers like Elmore Leonard and Ross MacDonald, but his own tough guy sleuth, Jack Prine, is an original. Prine is a compelling and entertaining narrator, an aging polymath well versed in violence but also Shakespeare and Buddhism. Brought to life in Davis's beautifully spare prose, he is hard to put down in more ways than one." — **SEAN MITCHELL, former reporter and critic for the** *Los Angeles Times* **and editor of Dallas's first alternative weekly,** *The Iconoclast*

"Davis's *East of Texas* is wild and sexy, his *West of Hell* harsh and lawless, but both needles in the compass remind us of the sort of invisible reality one single place can construct in perfect symbiosis." — **DR. RUBÉN OLAGUE, former CNN correspondent and vice president for news at LBI Media**

"In his long career as a journalist and author, Rod Davis has always been a master of place. In *East of Texas, West of Hell*, his craft is again on display, painting deep, tactile pictures of oil patch motels, sticky riverfronts, and gleaming Southern cities. This skill marries beautifully with Davis's particular style of noir, at once languid and propulsive. He expertly sets a mood while fully defining the cast of wayward souls we meet along the way. This deepens the thrill of Jack Prine's journey through his beloved South on a self-described 'doomed rescue mission and righteous killing spree.' This is Davis's greatest work to date." — **ERIC CELESTE, longtime city columnist and contributing editor, Dallas's** *D Magazine*

~~~

EAST OF TEXAS, WEST OF HELL

East of Texas, West of Hell

A Novel

Rod Davis

NewSouth Books

Montgomery

NewSouth Books
105 S. Court Street
Montgomery, AL 36104

Copyright © 2020 by Rod Davis
All rights reserved under International and Pan-American Copyright Conventions.
Published in the United States by NewSouth Books, a division of NewSouth, Inc.,
Montgomery, Alabama.

Library of Congress Cataloging-in-Publication Data

Names: Davis, Rod, 1946– author.
Title: East of Texas, west of hell: a novel / Rod Davis.
Description: Montgomery : NewSouth Books, 2020 | Series: Jack Prine; book 2.
Identifiers: LCCN 2019058707 (print) | LCCN 2019058708 (ebook)
| ISBN 9781588384164 (trade paperback) | ISBN 9781588384171 (epub)
Subjects: GSAFD: Suspense fiction.
Classification: LCC PS3604.A975 E22 2020 (print) | LCC PS3604.A975
  (ebook) | DDC 813/.6--dc23
LC record available at https://lccn.loc.gov/2019058707
LC ebook record available at https://lccn.loc.gov/2019058708

First Printing

Design by Randall Williams

Printed in the United States of America

Just give me one thing that I can hold on to
To believe in this living is just a hard way to go
"ANGEL FROM MONTGOMERY," JOHN PRINE
1946–2020

~~~

EAST OF TEXAS, WEST OF HELL

"All life is suffering."

— First Noble Truth

1

I squatted in the soggy backyard jungle behind the meth house and studied what was left of the two bodies. Nobody was around, and likely nobody had been. If so, they'd left the remains as found—half-devoured by dogs or raccoons or whatever else roamed this battered neighborhood southwest of Atlanta's big towers and big money. The faces weren't really there anymore. Neither was most of her torso.

They were slumped at impossible anatomical angles against a vine-shrouded oak. I couldn't tell if they had been tortured or merely executed and mauled. The entry and exit wounds on each remained obvious. The male corpse was black, maybe Latino. The female was white, so it wasn't Rose. Which was a good thing. But a very bad thing if Rose had been mixed up with them. Or with whoever had done this.

First time I ever saw a dead body I vomited. I was twelve, volunteering in my small Texas town to search for a popular high school girl who'd fallen into a flood-swollen river. Fish and turtles had gotten to her pretty bad.

All the kids had to write their names on sticker tags in case we, too, disappeared. My "Jack Prine" got blurred when I slipped into the water trying to get a better view, pissing off a fireman who had to grab me roughly by the arm just before I decorated his boots with my breakfast.

Subsequent years and jobs covering mortal mayhem as a TV reporter or covering up more extreme mayhem for the military had all but numbed the impact of witnessing human remains. Still, this was fucking barbaric.

Night was descending fast and I needed to move along, but I couldn't stop staring. I knew that led nowhere good. I shouldn't have been there in the first place. But I was. Elle had called.

It was almost 5 a.m. She was so shaken she could barely talk. She asked me to check on her "runaway daughter" without so much as a hello or hope-I-didn't-wake-you-up. As if we'd had regular crack-of-dawn conversations instead of once-a-year awkward small talk around the holidays.

Could I come to Atlanta as soon as possible? She said she had been up all night making phone calls to Rose but nobody answered and now she thought Rose may or may not have been kidnapped. May or may not willingly have moved in with some kind of artistic wannabes, who may or may not have been dealing meth. She couldn't call the police either way. I made a lame joke about having heard that about the police three years ago, when I found her brother Terrell dead in a New Orleans gutter. How we met. But it just fell into a silence that confirmed how scared she was.

Flights were full and I barely booked one at double the usual fare on Delta to the Hartsfield airport. It got me into Atlanta by sundown and then to the address Elle had given me, which she said was the only thing she had.

Now darkness was closing in and I was staring at gore behind a house I almost couldn't find in a neighborhood that no longer mattered. I could hear thunder in the distance. Storms had been sweeping through the South for two weeks.

I eased slowly around the corpses. Waist-high weeds squished under the soles of my old Luccheses. Heavy rains had transformed the yard into a Rousseau canvas, primeval and lush and vivid and latent with violence. If the city had ever cited the place for code violations, nobody'd done anything about it.

A dog barked somewhere down the street. That meant other dogs might still be in the yard. The gate at the side of the house was wide open. I'd used it coming in. No canines, but it seemed likely that strays or worse would return with the night. I shifted my attention to the surrounding neighborhood, listened for any unusual sounds—alarms, loud voices, sirens. It was quiet enough for me to hear my own footfalls. The only real noise came from interstate traffic in the distance.

The house itself was also dark, except for the faint glow of an electric light, probably from an inner room. It gave just enough illumination to convince me the best and maybe only way to go in was from a torn screen door hanging ajar at the back porch, which was basically a concrete slab. I started walking that way when I noticed something in the shrubs nearest the tree.

I hoped what was sticking out wasn't another body part, and it wasn't.

It was a machete. Blood and gore on the blade almost to the hilt. You can't carry sidearms on planes, so among other haste-driven omissions, I'd come here without any kind of protection. This would do as a field expedient. I wiped it as clean as I could on the grass and went on to the house.

Behind the screen, the plywood door sported a smashed-in hole about the size of a good boot kick. I pushed it open and stepped into a bare room with chipped concrete floors and an old porcelain sink next to a washer and dryer. It was a basement utility room, probably used at some point in the old house's life by the "help."

I took narrow, uneven wooden steps upstairs to a faded linoleum-floored kitchen that looked like it had been attacked by feral hogs. The living room was similarly wrecked—broken TV, overturned couch, carpet wet with wine, urine, and blood. I paused to listen at a stairwell leading up to the second floor. Nothing.

Upstairs the three bedrooms told the same story. The light I had noticed was from the bathroom. The shower stall was blood-spattered and the curtain in tatters. The wall tiles were punctured with bullet holes and what looked like a shotgun blast pattern.

I opened the closet doors in each room, machete at the ready, but found nothing except a few clothes, women's and men's, snaking down from wire hangers, as if they had been not quite in the grasp of whoever had left in a hurry. The only body belonged to a yellow lab on a floor mattress, curled up over a big wound in its abdomen. Its only crime probably had been to bark, or be alive in the wrong place.

I went back to the stairwell landing and leaned against a wall, catching my focus as much as my breath. At some point in the future a cop might be in here doing the same, trying to figure it all out. I wasn't one, and didn't want to run into one. I didn't especially like or trust them, and in any case didn't have the same professional motive. The sooner I was gone, the better.

I walked downstairs, rinsed off the machete in a stained sink next to the washer, and wiped it with paper towels. I also wiped the door handle and faucet, the only other things I'd touched. I went back outside and tossed the machete back into the shrubs, then stuffed the towel I'd used into my jeans. I looked over the scene a last time and walked to the gate, taking advantage of the knee-high weeds to wipe spots of blood and mud off the soles and heels of my boots, the way I'd learned as a boy to clean off cow shit.

I crossed the street to my rental car, a boxy brown Dodge, alert to anyone or anything around me. I unlocked the car door, reconned the area again. I eased away from the curb as normally as possible, glancing into the side mirror to see the house recede in the yellow haze of the emerging streetlights.

After a few blocks, I called Elle. Just to relay the basics. I'm not sure even she took a breath until I said Rose wasn't there. As for the two corpses, I gave a quick description and Elle said she had no idea who they were. I added that I was okay. Not that she'd asked. I said I'd be at her place in an hour to elaborate but didn't want to talk more on the phone.

Her house in the Highlands wasn't an hour away, but I took the time to lay a false trail to see if anyone followed. It seemed a prudent precaution and not just military spycraft. If I'd been spotted I'd have ended up dead or in custody.

That gave me plenty of time to consider what I really had witnessed. What business, if any, it could be to me, or to Elle, or to Rose. Nothing popped up because I had no frame of reference. The only thing I knew for sure was that the imagined serenity I had been creating in the Big Easy since I'd last seen Elle had been deconstructed to hell.

<center>~~~</center>

2

A little before nine, I was knocking on the door on the wrap-around wooden front porch at her white- and yellow-trimmed house. A light came on and she came out, framed like an angel. She gave me a hug and quick kiss on my cheek. I took it and liked it. It was the kind of greeting you give to an ex that means it's going to stay that way—but with just the slightest extra movement in a muscle in the lips that says there is still a crack in the defense. You can tell you've been in love when you think like that. There are a million songs about it.

I wiped my boots on the doormat and followed her inside. The wooden floors were polished and gleaming. I hated to clunk across them. She didn't care. She asked me if I wanted a drink. I said I did. In the kitchen she poured me a Jack and water. I liked that she remembered. She'd already been working on a glass of red wine.

We did a quick and somewhat awkward toast "To Rose." I downed most of mine with one swallow. "Might as well see the house," she said. Shrinks like her would probably have labeled the offer of a tour of the two-story house a deliberate evasion of reality. But I was okay with it. A little evasion gave us time to breathe.

It was much larger than my rent house in the Marigny, and almost as spare in furniture and accoutrements, but hers had quality and taste. I knew from our few contacts in the last couple of years that Atlanta had been good for her. She'd set up her own practice as a counselor. A side deal with the school district gave her plenty of extra work with kids from troubled backgrounds. She didn't need the money, of course, as the sole living heir to the Barnett estate.

The walls of every room were painted different colors, ocean blue to crimson. Both bathrooms glistened with stainless steel and glass. Her bedroom was lavender with little more than a queen-size bed, dresser, and expensive-looking striped chairs. Not a room in which I would be spending the night. I had an open return flight reserved at 11:30 p.m. that would get me back to New Orleans pretty late. It was the best I could book on emergency notice.

The tour took maybe five minutes, as did the illusion of normality. We settled in the downstairs study, also perfectly appointed with the desk, walled bookshelves, matching sofa and chairs, and marble-topped coffee table for visitors. It occurred to me she might sometimes use the room for clients. She said she did but only for special cases. She was connected to a group of doctors and therapists who occasionally did off-the-books volunteer counseling with abuse victims who didn't have money for hospitals or whose legal troubles prevented them from going there.

For now, the coffee table was covered with photos of Rose. More were in a wicker basket. We sat on the sofa and sifted through them. She said she'd been doing this since she called me. She excused herself for a moment and went back into the kitchen. I gave her my glass. She came back with a refill and a faux antique postcard that had been pinned to her fridge. It was postmarked Beaufort, South Carolina—not far from Parris Island, where the Marines train.

On the front was a retro Kodachrome-style image of some quaint downtown "Shoppes." On the back, delicate handwriting that said, "Hey, Mom—checking out the beach life here in S.C. Beaucoup high-end restaurants I could work in. Strange voudou town they call Alafia just down the highway. Auntie knows about it and they know her. Now up to Savannah with Kirby for a job interview. Don't worry—Rose."

I looked at every picture. At nineteen, the girl had grown into a beauty. Her eyes were like her mom's, but with enough sadness around the edges, at least in that shot of her on the porch swing, to let you know it hadn't been a picnic coming up in a foster home.

I could see in Elle's quick-changing expressions that she was absorbing the news of what I'd found about as expected. Hard. Of course, she was glad that Rose wasn't among the horrors, but she was considerably anxious about where her daughter might be. Who, she said, actually wasn't a runaway. It was just something she had told me when she called because that was how scared she was. Rose had actually been living at home, although she often went on trips or spent the weekends with friends.

I let the "runaway" lie slide, chalking it up to Elle's fear, which was palpable. More important was where she'd gotten the tip about the house. She said it was from a friend of Rose's that she barely knew. I pressed. She said it was from Kirby, the one mentioned in the postcard. Elle had only met her once, briefly, when picking Rose up from the restaurant. Kirby was blond, cute, funny. I said the dead woman at the house in Atlanta was white but had black hair. Her face was unrecognizable.

Elle walked to a window facing the street. She said she wanted to go out on the porch and listen for the storm coming in. I said I hoped it waited until after my flight. I helped her put the photos and postcard back in the basket.

The night had cooled just enough to be tolerable and we sat on lacquered black wicker chairs at either side of a matching table. It seemed impossibly Southern and pleasant.

You'd think the alcohol would have helped but it didn't. We stared at the stars when the clouds briefly parted and exchanged quick sentences about what we'd been up to in the past year. Mostly just awkward pauses. I don't know if she was thinking about how it had all started between us, but I was. The beating, the shooting, the chasing, the stabbing, the bodies from New Orleans to Alabama and back. That Rose's father, Trey Barnett, was the decadent white scion who had raped Elle. Who had murdered her brother Terrell. Who was half-brother to them both. Whom Elle and I had killed in his trendy art studio in New Orleans by plunging a screwdriver into his chest. And whose complicated family fortune all ended up with Elle, the sole survivor of incest, "mixed marriage," heartbreak, and infinite layers of deceit.

We didn't venture into that at all. Nothing was there anymore anyway.

The small talk was weird, but sometimes people have to say things around the edges before they get to the heart. For Elle, the heart was Rose. Always was, always would be.

Looking out at the night, she told me again how she and Rose had reconnected. I would say how she had "found" the daughter she had given up at birth, but it was actually the other way around. Rose had turned up two years after running away from foster families and living with so-called friends from Athens, where the last fosters had raised her. Then on an ever-changing circuit to Nashville, Charlotte, Birmingham, and even Oxford, Elle's hometown.

During that time Rose had mastered the itinerant's ways of making do. With her looks she had easily found jobs—mostly as a waitress, a couple of times in a short-order kitchen. Eventually, the grapevine of relatives and acquaintances had informed her of Terrell's murder and her mom's whereabouts and inheritance. She just rang the doorbell one afternoon. Stayed. Started working it through. No way she'd go back to high school so she breezed a GED and enrolled in an Atlanta culinary college two-year program for budding chefs. That led to a good gig at Viktor's, a pricey steak house in

Buckhead. And that led to—pretty much what I was trying to figure out.

All under an assumed name: Carla Simms. Easy to say and easy to forget. Something else Rose had learned that was important to survival. She told Elle that some of the people she'd lived with before coming home didn't need to know where she was anymore, or ever. Elle had waited for elaboration, knowing the hurt was hard to cough up. She didn't like the fake ID, but she couldn't disagree with the motive. And she didn't challenge Rose on it. The mending hadn't gotten that far yet.

Rose going to Savannah wasn't the surprise, Elle said. The surprise was how a job interview got routed through a meth house in Atlanta. If that was how it went down.

I leaned on the rail of the porch as she finished the story of their past. I let it settle before I got to the present. It wasn't good. I told her answers wouldn't come easy—and if she really thought the trail led out of the carnage in the yard, the answers would likely be very bad. Her look at me was hard enough to snap steel.

We stared a little longer into dark clouds and space and the tree-lined street. It wasn't "like" something wasn't being said. It was definitely that something wasn't being said. I was going to need a good deal more information. But I couldn't see getting it right away.

WE WENT BACK TO the study. Elle said she remembered a few more photos, more recent, and said I should look at them. Especially the one that showed Rose and Kirby together outside a coffee house in Atlanta. She pulled them from a drawer in her desk.

They were gorgeous. All smiles at the coffee shop. But the free-spirit thing they fronted for the camera wasn't convincing. Kirby was strikingly thin. Elle said the shot was taken two weeks ago. She saw the expression on my face.

"What?"

"Any chance she could have dyed her hair? Kirby, I mean?"

"I don't know. She could have. She did that a lot."

"Did she do meth?"

"Who?"

"Kirby."

Elle looked away the way someone does who knows the answer but doesn't want to say. "I don't know."

"She has a look."

"Rose didn't do drugs at all. She was over all that."

"Kirby, though?"

"You think that girl was Kirby? At that house? You said she had black hair, not blond."

"I didn't know what I was looking for."

"Jesus."

"Yeah." I put the photo down. "The tip you got for me. You never told me who it was from."

Elle diverted her eyes. "You wouldn't know who it was anyway."

"It was a friend of Rose, though?"

"Of Kirby."

"Who? What kind of friend?" I could hear my voice sharpen.

"Blaine someone. He was Kirby's boyfriend. An ex, I think. You know how they are these days."

"And he called you . . . why?"

I was unconsciously tapping my finger on the desk. She put her hand over mine until I stopped.

"All he said was that he was trying to find Rose and wondered if I had heard from her."

"Yeah?"

"And I said I thought she'd gone to Savannah with Kirby."

"What did he say?"

"He said he thought they actually might be in Atlanta, at a house of someone Carla—that's what they all called my baby—knew from culinary college."

"Fuck."

"I knew the house. Rose had gone over there before after her car battery died and I had to pick her up. The yard hadn't been mowed in ages and it looked like nobody lived there. I wrote down the address in my day planner. That was a couple of months back. But when Blaine called—it was two days ago—he said Kirby wasn't answering her phone, and would I try to call Rose? I said I would. She didn't answer, either. I gave it another day and then I started freaking out. And that's how I ended up calling you."

I looked at her.

"I would have driven over there myself," she added. "I don't know. If I hadn't reached you I would have. But I did. Reach you."

I could feel my jaw muscles working. "It's okay. I had a free evening."

"And so."

"And so."

Again, I didn't rebuke her for shading or omitting details. She was wrapped up bad. Real bad.

I checked my watch and asked her a few more things about Kirby and where they might have gone in Savannah. She didn't know much and said she would try to find out where they might have stayed for the job interview. We both knew the timeline for missing kids. The only question was whether she was missing or had just gone dark on her own.

There was just enough Elle still didn't know about Rose to keep the answers vague. Except for what I had just seen. I wasn't vague about that.

I told her I would go home, get my stuff in New Orleans, and drive back to Savannah right away. I said she should call me any time she found out anything more. She was now officially terrified. She wanted me to pick her up on the way back from New Orleans, but I said definitely not. Whatever this was going to be, it wasn't going to be for her. We'd been down that path together once, and we were lucky to have lived through it. "Find her," was all she said when I walked away. I couldn't answer.

I sped and ran a red light to the airport but made it to the gate just as the clearly annoyed ticket agent was about to close the jetway. The plane was nearly empty. It was easy to get a window seat. Looking out at the stars fleeting past the wing, I was almost happy.

There had never been any doubt from the moment I took her call back in New Orleans that I would drop everything to help. Until I had found the bodies, I thought it would be what Elle hoped against hope—a false alarm. Still, I was utterly confident I could handle all variables. That I'd bring the girl home to mom. Save the day, damn the cavalry, fools rush in kind of thing.

I would have settled for any of that.

~~~

3

I slept in later than usual the next morning, tired from the flight. I showered, dressed, brewed a pot of chicory coffee. I had no appetite for food. After a second mug I called her. She said there was nothing about the bodies on the morning TV, or in the Atlanta paper. I said I hoped it would take the police a long time. I asked if that storm had come through last night and she said yes, a big one, and I said that was good, too. It would keep the police busy and wash away any footprints I might have left.

What I didn't say was that it would give more time for the scavengers to do their work on the corpses. If it involved cartels or major players or even local scum, it would go into the unsolved case files. The big boys had a way of eradicating their own. No one would care. Like most of us, the cops figured drug dealers exterminating other drug dealers were not doing society a disservice. I told Elle to keep watching, though.

By eleven, I had loaded up my black Jeep Grand Cherokee, my one big splurge after getting rid of the Explorer that had carried Elle and me on the trail of Terrell's murderer. In it were provisions for a long road trip, as well as my small arsenal: a new Remington 12-gauge and a new Colt .45, the military M1911 model, and ammo. All bought from a gun show outside Shreveport where they didn't pay much attention to official forms. One dealer tried to convince me to get a Glock and maybe he was right, but I stuck with old school. The weapons nixed any passing thoughts I'd had about flying back to Atlanta and renting a car. Also, I didn't have any idea where I might be headed, or for how long, other than Savannah. I didn't know how much it would all cost, either, but I had an envelope with a few thou in cash and a barely used credit card I'd set up under an alias a couple of years ago just to see if I could.

I closed the back hatch and looked up and down the street. My mind went into a kind of neutral gear, almost like a daydream. It took me a moment to realize I was just standing in the hot sun on a sidewalk in the

Marigny. Dissociating myself from my physical surroundings had become a thing in the last couple of years. The Buddhists teach you to do that on a Zen cushion, but I'd expanded the boundaries. I don't know exactly why, but at least I was aware of it.

Next thing I knew I was walking into the Quarter. I told myself it would be good to get another coffee and some food before taking off. The hypoglycemia had stabilized because I worked at it, but it could still jump out if I didn't eat right. Mostly I just needed a minute. I needed to get my head straight, and fast.

The Vieux Carré could be good for that. Noisy streets crowded with strangers. Shadows and secrets behind each door. Violence every night. Confession and regret every morning. The constancy of the river's daily redemption.

A bearded guy on a bicycle almost hit me as I crossed a side street headed for an open-front deli bar near Pirate's Alley. A block later a tourist lady in shorts carrying a bag of swag bumped into me and only apologized when I glared like I owned the Quarter. Actually I had probably bumped into her.

I turned a corner and got in the to-go line at the deli. It moved quickly enough. I wolfed down a double egg and bacon croissant within a half-block, then started on the café au lait. I turned down Royal toward the Marigny and on the way paused along the fence behind St. Louis Cathedral to ponder the statue people called Touchdown Jesus. I looked at it the way I had stared at the street outside my house.

June 2003 already. Had it really been three years since Elle and I met? Less than that since 9/11. My high-end tourist business idea had turned out to be about as foolish as it now sounds. So much for the dawn of the new century. The wars in Afghanistan and Iraq didn't help. I'd already lost three friends there. I continued the occasional unauthorized PI work for my Army buddy and lawyer Ray Oubre, mostly to help him out. A little freelance writing and a few road trips here and there to avoid feeling cooped-up. A fleeting and fairly stupid romance with a flight attendant that ended in a draw.

I rarely saw Big Red. It was his insider market tip that tripled our money from Elle, and we were both set up far better than either of us deserved. I moved out of my old apartment, but I liked the Marigny, so when a cottage came up for rent a few blocks away I jumped at it. The owner was a client of Ray's, an expat engineer off in Thailand for at least two years. I liked the place especially because it was surrounded by a spiked black iron fence and a solid steel gate at the driveway.

Once while drinking in a dive on Frenchmen Street, I told a woman with a yat accent on a stool next to me that I was adapting to my adopted city. For some reason it really pissed her off and she moved down the bar as if I'd just farted in her face.

Maybe so. Maybe I was a passing tourist in my own way.

This time it was a fat guy in a purple muscle shirt and orange shorts who bumped into me. I was glad for the disruption of my reverie, even though it caused me to spill coffee on my jeans. I dabbed the stain away with a napkin and threw the coffee cup into an overflowing litter barrel. I marched back to my house like I was late for an appointment. There was nothing more to evaluate. Nothing more to plan. There was only get in the Cherokee and drive.

<center>~~~</center>

4

No matter how many times you move across the South, it's always the same and different. Lush, verdant fields and forests, lonely blacktop, cracker-infested small towns and retail strips. Here and there the cities and towns where segregation and Confederate flags are preserved as "history not hate" and nothing has or ever will change. In other places, fading mercantile-era streets have morphed into yuppie enclaves. Suburbs thrive on low-wage industries and the whiteness of their schools. Old South. New South. Same as it ever was. I had grown up in variations of all this in Texas. It was unspeakably familiar. It birthed bone-deep anger that lodged in my soul. I think everyone in the South finds ways to accommodate that anger, or nurture it, or rail against it, and it marks us for life.

I took the fastest route to Savannah—east on I-10 flanking the Gulf Coast and Redneck Riviera with a hard left to the north on I-95 at Jacksonville. I planned to stop for the night somewhere near the Savannah River and in the morning go over to the address Elle had gotten from Blaine, and probably then the restaurant where Rose might have interviewed. Elle called me on the road to say that Rose had once mentioned a place called Topper's, favored by both trendy and old school.

Someone there would probably know her if that was where she was trying for a job. As I got closer to the old city, though, I kept remembering the postcard about the voudou compound. If it had a connection to Lenora, then Rose very likely would have been there, too. Elle said the two were close. Elle said Alafia was off I-95 up toward Hilton Head or Charleston, near Beaufort. I had a feeling I would be venturing that way.

It was nearly midnight when I got a room at a decent chain hotel near the airport. I was tired but took the time to take the backpack with my clothes and the bags with the weapons into the room. I also took in the bottle of Jack I'd picked up earlier and poured myself a glass, used it to wash down a couple of protein bars, the only food I'd remembered to bring, and then I fell asleep in my clothes and stayed that way until I woke up at seven. My head was cloudy with a bad dream that I knew had come out of New Orleans. In it, I had lost Elle rather than saved her from Trey's greed and perversions. It seemed like I had been screaming at someone in anger but I was pretty sure it was in the dream and not my real life. Then it occurred to me I might have been dreaming about the future.

I WASN'T VERY FAMILIAR with the city other than having been to some of the parks and bars in what was essentially the Gothic and antebellum *Midnight in the Garden of Good and Evil* scene around the historic section and the river. The address Blaine had given Elle was south of all that and several steps down the socioeconomic ladder. What they call a transitional neighborhood. Hard to say in which direction. But pretty obvious for the ranch-style brick at 1358 Westview, stuck between a vacant rundown duplex on one side and a nightmare of cheap aluminum siding and a busted down

RV in the carport on the other. All three dwellings needed a lawn mower, a hedge trimmer, and hundreds of hours of basic maintenance.

Oddly, as things can be in Southern cities, only a block away the juggernaut of gentrification was spiffing up a retail square with a mixed bag of venues including a laundromat, convenience store, beauty shop, hipster clothing boutique, and a brightly painted bookstore called Bama Savannah that specialized in SEC sporting posters, children's books, and, according to a hand-lettered sign in the spotless front window, poetry readings.

One of the main draws for shoppers was free parking across the street. The main draw for me was that the lot provided a near-perfect view of the house. I parked and walked over to the Speedy Mini for a coffee and breakfast sandwich, then back to the Jeep to eat and surveil. Since it was a weekday morning, nothing seemed to be going on and everyone seemed to be gone for the day. I wasn't sure if this was a street for poor families or young professionals or itinerant transients. Whichever, it figured for a place where no one knew much about their neighbors or cared. Maybe that's what accounted for the anomaly that dominated my attention. What cars were left in the driveways were older Chevys and Dodges and Hondas and Toyotas. Not at the address Elle had sent me to. Parked there were a bright blue tricked-out Ford F-250 pickup and a shiny new black BMW 700 series.

My impulse was to ring the doorbell and see who answered. Depending on what they looked like, I had a phony line that I was looking for a guy named Curtis, or a real question, designed to provoke, wondering if two young women, one black, one white, might be staying inside. But my training said to watch and wait.

To kill time, I went back to the convenience store for another coffee and also a small box of laundry detergent. I went into the laundromat. No one was there except an older woman, probably the attendant, reading a magazine. I put quarters in a washer, poured in soap powder, and turned it on. Then I walked back to my car, got a perfectly clean sweatshirt out of my travel bag, and went back and dumped it into the washer.

Probably should have changed the order of doing all that, but I was improvising and it didn't matter. When the wash cycle was done I put the sweatshirt in a dryer, window-shopped around the other stores, then went back to the Jeep. Everything I did let me keep a good line of sight on the house. I couldn't do this much longer without being noticed.

Just after noon, a middle-aged guy, black or maybe Latino, wearing a gray tracksuit, came out of the front door. He was talking on his cell and seemed in a hurry. He got in the pickup and backed out of the driveway while still talking, headed off in the direction of the interstate. Nothing happened for the next fifteen minutes. Shoppers had started coming into the parking lot and the street got busier. My gut said it was time to move.

I went back for my sweatshirt. The attendant glanced at me without interest and kept reading. I stowed the now immaculately clean sweat in the Jeep trunk as cover to unzip the duffel that held the pistols and ammo. I put the Colt inside a weathered khaki shoulder bag that I used instead of a briefcase. I locked the Jeep and headed for the house. I was aware of the danger and perhaps folly of what I was doing. But I wasn't swimming in fresh options or hot intel.

I slowed as I got to the driveway. I looked through the Beemer windows and tried the passenger door but it was locked. The house was quiet. I walked up the sidewalk. At the slab porch I pulled the rusty screen door back just enough to rap on the cheap composite one. It wasn't locked either. I pushed it slightly. I could hear music, something with a beat, but not loud.

"Hello?" I tried that three times. No answer. I pushed the door farther and listened again. Still nothing. I took a quick glance back at the driveway and street. I pulled the Colt from my knapsack and went inside.

~~~

5

It was what it appeared, a cheap rental in bad shape. Thread-worn beige carpet with dark stains in the front room, random lamps and a coffee table strewn with ashtrays, playing cards, and what I was pretty sure were tweaker spoons. Also a lighter, needle, and syringe. But mostly what I saw was the half-naked body of a young white male sprawled on a fake leather couch.

I instinctively dropped to a defensive crouch, listening yet again for movement. I could see the kid well enough to know he was breathing. After a few moments I stood up and visually swept everything else. The kitchen behind the couch was cluttered, dirty, and stinking of onions, beer, and trash. A narrow hallway littered with cans and bottles led to bedrooms. The music was coming from back there.

The kid's face was banged up bad and coated with dried blood. He wasn't moving. I went down the hall, pausing at each room. The first one was empty except for an unmade bed and some empty cardboard boxes on the floor. Across the hall from that was a bathroom. Nothing there except a stopped toilet and more stench.

The bedroom next to the bathroom was completely empty. One of the walls was covered with graffiti, mostly nicknames like "Chuy" and "Pookie" and "Little Flo" and "Trainstop" and meaningless snippets and drawings of people fucking each other, animals, or in one case a rainbow. Two long blood smears, like someone had wiped his or her hands along the wall to rub something away, covered some of the words. The radio was plugged in on a window ledge. I kicked out the plug.

That left one more bedroom. Even as I walked in, I wished I hadn't. It was the Atlanta house all over again, except with one fewer bodies. This one was female, nude, sickly thin, propped against a wooden bed frame with a futon mattress leaking its stuffing. She was in no danger of falling over because of the machete pinning her chest to the frame. Probably it had been used to slit her throat, which was easy to see because her head had fallen unnaturally backward against the mattress. She probably had been very beautiful. She definitely was a blond.

I returned to the living room. There was nothing to be done for the girl. The young man still hadn't moved, but he was alive enough and I leaned down to shake him hard. His left forearm showed fresh needle marks.

I pulled him up to a sitting position. He groaned and sputtered up some spittle. His eyes opened in what looked like pain or fear or both. It wasn't until then that I noticed his right leg. The shin wasn't aligned right, and his cargo pants were caked with blood. I touched the leg enough to feel the sharp edges of bone. His ankle was bent to an L-shape.

"Please . . ." His voice was almost inaudible.

I pulled pillows and a dirty blanket off the couch and floor and propped them on both sides to keep him from falling over. "I'm not going to hurt you. I was looking for someone. Can you understand me?"

"Please . . ."

"Can you hear me? What happened?"

His eyes opened slightly through yellow crusts.

"What happened? Who are you?"

"It hurts."

I swept the trash off the coffee table and sat down on it. "I'm sorry." I looked at him for longer than I wanted. And kept listening for anything coming from the outside. After a minute I leaned over to him again and slapped his face fairly gently. It drew a reaction. Anger. Quickly replaced by resignation.

"You didn't have to kill her." His eyes open now. I could tell that might not last long. Maybe he'd been in shock. Maybe he hadn't gotten there yet.

"I didn't. I don't know what happened."

"You fucking killed her. Fucking Topper."

"My name's Jack. I just got here. I was looking for a girl."

"You fucking killed her."

"A girl. Rose." I pushed on his leg slightly. He howled and I let off. "Rose." Then I remembered. "And Carla. A girl named Carla."

"Kirby."

"I know. She's in the other room."

"You killed Kirby."

I could see where this was going. "Okay, I killed Kirby. But why?"

"I told you we didn't have anything. We were just fucking visiting Lester. We were just here." His speech was thick but I could make it out.

"You and Kirby."

"And Carla. Did you kill Carla?"

"No."

He nodded his head like that was good.

"Where is everyone?"

"They're dead."

"All of them?"

"You killed Kirby."

"But I can't find Carla."

"I know."

"How?"

He leaned forward to scan the coffee table. "Is anything left? I really need a bump."

"No, it's gone. But where is Carla?"

"Fuck."

"Yeah, fuck."

"They fucked me up, too."

"Who?"

"You did."

"Okay. Yeah. But why? So I don't have to do it again."

"Topper."

"Who is Topper?"

"He was going to give Carla and Kirby a job."

"Topper beat you up?"

"You did."

"Right. But I mean, I keeping forgetting why. I have to fill out a report."

He seemed to think that over. "You beat me up so Topper would find me like this."

"And Kirby?"

"Yeah, you killed her but you didn't have to. Topper, he would have fucking paid you."

"You think?"

"He's loaded. This was all just bullshit. And why did you take Carla with you?" He laughed to himself. "I mean he likes her but not that fucking much."

Blood and more spittle came out of his mouth.

At that exact moment, I could hear a car pull up outside, and an engine idle. I let the kid fall back against the couch and hurried to a place along the wall near the front door, Colt at the ready. He groaned slightly but that was about all he could muster. If they came in, I'd just shoot them. Nothing else could come of it.

I heard a car door shut, some footsteps, and another car door open—the BMW. Then that door shut and the engine purred up. In a couple seconds I could hear the gears shift and the Beemer backing away. Then two vehicles leaving faster than they should if they wanted to go unnoticed. Or cared.

I stayed hidden until I was sure they were gone, and then gently lifted a slat on the dirty blinds of the front window. No one. Nothing. Maybe you really could do anything to anyone for any reason in an American city these days.

I went back to the kid. "I'm still here," I said, settling again on the coffee table.

His head was tilted back on the top of the couch, almost as much as Kirby's. I reached out to touch his forehead. Clammy and cool. If he hadn't been in shock he was now. There wasn't anything I could do, or wanted to. And I definitely didn't want to stay there any longer.

It occurred to me that he might have some ID. Sure enough there was a wallet in his pocket. With a driver's license. It was from Florida, and he was Damon B. Weston. I hung on to the wallet, since it now had my prints.

I knew I needed to check the third bedroom again although I didn't want to. It didn't take long. If Kirby had brought anything with her, including her clothes, it wasn't there anymore. I thought of covering her with something but was already berating myself for touching Damon's wallet and the coffee table. So I left her.

In the kitchen I picked up a reasonably unsoiled towel next to the gas stove and wetted it. I used it to wipe anything I had touched. But it was a nervous reaction and I gave it up. Whoever would eventually come to find Damon and the girl would have no interest in alerting the cops. I finished and walked back to my Jeep. I sat in it until I was sure no one was watching or following, then drove away and toward the river. I needed somewhere to park and think.

Only good thing in all the bad was that now I knew, more or less, where Rose was. Or recently had been. What I didn't know was if she was alive.

~~~

6

I'd already checked out of the hotel so I didn't need to go back, but I did need to spend some quality time on the phone with the woman who'd gotten me into this. I recharged my cell while driving to the riverfront and parked in a small public lot. I generally favored hiding in plain sight. I found an unused bench overlooking the river and what I could see of South Carolina on the far shore. A row of "Keep Savannah Clean" litter barrels gave me a place to toss Damon's empty wallet. I cut up the driver's license with a knife from my glove box and put the pieces in different barrels.

A few barges and a couple of cargo ships slid along the sunlit water. People walked past on the sidewalk and also down below along a string of tourist bars and restaurants. My mind reviewed the past few days without much result. I kept trying Elle's phone but no answer. I was ready to move, so I walked across a busy street to an upscale hotel that looked like it might have a concierge. It did, and I asked him about Topper's. "Good Southern food, but a little pricey," he said, giving me a mildly deprecating eye, then grudgingly explaining how to get there.

It was a short drive down the edge of the park, on the first floor of a two-story red brick building covered with moss and ivy. Business and law offices above. An appropriately sedate wooden sign, "Topper's," hung from a chain by the front door. It looked like a trendy café in London, and maybe that was the idea.

I walked in, and took a moment in the cool, dark foyer to let my eyes adjust from the bright sun. From there, a reception lounge with six stools facing shelves of expensive liquor behind a polished mahogany bar opened into the main dining room. It was appropriately cozy and tasteful down to the white linen tablecloths and French paintings. I was early for the upper crust lunch crowd, but not for an older man in a tan suit and straw fedora anchored at the end of the bar. More interesting was the busty, middle-aged blond in a floral dress at the other end. The man looked like he lived there.

The woman seemed both part of the scene and too good for it.

A young waiter who turned out to be the manager asked if I wanted to be seated, because lunch wouldn't start for twenty minutes. Like I was supposed to know that. Or I was welcome to wait. He gestured at the bar. I said I had come for an appointment with Topper. He looked me over like the guy back at the riverfront hotel. I thought for a minute he would tell me I needed a jacket, but instead just asked me if he could help. I said no, and apologized for my casual dress, which seemed to make him more comfortable. I said I was just a friend of Topper from the old days and had popped in to say hello.

Since he couldn't know if I was lying or telling the truth, the only safe route was to humor me. He explained that Topper wouldn't be showing up until about two, if I wanted to come back. I almost agreed until I noticed the woman's head turn slightly my way at the mention of being Topper's friend. So I told the manager I'd have a drink. He said that would be fine, then went back to the kitchen.

I took a seat next to the woman. She seemed used to men doing that. "If that bastard owes you money, too, you'll play hell catching him on a drop-in," she said, after a sidelong glance. Her voice husky and honeyed. I heard a slight cough, or chuckle, from the gentleman down the bar.

"You know Topper?"

"Who doesn't?"

"I was just hoping to catch him."

"You knew him from what old days? What's his full name?"

The blue eyes in the beautiful face narrowed and locked hard on mine. I knew I was busted.

"I just said that. I'm actually looking him up for a friend."

She laughed lightly. "Doesn't narrow the field much." She took a sip of her cocktail.

"It's the friend that actually knows him. Not me personally."

"So you're what? You don't look like a cop."

"Not hardly."

She smiled.

"I'm just helping."

"But it's about money?"

"No."

"Everybody looking for Topper is about money."

"Yeah?"

She indicated to the bartender she wanted another. Which is the first time the bartender noticed me. "Anything for you?" She was a pretty young brunette, Latina, wearing the uniform of black pants and white shirt with suspenders. I told her I wanted a beer. If she thought that was downscale she didn't say anything. "Draft?"

I nodded.

"Meredith Topwynn," my new friend said.

I turned my head back to her.

"The name he was born with. Florida, originally. Some kind of very weird, and fairly well-off family. Orlando. Or maybe Tampa Bay."

"I see."

"Do you?"

"I mean you must know him pretty well."

"At one time. But you—you don't know our boy at all." She paused. "I hope your 'friend' actually does."

"If you have any idea where I might find him, it could help a mom feel a lot better about where her daughter might be."

That got her attention in a way I hadn't expected. She straightened up a little on the bar stool.

"Tell me what you mean."

I think we had decided to trust each other. Or at least use each other. "I mean a young woman is missing. I'm trying to find her. Time is kind of an issue. I just thought if I came here I could ask him in person." I looked around, kept my voice low. "Kind of been hard to reach."

The bartender brought a fresh drink and my beer. We waited until she had gone.

"You from around here? You don't sound like it."

"I'm not. Grew up in Texas."

"There you go."

"Nobody's perfect."

"Cheers." She raised her glass and I my mug.

"I hadn't expected to find someone else here who knew him. I mean other than employees."

"Well I'm not hard to find." At that, she did a royal wave to the guy at the other end of the bar, who seemed to be doing his best not to eavesdrop. Then she lowered her voice.

"But of course Topper is hard to find. I've been trying to get to him for a couple of weeks. See, it is about money with me. He owes me a fair amount." She looked past me, and lowered her voice again. "Close to twenty grand. He said it was to fix up the kitchen." She looked over that way. "Trust me, it isn't fixed up."

"I heard this was a high-quality joint for food."

"I guess. Just don't look at how they make the sausage."

Permutations ran through my brain. "So does he actually live around here?"

"Technically. He has a nice house over on Corker, but he barely goes there. Spends most of his time across the state line. Around Beaufort, more or less. Five bedroom ranch-style in the woods. And some"—she took a sip of her drink—"outbuildings. He calls it his compound. Kind of hard to find and he likes it that way."

"You've been there."

Her face went taut. "A few times." She swallowed hard. "Not recently."

"Do you think you could draw me a map?" I slid a cocktail napkin across the bar top and pulled a pen from my shirt.

She thought that was humorous. It took her about a minute to make a line for I-95 and then four turns leading to Topper's South Carolina compound. "When you get there, you'll know right away. It's surrounded by creepy mossy trees and then down a long lane and a black iron fence. The front gate is painted gold, with a 'T' in the center of it."

"I thought it was a hideaway? Sounds ostentatious."

"Yeah, well. He's a man of complexity."

I put the map in my pocket.

"What about his place here?"

"On Corker, like I said."

"I mean maybe an address?"

"I don't know the number. Just off the corner of Corker and State. Ivy-covered, kind of like this place. Gray stone, green and yellow trim. Two stories. You won't be confused."

"Thanks. I know you didn't have to give me this."

"I have a certain amount of self-interest."

"I'm not a bill collector."

"But you are a hound dog, right?"

I looked at her.

"On a trail, I mean."

"Right. A trail."

Her eyes fixed on me as if she were on a trail herself. Then she looked away and laughed deep in her throat. "So now you have to finish what you started."

"Meaning?"

"Meaning what's a fit-looking guy with a dashing scar on his cheek doing looking for a young girl that you say is really a favor for a mom?" She smiled like a cat. "Whew. A mouthful." Our eyes met but only for a second.

"It's complicated."

"Spill. Tit for tat. Oui?" She wasn't kidding.

"Fair enough." I lifted my mug in a faux toast. "This girl is from Atlanta. She disappeared a few days ago and supposedly was coming here for a job interview. Her mom is a friend and is worried."

I could see churning in her brow. "Can you share the name? A description?"

I told her. The brow went into full furrow. She took a long drink. The conversation went on pause. Finally she put her hand on mine.

"This girl, you know her yourself?"

"No. Just the mom is my friend."

She pulled her hand away slowly.

"You seem to know her."

"I've seen her. I think. I don't know her."

I leaned close. "You saw her here? The girl?"

"Here. There."

Now it was my turn with the hand. But more in the way of pressing hers against the bar top. "This is serious."

"You're right about that," she said, pulling free with a sharp look. "I guess maybe you should get on with your search."

It was a bad move and I knew it. "Look, I'm sorry. I just really need to find her. How was it that she was here?"

"She wasn't a stranger. Usually with a friend. A cute blond girl. About the same age, I guess. I never really talked to them. But they stood out. Been coming here off and on since last winter, more or less."

I nodded.

"Topper was intrigued."

"As a boss? Or a player?"

"More the latter." She looked around to see if anyone was listening. If the older gentleman was, he wasn't happy about it and kept turning away from us. I noticed just the edge of concern, more probably fear, shaping her expression. Like the booze had opened her mouth a little more than she had intended. Occupational hazard for barflies, but I was starting to doubt that's what she was.

"Can you be any more specific?"

She looked away, then back. "That's a good map I just drew for you." Her friendliness all but frozen.

"Maybe I might find her there?"

"Or maybe just Topper."

She looked at me in a way I knew was a strong wish that I would leave. "Well, if you do see the big guy there, tell him to call me," she said, a little louder than normal, mimicking a phone with her fingers. Then she turned her body to the bar and away from me.

I downed the rest of my beer, not knowing what to say, and dropped a ten on the counter. As I got up and pushed my stool against the bar, she leaned toward me, her voice so low I could barely hear: "If you can't find him there, go up to that little voudou village, Alafia, near his house. It's easy to find. Signs on the highway. Ask for the Chief. He'll know. Tell him Ginger sent you."

I watched as her eyes darted around the room to see if anyone was listening, other than the old man, who didn't seem to be able to hear her whispering voice. Not so sure about the young bartender. I thought maybe I should try to find a way to talk to her, too. But it would never happen while she was on duty.

I left the bar with the map given to me by a woman whose name I had just heard, although she never heard mine. The sunshine nearly blinded me and caused me to sneeze. Meredith Topwynn's cottage in the South Carolina woods was probably an hour's drive.

<center>~~~</center>

7

I tried calling Elle and left another message. It wasn't until I had crossed the state line and turned off I-95 onto a two-lane highway that I heard back. She said she'd been helping with one of the special clients she'd told me about. Basically she had zip. Nothing from Rose, although there'd been another call from Blaine. He seemed more interested than an ex or even a boyfriend might be. He said it was important that he talk to "Carla" as soon as possible but didn't say more.

I summarized what I had found in Savannah. She listened with barely a comment. Just a few heavy breaths and oh-my-gods. Twice, she made me confirm that Rose wasn't among the casualties. I asked if the name "Damon" meant anything to her and she said no. I told her I was on my way to this guy Topper's. I told her that I thought Rose had known Topper already and that she might be there, and if so, I would bring her back to Atlanta immediately, even if I had to tie her up. I said I'd check back within two hours at the latest.

What I really thought was that if Rose were alive, she might be in bad shape, maybe as bad as Damon. I figured if she were dead she'd have been left back at the house. Whoever had her now was keeping her alive for reasons that could only add up wrong. Somewhere in those calculations was a kid back in Atlanta named Blaine who I was going to have to brace pretty hard no matter what.

But for now the thing was to drive and stay focused on what I might be finding next. Eat when you eat, sleep when you sleep, the Buddhists say. For me, it was going to be shoot when you shoot, die when you die.

I turned into a long, tree-lined gravel lane up to Topper's house about three or so in the afternoon. En route I'd noticed a road sign for "Alafia" but I didn't stop. It was even hotter than Savannah and extra humid from suffocatingly dense foliage. I rounded a sharp curve and as soon as I saw the "T" on the gaudy golden gate I was relieved that it was as Ginger had described.

I drove slowly through the lane seemingly carved from raw nature itself until I could barely make out part of a house and some kind of SUV parked near it. As I got closer I got the full view. Definitely a big house, with a detached garage off to one side, and some other buildings. Very much a compound, again just as Ginger had said. Both the garage doors were open but I couldn't see anything parked inside. If I had expectations of violence, none was apparent.

I eased closer, stopping again where a circular driveway surrounded a freshly mown lawn and the house like a gravel moat. Not much point trying to hide my approach. I waited for a minute or two just to see if any hornets might fly from the nest. Nothing but quiet.

I parked at the top of the moat. A cobblestone walkway led to the house. All still quiet, and I was less than comfortable. I got my Colt and shotgun from the Jeep and approached the front door. Still no movement or noise. I looked for places to duck if I had to. There weren't any.

I knocked heavily when I got to the front door. Maybe I was a little too lax in my security, but my sixth sense said nobody was home. I pounded the door two more times. Then I tried the brass door handle. It wasn't locked. I went inside.

A rush of cool air came my way, which told me either Topper left the a/c on all the time or somebody had recently been there. The room was soft-lit by the afternoon sun but no electric lights. For a few moments it reminded me of a rich guy's hunting lodge—dark-stained walls of pine or oak, expensive leather couches, heavy stone-topped tables, a Bose audio box and big screen Sony TV next to a brick fireplace. Lavish kitchen at the far end, fitted out with a high-end gas range, huge steel-door refrigerator and freezer, and a bar counter over which hung a Williams Sonoma dream cloud of pots and pans and culinary equipment worthy of the owner of a fancy restaurant.

I couldn't hear any kind of noise. Still, I brought the Remington to port arms and clicked off the safety. But I was definitely alone. Through a side window I could see the SUV. It was a Land Rover.

What was this, the third house I'd entered in the last seventy-two hours expecting one thing and finding another? I looked down the hall toward what I assumed were the bedrooms. I could see a glimpse of a large, enclosed area at the far end, probably a former screen porch that had been enclosed and remodeled because nobody liked to sit out in the open anymore.

I moved slowly, the pine floors creaking with each step. All five bedroom doors were closed. I opened each as I passed. Unlike Savannah, there were no surprises. Same hunting lodge motif, and three bathrooms. The kind of place the landed gentry rent out to corporate types during deer season.

When I got to the back of the hall I could see the back porch had become a man cave. Deluxe. The door was wide open but had several locks, indicating it was usually closed off. As soon as I walked in I could see why.

A hunting lodge all right. For monsters. Thick maroon drapes covered what may have been windows. The lacquered pine walls were plastered with black and white framed photos of humans, mostly women. Next to each was a glued-on patch of what looked like flesh and hair. One wall was decorated with glass trophy cases of mounted human bones, and skulls. A huge steel pot as big as a fifty-gallon oil drum sat in front of a mantle, with several smaller pots next to it. Bones stuck out from all of them. A copper cooking pot, the kind people used to use to boil down lard, was off to the side. The rest of the room was filled with leather couches and tables much as in front, but the floor was made from stone instead of wood. It was slightly discolored.

I made my feet move. On closer inspection the photos were even more disturbing. Up close I could see the eyes and the expressions. In none of them did anyone look as if they were in peril. In fact, all of the subjects were smiling, as if at a fashion shoot.

The skulls and bones were a whole 'nother story. I realized I wasn't breathing and stopped to take a few. Whatever I had thought I would find at Topper's wasn't going to be inside the house.

But there was plenty more to check now that I was here, and it would be an understatement to say that I had a bad feeling. The only choice was to nose around. The only hope was that I'd find nothing useful, that Rose had never come anywhere near. The room had a back door, a private entrance strictly for psychopaths. It also had dead bolts. A few butt strokes with the shotgun busted the door frame. I didn't care about noise anymore.

Outside the birds had started to sing again but otherwise no movement. I moved across the yard and gravel drive to the garage. Clean, sturdy concrete floors. The usual scene of tools and yard equipment. A new emergency generator in one corner. Most of it was open space for parking. Along the back wall was a door. It, too, was locked, and also susceptible to a butt stroke. Thanks, Army, for the training. Like algebra, you just never knew when it would come in handy.

The door opened into a small room, with a few more tools hanging on the walls and a concrete floor like the rest of the garage. But with yet another door. It was like peeling an artichoke, or going into one of those Russian nesting dolls. This door wasn't locked and within seconds of opening it my eyes were tearing up from a stench that could only have one cause. I went back into the main part of the garage to catch my breath. A pile of red work rags were on a work shelf. I tied one around my face like a bandana and went back to the inner room.

The scent of decay led to a concealed flight of stairs and a basement. At one time it might have been a storage room for fruits and vegetables or maybe venison or game fowl. I heard a low mechanical hum and proceeded down, shotgun ready.

A light switch was at the base of the stairs and I clicked it. First thing I saw were four large white storage freezers arrayed against the walls. In the center of the room stood a large table with a wooden and metal top. It looked like an expensive butcher block for a commercial kitchen.

On the table was something I don't like to think about anymore, although I sometimes do. The head, sans hair or skin, was separated by several inches from the neck. The legs were neatly stacked below what remained of the abdomen. It was a guy, but no balls, no dick, no entrails. The arms were gone, too, and lay on either side of the torso. Probably had been a young black man, although the discoloration made everything unduly purple and in some parts green and pale brown.

I looked back to the stairs to be sure I wasn't being sealed in. I wanted to leave but I knew I had to check inside the freezers. They contained about what you would expect. Body parts in clear plastic bags, including more severed heads. One freezer seemed devoted exclusively to women. Another was reserved for sexual organs of either sex, also in freezer bags.

I cleared the stairs in three bounds. I wasn't a cop and I didn't need evidence. I did need to survive. I didn't bother to lock or even close any of the doors behind me. I had touched stuff but I didn't care. I got out of the garage and leaned against its walls until I could breathe the fresh warm air normally.

Which is when I heard the dogs. Two. Big black Dobies. They came on me fast, but one was enough in the lead that I took him out easily with the shotgun. I got the other about four strides before he could leap and tear out my throat. In a matter of seconds, both lay blown to shreds just yards away.

They had expensive-looking collars with electronic tags. Out in the woods somewhere were wires or relays that stopped them from leaving the property. Maybe they'd been out terrorizing the woodlands or just doing dog things and had come back in on hearing me opening and shutting doors. I couldn't know. All I knew was I'd had to kill them, and it made me feel like crap.

But no time to dwell on animal cruelty. I turned my attention to the Land Rover. I could see now that one of the doors wasn't completely closed. I figured, what the hell, I'm becoming the fucking trailblazer of gratuitous dead bodies and no doubt I could increase the count by opening the door all the way. But the inside was clean. A slight hint of cigarettes.

I leaned against the side of the Rover and took more deep breaths. This was turning into a hell of a favor. And it was a devil's crapshoot if any of it involved Elle's daughter. But there was no mistaking the look on Ginger's face when she told me that Rose and Topper had known each other.

<center>~~~</center>

8

The second and third shots cracked plenty loud as I stayed low to use the Rover's driver-side door as cover. Not so the first round, which had nicked me just above the ear. I expected more shooting. Instead came a shrill, upper-class Southern voice at max volume: "Goddammit, you mule-fucking redneck peckerwood, stop shooting at my fucking Land Rover. Are you fucking nuts?"

I touched my face and felt the thin red line of blood. The crease wasn't deep, but it had the capillaries working overtime. A moment passed. Then the same voice called out, this time for me. "Who the fuck are you, Louisiana license plates, and what are you doing at my house?"

I raised up just enough to see through the windows of the Rover. I wasn't really surprised to behold the same tricked-out F-250 pickup from the house back in Savannah. And two guys standing on either side of it. Apparently unconcerned that I might return fire.

"Look, if you're here for the *palo*, just say yes. And I'll make amends for all this shit. If not, you better have a fucking answer."

I wasn't sure what kind of ordnance they might be carrying. Probably just sidearms or the car and I already would have been riddled. They were a good fifty yards away. Bad range for them, unless they were expert marksmen, which I had no reason to assume.

"I'm waiting, whoever the fuck you are." Another pause. "This is my goddamn property and I can shoot your ass and no one will care."

I made a quick calculation how far it was to the side of the house. The angle would give me just enough cover from where they were parked if they stayed put. I needed to move. I could hear some kind of bickering. I tucked the shotgun to my chest and rushed for it. I was already behind cover when the next two shots were fired. Neither of them sounded like they found anything other than air. More bickering. All I could really make out was, "Stupid fucking peckerwood . . ."

I pressed my back against the red bricks, but didn't try looking around the corner. No point letting them know where I really was. I bent down to pick up a stone from the flower bed I'd stepped into. I heaved it in the opposite direction, toward the other side of the house, and it made the predictable noise.

The level of bickering increased and then the shrill voice came back: "Don't be a fucking idiot." I think it was directed at the mule-fucking redneck peckerwood rather than me. I still hadn't said a word. But it might help to talk to Topper, assuming that's who was fuming out there in the driveway.

"I'm not looking for trouble," I called out. "I just came to try to find a friend."

That shut them up. For maybe a ten count.

Then, "So you're not here for Mr. Sanchez?"

"I don't know who that is."

"Then who are you, asshole?"

"I need to talk to Topper. Is that you?"

"What 'friend'? Don't make me keep asking."

I took a breath. This could go on all day.

"A girl. Her name is Carla."

Silence. Then, "You know Carla?"

"I'm just here to find her."

"What's the connection? I can see you're a white guy."

"I'm helping someone else."

"So Carla's not your friend. More a friend of a friend." It's hard to sound sarcastic when yelling, but he was pretty good at it.

"So can you tell me where she is?"

He coughed several times, and then silence. Then some dialogue I couldn't really distinguish.

And then footsteps running in my direction.

The peckerwood, a white guy in black jeans, matching T-shirt, and purple hair, was coming straight at me, waving a pistol in his left hand. Either he didn't think I was where I was, or he really was a stupid peckerwood, or lit up with meth, or all three. I waited until he was about ten yards away and stepped out.

He hitched his stride a couple of steps as if trying to decide whether to turn or keep coming. Bad move. I put the first round from the shotgun into most of his midsection. He stumbled a few more steps and I added a second load. This one pushed him back until he dropped, and the pistol careened out across the grass and into the gravel moat. I stepped back behind the brick corner again.

"Goddamn!" came the voice. "What the fuck?"

It was a safe assumption that I'd just killed Topper's bodyguard, or at least his thug of the day. Which meant he probably wasn't ready for a firefight on his own. Maybe while acquiring his skills in dissecting human beings he had also taken time on a target range, but my guess was no.

I stuck my head out enough to see him. At least six feet, a shock of bleached white hair pushed back over a fake tan, orange-ish face, tropical shirt and matching slacks. Not terribly threatening in appearance but I couldn't see his eyes, and that's usually where the action was.

He seemed to be staring at the body of his late protégé, then opened the pickup door and got inside. I could hear gravel crunch as he slammed into reverse, narrowly missing my Cherokee before the pickup lurched forward down the lane.

I would have stayed to tie this up one way or another. I could have tried some rounds with the Colt as he sped away. But it wasn't accurate at a distance. And I didn't want to kill Topper. I wanted to grill him. Find out where Rose was. And then kill him.

My guess was that he was going for backup. I had taken him by surprise. Maybe he was connected to the county law or some kind of private security outfit. He had to have some kinds of low friends in high places in order to have kept this human abattoir operating. I had no way of knowing. Which also argued against trying to follow him.

I held back until he was out of sight, gave the area a quick visual recon, and walked out to the Cherokee, past the Dobies, past the peckerwood. Definitely ripped apart, definitely stone dead. I was aware of my callousness. I'd just killed a man and the dogs were what bothered me. I stowed the shotgun in its bag in the trunk of the Jeep but put the Colt in the glove compartment. Moments later I was turning out of the driveway.

I was as mystified as glad that I was still alive. Also mystified where to go next. I still had nothing of value on where Rose might be, and now I was arguably a homicide suspect and witness to a den of horrors. And still bleeding, though not badly. Just before the highway I pulled over to a worn-down patch on the lane. I used a paper towel from under the seat to dab at the wound like you would stanch a shaving cut. I let my head lean against the steering wheel. Just a minute to think.

Fuck, it was all just guesswork. Topper would need to get his pals to secure the scene at his butcher farm, and get rid of the body of the mule-fucker. The whole thing was smelling more and more like a drug ring.

Very likely he also was selling black market organs out of those freezers, but that question about *palo* came out of left field. I knew a little about *palo* from Lenora—some kind of hardcore religious practice from Kongo. That sometimes used human bones to activate spells. He thought I'd come for that?

I pulled myself back from that rabbit hole of distraction. The quandary wasn't Topper's loathsome enterprises; it was the whereabouts of Rose Meridian. I should have spent more time in the house. I should have looked harder at the photos on the wall. If she'd been in the house, as Ginger had implied, maybe something would have jumped out at me.

On the plus side, I was reasonably sure that parts of Rose weren't in any of the freezers. She'd been seen yesterday in Savannah. There wasn't enough time to have wound up on the butcher table and then in a baggie in Beaufort.

None of it added up.

If Topper had gone back to his house in Savannah or his restaurant, I could find him and we could have a chat at any time. If not, and assuming I could find his house, I could break in at least long enough to see if there was evidence that Rose had ever been there. If neither of those yielded anything . . .

I needed to go back into the house. I must have missed something. I had to know for sure. The time clock on missing persons was ticking. It already had ticked too far.

I parked at the back door and reentered the nightmare I never wanted to visit again. I started with the front room and worked my way through the bedrooms. I tried to be fast, but methodical—furniture, tables, walls. If it was there, I'd find it. But I found nothing I could use. No bracelets, necklaces, shoes, socks, panties, bras, purses, phones, sandals. Nothing that might have belonged to Rose.

All that remained was the trophy den. The mounted and framed bones and strips of skin could be evidence in some future trial if Topper ever got arrested but were of no use to me. Nor were the various portraits of young men and women, all presumably dead, and none resembling Rose.

I was backing out of the room, eyeing it a final time, when I noticed a small pile of glossy print-outs on a slate-topped end table next to a worn and cracked black leather chair. There were eight. The only one that mattered was of a young black woman and a young blond woman, both in T-shirts and shorts, standing in front of the house. They were facing away from the camera, but I knew who they were. I put the photo in my back pocket along with the ones Elle had given me.

I pulled a green throw rug off a couch and used it to wipe down the few things I might have touched. I got out. At the Jeep I paused to scan the compound and the garage. I wasn't going back there.

I checked the clock in the dash and calculated that I could get to Savannah in time to maybe run into Ginger at dinner or happy hour. Maybe Topper would be brazen enough to go back to his own restaurant. Serial killers often had that kind of arrogance.

I'll never know how that might have gone. Before I could take off, I felt a sharp zing in my left hamstring. I reached back to feel what it was, and touched a metal shaft and feathers.

Fucking dart.

I never thought of a fucking dart. Nor could I see anyone out there with a safari hat trying to bring down a lion. For that matter I couldn't see much of anything except daylight and before I could get around to the trunk hatch for my binocs, which were really good for spotting lions and safari hunters . . . my leg began to tremble all the way up to my skull.

I worked at standing up, and then at just holding on to the side of the slippery metal-and-glass door of the Jeep and then just leaning against it, and listening for lions or whatever they were trying to hit instead of me . . . but my fingers weren't working, or my arms, and then neither of my legs and I knew I was falling down and my back hurt but also my brain was on fire and all I could see were a million bright prisms inside a diamond honeycomb.

~~~

9

No real reason I should have woken up. Ever. Not that I wanted to. My head felt like it was exploding and a wet coldness numbed my back. The muscles in both arms cramped in spasms complemented by a blunt ache along my lower shins and ankles. I tried to sit up but couldn't. After several blinks to clear my eyes of matted goo I saw the reason for the physical hell. I was flat on my back and chained to a table. Flanking me like prison guards was a square line of white storage freezers. Above them shelves with big jars of the kinds of things you see in med school training labs. And bottles and pails of chemicals.

I knew where I was. I just couldn't put together how I got there.

My incoherence went on for about an hour, maybe three, I have no idea. Some of it passed while I drifted into bizarre dreams and nightmares, but an increasing amount of it was fully conscious. That was the fun part. The bad part started when I heard voices from behind, one of them the syrupy drawl.

"He's awake," said another voice, also with a seriously Lowcountry accent, but not the upper-class version.

"No shit," said the syrupy drawl. And then the face that went with it appeared in front of me. "Guess you trespassed on the wrong property."

I tried to answer but my mouth seemed to stick together and my throat was full of sand.

"Tranks'll do that to you," said the drawl, which my brain finally acknowledged as the guy from the house of slaughter and the owner of the restaurant, which reminded me I was hungry, which reminded me I smelled like I had thrown up. Topper leaned closer. Giant fake-tan face and thousand-watt whitened teeth and all. I was in an eighties disco.

The Lowcountry lowlife worker bee laughed. "Shit'll bring down a fucking panther."

Topper's face kept getting bigger. Damn near big as the moon. If the moon smelled of alcohol.

"Still, except for Benny, glad you stopped by," the face said. Then, to the worker bee, "Set up the buckets and get the tool box. If he nods off again give him another shot of wake-up."

"Shit do put him out. Definitely might take a little extra zap to keep him awake for the fun."

I tried to move, which got both of them laughing.

As a punch line, Topper slapped my face, hard. It made the hairline crease from the bullet start to bleed again. "Fuck. Hubert, get something to slop this up. Shit gets messy enough as it is."

I let my head rest on the table and tried to get my mind fixed on the certainty of what was to come. My brain was a combination of trank and speed fighting for dominance. Maybe the worst thing I'd ever felt in that particular organ. I felt Topper's hands glide along my chest, stomach, across my groin, and down the length of my legs. "All good. All real good."

I could sort of think, but my mouth didn't work at all, except to expel a hoarse cough.

"Don't strain yourself. Not all that much point."

I could hear things being dragged across the concrete floor behind me and then I could see my new buddy Hubert along my left side. He was an ugly shit, thick dark hair and a scraggly beard. He gave me a close look, like I was an engine about to be removed from a chassis. "Yeah, should work out great. You want to drain him right off or let him feel it?"

"Let's do this one a little slow. I am interested in a conversation first."

"It might be an hour before he can fucking talk right."

Topper's face was in front of mine again. "Yeah, you're right. And it's already damn late. Shit, did you use the big dart?"

"Well, yeah."

"That actually *is* for panthers, asswipe. And bears."

"We've used it on people."

"I know."

"Shit, I was back in the woods when I heard all the fucking noise. All I had."

"I know."

"And then I seen Horse and Buggy."

"I know."

"I mean goddam. They was good dogs."

They looked at each other.

"And Benny."

"Yeah. Benny. What a fucking moron."

It didn't seem like Hubert took that well, but I wasn't in a good place to judge.

"Well, he didn't need to get killed."

"That's true," Topper said, grudgingly.

"So anyway I had the trank gun from looking for that panther, or bear, or whatever the fuck it was you thought you saw last time you was here."

"Thought?"

Pause in conversation.

"Well, I been looking . . ."

"*Thought?*"

Pause.

"Anyway that's what I was looking for."

Another pause. My guess was Hubert was getting the same kind of look Benny used to get.

"Good," Topper finally said.

"Yeah."

"Right, then. Right."

They let it settle a little more. "So it all worked out, my friend. Maybe even better this way." His face was inches from mine again. "Pupils are like fucking hubcaps. Pale as a ghost."

"We could just come back in the morning," Hubert said. "He ain't going nowhere."

Topper grunted, moved to the end of the table, looked me over from a different angle. "Well, that is true."

His cell phone started ringing. "Fuck. Fourth time he's called tonight." It rang some more, then stopped. He said something into it. "It's late, Chief, what do you want?"

I think he was listening to something. I could hear a faint voice or static through the phone speaker but too foggy to make out.

"Well fuck that."

More listening.

"You got to be shitting me."

More listening.

"No, no, fuck it. Just fucking do it."

More listening.

"No, I have no idea where she is . . . That's what I just said . . . Yes, she was, but now she's not . . . I just said I don't know. You can tell the bitch that's what I said."

I could see him hold the phone away from his body and then put it back to his cheek, but then my neck wouldn't support the effort and my head dropped back on the table.

"I said okay, all right? . . . Yeah, it'll be open . . . No I don't like it at all . . . Just do it. Yeah, like Nike. Just fucking do it."

The phone clicked shut.

"Close it up," Topper said. "We're leaving."

"What?"

"Just fucking do it."

I could hear them climbing steps and raised my head once again just long enough to see them going out the door. I think. Then the lights went out and it was dark and I was chained to a butcher table. I tried to stay awake but I couldn't. It wasn't sleep. Something other than sleep.

~~~

10

It seemed to be early morning when I woke with something akin to normal cognition. I say that because of the soft light coming through a small shoulder-high window along the wall and also because I could hear a rooster crowing. I wasn't tied down anymore, and I wasn't on a table. I was on a fold-out cot at the side of what seemed a one-room cabin or maybe a motel room. The plain plywood walls were painted robin egg blue and there was a woven straw mat on the concrete floor next to the bed.

I tried to sit up and found that I could. My legs almost knocked over the lamp on the tray table next to me. A bigger table was on the other side of the room next to a mini fridge. Next to that was a small sink with a single clear glass on the edge. On the table were a loaf of white bread, a jar of peanut butter, and some small bottles of water and orange juice.

I noticed that I was wearing a long white robe that hung down to my calves. No idea what happened to my clothes. When I felt less woozy, I stood on my feet. It wasn't as easy as it sounds.

My mouth felt like cotton and all I could think of was the water on the table. So I drank it, then downed the OJ. It made me light-headed again so I went back to the cot. At some point I woke up again. I was too weak to do much but I managed a few steps to the frame door at the front of the cabin to see what was outside. It was locked.

The window was locked, too, and even had rusty iron bars on the outside. But I could see through it well enough. I was inside a forest. I couldn't understand why Topper had moved me in here. Maybe he wanted to fatten me up before the slaughter. It seemed funny at the moment.

An air conditioner kicked on somewhere and I felt a cool draft coming from a vent in the ceiling, which made me think this room was connected to another building. Was there an annex in the main house I had missed? Maybe an upstairs space hidden from view?

I guess the headline was "He's Alive." Unless it was "Why Is He Still

Alive?" I had no answers. What I did have was a throbbing headache and a rumbling stomach, and a sudden urge to throw up. Which I did, in the sink. I rinsed it away immediately because just smelling the contents of my stomach made me almost throw up again. Then I went back to the cot. I tried not to let myself fall asleep, but I did anyway.

When I woke up again I judged it to be midday. Now I was hungry. I doubted they would kill me with poisoned peanut butter and Rainbow bread, so I made two sandwiches and stuffed them down. By then I had to pee and used the sink for that, too. I paced a few minutes to try to get my muscles loose, then sat on the bed again. This time I really was awake, and thinking, and starting to get the idea I was in a whole different ball game than back at Topper's. Now all I could do was wait for someone to tell me who was playing whom.

What the hell, why couldn't I just break out? The window was too small to crawl through, but the door might go down with a couple of body slams. And then? I'd be barefoot in a white robe somewhere in the Carolina boonies. A very decent target for whoever had put me in here in the first place. I would need to give that a little more thought. On the other hand I needed to get the hell out of anything around here.

I don't know if whoever had taken me out of Topper's chop shop had a way of monitoring me, but after what seemed only a few minutes a folded sheet of white paper sailed under the door like an invoice from a hotel. The handwriting was clear and deliberate.

"You are safe. I will be back in one hour and will explain and let you out. Chief William (friend of Lenora)"

As notes go, it was effective. I looked it over repeatedly, as if more information would come, then tossed it on the table next to the peanut butter. An hour seemed like a long time. I looked at the door again. Tempting, but I still couldn't be sure what was out there. On the other hand, if anyone intended to harm me, wouldn't they have just left me on Topper's table?

I had little choice but to wait it out. I did a few push-ups, sit-ups, some core and leg stretches. Then I drank two more of the water bottles, peed again in the sink. I spent a good bit of time looking out that high window but all I could see were the trees and birds, the sun, and a little of the cloud-dappled blue sky of a land that could hold all this.

I sat back on the bed, cross-legged, meditating after a fashion, which I probably should have been doing a lot more lately although this was no time to get into all that. After about fifteen minutes, or a couple dozen ten-count breathing exercises, I heard a key engage what sounded like three tumblers unlocking the door. I jumped up. Whatever was incoming was overdue.

The last thing I expected was a black guy dressed same as me, but with a white cap and a gray beard. And a smile that seemed wholly out of place.

"Easy," he said. The light from outside caught me and my dilated pupils off guard, and I had to blink through involuntary tears. "It'll wear off."

"You are William, or Chief?"

"Chief William, I'm called. I'm a priest. The Yoruba religion."

"The voudou village?"

"Once upon a time. Not now. You are on my own property. My own farm."

I tried to look tough, which the tears didn't help. "Last thing I remember was lying on a table about to be cut up."

He nodded, and I could see it was sympathetic. "You can sit back down if you like. You might get dizzy if you stand too long."

"Mostly I'd like to know what the hell is going on. And how do you know Lenora?"

"Please," he said, indicating the bed. "We have a lot to talk about."

"I'd rather stand." I held up a hand indicating thanks. "Actually, I'd like to get out of this room. I'd like to stretch my legs."

"I understand. Wait here a minute."

He left the room, the door open. I could see more woods, but in front of it a fenced-in garden with corn stalks, tomato stakes, and maybe some lettuce. Just past it a red, pre-fab storage shed alongside a small suburban-style tractor. I could hear bird racket from the trees, same as back at the Topper compound. It unnerved me. I made a mental note to remember that maybe something had happened to me that I didn't want to deal with.

It wasn't long until Chief William was back, holding a pair of beach sandals and a plain black ball cap. Very much like one I kept in my Cherokee. He tossed them toward my feet. "You'll need these." I picked up the cap and slid my feet into the sandals. "Where did you get this?"

"It's yours. It's from your car."

"You have my Jeep?"

"Now I do. We had to go back for it but your key was still in your jeans, turns out."

I looked at him with what must have seemed naiveté.

"We had to throw all those clothes away. That's when we checked your pockets." He smiled slightly. "Topper's never been too good with getting good help."

Another memory swept through and I might have grimaced.

"It's okay. That's all done," he said.

I swept my hand down across the robe. "So this is the result."

"We had to wash you down." He shrugged. "Actually it was a hose. You were pretty covered in blood and shit."

"Shit?"

"A trank will loosen the bowels."

I looked away. I had no real idea what might have happened since late yesterday afternoon. Just flashbacks, mostly of lying on that table and having some kind of conversation with Topper and his pet thug.

"I never knew any of that."

"I know. Have you ever been anesthetized for surgery?"

"Yeah." I flashed on my appendectomy, and also the way I got the scar on my face in that alley in Korea.

"Think of it like that. You'll drift in and out." He walked out the door. "Follow me. It's okay. They're all gone."

11

I followed him and had no plans to go back in that room. He led me along a cleared area toward the garden. I could see the shed or cabin was indeed attached to a larger house. Not a big or fancy one, just an old ranch-style that may have once seen better times but was now a home to this strange priest. The exterior was painted green, and so was a freestanding garage next to it, with a green late-model pickup truck inside.

"We'll go up this path around the edge of the farm," he said. "It's ten acres. Mostly just pine trees. But it's safe."

"If you say so."

We proceeded along, side by side, joined by three dogs, lab and hound mixes. Friendly. Not like the Dobies. That still bothered me but I was glad I could remember it. And now more of what had happened.

"Gigi, Normal, and Eufala—good dogs. But not if they don't like the way you smell. Or if you're not with me."

"People here are into dogs."

"I saw the Dobies back at the cottage. And the man."

"I didn't have any choice."

"I know. I just didn't want you to worry about these big babies." At that, the brown one jumped up in front of Chief William and got a quick head pat and then was off again. The spotted one tried the same with me and I cuddled her ears and she left, immediately followed by the black one. All three loped ahead of us like kindergarten kids at recess.

"My wallet. My cell phone. I left all that in the glove box before I went in."

"I imagine all that is still there. We didn't take anything."

"I didn't mean that. I meant . . ."

"Things will come back to you. It's okay. We've never had anybody straight off the tranquilizers, but I know what they do to animals."

"So I can call Elle."

"You can. Although she already knows you're here."

"You called Lenora?"

"I did. Right away. And she—"

"—called Elle. I get it. I've been in that grapevine before."

"Yeah, it stretches out pretty far."

"Then I'd like to call her anyway."

"Be my guest."

"I guess I should say thanks."

"It's up to you. It's always up to you."

I looked at him. He exuded a confidence that I hadn't expected. Not that I had expected anything. I just met him and didn't actually make my own reservation at his guest room. But I felt just the slightest kind of good connection.

"So about me being here."

"You want the short version or the long one?"

"The short one now because I have no fucking idea what I'm doing. But the long one later."

"Fair enough."

"And at some point can I get some clothes?"

"You're wearing the robe of an initiate. It is clothes."

"I just meant . . . "

"I understand, Jack. If I can call you that."

"Of course."

"The basic is that I got a call from Lenora that her niece, Elle Meridian, thought you might be in trouble in Savannah looking for Rose."

"You know all of them?"

"I know Lenora. I've met Elle. And I know who Rose is but never met her. I also know how you got Elle and Lenora out of that mess back in New Orleans."

"Huhhn."

"Lenora and I work together often enough. Spiritual things." He looked up into the branches over us. "And once upon a time Lenora and I might have worked out."

I gave him a sidelong glance. Sure, I could see that. But that wasn't really the question of the moment.

"I wasn't sure why she called me until she mentioned Topper. She said it was a name that Elle had gotten from a friend of Rose's. As soon as I heard Topper's name, it clicked. All the way through."

"You know all of it from that."

He glanced at me. "Did Elle ever tell you about second sight?"

"Yeah."

"So I have that, too. But I also made a couple of phone calls to people I know who know Topper and one who'd seen you at his restaurant . . ."

"Ginger?"

"Who?"

"Ginger? Late forties, blond, good-looking. Likes to drink."

He smiled. "Simone."

We looked at each other and nodded.

"Didn't think that was her real name."

"Anyway, I became really sure you were headed to Topper's little summer place—" he smiled to himself—"and once I knew that, I knew things might get bad."

I nodded as if I understood.

"So I started calling him on his private cell. He never did answer or return my calls."

"That was you on the phone."

"Until that one time when he did answer."

"Shit."

"Actually him answering was the opposite of shit. It was your reprieve."

"Right."

"But I know what you mean."

"Yeah."

We walked farther.

"But what did you say to make him—To make it . . . wind up like this?"

"Instead of you checking out?"

"Yeah. Instead of that."

"It's complicated but basically we have some business arrangements."

"You're in on that stuff?"

The path we were on curved a little to the left as we reached a wire fence that I guessed was the property boundary.

"The stuff you saw? No. In fact, until we came for you, I had only heard rumors."

"But something else."

"Sometimes I have clients, or other priests I know have clients, who need some of the things Topper has. They pay a lot of money for a bone, let's say. Even more for something stronger."

"Body parts."

"Some of them do. I don't do that, and I tell the other priests to stay away from it, but they don't have to listen to me."

"So you're the middle man."

"In a way, I guess." His jaw tightened. "But not anymore."

"Fuck. I don't get any of this."

"You don't have to. But to answer your question, I let Topper know that I knew you were there and that other people knew, too. I told him you weren't from the Mexicans and only trying to find someone important to Lenora. He knows who Lenora is, although they don't do business together directly. Lots of people in this part of the spirit world know who Lenora is. She's practically a goddess herself." That seemed to strike him as humorous. Inside baseball, I guess. Meanwhile I made a mental note about the "Mexicans."

"Anyway, he did the mental computations and figured you weren't worth the threat to future sales." A glance at me. "Sorry."

"No, that's fine. Nice to know my value."

"After that it was just a matter of getting over to pick you up and get you out of there. My friend from the village, André, came to help me. And then he went back for your Jeep after we found your keys."

"All this time I was unconscious?"

"I'd say knocked out with a powerful drug was more like it."

"Right."

"So we cleaned you up, put you in the guest room."

I thought that over. "And locked the door."

"We had to. Couldn't risk you getting out and wandering around in your condition."

"I guess."

"I told Topper we'd be taking you back to Atlanta so he'd leave it be.

For all I knew he'd be watching, or you might do something stupid like go back to the compound. So we kept you overnight."

I mulled that over as we kept walking.

"Okay," I finally said.

"Plus you were knocked out."

"But I can go now?"

"You can stay or go. You have Lenora's blessing and that's a gold pass to me."

My left leg buckled slightly—enough for him to reach over to help me keep my balance.

"You can stay another night. It might be best. I don't know what they put in their darts or what else they might have given you. I would say, though, that driving in your condition might wind up with you getting pulled over."

I thought about that. "Well maybe we could start with some clothes."

"We can get that. André can go to the Wal-Mart."

"I was thinking of some of my own. From the Jeep."

"Right. Of course."

"Speaking of which . . ."

"André still has it. We thought it best."

"So I couldn't break out, find my keys, find the Jeep, figure out where I was, and take off in the night."

If he had a reaction to sarcasm, it didn't show.

"Anyway, I can call him and he'll bring it right over."

"That would be great. And maybe he can bring something to eat. And some coffee. A really big coffee."

"Yes."

"And maybe we can talk some more."

"If you want."

"Here's the thing. In that back room or den or whatever at Topper's house—"

"—I've been in there—"

"—in that room there are photos on the wall."

"Yes."

"And there are some photos not on the wall."

He stopped and looked at me.

"I found them on a table. One of them is of Rose. And a friend of hers."

He kept looking at me.

"I found the friend of hers, the one from the photo, dead in a house in Savannah two days ago. Her name was Kirby. Mean anything?"

He shook his head, kept walking. I caught up.

"The information I have is that Rose is long gone from here," he eventually said.

I touched his arm to stop him. He looked at my hand but that was all. I pulled it away.

"Sorry. But you know where she is?"

"I don't. That's just what I was told."

"By whom?"

"Do you want to know?"

"Of course I do. That's the whole fucking point."

He nodded and resumed walking.

"Topper."

He knew that had to settle in and so did I. We rounded what I figured was the far end of the property. Around one curve in the path I saw a clearing with a circle of small log benches surrounded by several carved and concrete statues. One held a bow and arrow and looked fierce.

"Ochosi," the Chief said, following my gaze. "He's my main spirit, you could say. That's why all the green around here, if you wondered. It's Ochosi's color. He's one of the two warriors, we say. The other is called Ogun. Their jobs are to protect the religion. Which is what I do, too."

I nodded. I knew it meant something but it was far from my immediate concern. We resumed walking. I was working up a decent sweat, and attracting mosquitos. I wanted more water. And some repellent.

"What exactly did he say? Topper."

"He said you'd be wasting your time and to tell Lenora 'the bitch was gone to Texas. Like Davy Crockett.' I remember that last part because he was laughing when he said it."

"Did he say where in Texas?"

"No. All he said after that was, 'Fuck you, Chief. I won't forget this.' All I said was, 'Thanks. We'll catch up later.'"

He looked up at something passing in the sky. "I got over there pretty fast to pick you up but Topper was already gone. By the time André got his girlfriend and went back to pick your Jeep, the dogs and Hubert were gone, too. André tried to get into the house for some sheets or towels to wrap you in, but everything was locked. That's why we had to clean you up back here. André didn't hang around. And I'm not going back there anymore."

We walked the rest of the way mostly not talking. The forest seemed endless. He said it was part of Africa, not the U.S., and who was to say otherwise. As long as you stayed inside, it could be anything. That's what he wanted to do, keep me inside. Even though I told him I was an erratically practicing Zen Buddhist, he thought there was something in me that could connect with his own world of spirits and gods and goddesses and potions, and, when necessary, sacrifice.

WHEN WE GOT BACK to the main part of the compound he said I could take a shower and wait for André to bring my Cherokee and clothes. It didn't take long. André was a young guy, big and muscular. Chief said he was training to become a priest, like him, but to Changó, whom he joked was the macho spirit. Always a leader. I could see that in the kid. When he talked, I could also hear, from his accent, a young boy from Alabama or Mississippi just trying to make it through a hard life.

It was good to be back in my own jeans and shirt and shoes and skivvies. I tried calling Elle right away but of course the phone batteries were dead. With summer evenings, it was far from dark yet, but I was getting tired again, even with the coffee. William said I dozed off for about an hour but woke up around nine. He asked me again to just stay the night and leave in the morning. He said we could talk and catch me up on things a little more. I could stay in the big house. I was happy to.

We passed the rest of the evening at a table next to a big window in his kitchen. He said he had built the window himself and used it often to meditate, pray. The rest of the house left no doubt it belonged to a priest. The living room was mostly clear of furniture. A long table along one wall was devoted to the kinds of things I had seen in Lenora's house—vases, pots, statues, a few photos of him in what I assumed were his ceremonial trappings, and lots of incense holders. He said he did readings and counseling with clients there. And sometimes in the clearing outside.

I asked him about the place called Alafia and he said he learned most of what he knew there, and also from a trip to Nigeria, but that his spirit Ochosi had led him to move apart from groups and find shelter in the forest. And that's what he had done. Maybe that's what he wanted to tell me about before letting me leave. Which he knew I was hell-bent to do.

<div align="center">~~~</div>

12

I was slow waking up but for the first time in the last two days my head was clear. The clock said eight thirty, and the Chief was outside tending his kingdom. He'd left blankets and a pillow on a sofa. Also a note on the table next to it telling me where to find the coffee and bread for toast. He was by the shed, talking to the driver of a flatbed truck in the driveway filled with cages of chickens. He saw me and waved when I came outside. Then he carried on with the business of unloading the birds to a place behind the shed. It occurred to me it wasn't about the eggs.

Everything in the Jeep was intact, and my phone, on the driver's seat, had been charged. I went back inside for more coffee and waited until the chickens were sequestered and the truck had pulled away. William asked if I'd slept well and said he knew it was time for me to go. He said I should come back sometime because he wanted to introduce me to Ochosi. He said that was our bond. I asked if that meant I was an Ochosi and he said the spirits would have to decide. I said I might take him up on it. I eased away with the window down. He said that if he heard any more about Rose he would call me. We had each other's numbers.

I TOOK MY TIME getting to Savannah. I was at a dead end finding Rose unless I got something from Topper. What he'd said to the Chief was proof that he had some idea where she was. But I didn't really know if I could find him. Nor was I even sure Rose was alive. It all depended on what had happened between South Carolina and Savannah in the past two days. When I was zoned out.

I got to the city a little before noon and went for another walk along the riverfront. It wasn't the Big Muddy, but it had a similar calming effect. The morning was hot and sticky and I quickly sweated through my T-shirt. A trendy-looking place across the street had iced coffee, which I usually don't like but it hit the spot. After killing half an hour listening to the idle chatter of patrons I figured it was a good time to go see if Topper was at his namesake bistro, and if not, if Ginger/Simone might be.

He wasn't. She was. She seemed surprised, to put it mildly, to see me. Not unhappy. Just surprised. She motioned for me to join her on a stool and I asked her if we could grab a table in the far corner instead. That light in her eyes told me all I needed to know and even if I were taking advantage of her attraction, I also knew she was a big girl and could take care of herself. Also, seeing her again wasn't bad. I had been without a woman far too long and Elle would never be mine again.

A waiter led us to Simone's table of choice, and not without giving my outfit of jeans and damp T-shirt a once-over. The old gentleman from last time was at his regular stool. You have to like that about the South. There's a solace in patterns. Even the ones you don't like, you can predict like the afternoon rain in summer. Rain can cleanse or drown you.

I noticed the young female bartender emerge from the kitchen to serve the old guy.

Simone and I sat.

"First you," she said, keeping her voice low.

"I visited your friend. At the place you told me about."

"He's not here," she said. "He was last night, late, sort of in and out. Or so I'm told."

"Coming back? Today?"

She shrugged. "He usually does. I know he's at his house. It's real close."

"You sure about that?"

"I know he called from there last night because it's on my cell."

"Called you?"

"You know."

"I thought . . ."

". . . Yeah . . . But he still calls anyway. Sometimes." She paused. "When he can't find somebody else."

"Jesus."

"I never answer. If you wanted to know."

"I believe you."

She shrugged. "But back to your meeting up at his country estate?"

"You ever been there?"

"Like I said earlier. A long time ago."

"Why'd you stop?"

"I think you know. Let's get on with the story. Did you talk to him? Did you find that girl?"

I looked around the room.

"We talked a little. He's a fucking piece of work."

"He's fucking insane."

"He tried to kill me."

That stopped the conversation just in time. The bartender had come over to ask if we wanted a drink. She was very professional, in her white shirt and black slacks, but her dark eyes gave her away. She had something to tell me. Something in private. I ordered a beer and Simone got her usual starter, a Bloody Mary. She shared a greeting with the girl, whose name was Elena.

"Damn," Simone said when Elena had gone. I was glad my time at Topper's compound was a surprise to her. Until then, I really wasn't sure.

"I'll spare you the details, but it was bad. And this guy is into way more than trendy restaurants."

"Like I said, I stopped seeing him long ago."

I looked at her harder than I meant to. "You're afraid of him."

She looked at me even harder. "Some."

"And that's why you use 'Ginger?'"

"Sometimes."

"But you still come here for drinks."

"It's close to my house. I see a lot of my friends here. And I'm too old for those other bars."

"I see."

"I doubt you do. But nothing will happen to me here. It's his place. He likes to have regulars."

"That he can booty call."

"He has no boundaries. And he's nuts. More nuts all the time."

"What a fucking town."

"I'll drink to that." She raised her water glass and set it down. Looked out one of the windows. We both sat silent for a minute or so to let the conversation de-escalate.

"So far I haven't found the girl. But I'm pretty sure I know where to look."

"You think he's going to talk to you?"

"If I can get a face-to-face, yeah, I do."

"So you didn't come because you missed me." She laughed. Pretty mouth. Perfect teeth.

"The thing is, time is important. It's nice to see you but I really need to find him fast. I think you already answered my question if he's really at his house. And those directions you gave me are good."

"Check, and check."

"Given what just happened, I'm surprised he's so open."

"He's incredibly arrogant. Incredibly vain. And incredibly insane. It probably never occurred to him. Does he even think you'll want to find him again?"

"I would imagine so." I didn't want to draw her into any more.

"Well, then, there you go."

"Yeah."

Elena brought our drinks. "Do you want to order? Tommy isn't here yet but I can take care of you."

"I'll have the lunch salad and soup," Simone said. She looked at me. "You need a menu?"

"Decent burger, anything like that?"

"Angus beef."

"I'll take it."

The food came out fast enough. The conversation slipped into Simone née Ginger telling me a little about how Topper used to be just a weird but seemingly interesting guy. But then he got "stranger and stranger." I asked if he had ever hurt her. She didn't answer directly but I figured he was a hitter. She asked me to keep her updated if there was any way she might still get her money from him. I said she should hire a lawyer. She said she was thinking about it. There was something in the way she talked that reminded me of something I couldn't quite pin down.

"You know I have another name, too," she said, breaking an awkward silence.

"Must be hard to keep track." I tried not to be too snarky, or surprised.

"Ha ha. On my birth certificate it says Briquelle Simone Marie House."

"A lot to remember."

"My mom was half-French and a little pretentious."

I realized how hungry I was as soon as a young guy from the kitchen set the plate in front of me.

"Kids basically called me Brick. By the time I was in high school I got these." She glanced down. "So then it was Brick Shit House. And in college just Brick House, like in the song. It became an issue when I started working. That's why I went by Simone. I picked it because of Simone de Beauvoir, you know, the writer."

"I know."

She looked at me like I was the first person who'd ever said that.

"Does that make me pretentious, too?"

"It makes you smart."

She smiled, raised her glass. "Cheers. Anyway, nobody really calls me Brick anymore except from back in the day and some very close friends." She stopped, looked over her plate and mine. "And Topper."

The burger came with cole slaw. It wasn't bad. "But now it's Simone. I mean professionally. And here."

"Yeah."

"So I shouldn't call you Brick?"

"You can call me whatever you want."

Our eyes connected in a way I hadn't expected.

"I like Brick. It suits you."

She raised her eyebrows. "Whatever you want."

That lingered in the air.

I wolfed down the rest of my meal and beer. She dabbled at hers, smiled a lot, said little.

I told her I'd be calling on Topper now. She said I'd know if he was at the house if his Land Rover or BMW were parked there. Before getting up, I took a business card from my wallet, wrote my cell number on it, and put it in front of her plate. She wrote her number on the back of the drink special list, tore it off, and handed it to me. Slight tingling when her fingers touched mine.

On the way out of the restaurant I stopped to pay Elena the tab, and Ginger/Simone/Brick went to the women's. I asked Elena if she had a minute.

"In back. Parking lot. Give me five."

~~~

13

I waited on a wooden bench, out of view of any restaurant windows. The heat and humidity kept getting worse even in the shade. Five minutes passed and I was about to walk over to my Jeep when I saw Elena rounding the corner. She was petite, almost like a kid, but her gait and demeanor were all about muscularity. Decidedly tougher than the forced politeness of her job.

She sat next to me.

"It's Carla you're looking for, isn't it?" she said, skipping the small talk.

"What makes you say that?"

"I overheard a couple of things. And Simone gave me a couple of clues, too. She knows I know Carla."

I tried to watch her expressions closely.

"Yes, it's Carla."

"She was going to start working here. I met her when she came down a couple of months ago for the first time, with a girl named Kirby and some guy."

"And you stayed in touch?"

"Yeah, I even went to Atlanta once for a weekend. And Carla stayed once at my place here."

"She came here a lot?"

"Not a lot. Half a dozen times, maybe."

"Seems like a lot."

"She was fun. She was really trying to get the job here but we didn't have an opening for a while. I think she was also thinking about going to SCAD."

"SCAD?"

"That art university downtown. They call it SCAD." She shrugged. "I don't know why. She wasn't really an artist. Maybe just some kind of excuse to get out of Atlanta. That was the way I thought about it."

"I should check it out."

"I guess. But she never got around to enrolling. She wound up having drinks with Topper one night. I told her he was creepy but she did it anyway."

"And then she got the job."

"Yeah."

"Then why isn't she working?"

"She hadn't started yet. Something about not being ready to move for a few weeks."

"But she came up here in the meantime. To see you or Topper."

"Me. But then she would also see him."

"How about you? Did you ever 'see' him?"

She shrugged like it was nothing.

I looked away to get a picture in my head, then back at her.

"What about Simone? Doesn't fit the pattern."

"Well . . . they went back a ways."

"I'm not trying to be brutal. But you and Carla. That pattern. How many fit into it?"

"A lot, over the years. They come and go."

"But you're still here."

"I am."

"So that means there's a condition to your employment?"

"Fuck you."

"Look, I just want to find her."

She pulled a lone cigarette from her blouse pocket and a lighter from her jeans. She blew a puff of smoke my way.

I ignored it. "Do you know anything about what he does?"

"Some."

"So do you think Carla is involved in some way?"

Another exhale. This time not in my face.

"Not that sick stuff. I don't know what else. Her friend Kirby seemed to be a bad influence. Or that's what I got from the way she acted. I think maybe she sold some pot, that kind of thing."

I wasn't going to tell her any more about Kirby. She didn't need to know.

"So you don't have any idea where Carla might be?"

"I don't."

"Not at Topper's compound?"

"No." She looked away fast, took a drag.

"How can you be sure? I'm sure she was up here."

"She's not at Topper's." Another drag. "Look, I don't have a lot of time for my break. She's not at Topper's because he was at my apartment last night. Late."

Her eyes had infinite depth but I couldn't make out anything.

"Does that happen a lot?"

"Not anymore. But he was seriously wired last night. I don't mean on the usual blow. He was antsy, you know. Just one thing on his mind. He said he'd already called Simone but she didn't pick up, so now I was the lucky one." She looked off. "And then he fell asleep. Didn't wake up until just before I came to work."

"Did he say where he was going?"

"He was going home. He was a mess. He's very vain."

"Do you think he is there now?"

"Probably. He's not a morning person. Probably crashed again. I don't think I'd ever really seen him like that. And he always goes into the restaurant at two to check on the money and talk to the chef."

"Is anybody else in the house?"

She shook her head.

"Any special security I should know about?"

"I think he has one of those home alarm things but he doesn't use it a lot because it always goes off when he's not there and the neighbors get pissed."

"So I might be able to get in to see him."

"Sure."

I played out some scenarios in my head. She took a final puff and ground the butt on the concrete in front of the bench.

"I don't suppose he said anything about Carla," I said.

"No. Just went on about being sick of the idiots working for him out at his little farm, or whatever you would call it. And he would have to get better help. Then he went off on some long thing about the failure of human resources and the lowering of the skilled work force and gene pool, and then of course he went on his race thing."

"Race?"

She stood, stretched. I could hear the bones in her neck crack when she rotated her head. "I get all tight working in there," she said. "Yes, race. He's famous for that, at least when he gets drunk or high. He'd talk about a book he read a long time ago. *The Bell Curve*. I can remember the name because he said it so often. He said it turned the light on in his head, something like that. Then he sort of just got more into the whole white people superiority thing. Really off the deep end. Saying that to me, right?" She looked off into the street, took a breath. "I don't know if you saw any of that at his place up there. It was one of the reasons I try to stay away from him. Fuck him."

"Except last night."

Her eyes flashed at me.

"Well, fuck you, too. You wanted to know, right? I'm just telling you there's something wrong with him. You know, scary. Carla and I had to handle it sometimes. You don't get to judge, right?"

She sat down, looked out at the street again, watched the traffic. "So anyway, I need to get back to work."

"Sorry," I said. "I'm not judging you. I just want to visit him."

"I figured you'd want to. 'Visit him.'" Air quotes. "That's why I came out here. I mean, I was hoping you would."

"Why?"

"I want to know where she is, too. And is she okay."

"You want me to come back by?"

"Not really."

"I could call you."

Thoughts passed across her lineless face. Then she reached into her pants pocket and brought out a Topper's business card. She wrote down a number and gave it to me. "Yeah, do." I took the card in my hand. "But just for that, right?"

"Right."

She stood to leave. "And by the way, Simone has been through some shit. You should be nice to her."

"You're friends?"

"Not exactly. But she's in here a lot and sometimes we talk. Once she was here late and Topper was gone and we had a couple of closing time drinks. Anyway, I like her. I wish she wouldn't come here anymore but I think she is one of those people around here who have run out of ways to change and so they just do the same things over and over. It sort of makes them happy." She grinned at her assessment, then shrugged. "Bye."

I checked my watch. One thirty-seven. If the late-night rambler's habit was to drop by his restaurant at two in the afternoon, time was up. I wanted to catch him off guard, and on his way to his work routine seemed as good as I was likely to get.

~~~

14

Daytime wasn't best for this sort of thing, but what was? I was acutely aware that I was bouncing from one bad scene to another, in charge of nothing, finding no one. Every day, every action was coming down to blind luck or bad karma. And no Rose.

I found Topper's street pretty easily thanks to Brick's directions and eased to the curb a couple of houses away. Not too far from the city's main hospital, Topper's house fit the mold perfectly—gray stone, green and yellow trim, two stories, lots of ivy and moss. A magnolia. Like his eatery, it spoke classic Southern bourgeoisie, full of doctors and people wanting to live around them, right down to the manicured shrubbery, perfectly shaped flower beds, freshly mown and edged lawn. Also a detached two-car garage on the right side of the house. The doors were open and inside were a tan Land Rover and black 700 series Beemer. I was familiar with both.

A security company's warning sign ran along the sidewalk leading to the front door. I had little confidence in those devices. I guess they scared off impressionable teenagers but meant nothing to a reasonably competent break-in artist. Still, I had to give this some thought. I didn't want an alarm going off even by accident.

I wouldn't have to wait long for him to leave, assuming he would keep to his schedule to be at the restaurant at two. I felt unnoticed where I was parked, with a good enough view of the garage, so I spent some time in my head trying yet again to make sense of anything. I checked my Colt. I looked at the clock like time had meaning.

When it said two I got out. I locked the Jeep, and walked along the tree-shrouded sidewalk with my cell to my ear like I was a neighborhood regular. I was almost at Topper's driveway when I heard a side door open and that damn voice, which seemed to be scolding a cat or a dog named Myrtle. He crossed a short walkway into the garage. I hadn't thought of a dog and hoped it was the former.

I needed to move fast but he saw me from about ten yards away. He was putting something on a shelf, or maybe taking something off. I raised the Colt to my side but enough for him to see it and closed the gap to him within seconds. He didn't say a word. Didn't raise his hands. Just looked at me. Somewhere between surprise and fear and cold, dark anger. About what I remembered from previously.

"Yeah, it's me."

"What the fuck?"

"Don't do anything that could get you shot."

"Fuck you."

"You know, like your boy back there at your farm."

"It's an estate."

"Jesus."

"Fuck do you want?"

"A few minutes of your time. Let's go back inside."

"I just set the fucking alarm. Can we talk here?"

"You can unset it."

I could see an idea crossing his mind.

"I can use this as a tool for cracking your face as good as for shooting you. A Colt is versatile that way." He did a mental calculation to see if that could happen. The math was on my side.

"Fine. Let's get this done. Whatever the fuck you want."

We took the short walkway back to the house. Instead of turning off the alarm button he opened the door and paused at the threshold. I waited for the siren and braced to fulfill my threat. I wasn't leaving him here intact no matter what.

But he turned to look at me. "Dumbass." The broad smile seemed wholly out of place. "Sometimes I don't bother with it." He walked inside.

I knew that this was going to get ugly and that's the way he wanted it. I followed him in.

The door was to the kitchen, one of those clean, well-equipped models not unlike the one at his "estate." Maybe a little bigger. But the copper pots hanging from hooks and the Viking range and giant steel fridge and adjacent wine-cooling box didn't look used. More like for display. Maybe this whole setup was just for impressing high-dollar customers or investors. Or young girls.

"This is far enough," I said. He stopped at the cooking island and turned to face me again. He was about a head taller, but soft and flabby. The math was still in my favor but I stayed an arm's length away.

He didn't seem interested in making a play. Mostly, he was annoyed. As if I were the help barging in to complain about not getting paid. Now that I could see his dilated pupils, I figured he was medicated.

"Sorry about that back at the farm. Nothing personal. Just business." Again with the smirk.

"Absolutely." I could barely utter the word.

"And to what do I owe this pleasure?" He leaned back against the island's thick hardwood top. "I really need to get to work."

I took a step back, too, and leaned against a pantry door. I was trying to figure his cool. Drugs covered most of it. The rest I didn't care.

"Where's Carla?"

His eyes came into focus and his body stiffened slightly, although he clearly wanted to retain the casual pretense.

"Carla," I repeated.

He still didn't answer.

"I don't have a lot of time either," I said, and waved the pistol barrel slightly.

"You're with the Jovenes?"

"I don't know who that is."

"Right."

"I'm not."

"Right."

"Look, I'm here to find Carla. Period."

"She's quite the little firecracker."

I didn't smack him but I wanted to.

"So where can I find her?"

"Hell, I'm looking for her myself."

"Look, I know she came here to find you. With some friends."

The smile evaporated. "Yeah, what about it?"

"You know, that house where your car was parked."

"What about it?"

"This is getting tedious."

"What about it?"

I took a step and struck him hard just above his left cheekbone with the barrel of the pistol. He stumbled against the counter but regained his balance, touching his face to feel the welt. "Asshole."

"I have a problem with patience."

He managed both a glare and a so-what shrug.

"Next thing will be the kneecaps. That really hurts. So I'm told."

"Should've taken yours."

I think that's the exact moment I knew I definitely wanted to shoot him. But not yet. "Look, whatever you're into, it's not why I'm here. I want to get Carla. That's it. Nothing else."

"You don't want her any more than I do. Little bitch."

"Meaning?"

"Meaning she's got something I need." He touched the welt again, which was turning a deep red.

"How's that?"

"Not her pussy. Already tried that. Very tasty."

Maybe the first shot would be to his balls. "Then what?"

"You know."

"You mean drugs? How so?"

"I mean drugs. 'How so' is all her fucking friends." Blood started to trickle from the side of his head. He held up two wet red fingers to show me. "By the way that dumbshit Damon didn't make it, either."

"I don't know about that."

"Sure you do. Carla knows you're trying to find her. Hell, her mother must have left a dozen messages on her cell. Only thing is she doesn't have a clue. The mom." There was a linen napkin on the countertop. He pressed it to the wound. If he had in mind stopping the bleeding, it wasn't working.

"Carla came here looking for a job. And her friends that came with her are dead. And she's gone. Tell me how this adds up."

"Jesus, is everybody around here stupid these days?"

"Humor me."

"Why?"

I noticed his eyes flick toward a line of chef's knives hanging from a magnetic strip over the island.

"Go for it."

"I just want you out of here. The fuck more do you want?"

"I want Carla. That not getting through?"

I heard a metallic noise and suddenly his eyes trained on something behind me. By the time I turned my head to see what it was, Elena was stepping through the door from the breezeway. Her right hand held an automatic aimed at Topper.

That was also exactly the moment that a very large tabby cat leapt from behind a metal serving cart near the kitchen door trying to get outside like it knew what was coming down.

It slammed into Elena's face screeching and clawing, knocking her off-balance enough to lose her footing on the smooth tile. She fell hard on her right side. I could hear the crackling thud of her head. When her elbow hit the floor, the pistol discharged. Topper yelled and fell backward against the sink at the end of the island.

My reflexes worked a lot faster than my brain and as Elena's body skidded from the recoil I stepped on her wrist and kicked the gun loose, then repositioned myself against the wall with my Colt covering both of them. Topper was looking at his arm and holding it. "The fucking whore. That fucking whore." I couldn't see any wound but maybe he had twisted it.

The screeching and clattering and yelling and shooting were like bizarre burglar alarms for the neighborhood and I took a step out through the door for a quick recon of the yard and street. But I took too long. This time the noise was clanging metal followed by heavy footsteps and a ferocious grunt. Topper was kneeling on the floor next to Elena's body.

He looked up at me with the kind of expression that only can come from someone who carves up bodies and puts them in freezers. He didn't care if I saw it. A metal carving-knife handle stuck out from Elena's left eye socket. The tip of the blade jutted from her neck below the right cheekbone. She was gushing blood.

I hit him full strength with the pistol butt, this time directly on his forehead, although I was going for his nose. He fell back against the island counter again, but, to my surprise, didn't drop. Instead, he staggered to his feet and grasped toward the magnetic knife rack, pulling down a cleaver.

But he was dizzy from the blow and didn't have his balance. He stepped into Elena's growing pool of blood with the wrong foot, slipping and flailing his arms like a vaudeville comedian on a banana peel. Not that it was funny. On the way down his chin caught the lip of the countertop. He crashed onto the floor, more or less upside down to Elena's body.

This took less than thirty seconds.

From the back yard, I heard two cats meowing their lungs out like one of them was in heat. It was enough to break me from staring at the bodies and trying to compute what the fuck had just happened.

I pulled the door shut, as if it would matter anymore. Topper's chest was moving but he was out cold and bleeding from his head. It looked like his arm or maybe his wrist was broken. I was careful to stay away from the spreading pool, which was flowing in a single direction toward the sink. So the house foundation was tilted. What was I, a real estate salesman? I don't know why I do this in the midst of violence. Notice the irrelevant. A coping mechanism, but not a good one.

I got close enough to assess Topper's chance of survival. He was pale and probably going into shock. At the least, a concussion. The cleaver he'd grabbed had slid a foot or two away on the floor. I thought how easy and justifiable it would be to chop his throat.

And Elena? What the hell? I studied her again, sprawled and disfigured. The pistol was a Beretta, military issue. She was still in her bartender uniform, but now it looked more like a disguise for a spy. This was the girl I had talked to less than two hours ago, the friend of Carla/Rose, the chatty pal of Ginger/Simone, the hot but classy bartender at an old-school, high-end bistro who appeared out of nowhere to presumably shoot either Topper or me, or both, and was dead for her efforts.

I needed to get out. Maybe by some miracle of midday city noise the shot hadn't been noticed. And it was Savannah. Like New Orleans, a place where people had a high tolerance for freaky. But it was a good bet Elena had left a car on the street, or that someone would notice my Jeep.

Problem was I had to stay. I wasn't there to interact with Topper, or kill him with overwhelming justification, but to find out what he knew about the girl I was hunting. Just like back in South Carolina, I had to resist my instincts and common sense and make a quick walk-through of a vile lair if anything was to be salvaged. I had an unwanted feeling maybe I owed it to Elena as well as Rose.

~~~

15

The living room seemed clean enough, and I zipped through the two downstairs bedrooms. One was like a four-star hotel: neat, clean, and impersonal. The second was almost empty except a single chaise lounge in front of bay windows. The floors were polished and clean, except for a series of fresh-looking scratches running from the louvered-door closet to an opposite wall. The closet held nothing but coat hangers and a cardboard box. I opened it to find a single running shoe.

The other two rooms were upstairs. His, the master, faced the street and was anchored by a king-size bed on an oak frame, surrounded by leather chairs, a TV and stereo cabinet, and a treadmill. It had its own bathroom. Dozens of prescription bottles in the medicine cabinet but nothing that stood out. The towels, washcloths, and even the duvet were black, or dark gray. Guy was a player.

The other upstairs room was different. The wooden door was reinforced with metal plates around the locks and handle and along the door frame. It was open or I might not have been able to get in.

The inside was what real estate agents might call unique—a large room with a single bed, a sitting chair by the window, and an antique dresser. What made it unique was the metal staircase, painted black, along the far wall, facing the rear of the house. The staircase led to a door. To a third level.

The last secret stairs I found took me down to a basement of horrors, and although these went up, I knew they wouldn't land anywhere good. The steps were narrow and without railings, as if daring someone to fall, and I nearly did. The door at the top also had metal lock plates, and it also was open. Obviously Topper hadn't been expecting company. He probably was hurrying to go to the restaurant when his day changed forever and he never got back up here.

I went in, bowing my head slightly until I realized the clearance was plenty high. It had been designed for the attic so you'd never be able to see it from the street. It had one window, but the blinds were drawn and in the diminished light the room, although clearly an office, resembled nothing so much as a hidden turret in a medieval castle.

The walls were filled with sticky notes, posters for the "Salvation Brigade," and a large map of Texas. A battered wood desk was covered with folders, papers, and a serrated combat knife used as a paperweight. A computer screen and keyboard anchored one corner. The rest of the room was filled with bookcases, metal file cabinets, and cardboard boxes bulging at the sides.

I stopped a moment, listening for any noise from downstairs. I'd given myself fifteen minutes max to finish this and get out and had about half of that left. I quickly rifled the various shelves and drawers. Most of the contents concerned the restaurant, real estate, or the food business. Completely out of place were a couple of photos that might have been Topper as a kid with a brunette woman and a fair-haired man, presumably parents.

The desk held more promise. Especially a wire basket near the knife filled with handouts and flyers for the Brigade, and a couple of letters. A quick read made it clear he was connected to some kind of homegrown militia out of Texas, probably Dallas or Fort Worth. Then I noticed a thick brown folder, not in the basket but next to it, as if recently used. Top of the stack inside was a copy of the same four-by-six photo of Rose and Kirby I'd seen at Topper's compound in the woods. "Them," said the handwritten sticky note on it.

I grabbed the folder and a few other things that might be of use, including a letter with a return address, postmarked Abilene, also apparently from the

Brigade. I thought, fuck this, and gathered everything I could carry. Then I remembered the computer. I was out of time but I had to look. I pressed the spacebar and a screen saver popped up showing a real-estate promotional photo of Topper's compound.

I tried clicking a couple more keys. The screen saver faded and I had a full view of the desktop. Two rows of folders and files. For such a secretive office, you'd think he'd have had a password. Or maybe, as with the locks, he had planned to be back soon.

Most of the files seemed to be about food business, and I didn't bother to open them. But I took a chance on the one labeled "S.B. 2." It opened to another file called "Salvation Brigade." Inside was a long list of other files. I was out of time and popped out the disk without reading it. I put it and the paper folders under one arm and headed down the stairs and almost fell off them again.

Downstairs I had another look at Topper. Still unconscious but breathing and bleeding. Odds were he'd be dead by the time anyone decided to check in to see why he hadn't shown up at the restaurant. But what if he lived?

My gut told me that wouldn't be a problem because he was hip deep in his own criminal shit and would more likely try to clean up the mess than reveal anything. Or, if someone else found him, he'd have a good case for a crazy employee seeking revenge for him having taken sexual advantage of her, or maybe two-timing her. He was only trying to defend himself from her break-in and his own injuries came from that.

It was actually a pretty good alibi, and this was a town where he had some sway. He'd get away with it. But the really smart play would be to tell no one, get rid of Elena's body, and tell his doctors he'd hurt himself in a bad fall in his kitchen.

Then I started to think of other ways it might look . . . how the cops might find out anyway . . . Maybe I should give the house a good cleaning to erase any trace of my presence. Second thoughts were a lifelong enemy. I needed to keep moving. I was already late.

I let myself out through the breezeway door, had a quick and unpleasant look at the Rover and the Beemer in the garage. Then I scanned the street again and walked to my Jeep. Two cars passed, neither of the drivers gave me a glance. People in upscale neighborhoods gave even less of a shit about their neighbors than in the torn-up ones where I found Kirby and Damon. Unless it's about property. But I wasn't stealing anything.

~~~

16

By the time I reached the interstate to Atlanta, I had enough charge on my cell battery to punch in Elle's number. I told her I needed to find Blaine. I summarized the progress as having "a good lead on Rose." I said that meant she seemed to have left for Texas, but I didn't know how or why. Elle snapped at me in frustration and then apologized.

I couldn't tell her what really had happened. Sometime later, and not over the phone. I didn't want to keep things from her, but things had gone so off-mission that prudence was best for her and safest for me. I would pass along only what seemed plausible, or necessary. I was in the field and could see and touch and feel the reality. All she had was her imagination. And her fear.

It was a fine line, because I depended on Elle to tell me everything she knew or heard from Blaine or anyone else who might be involved. I couldn't risk her losing it in the process. She was a seasoned counselor who dealt in the grief of her patients, but this was personal. As for myself, I'd gone into some kind of calloused numbness, and more than a little adrenaline-fueled anger. Hell, I nearly got chopped up and sold in specimen jars.

She said she'd get in touch with Blaine to set up a visit. I said for her to tell him that I knew where Rose was. Elle reminded me her friends still knew her as Carla. I said that by either name, he would definitely want to see me. Elle asked why he would be more interested in Rose than anyone else. I told her it might have something to do with both Rose and Kirby, that maybe something had gone on between him and either one of them.

Elle said that didn't sound right and I said that I was hoping maybe I could just get Blaine to cough up what he really might know about where Rose had gone.

Elle said I shouldn't lie to her. I said I wasn't. She said I shouldn't cover anything up. I said I wasn't.

So that was our new understanding. As for being plausible, the most plausible thing to me was that a Southern preppie shit named Blaine Warner knew exactly what had happened to Rose. Maybe even knew what happened to Kirby and Damon.

He was going to tell me. Among the other items in my backseat duffel bag was a blackjack I'd bought at a garage sale in Metairie. It belonged to a young woman who was moving out of her apartment, and out of New Orleans. She told me it really wasn't hers but she was getting rid of everything that belonged to "the asshole ex." It was a steal at five dollars. But I only had a twenty and she didn't have change. She told me to "just take it" and her eyes were a mix of fear and rage. I took it, held out the twenty, and told her to keep the change. She looked at it, then pushed my hand away. "Just go," she said. "Take the fucking thing and go. Go. Use it on some other asshole." The expression on her face told me she wasn't expecting an answer.

I was in Atlanta by 8 p.m. and found a motel in Buckhead, near where Blaine lived. I wanted to go see him right away but it wasn't the best time to drop in on a guy who might be up to anything. Guys like that needed to get a wake-up call, not an evening doorbell. And I was hungry and tired. I stopped at a deli in a bland retail strip for take-out chicken and bacon salad. Then, from a package store across the street, a bottle of cheap Cabernet and a couple of fifths of Jack for later on.

I went back to the motel, knocked down a good chunk of the vino, and read through the folders from Topper's, which didn't amount to much other than that the Brigade militia or whatever it was definitely headquartered in Texas and used a P.O. box out of Abilene, at least for what I was looking at. I set the alarm for five and fell asleep around ten. I woke at four, flushed and angry from a nightmare. I was on a tourist boat to some place on the Amazon and running through the rainforest without any clothes.

BLAINE'S PLACE WAS MORE a high-end condo than an apartment; lucky enough for me, because I didn't have to worry as much about neighbors. But I didn't plan to linger. I only had a few questions and he only had a few options. I parked down the street and walked to the white stucco building with unit 18B. It was separated from 18A by a tiny rectangular courtyard with a wrought iron table and two matching chairs shaded by a red-and-white striped umbrella. I pulled out my cell phone and called the number Elle had given me.

He answered grumpy and groggy. I said I knew it was only six in the morning and was sorry to call so early but I was a friend of Carla—damn near said Rose—and she wanted me to drop off a package as soon as possible and I was headed out of town. That seemed to change his attitude. He said to leave it by the door. I said I was supposed to give it to him personally, her orders. He cursed in the receiver and said to hold on. It took a few minutes before I could hear him behind the peephole. "Who are you? How do you know Carla?"

I said I knew her through her mom. More cursing. Then, "Look, just leave it there. I'll get it in a minute."

"It's not something I feel comfortable leaving. Or that you should either."

"Look, you'll wake up the neighbors. Just leave it."

"If you'll open the door I'll just pass it to you. I don't want to stand around here, you know?"

I could hear him slump against the door.

"Well?"

He didn't reply, but after a moment, the deadbolt clicked. The door came open but stopped at the chain. I body-slammed it with all my weight and the door popped open like a cheap necklace. The force pushed him back and off-balance and when I was inside I hit him fast in his throat. He fell back, gasping. He rolled over on his stomach and tried to raise his body. But I was faster and before he could get even to his knees I kicked him in the gut hard enough for him to fall over on his back again, breathing harder than before.

I pushed the door shut behind me and readied for another kick. But he was occupied with trying to breathe.

I pulled the sap out of my jeans pocket and just for good measure slammed it against his left thigh. It would leave a bruise. He cried out in pain and tried to ease away on his back, like an overturned turtle. Mood lights by the fake fireplace were on low. I needed it brighter and, with an eye on Blaine, hit a switch by the stairway to the loft, which connected to an overhead panel that lit up the whole room. The sun was coming up outside and I could have just opened the curtains, but this needed to be a private party.

He wasn't a big kid—maybe five-nine or -ten and slender like he either worked out or watched what he ate. Medium blond hair that probably was a source of vanity. I slapped weighted leather in my hand a few times so that he could see what was causing him distress. So that he could see he could get much more.

"I need to know about Carla. You're going to tell me."

"Who are you?" Still on his back but no longer squirming. I had a decisive advantage standing over him.

"It doesn't matter. I know who you are. I know a lot of people who know who you are. But I'm looking for Carla. That's all you have to be thinking about."

"Fuck," he said, rubbing his thigh, trying to wake up. "Okay. Carla? Carla Simms?"

"Yeah. Carla Simms." I had forgotten the alias last name. Lucky break.

"Give me a minute. I was really fucked up last night." I could see him look up the stairway. "I think somebody is up there."

"You think?"

"She drove me home. I was out of it, man. I can't remember if she stayed. You fucking woke me up."

"Think hard."

"Yes. I mean she is. But she's passed out."

If she woke up and came downstairs I'd have to deal with it. But if she was passed out, maybe she'd sleep through it. I didn't have a lot of choice. And I needed to work faster.

"Keep it down and she won't get hurt." I paused. "As for you . . ." Another slap of the sap in my hand.

"Are you with the Mexicans? Or Topper?"

I almost laughed. Mexicans again.

"Neither. Like I said."

"You just want Carla? Why?"

I squatted next to him and smacked the top of his hand. Something may have broken. He started to cry out again so I covered his mouth with my free hand and pushed his head back hard against the gray tile floor. His eyes told me he was scared enough and hurting enough. I just didn't need the sounds.

"No more questions. Just answers. You need to trust me that I am completely worn out with all this shit and I have no time."

His look told me he understood.

"Now sit up."

He did, slowly. I let him scoot a little back to lean up against the edge of a blue couch. I stood, staring down hard. For a second I thought I heard something from upstairs. Panic flashed in his eyes. But it was nothing.

"Let me begin the story," I said. "I'm helping a friend. Her daughter is gone. We don't know where. By the way so are two people you may also know. A good-looking blond named Kirby and a street rat named Damon."

His head cocked slightly. "Kirby and Damon?"

"Where do you think I met them? And you only get one chance to answer. Make it good."

He looked at me with what I guessed was his honest face. "Savannah?"

"Correct. Now what on earth were they doing there?"

"I don't know."

I dropped to a knee, cracked his ankle. He yelped. I reached for a small pillow on the couch and pressed it to his face. "Do that again and you won't have any teeth."

"Jesus." Muffled through the pillow. "Okay."

I took the pillow away and he took some fast breaths.

"This is about them?" Face struggling to hold back the pain.

"Yeah. It's all about them."

"Jesus."

"Jesus has left the building, asshole. Now, why were they in Savannah?"

He had to make a decision and it was to not get hurt any more.

"They were there to find Topper."

"Carla went with them?"

"They all went."

"Not you, though."

"I was going to meet up with them later. But I haven't heard in three days. No, four. Look, I want to know where she is as much as you."

"That's why you've been calling Elle. Because you are concerned."

"Yeah."

I thought of hitting him again to advance progress. Watched his face go through permutations. I glanced at the stairs. "Nobody's really up there, are they?"

He didn't answer.

"I can break your leg and check it out myself."

We exchanged looks. He was more devious than I'd given him credit for. Fair enough. But he knew I didn't need to be devious about hurting him.

"No."

I walked to the base of the stairs anyway, cocked an ear. He looked away. If there were someone up there he'd have given it away with his eyes.

"Look, exactly what were you up to?" I said. "I've been to Topper's place. I know what he was into. And by the way I visited a house here in Atlanta where a couple of people were left pretty fucked up. Somebody thought Carla might have been there, too. You're a dealer, right?"

He hesitated. I crouched next to him again and hit his right knee hard enough to hear a snap. Instead of screaming, his mouth opened and nothing came out but a loud exhale, and then something that sounded like, "Oh, god."

"Yes or no."

He nodded. His eyes were wide and watery. He leaned forward to touch his knee but it hurt to do that so he dropped back against the couch.

"Why are you doing this?"

"I'm not. You are. You can end this any time if you just tell me what you know."

He looked at the front door as if there were a way out. Then his head dropped back again. It reminded me a little of Damon. Who had been hurt a lot worse.

"It wasn't supposed to be anything like this." He pushed himself up straighter with one hand. Probably the pain was shooting through his leg in waves, but for now the shock was preventing it from registering. It would, later.

"Meaning?"

"Okay, look. We're not dealers. Just this thing happened. I found out about a big load of meth and a little crack or maybe some dragon out of Afghanistan that somebody wanted to unload. It was worth like maybe four or five million, they said. It was a complete fluke."

"Right. You hear about that stuff all the time."

"I mean I sell pot, mostly to friends and a few suburban types, you know, yuppies, that kind of thing."

"Except for the speed freak grapevine."

"It was more another thing. I had a friend from back at college. He was into major stuff but I lost track. He showed up out of nowhere and said if I could unload it he'd only ask for half the money. I mean, I talked him down to a million, his end. The rest for me."

"I don't care. Where does Carla fit in?"

"Kirby is my girl. Carla is her friend. I asked them to go to Savannah to talk to this guy I sort of knew—Topper. Just through normal social circles. I mean I grew up there."

"So Carla and Kirby were going to set up a huge drug buy?"

"No. No. I just wanted them to go meet Topper and set it up so I could come. They took just a few tabs of the meth and a little of the crack. Kirby didn't want to but Carla was looking for a job with the guy—foodie kind of stuff—and Carla said it would help get the job. But they weren't going to do anything more. Once it was set up, I'd go down and finish it up."

"What about this other guy, Damon?"

"He was Topper's go-between. You know, he'd never meet anyone straight on." He coughed. Then winced. I knew I had to finish up before he either passed out or just couldn't talk.

"Damon is dead. So is Kirby."

He looked at me, mouth open.

"I found them in Savannah that way."

Whatever fear I had instilled in him shot up about twenty-fold.

"You didn't say they were dead. Kirby? Damon? How—"

"Looking for Carla. Remember? All l care about is finding Carla."

"So she wasn't there?"

"No shit."

He shook his head. "Kirby . . ."

I gave him ten seconds to grieve.

"So you were saying."

"You're sure it was her?"

"I am. I checked. And him, too."

"Oh Jesus fuck. Oh fuck, oh my god . . ."

"Tell me how you got that dope."

"My friend."

"Yeah, well, why did he come to you?"

"He knew about Topper."

"Knew what?"

"You know, that he was . . . expanding . . . you know, trying to set something bigger up, here and in Savannah. Word gets around, you know, in the business."

"Uh-huh."

"So he had all this weight and came to you."

"Well, he said it was a fucked-up deal and he wound up with it and didn't want it and wanted to get rid of it fast. He thought maybe it belonged to the mob or someone. But he also wanted to make some money off it. I didn't ask him where it came from and he wouldn't have told me anyway. He just said it was a fucked-up thing and now he had it."

Finally something sounded true. "By any chance did he stash it at a house over on the southwest side?"

He looked at me with that fear again.

"Yeah, okay. That's right."

"The house where two people got killed and all cut up? That house?"

"You know about that?"

"Of course I do. Was Carla there?"

"Sort of."

I balanced the blackjack in my palm. "We have to move this along, bubba. Let's assume I know about the house and saw what happened. But let's assume I want to know how that connects with where you and I are sitting right now."

He tried touching his knee again, and wiped some blood from his mouth. Then he sat back. Whatever was being held inside was coming out.

~~~

17

"The house, it was two skanky dealers lived there, Irv and Becky. They mostly did pot, pretty low-key. I bought from them off and on. I promised them five grand if they could just hold some shit for a few days. It was all wrapped up in plastic and so I just told them it was a couple bales of Mexican brown. One of the reasons they lived in that old house was that it had a hidden half-basement down under the back porch. It was pretty cool. They kept a workbench and rug over the trapdoor and you'd never have a clue. So we just put it there. I mean, fuck, all I had to do was pick it up and drive it to Savannah to leave with Topper." He paused. "I mean, fuck, maybe Lester knew. Maybe he knew what would happen."

"Lester, that's your buddy?"

"Yeah."

"What did happen? I mean beside all the gore."

"It wasn't the mob. It was these Mexicans, out of Texas or maybe Mobile, somewhere like that. I guess it might have been their shit. Anyway they must have found out."

"From Lester."

He shrugged, like it was a bad thought.

"Maybe. I don't know. All I know is these Mexicans showed up before we could get everything moved down to Topper and I guess they went bat-shit.

Jesus. Irv and Becky. They were actually pretty nice. Real laid-back, just pot dealers, not this stuff. You saw them?"

"Yeah. You?"

He nodded. "I was supposed to come over, but when I got there, it was a mess. I don't know what happened."

"I'd say there was a fight. Your friends lost. When were you there?"

"Wednesday. Last Wednesday. No, Thursday."

"I got there Saturday. So you just left Irv and Becky to rot?"

"What could I do?"

"But get your stash and get on with business."

"Yeah . . . yeah . . ." He stopped and things ran through his brain that I could see, a little. "And so I got out of there right away."

I looked him over.

"And then you got Carla and Kirby to rush down to Savannah? After all that? Really?"

"I know. Stupid."

"I oughta crack your head right now kind of stupid."

"Look, I'm telling you everything I know. Are we done?"

"Not really. Aren't you leaving something out?"

"What?"

"The drugs, shit brain. Obviously the Mexicans didn't get the drugs."

"No. They didn't find the basement."

"Seems like they would have."

"Maybe. Or maybe they had to leave. I mean I thought of that, too. But that trapdoor really wasn't easy to find."

"Just to speed this along . . ."

". . . So anyway when I went over there I saw the shit was still down in the basement and I called Kirby and we loaded it into the back of my pickup."

"Five million worth. In your pickup."

"We were scared. We just wanted to get out. I just threw a tarp over it and nobody would notice."

"And you and your sweetie did that right away?"

"Yeah. And don't make fun of her."

I let him have his moment.

"Look, if she hadn't answered I don't know how I would have done it myself."

"So she was with you and she saw all that? Was Carla with her?"

"No. Carla was working or out with friends or something. It was just Kirby. She threw up when she saw Becky. But I made her keep going until we loaded it out. I think she was more scared of leaving it than sick from seeing those bodies. I told her to forget all about it and she'd be okay."

"And then what did you do with it?"

"I brought it back here. Parked it in the garage. I called Topper right away."

"So he picked it up?"

"Well, no. I mean that was the whole problem in Savannah." He looked at me like I was a dumbass. Maybe I was.

"Then where is it?"

"I hid it."

"Right. Where?"

He knew he was about to be hit again if he delayed. "I have a storage shed."

"One of those U-Haul places?"

"Not exactly. It's behind a house I own and rent out."

"You put five million in drugs in a shed behind a house?"

"It's just an old guy lives there. He doesn't have the key or anything. He's not even in town. He's down in Florida. He goes there all the time for the horses or some shit like that."

"Un-fucking-believable. How do you people ever survive this shit?" I flashed on Topper yelling at Benny and Hubert back in South Carolina. It was a workforce problem, for sure.

"It's safe. I mean for a little while."

"And you figured Topper wouldn't know where."

"He doesn't."

"But Kirby did?"

It just occurred to him. "Shit."

"As far as you know it's still there."

"As far as I know" took him a long time to say.

I took a breath to stay focused. "So you found two dealer buddies mangled to shit, took back your secret stash, and then you sent Kirby and Carla to Savannah to talk to Topper, except they only got as far as Damon. That leaves whoever killed Kirby and Damon. And whatever happened to Carla."

"Maybe Topper has her."

"He doesn't."

His brow knotted up. "Well, who killed Kirby?"

"Guess."

"The Mexicans?"

"It wasn't Topper. And your girl Kirby didn't tell the Mexicans, or she died before she could, because she looked damn wasted away from what I saw of her. Who the fuck knows. What I do know is that if Topper had the drugs we wouldn't even be having this conversation. So they must still be in your shed."

"Jesus."

"You've got a bigger problem than me."

"Are you gonna take them?"

"The drugs? Hell no. I don't want anything to do with them. Do you remember? I'm looking for Carla."

"Maybe you could trade?"

"Fuck. You're an idiot."

"I just want this to be over."

I looked at him. "Don't wish for what you can't handle."

"This was supposed to be quick and easy. Win-win for everyone."

"Yeah. Didn't work out that way."

"No." He looked forlorn, under the circumstances.

"Okay. I'll make it simple. Topper doesn't have her. Topper has his own problems. But while I was visiting him—"

"You? Topper . . ." Blaine's expression cratered again.

"Yeah, well, we met. And turns out he had some things that make me think he's tied into some people from Texas. That make sense to you?"

"He did have some kind of thing there." It seemed to spark a memory and he rattled it off. "It's like what Carla and Kirby told me. The rumor mill in foodie world was that he had gone all crazy, white power kind of thing, hated black people, Mexicans, hated immigrants, America under attack, all that. He thought they would destroy his business and everyone else's.

They said he was hooked into some crazy Texas militia or rednecky thing. It was weird and strange, but Carla still wanted to work there because his restaurant was still hot and it would look good for her next job, which she hoped would be back here in Atlanta, or maybe even Miami or New York."

"So to simplify the point, do you think Carla might be in Texas? And where might that be?"

He sat up as if expecting something. "Look, they never told me that, or at least Carla never told Kirby and Kirby never told me."

"How about Dallas? Fort Worth?"

"It's a food scene."

"I don't think this is about food anymore. Could those rednecks be there?"

"I guess."

"And so could they be handling drugs for Topper? Think of them as a gang."

"I guess."

"And now here's the big one. Your buddy, I think Luther is the name."

"Lester. It's Lester."

"Lester. Fine. Is Lester connected to the rednecks in any way? Is that where maybe the drugs came from that he needed to unload through you?"

"I don't know. But I mean why would he do that? Wouldn't they just give them to Topper straight up?"

I heard myself laughing and didn't even know why.

"Fuck if I know. You ever heard of drug dealers who wouldn't double-cross their mother?"

"I guess. So the militia guys are dealers?"

"Where do you think Lester is?"

"I don't know. Dead."

"But you don't know for sure."

"No. But I can't see how else the Mexicans knew about the house."

I glanced at a clock on the wall. I'd been there a half hour. I stood.

"Don't kill me. Please don't kill me. I don't know where she is. I didn't know any of this would happen."

"Sure you did. You let it."

"Kirby," he said, almost to himself. "Kirby."

"Okay, here's the deal, asshole. You need a doctor. You know one without going to a hospital?"

"Yeah."

"Huhhn."

"I mean, I do. He's sort of a client."

"Of course."

"But he's cool."

"Cool? Are you shitting me? You can call him and you probably should. You can make up a story about falling down the stairs. But let's be real clear: you'll never talk to anyone else about this. You have to stop calling Elle. I mean unless you know exactly where Carla is. Do call for that. Don't fail to call for that. You call for anything else and someone will drop by and visit you and then you can spend forever with Kirby. If she'll have you with all the parts that will be missing."

"I didn't mean . . ."

"Of course you did."

I kicked him in the knee. Just enough to retrieve the pain. It did.

"I don't even know who you are."

"And you won't. And don't ask."

"I won't."

I looked around the room, got my bearings again, walked to the door. "Who was that masked man?" I actually said that under my breath. Followed by, "unbelievably fucked up . . . unbelievably fucked up." I had now crossed so many lines of right and wrong, smart and stupid, fantasy and reality and all points in between that morbidly recalling a childhood hero almost created a fulcrum on which to balance normal and sane. Except that something was happening to me that was as far beyond balance as time and space are from a black hole.

I left the entitled kid turned drug dealer to the fast crowd sitting in his living room about to pass out and probably dividing his remaining consciousness between choking on the thought of what happened to his girlfriend and wondering if he would ever walk again without a limp.

From my point of view, all I had racked up on my quest for the damsel in distress so far were four days of death and evil. In which my own part was subject to serious examination. Which wasn't the reason I had left New Orleans for Elle at all. But maybe it was the reason I was going to Texas.

~~~

18

Texas was the place. I believed Blaine in his pain. Also what I'd found in Topper's house. I hadn't looked at the disc from his computer yet, but I had a feeling it wouldn't add much to what I knew. Maybe I was wrong, and if so, all I had to do was turn around. But I was right. I had to get as far ahead of the curve as possible if I had any chance of getting to Rose before somebody turned her into Kirby.

Only problem was that Texas is a big state, and I was still in Georgia. I needed to hear from Elle, but the atmosphere or the satellites or the weather were making it hard to get a connection. I thought of going by her house on the way out of Atlanta. I wanted to see her, but it would be just as awkward as before. Or more so. For right now I only needed to know what she knew about Rose. And I needed to keep moving.

By mid-morning I was at the outskirts of Birmingham and pulled off at the exit for Vestavia for gas and to see if I could get the damn phone to work. It did. She picked up at the second ring. Once again, straight to it. No *How are you? How's it going? Kill anybody today?*

"Rose finally called. Jack, she's been kidnapped. They want a million dollars. In seventy-two hours. No cops. You know."

Case study in flat affect voice.

"And she's in Texas of all places."

"That was it?" I tried to match her tone.

"That was it. I think it took about a minute and then she hung up."

"No doubt it was her?"

"What?"

"It was her? You're sure?"

"Jack." Now I could hear the break in her voice.

"You have to be sure."

"I'm sure."

"How did she sound?"

"She was scared, Jack. Jesus."

I paused.

"Try to think. How scared?"

"I can't evaluate it. She was scared."

"Okay. Leave it for now. Did she say where in Texas?"

"No. Someone took the phone. A man's voice. Older, I think. Or maybe just hoarse. Not sure about that."

"What did he say?

"All he said was he would call back tomorrow."

"Did they say why?"

"I asked and he said I could 'fucking figure it out for myself' and then he hung up."

It sounded like something Topper would say but that didn't make sense so I let it go. "What do you think he meant?"

"What the hell, Jack?" I had to hold the phone away from my ear. "That's why I hired you."

"I didn't realize I was hired."

"Don't get pissy. You know what I mean."

"Okay. Look. How are you?"

"How do you think?" I heard a loud clunk and then shuffling noises. "I can't even hold on to the phone."

"It's okay." I didn't know what else to say. "How long ago was this?"

"About an hour. I tried calling you."

"Sorry. My stupid phone."

"Jack . . ." I could hear her taking a breath.

"I know."

"What can we do?"

"Well, let's work on it." I gave her CliffsNotes on what I had learned from Blaine.

"So, drugs."

"Drugs, and whatever that militia is."

"Jesus. Racists and meth. How, Jack? She wasn't into any of that." I didn't respond. "Blaine might have been making that up."

"I don't think so. He's definitely on the dark side."

"I should have seen it."

"What would you have seen?"

She didn't answer. "What did you do to him?"

"Nothing. I just scared him. I'm sure he was telling me the truth."

"Hhhn."

"That's why I'm on the way to Texas."

"What? Where are you? You're not in Atlanta?"

"No."

"Oh." More silence. "Okay."

"I just thought it better to keep moving. You know."

"Look, I'm sorry I said that about hiring you."

"Technically, you sort of did. Hire me."

"Come on."

"But that's not what I'm doing it for."

"Okay. Okay."

"Now I'm sorry I didn't come to your house."

"No, you're right. Better you're on the move. I'm a mess whether you're here or on I-20."

"I'm going to find her."

"I know."

"There's a reason she's still alive—" I held back. "A reason she's okay. I mean, these people might not be all that smart."

"But how did they know about me? About having enough money for a ransom? That's what I don't know."

"It's probably people like Blaine, her other friends. I think she just got caught in something that had nothing to do with her. They don't know what to do with her now, and so they think they can use her to get money. I mean, if that's it, we can take care of it."

"I don't know who might be with her. Jack, I don't know anything.

Except that guy Topper in Savannah is a psychopath and she was all set to work for him. And that's when everything started going to hell. I mean, that's all I know."

"So I'll just keep driving. She's probably around Dallas or Fort Worth."

"I guess. But drugs. What the hell."

"I know. That's why I had to see Blaine. He really wasn't in the loop, but he knew where the loop was."

"Knew? Did you kill him, Jack?"

"No. Of course not. We just had to talk. Mostly about Topper."

"When I told Lenora to call Topper to check on you, I could tell by the tone in her voice she was worried. Just what kind of freak is he? Is he a big dealer or something?"

"Yeah, he's a freak. And, yeah, he's a dealer."

"But Rose wanted to work for him."

"I don't know about that for sure. But his restaurant is big with the locals and you'd never really know he's a psycho just by seeing him or talking to him casually."

"Yes, I would. And I think Rose would, too."

"I don't know."

"I do. That's why I can't sleep. Rose knows. Like me."

"Second sight?"

"Same as Lenora. It's a family thing."

"Maybe she thought it would be okay. Maybe she felt safe with her friends with her. Or maybe it was just a trip to Savannah."

Something like an angry snarl of breath. "Yeah. That's exactly it. Except, you know, she's here one day ready to make her move on the world and the next she's gone. And the next, and next, and next . . ."

"I'm bringing her back. It's not a cartel or the mob or any kind of professionals."

"You really think that?"

"What I think is a drug deal went wrong and Rose got caught up in it and somebody dropped a dime that her mom had some bucks and now that's how they want to make up for the lost drugs. But whoever they are, they're in a rush. Cartels or the mob, they can be patient."

"I don't know."

"I don't even think it's a kidnapping, straight up. I'd call it an extortion."

"Like in Mexico."

"Well, yeah, like that."

"You just said it wasn't cartels."

I didn't answer right away.

"You're trying to make me feel better."

"I'm not. But this isn't cartel stuff. Somebody wants your money and if you can get it, then we can get Rose. They don't want Rose. They want a million bucks."

"So you keep driving," she said.

"I think that's best." I took a breath to get recentered. "About the money. Can you really get it from your bank? They might have questions."

"It won't be a problem."

"Whenever they call again, always ask to speak to Rose. Each time. I mean unless they call her Carla."

"They do."

"I need to keep remembering that."

"Jack . . . I'm scared."

"It will help her to know we're out there. For that matter try to talk to whoever gets on the phone as much as you can. Listen for anything you think might tell us anything."

"At some point they'll have to tell us where to meet."

"I know. But whatever you can hear is good."

"We need a new plan."

"I know."

"Jack?"

"Yeah."

It felt like she was searching for something to say. "You have somebody who could help you."

"Who?" It hit me at the same time.

"I mean, he kind of owes you, right? And me, a little."

"I would never put it to Red that way."

"But you could ask him. You know this is more than you signed up for."

~~~

19

I changed my route to slide down I-65 toward Mobile and the coast. I wasn't in a rush. What was the saying, "I'm lost but making good time?" I could get to Texas via the northern route of I-20 toward Dallas or down the southern route along I-10. It was a toss-up but Rose could be anywhere from Texarkana to El Paso. Coming in at Houston seemed reasonable, and I preferred that drive anyway.

And Red was in Biloxi. Just before I got to the exit for downtown Montgomery I dialed the number I hadn't used in months.

Of course it was an answering machine. I didn't want to proceed much farther without hearing from him. It was midday and I knew of a decent meat 'n' three not far from the interstate. Turned out it had gone out of business so I took a chance on a burger joint nearby and wolfed down my lunch. Now I had to kill a little time, waiting to see if Red would return my call.

I drove a few blocks to Washington Avenue, the main downtown drag. I parked, fed the meter, and walked most of the way up to the capitol, turning back when I got to the first church where Dr. King had been a pastor. Then back to my Jeep, a meandering route that included the bus stop Rosa Parks made famous and the old Greyhound depot where the racists beat up Freedom Riders.

The former capital of the Confederacy had changed, as had the state around it, but footing in the New South remained unsure if not treacherous. None of this had anything to do with looking for Rose. Still, the history of righteous struggle in these streets gave my soul a lift, and I didn't mind stretching my legs while waiting for Red's call. I hadn't exactly made time for exercise.

I'd just about gotten back to the Cherokee when the phone rang.

"How the fuck you doing, Shakespeare?"

"Great, absolutely fucking great. That's why I'm calling."

He chuckled. Slightly.

"So I'm guessing it's not just to shoot the shit about how we're spending all that money." I heard a burp. "I mean investing."

"I'm about to have a couple beers myself."

I started walking again, deeper into the lower and seedier part of downtown, phone to my ear.

"So what's up?" Pause. "Still got a job opening, you know."

"About that. You got a minute to talk?"

"I got lots of minutes. Taking a couple weeks off from trouble, you know?"

"I do."

"So talk to me."

I rounded a traffic circle and moved out of the way of an old man on an older bike riding on the sidewalk. "You remember Elle's daughter, Rose? That she was trying to find?"

"Came to Atlanta to live with her a year or two ago, right?"

"Right."

"Hope that's all going okay."

"It's not. It's not a lot. That's why I'm calling." I glanced into the window of a coffee shop. A woman sitting alone at a table looked back at me. "Okay to talk on this phone, right?"

"It's safe, if that's what you mean. Jesus fuck."

"Okay. Had to ask."

"And you did . . . Kind of dick-ish."

Now I was passing under the shade of an awning in front of an office supply store. It was that moment in a modern Southern summer day when the air-conditioning that's been insulating you wears off and hot, muggy nature begins to squeeze mortal existence from your pores. "Forget I asked. The bottom line is, I'm in a big pile of shit looking for Rose. Way bigger than I thought. And I might need some help."

"Huhhn."

"Okay to tell you about it?"

"It's your dime. Cough it up."

So I did. What got his attention was the part about Los Jovenes, the so-called Mexican gang. He'd heard of them. But he said they were Americans.

When I was done, kind of a silence, ending with, "How does a guy who wants to stay out of everything get so mixed up in everything?"

"It's a gift." I heard him take a long drink. It made me thirsty and I started looking for a place to get some water.

"I think I might want to run this past some of my associates. This is the kind of shit they hate. 'Los Jovenes' my hairy ass. They won't put up with it."

"The only thing I'm interested in is Rose."

"From what you said, Mexicans might be, too. As for those militia fucks. I've had to deal with some of them before. What they really get into is running girls and dealing meth." He was quiet for a few. It was like I could hear his brain whirring. "Goddamn, Jack."

"I need to find them and where they have Rose."

"I guess. It's a fucking long shot at this point."

"It is. But it's Rose. And Elle."

"I get it."

"So here I am. Calling you."

We let that sit a moment.

"I can make some calls. You have to give me a few."

"I don't have a few. I've got seventy-two hours. Ticking."

I saw a sign for a convenience store a couple of blocks up and headed toward it. When I stepped into the crosswalk I had to jump back as a jacked-up pickup veered to one side and laid on his horn.

"Where the hell are you?" Red said.

I watched the truck. Sometimes those assholes back up.

"Montgomery. Stopped for lunch." I kept walking.

"So you're already heading down this way?"

"Sort of."

"Damn, Shakespeare. You sound like you're in a hurry. Especially when you don't know where you're going. And assuming about things and all that shit."

"I am in a hurry. But I'm not assuming. I'm just asking."

"Who said seventy-two hours?"

"Elle said that's what Rose told her."

"You believe it?"

"Not much choice."

"Maybe. Sounds funky, though. You know?"

"It does. But it's all I've got."

"Roger that."

I reached the end of another block and made sure nobody was going to run over me for crossing the street. I could see the convenience store was either closed or gone out of business. I kept walking anyway.

"What I'm saying, if I get backing from the family, it will make things easier."

"You mean if they let you do it."

"Plus, you know, I'd get credit. Putting out a fire kind of thing."

"Like with the painting and Trey Barnett."

"Don't get a big head. That was one-off."

"I wish you'd get my jokes sometimes."

"Don't count on it. But look, on this one, if they like it, they'll want it done quick."

"Roger that."

"And decisive."

"Completely."

"By that I mean that if the family gets involved, through me, everything gets cleaned out."

"You mean that could include civilians."

"It's how it would go."

"Roger that, too."

"Make sure you do, little buddy."

No place I could buy a soda or a water. Maybe times downtown were harder than I'd thought. I turned around and started the hot hike back to my Jeep.

"I'll be honest. I don't really know how deep this gets. Just being clear."

"Look Shakespeare, you're good at this shit. Like I told you. Can't be any worse than the cowboys you ran into down in Honduras or Korea or wherever when you were an Army spook."

"You overestimate me."

"Maybe."

"I'm going to head down your way. No percentage in my just waiting around twiddling my dick."

"Fair enough."

"You're still in Biloxi, right?"

"Quarter mile in from the coast, over toward Pass Christian."

The old man on the bike was coming back my way, still on the sidewalk.

"I could meet you there, at your house."

A longer silence than I had expected.

"Yeah, okay," he finally said. "But not to my house. Hole up somewhere near. I ain't being rude. It's just a precaution."

"Sure."

"Anyway, my house ain't exactly ready for guests."

"No doubt."

"Just keep me posted on where you are."

"And you."

"Fucking A. This is all headed the same way with these pissants, sounds like."

"I hope."

"You hope it all goes south?"

"I hope it all takes us to Rose."

I was back at my Jeep. I turned on the a/c and felt the cool air on my damp shirt. I tried to visualize at least the next few hours. So far on this little trip that's as far out as I'd been able to plan. The old man on the bike coasted by again, and this time looked at me through the window and touched the bill of his tattered blue ball cap. I nodded back. It felt like a good omen. Or maybe I needed it to feel like it did.

~~~

20

The drive was fast, and not unpleasant. Central and southern Alabama are all forest and rivers. Except for the highway, you'd think you were in the land that time forgot. It calmed me and helped pass the hours waiting on Elle's call. She in turn was waiting on Rose's abductors.

I tried to put my mind in neutral. Awareness, mindfulness, consciousness—states of connection with the universe and the void that the Buddhists seek. Like I had a right to any of that. What had I just done to a young guy in Atlanta? Or had precipitated in Savannah? Would it balance out in light of what they had done, were about to do, and all who would suffer for their greed and evil? The Buddha doesn't juggle karma. He doesn't rationalize. You take the path; you go where it leads, hot or cold, smooth or jagged. All I could see around me were cars, yellow and white lines on the concrete, and oceans of trees. The calm would not stay with me. Nor I with it.

That's about when Brick called.

She said she had put it off but now she was scared. She'd gone over to see Topper on a last-minute impulse on her way to the bank, thinking about what we'd said. It had made her concerned about Carla and for that matter Elena. He could be up to anything with them. She knew all about that. And she had gotten pissed off again about the money he owed her.

She must have gotten there about an hour after I'd left. Elena was bad enough, she said, but the real horror show was Topper. He wasn't dead. He wasn't dying. He was conscious. And bleeding. And cursing. Bleeding a lot, because he was a bleeder, but basically it looked worse than it was. She recounted what he told her had happened. I said his version was close enough.

It took a moment for her to digest that.

Then she went on with her own story.

She had started to leave, over his pleading and cursing, but only got as far as the front yard when it occurred to her that if she did he probably would die. She went back inside. They struck a bargain. If he gave her fifty thousand cash on the spot—about half what he owed her—would she get him to a hospital? She said only if he had the money on him. He hesitated and she started walking out.

Fuck it, he yelled, he had seventy-five, would that change your mind, you bitch? Upstairs in the desk.

She said the bitch said yes, it would change her mind. Then she checked. He had a hidden safe in his bedroom closet. He gave her the combination. The cash was there. I rolled my eyes at myself that I'd missed it, but mine wasn't that kind of search.

She made a compress to stanch the biggest gash and told him to press it as hard as he could, and helped him lean against the countertop while she pulled kitchen towels from a drawer to sop up the blood and clean his face. Always watching for the slightest indication he might try to turn the tables by killing her for her kindness. But he was in no shape for a battle and she was plenty fit and strong enough to hold her own.

She helped him navigate around Elena's body getting to the garage. Neither of them said anything, though she had to look at the poor girl's butchered face. She'd thought of taking his Range Rover but then decided on her Mercedes. She didn't want to leave anything of hers anywhere near the house.

She scanned the streets quickly but saw nothing. She got him to her car and buckled him in the passenger seat. The back seat would have allowed him to rest better, but she couldn't have watched him continuously. She made him lean his head forward over a wad of towels in his lap so as not to leave blood on the seats. His expression bothered her so just before she started the ignition she rapped him sharply on his broken wrist. He recoiled against the door, then sat up and stared straight out the windshield, clutching a towel with his good hand. She didn't have to look to know what his face looked like.

At the hospital ER they told the nurses and very young doctor he had slipped in the kitchen and hit his head on a counter. Which was true, sans context. The doc, probably an intern, patched him up with a few stitches, gave him a painkiller shot, and wrote him a 'scrip for some good drugs. Topper told him he had a free meal any time he wanted to come by the restaurant. The intern was impressed.

Brick called for a cab, had a few closing words, and walked beside Topper in silence as a nurse wheeled him outside. He said a couple more things. Then she left. She wasn't going back to that house. Ever.

That was the story. It had come out so fast she was breathless. But there was an epilogue. It was what Topper said, high and chatty on the pain-killer, waiting on the cab. He told the nurse to give them a minute, nodded his head for Brick to come closer. He half-whispered that he was going to get the drugs "those kids" had stiffed him about, and take them to "those rednecks in Texas" himself.

I could hear her lungs working hard again, trying to catch up to her adrenaline. "His exact words were, 'I can't wait to put a fucking bullet in Blaine's pretty little face while I'm at it. And you know, you have a pretty face, too.'"

I waited a moment. "Fuck that. He's too fucked up to know what he's talking about. Anyway, you'll never see him again."

She was still breathing hard. "It really did look worse than it was. By tomorrow he'll be evil incarnate like he never missed a beat. But I hope you're right."

"So I shouldn't have left him alive."

"You should have killed him, Jack. Yes."

"Maybe," I said, with some effort. "But that's not what I'm after. I have to keep reminding myself."

"You don't even fucking know."

"And you? You could have just left him in the kitchen to bleed to death."

"I think I just told you about all that."

"Bottom line is nobody killed him. I feel confident that won't always be the case."

"I guess that's why I called. Mostly."

"I'm glad you did. Mostly."

"Okay."

"More than okay."

"So 'those kids,'" Brick said, letting my moral quandary fall where it belonged. "That would include Carla, right? And her friend Kirby?"

I said it would.

"And you still haven't found her."

"No."

She was quiet a long time. I stayed in the right lane, the interstate just a movie screen. The real view was in my head, in her words.

"Brick?"

"Yeah."

"Are you okay?"

"I told you I'm not. I mean he could just as easily come back for me. I doubt I'm worth seventy-five thou to him."

"Can you leave town?"

"You think that would help?"

"I do."

"You know you're going to run into him, Jack. Again."

"Planning on it. So do you think he was going to Atlanta, definitely?"

"Rather than wait for that boy to drive all the way back down here. I mean, assuming he would. Which he probably wouldn't."

"Topper's smart enough to know Blaine won't come to see him in Savannah if he doesn't have to. It'd be a death wish."

"So he'll go get him."

"It's what I'd do."

"Go to Atlanta and handle it."

"Definitely."

"This is getting bad."

"It's already bad."

"Well then, you know where you need to be."

"I do."

"I like hearing you say, 'I do.'" She laughed.

"You be careful. I'll be in touch."

"Okay. I'm only joking because I'm scared. It's a thing I do."

"I know all about it. But just get out of town. This will pass, as they say."

"Sure. As they say."

We said goodbye, awkwardly, and I put my mind back on the road when I realized I had veered across two lanes almost into the median. Brick told a hell of a good movie. I had no idea where she might go, or for how long.

And that was best. I mean, if things turned around and I wound up on a table at Topper's farm again, the less I knew the better. I'm pretty sure she had the same feeling.

<center>~~~</center>

21

I passed Mobile by late afternoon and swung west to pick up U.S. 90 as it hugs the coast. Biloxi was all casinos, hotels, and retail clutter and then beaches and Old South mansions leading to Pass Christian. Not far out of town, I found one of those retro "tourist court" motels, the Tern Inn, that looked clean but forgettable. It was just across the highway from a clump of wind dunes leading to the beach. I had a thought to press on to New Orleans, but I didn't want to go to what I called home. I didn't want time to reconsider how far down this rabbit hole I'd fallen.

I checked in and spent a little time in my room going over all my travel gear and weapons. Made a mental note to buy more Advil. And I was hungry. My appetite had come back after a couple of lean and ultra-stressful days. The smell of salt air helped. I'd passed a seafood joint on a wooden pier about a mile away, so I changed into shorts and headed out on foot. It felt good to loosen my legs.

I crossed the highway just in time for the wind blast from a passing eighteen-wheeler to kick a discarded burger wrapper into my face. Which blinded me just long enough to have to dodge out of the way of a Chevy Tahoe trying to cut into a beachfront parking zone. It found one about twenty yards ahead. The doors burst open and three kids leapt out, headed for the water. They were from Texas, or at least their license plates were.

The last one out was a teenage girl, clutching a straw hat on her head. She gave me a quick friendly glance and rejoined her raucous siblings as I passed by. Then mom got out of the car and so did dad, who waved to me as a kind of apology for nearly splattering me on the pavement. I waved back. I mean, hell, it was my own fault.

I headed on for the pier, but seeing them having fun made me smile. I couldn't remember the last time I had. The closer I got to Tom's Ocean Grub the more the wafts of seaweed and suntan lotion and fried food filled the air. Seagulls floated overhead, fussing over whatever they fuss over. Something pushed almost imperceptibly at my brain, the way it does when you hear a song and forget its name. It keeps nagging, out there on the edges. And then you remember. And feel stupid for having been obsessed.

The diner was more crowded than it had looked. But I found a table with a good view of the beach. The waitress was tan and pretty and peppy. She wore shorts and a Hawaiian-style shirt tied up over her flat midriff. Tom Petty from the corner speakers.

I ordered a fish sandwich and looked toward the bar to see what they might have on tap. I almost ordered the Beck's when I noticed a row of "Special and Homemade Teas" to one side. Also a faux wooden barrel of "Real Deal Root Beer." I pointed and told her I'd have that. It sounded better than actual beer to quench my thirst.

She looked at me like I was some kind of geek, possibly a metrosexual, but brought it over in a frosty mug and said the food would be out short-ly. I downed it so fast it gave me brain freeze. I put the mug on a coaster while my head stopped aching, and stared out at the waves and the people. I thought of the teenage girl and the family by the beach and it made me smile again. That went away in a microsecond as images of the past week burned through my brain. The only word-thoughts that formed, repeatedly, were along the lines of "Jesus Christ" and "Fucking hell."

There was no point going back to Savannah. No point in lingering any-where in Georgia or South Carolina. There might not have been any point in striking out for Texas, or sitting out a night here, either. All I had to go on were a few papers in a pervert's house and the theory of a drug dealer unlikely to live out his next year. But at least it was plausible. Whatever had happened in Atlanta and the Lowcountry very likely flowed westward—Texas, Mexico, maybe both. Unfortunately most of the connections, never mind the validations, were dead. The logic of the search twisted around on itself. To find Rose, I had to find Rose.

My instinct said to catch some sleep tonight and keep driving, with or without Red. Answers and leads would come to me on the road. Which is where I was. On the road again. In a bar. In Biloxi.

Soon enough, the waitress brought my sandwich. She small-talked just enough to guarantee a tip, and refilled my mug. Still gave me the look, though. I added some of the house hot sauce to the fish. It was decent. And spicy.

I took a sip to cut the heat, then pulled the mug away from my mouth like the root beer had gone bitter and acrid. I couldn't drink it. I set the mug in front of me and sniffed the rim as if it were wine. But no adjectives came to mind. Only a picture. A scoop of ice cream on fresh-baked apple pie. In a blinding, formless space. The pie vanished, the space went from light to black.

I lost all track of where I was, when I was, and nearly who I was.

I don't know if anyone at the other tables noticed. I don't know how long I must have stared at the mug, the melted rivulets in the frosty foam, the roll of earthy aromatic waves, rising like golden wisps of angel hair to the sun, then incinerating, exploding in my skull, obliterating every trace of myself.

Eventually I blinked, and knew I had done so.

The only thing I could see was Rose.

I didn't recognize her at first. Then she appeared in full, a bright nebulous image with long brunette hair, innocent blue eyes, a face with freckles across the nose.

I said "Rose." People may have heard me. Maybe not. It didn't matter.

It wasn't Rose.

It was Ronnie.

I wanted to throw up. I looked around, couldn't see the waitress, couldn't wait even another second. I pushed back my chair, nearly knocking over the drink that had flashed up the memory. I pulled a twenty from my jeans to cover the check and tip and pushed through the busy tables and the customers waiting to be seated. I collided with two of them, who cursed me as I hit the door. Outside I sprinted across the parking lot, a football field of asphalt with cars the size of elephants and dirigibles and planets swarming around me.

I didn't stop until I reached shoreline. The water flooding my shoes popped me back into some semblance of consciousness. I sat on the wet sand. I caught my breath. It wasn't easy. I couldn't seem to get a handle on the oxygen. My heart was battering my rib cage.

I managed to stand after maybe twenty minutes and walked back to the motel. I only know this because I remembered it later. At the time, I had no more awareness or control of my movements and actions than a puppet hanging from the strings of an unseen master. A vicious, sadistic clown.

~~~

22

About sunset I realized I was sitting in a chair in a room in a motel. I decided I needed a drink. The booze I'd bought back in Atlanta was in the Jeep. It took me a minute to find my keys and get out of the room. The Jeep windows had been closed and on pulling up the hatch door the trapped heat sucked away my breath. I found the Jack and closed the hatch and clicked on the locks and started to walk back to my room to get shit-faced.

Ronnie was in front of my eyes, consuming the entire universe that I had previously obliterated, and then where Ronnie had been was a pile of ash and starlight and then nothing but light. I dropped the Jack. It landed on a clump of sand in the parking lot. I was so grateful it had not broken that tears formed in my eyes. At least I thought that's why they did. Nothing was real. Not time or energy or matter or existence or any kind of sensation in my body. Somehow I got back to my room.

I went to the window, opened the blinds, looked outside. I had a beach view. A scarlet-orange tinge of sky hovered over the Gulf, a thing of beauty. I tried to bring it inside my head to replace what was no longer there but the nothing wouldn't budge. At least I felt like a living being again. I could feel my toes and nose and legs and fingers. I might have stood staring at the Gulf for a half hour. And then it was nearly dark, and the water looked dark against the sand, and the people still out walking around were alien to anything I could grasp.

I can't say I had ever had that feeling before, not in the service, not in my reporter days, not even in hospitals under anesthesia or the hypoglycemic dizziness and passing out I'd experienced a couple of times. I tried to figure out what was wrong with me and then she was back and movies played in my head on swing sets when she was a little girl and dropping her off at school and saying goodbye and hello at airports on holidays and then those other times.

And then that one time.

I went outside to the motel ice box under the exterior stairwell and then went back to the room and poured the first drink. By nine o'clock I was on my fifth Jack and ice and then just Jack and water and finally just Jack. Apparently I was watching CNN on the TV but not really because I had no idea what any of the news was and certainly nothing about drug dealers getting knocked off all across the South. I had to pee and did that and then I was hungry and remembered I'd put some jerky and chips in my bag and devoured them.

I took my sixth Jack outside into the sticky warmth. I tried to figure why Southern nights evoked such acclaim and notoriety compared to nights anywhere else. I mean, it's the same planet, same sun, same air. I couldn't get a handle on the argument so I started walking toward the highway for a better window on the stars.

I crossed without looking or caring and within about twenty yards I was on the sand again and moving as best I could, barefoot, toward the water line. I guess the tide was out because it seemed to take forever and when I could feel the grains damp under my feet I sat down and nothing seemed real except the waves and whitecaps and just a hint of moonlight.

And Ronnie. It was good to have her back, here with me at this beautiful intersection of land, water, and sky. Southern sky. After twenty years.

I let the memory run. That's a lie. It implies volition. It wasn't my call. I wasn't even sure I could get out of it again, or if I wanted to. Ever. All of which probably sounds extreme. But the human condition is subject to no real boundaries or conceptions or rules or form and as surely as it can carry you like a leaf on a gentle wave it can hurl you as deep into hell as anyone has ever imagined. Stuff like that always made me wonder about karma. About God. I mean that was some cold shit to put on existence just to prove a point.

So Rose would have to wait. I knew why I had been so ready to help Elle. It wasn't about Rose at all.

~~~

23

For the rest of the night I could see nothing but Ronnie. Her memory settled across me as if it were reality, and I moved even further into the life I had known with her. It is called the past but I have serious questions about what that is, and when. She was with me at that moment, the entirety of her existence around me like a warm blanket that was also stabbing me with a thousand needle teeth. I wanted it the more it hurt, because the more it hurt, the more it was real.

And even with the Jack and the ocean and the sand and the night I knew the reality could only be within me. And so that's where I went, because what is in our mind is neither within nor without us. We choose to forget how it works. But now I was choosing to remember.

But there was a catch. Thanks, Yossarian. For me, getting to Ronnie meant going through not just myself, but her mother. Truth is, Rhonda Anita Prine was an accident. And yet we know there are no such things. Yet here we all are.

Annalisa was a woman I never should have married, from a match that never deserved to have been consummated. She was all about an academic career. I was filled with arrogance, propelled by illusions of invincibility, adventure, and purpose. Creating a family was beyond either of our interests or abilities.

She was Mexican-Irish, a babe with brains, we used to joke, finishing a master's degree in Latin American history at a university in San Jose, Costa Rica. I was on classified temporary duty there not long before my Army hitch was over. There was an attraction. She got pregnant. She wanted the baby and didn't want to go back to her home in San Antonio to have it. She said she wanted the kid to have dual citizenship, just in case. She stayed with the Ticos. I got recalled stateside for my last few months in uniform.

Rhonda Anita was more than a week old before Annalisa informed me of her existence. I had heard people say your life will never be the same after a kid. I thought they were exaggerating. What can't be exaggerated is how poorly prepared I was to be a parent.

I'd never given it a thought. Or maybe I had in that fleeting way that everyone is vaguely aware that they are born, grow up, get a job, think of a career, eventually become immersed in something called a life, and then die. But in truth I had none of that. I never had a real grip on the future. Just an assumption that it would happen and I would do this and that. I can't say it ever pointed to anything that mattered now.

Annalisa and I kept in touch and began seeing each other after she moved back to San Antonio with the baby, so she could get help from her mom. Meanwhile I'd gotten into TV thanks to a hook-up through an Army buddy at a station in Little Rock. We got married, lived there. Then I got a weekend anchor job offer in Dallas. Turned out I had a knack for the tube, the scar on my cheek notwithstanding—or possibly one of the attractions. It was an upmarket move and impossible to turn down. I became a Dallas TV guy.

Took less than two years for everything to unravel. Annalisa landed a tenure track from a private college in Memphis and took Ronnie, who'd just turned four, with her. Divorce papers followed. I didn't see them very often. I compensated by becoming a player, which as a TV reporter and anchor is pretty easy to pull off. I had it pretty good. What I didn't have was a daughter. Just a thread to something that had barely existed. Threads can be easily ignored, overlooked, forgotten.

What a miserable thing to say about your child. What a miserable, selfish, clueless metaphor.

~~~

24

Throughout the divorce years, I kept in touch and I paid my support. Rarely saw Ronnie. Annalisa got another teaching job, better rank and pay, in Houston. I was glad. Dallas to Houston was easy, thanks to Southwest Airlines. But not for Ronnie. I could see her more, but she cried after every visit, and I might have teared up a few times myself when I had to send her back to mom.

It's a horrible feeling, your kid slipping away. It's like you're holding her hand and she's slowly being claimed by the waves. Especially when you just let her go because your fucking life and career are so important and you couldn't find a way to get along with the beautiful woman that was her mother.

Annalisa remarried and custody visits became awkward. I didn't care much for Wayne, husband number two, although I pretended to feel bad when he ran his Jag off a highway to Galveston one night and got his head smashed in. As did the stripper who was with him. Annalisa said she didn't care if he was a cheater now that he was dead. But the truth was that something in her changed. Whatever had sparked her infectious vitality now seemed more like cold, hard steel.

Ronnie compensated by becoming stronger. For her it was behaving about as perfectly as you'd want. Good grades, lots of friends, outgoing, front row on trumpet for band. Generally warm and full of love, even for me. Then she turned thirteen. Or at least that's when I noticed. Which means I might have missed the warning signs.

She grew more distant, like her mother. Colder, in her own way. Or at least shut down from me. Visits became infrequent, almost polite. I knew I was losing my daughter but I figured it was because she was a teenager. It would work out eventually. I had my own life, my own work, my own self. I went through a few women, none of whom speak to me anymore.

I mentioned I was unprepared for parenthood? I couldn't even profit from on-the-job training. Later, it was obvious that something was wrong with Ronnie. Either I didn't see it at the time, or—far, far worse—didn't want to see it. A thousand times I have told myself that.

After me and the dead cheater, Annalisa married a third time, to Clayton, a successful if staid Houston corporate lawyer. It should have been a secure home, and maybe it was. But that's where Ronnie's changes intensified. Her crowd of friends changed gradually, then completely. Her grades dropped. Her appearance shifted to what passed for goth in the Houston suburbs.

Just after she turned fourteen, she visited me over Christmas and we both knew faking it wouldn't work for either of us anymore. She had lost weight. The black eyeshadow and lipstick and dyed hair and black leather jacket and jeans weren't exactly intended for subtlety. She told me what was happening in her life. Then she cried for more than an hour as we sat on the couch in the front room of my Dallas condo near White Rock Lake.

All I could do was hold her and try to find out what I could. And not show the anger rising in my chest. Not at her. Ronnie didn't get where she was all by herself. She didn't get where she was without people close to her knowing about it, and ignoring it, and perhaps even fostering it. Meaning her mom. I was furious at Annalisa and by extension, Clayton. From what Ronnie said, they barely paid attention to her and gave her anything she wanted. Under their watch, she was turning into a case study of a lost teenage girl.

We talked more that week. I thought we were making headway, finally getting through to each other after so long. We both made promises. Offers to help each other on our new common path. Resolutions about how to fix the mess, reel her back in from the waves. We made plans for her to move in with me when the school year was out. I saw some of the sparkle and smiles I had seen too little of late.

Just before I took her home, we went out for a root beer float. It was a thing with us. It started one summer when she was four or five and kept on going. Almost every visit we'd reach some point of happiness or, later on, conciliation, and I'd get the ice cream from the freezer and root beer from the fridge and we'd make a round like grown-ups might do with bourbon and branch.

As the ritual evolved, I'd say, "This is the best ever," and she'd answer "Indubitably," a word she'd learned in the sixth grade and liked to say because it sounded funny. Later she'd add it to our usual parting. I'd say, "Love you," when getting off the phone or leaving her at her mom's, and she'd say, "Indubitably." Or the other way around. Then we stopped making the root beers and nobody said "Indubitably." Sometimes even the "Love you" got dropped. I never drank root beer again.

As WINTER TURNED TO spring, and we made plans for Ronnie to move to Dallas, I could feel it slipping away again. Despite best intentions, the weekend visits ran into delays and postponements. When Ronnie did come, she seemed headed to isolation again, and not just the usual teenage stuff. There was fear in her eyes. Once I saw her coming out of the bathroom after a shower wrapped in an old beach towel, but I could see purple bruises on her legs and inner arms. Also a tinge of green and purple on her cheek, which had been concealed with makeup.

I asked her. She dodged the question but I kept at it. Finally she said she had argued with a boy, or boyfriend, about something and it had "made him get mad and we had a fight." These are words you never want to hear. And you know that they are never the whole truth. And you know she is being beaten.

I asked her again about drugs and since she couldn't really lie about the way she looked she said she was smoking a little pot, had tried some X, but was trying to keep away from it. In my need to feel better, I accepted that.

The last time I saw her was two weeks before the end of the school year. We took an overnight trip to Galveston to "have some fun" and talk about her impending move to live with me. She hadn't really told her mom yet and I said I would take care of that. I was pretty sure Annalisa wouldn't mind or would even be happy about it. Their relationship had hit bottom, to hear each of them describe it.

When I dropped her back off at their house on the southwest side of Houston, I actually felt pretty good. People said I was starting to look happier than in a while. I was even starting to see a woman who wasn't scared of a guy with a teenage daughter. It was all going to work out. I'd get a star in dad world.

I could have lived in that dream world forever, until the call a week later at 4 a.m. I remember Annalisa's voice, somewhere between agony and guilt, telling me how it happened. An argument at a party at some kid's house and then leaving with Eddie, the boyfriend. Skip to both of them found OD'd side-by-side on the floor at his house, parents away on a trip to the races at Lake Charles. Not even a note.

And then the next day another call, beyond all measure of pain, that the boy's parents said Ronnie had been pregnant and they'd been fighting. They blamed Ronnie and of course we blamed the boy. The funerals were separate. I only went to Ronnie's. Annalisa said she went to the other one, too, "because Ronnie would have wanted that." To which I thought and said bullshit. Little Eddie got her hooked on meth, which was found in her system along with the zygote, and I was glad he was dead. And I would never, ever, forget or forgive. Especially myself.

After that I never mentioned to anyone that I'd had a daughter. I never even told Elle. Thinking on it now, looking out at the Gulf waters under the moon, I almost had to congratulate myself on such a good job of traumatic amnesia. I mean I put a fucking *lid* on all that. Mr. New Orleans refugee, looking for a new route in life, hanging out in a city where forgetting and burying was the norm. Sir Valiant, who had helped Elle find her brother's killers and saved her in the process.

Great stuff to be proud of. So great I had even been called back into knighthood to find someone else. Another young girl who had fallen in with the drug netherworld and kept it secret from her mom, from anyone who loved her.

Ronnie. Rose. What was the difference?

~~~

25

And here I am with a bottle of Jack watching the waves. And my name is Jack. How ironic is that shit? And I'm sitting on the sand. And the sand is wet. From all that water. If I can walk on the wet sand maybe I can walk on the water. I mean, that's been done, right? I mean, if He could do it maybe I could, too? Right? I mean, I'm that kind of guy myself, right? Saviour of the weak, the oppressed, the endangered, the meek of the earth. All that good shit? Need a little of that sacramental Jack. Tastes good. Got to kick off my sneakers. Can't walk on water unless you are barefoot, everybody knows that.

I can hear music from that bar up on the pier and I need to go over there because I need to hear Johnny Rivers. Now. "Long distance information, give me Memphis, Tennessee . . ." And I'm headed there. It's not that far. Wait, I can leave Jack here until I get back. I need to hear Johnny because that is the greatest song ever recorded for assholes that lose their kids to their fucked-up wives.

And now I'm up on the pier and going into the bar and a big guy stops me as soon as I get inside and I tell him I need to play Johnny Rivers. He says I don't have a shirt on and no shoes so I'm out on two strikes from the rule so I have to go. And I tell him I need to hear Johnny. And he says forget it and blocks me with about two-hundred pounds of mostly muscle, some fat. But bulk for sure.

He says I'm a nuisance and under the law he is obliged to deny me service. Official and all and I try to get around him and then I notice on his left arm a big horse head, all black, and I step back and look at him. You were in, I ask? He looks at me real close and says, yeah, you? And I say fucking A and tell him where and he tells me where, and then I kind of calm down. I say again I just need to hear Johnny Rivers right now and he says look I can get you a Johnny Walker, how about that, captain? Then he says, use your ears man, no Johnny on that jukebox.

And I do and I realize this is a beach bar where they have Van Fucking Halen and Toby Fucking Keith and maybe even Shania Fucking Twain but they won't have my man telling us how he can't see his girl again. I stand there, thinking about this, and he signals a waitress and she comes over and then disappears and comes back with a go-cup for me and it's some whiskey crap but I don't care.

I toast my new big-guy buddy and he looks at me with something like pity and I leave. Some people are coming down the pier into the bar and they look at me like seeing some kind of beach trash and maybe I am but I keep going and I keep singing with Johnny Rivers, " . . . but her mom could not agree, and pulled apart our happy home in Memphis, Tennessee . . ." *And then I make it back to the beach because I left the bottle of Jack there and the light from the moon or maybe the road lights up on the highway glinted off it.*

So off into the waves. Water is warm, should be cold. But it's warm. Still too shallow to walk. I need to get a little deeper. There it is! Over my head for sure so if I just swim a little more I'll be able to get my footing after a few waves. Kind of like surfing. Just hop on the board when it's time and off you go. And who needs a board when you have feet of the saints. Feet that carry you to and from a little girl who only needed you to stay there. Not to let her go back into that world. Not to pretend she was okay, that she'd snap out of it.

Hey, Jesus. They don't snap out.

I CAME TO HALFWAY out of the water but not enough so that the incoming tide wouldn't fill my mouth and lungs and eventually make me spit it out and do the one thing I didn't want to do: breathe.

I must have, because I was lying on my back, looking up at the heavens, only there weren't any heavens. Just stars and planets and comets and asteroids and eons of nothing that could be easily confused with meaning and purpose and reality.

I watched. I could not pass out again. Not sleep. Not think. I could just watch. I could hear people walking nearby, laughing, on their romantic stroll along the beach front, and maybe they were laughing at me, sprawled out naked like some homeless wreck next to an empty liquor bottle. I guess I must not have looked dead, because the police would have been called. Probably. Hell, it was the Mississippi beach in the pre-dawn hours of a summer weekday not too far from the casinos. Human debris was no more uncommon here than in New Orleans.

When first light put a squint in my eyes I looked upon myself and indeed I had shed my shirt and also my shorts and skivvies and shoes and if I could have, I would have stayed here until the impending heat fried me and I could be at peace.

But a couple of wade fishermen passed along, and then a group of joggers, all fit and corporate-looking. One of them shouted something that sounded derogatory and I managed to sit up. My shirt was long gone but my shorts were close by. I think I had used them for a pillow. I managed to put them on. I found my sneakers, too, glad no one had stolen them. My back hurt and my right calf was cramped from the wet night on the sand. But I was able to walk.

I crossed the highway again to the motel. The cleaning crew saw me, didn't say anything. Ditto with an older couple loading up their Caddy to check out. I was lucky I had the room key in my shorts and so all I had to do was open the door and go inside and sit on the edge of the bed with my head pounding until I was able to shower off. I don't know how long the hot water ran over me but it left my skin boiled like a lobster. I dried myself with the scratchy motel towel, settled on the edge of the bed again, and didn't wake until the phone rang. They wanted to know if I was going to stay another night. I said I'd call them back in thirty minutes.

Then I looked at my own cell phone I'd left by the TV. There were a half-dozen calls. Five from Elle and one from Big Red. His was the one I listened to first. He wanted to know "Where the fuck are you? It's time to go."

The ones from Elle said to call her back right away. Then several hang-ups. I needed to call them both back. But I couldn't. I wanted to stay in the motel another day, at least. I wanted to go back to the water. I didn't want to be where I was. But I was. Where I was.

All I really had to do was get dressed. Get some food in my stomach. Make those calls. Get some gas. Get going. In my torment, I'd fallen into the hell of history. But this was the hell of now.

~~~

26

I didn't call. For a cheap mattress it felt damn good and I fell asleep again, until noon. By then I figured, fuck it, I'm staying. It's called a hangover. I'll get back to Red and Elle when I feel like it. I dialed the front desk to arrange for another night. Couldn't be done. Agribusiness machinery convention in town. Everything was booked. The clerk said I probably wouldn't find a room this side of Slidell, at least worth staying in. Unless I got lucky. I didn't feel lucky. I asked her if I could get an extra hour to check out. Reluctant yes.

I packed up my things, took another shower, slammed my fist into a door jam so hard it bled but didn't break. And then I left for Lake Charles. Might as well wait the night there for Red as anywhere else. It wasn't like I even knew where he actually was or where we were headed anyway.

I called him back from the road, told him I had wasted a day on some personal stuff about my daughter, which I then had to explain that I had. Did have. I told him just enough that he'd know. It was the first time I'd ever revealed anything about my personal life and he'd never told me anything of his, beyond a love of fishing. It seemed a little weird but when he said he was sorry about what happened, I knew he meant it.

I thought he'd be pissed I was AWOL, though, and he was, a little, but he said I caught a break because he was still waiting on the family about what to do anyway. Then he cleared his throat and his voice dropped lower and he said not to go so long ever again without returning his calls. Regardless.

He said Lake Charles was a good enough holding spot and he'd meet me there whenever any solid intel came through. He said everything right now was just an educated guess. Or blind chess. You have to have a feeling for it without seeing it. I agreed. But he surprised me when he said it really didn't matter where Rose was being held by the kidnappers anyway.

"They'll change the meet-up at least twice because that's what they see on TV. And they'll give us more time, if we promise them more money. These fuckwads are total fucking flakes."

"Copy that but I'd still like to know what they say."

"And copy that, but I'm still saying it'll be bullshit. For now. The cartels would already have killed her, or would kill her if you tried to change anything to get Rose. And then they'd come get the money from you anyway. Or the drugs, or both, or whatever the hell they may be after. Speaking of which, what's the news from Elle?"

"I need to call her."

"Shit, Jack. Call her."

"I will. Soon as we hang up. What about whatever you need to do if we need extra help?"

"Not a problem. The main thing is the Francosis. It's how they want to play it. Above my pay grade kind of stuff."

"They won't like the cartels, right?"

"They won't like anybody moving into their game, true dat. The question is how to handle it. Usually there's some kind of shit playing off one crowd against another. Whatever they call, I run it. That's my deal with them."

"You figure you'll hear by tomorrow?"

"I do."

"What'll they think about me?"

"They won't care. They kind of like you, for a civilian."

"Like last time?"

"Well, maybe a little easier this time. Last time you had to prove yourself."

I laughed. Slightly. More like an awkward chuckle.

"I don't see the humor, Shakespeare."

"I wasn't laughing like it was a joke."

"Either you got lucky with nailing Trey Barnett and getting that painting or you were real good."

"I'll go with luck."

"What do the mercs say, 'Who dares, wins?' I mean, what the fuck, Jack, you're right back in it again."

"So I'm a merc now."

"Wake up, man. You always were. Hell, we all are."

~~~

27

I passed New Orleans without stopping. Lake Charles wasn't all that much farther along. Late afternoon I pulled into a big casino hotel, which is about as anonymous as it gets. I endured the snotty scrutiny of the reception clerk and went to my room.

I had stashed about a third of the bottle of Jack in my bag yesterday when I was drunk and was surprised to find it. I poured a drink, not because I needed it but because I wanted it before calling Elle. Even with a hangover I knew that calling her would be a form of calling Ronnie. Not in any logical way. But that's not where I was.

She answered with that tone you sometimes get from people who are annoyed you haven't called them sooner. I was getting too familiar with it. I said I was sorry, there was a delay.

"Where are you?"

"Lake Charles."

"What about Biloxi?"

"This is closer to Texas."

"If that's where they are."

"If that's where they are. Have they called you?"

"There was a voice message. Some guy just says, '6 p.m. or whatever. You better answer, bitch.' Hangs up. It was the same voice from before. I've been waiting all day. And then you don't call either. Fucking call me back from now on, Jack."

I gave her an even shorter version of what I had told Red. I could practically hear her teeth grind.

"What else can I do?" she eventually said.

"Call me back whenever they call you. And I need you to get in touch with Blaine."

"You're drinking."

"It's just a beer. It's damn hot down here."

"Blaine? Why? I can't do that. And you already did."

"I should have spent more time with him. I thought I could figure out where Rose was from the stuff in Topper's house. But I can't. Maybe he can be more precise, is what I'm saying."

"I thought you said he was messed up."

"He is. But he'll talk to you. He pretty much has to. I went over that with him. Trust me, he'll talk to you."

"Jesus. What have you done?"

"Why do you care?"

Short silence.

"I'll call him."

"In person would be better."

"No. I just said that."

I didn't want to argue. "Okay. But if he doesn't answer . . . "

"Fine. Then I'll go over there. Satisfied?"

"We need an address, at least a city. Some way to contact them."

"He might not know."

"I've come to the conclusion he might."

It was nearly nine when she called back. I had fallen asleep fully clothed with the TV still on. She'd just gotten off the phone with the kidnappers. Same guy. She said they were probably trying to ratchet up her anxiety by being so late. She half-laughed and said she didn't have any more ratchets left.

The voice said they wanted us to meet them Monday, then someone said something in the background and the voice said Sunday. Repeated it. Sunday. The someone said Monday again and the voice sounded mad and said he'd get her the specifics later. But it would be at "a swamp lake in East Texas." The voice even dictated how the money should be brought to them. A metal suitcase, with locks and keys. Nothing else would do. They hung up. Rose never got to speak.

I said "fuck all that" to myself but not to her. She said she'd take care of the money details with a branch of her bank in Shreveport, but could get it from Houston, too, if they changed locations again. I said they would, but in the same general area because they'd want us close enough to bring the money to them fast. She said it would be ready whenever they were. She asked if she still needed to call Blaine and I said yes. In my business, two sources were better than one.

I called Red right away. He said I told you they were clowns, and to stay flexible. And that the family was in.

~~~

28

I woke at 4 a.m. at an airport in Memphis, Tennessee, trying to get in touch with my Marie, and then she was Ronnie and then I was sitting at a picnic table on the beach and watching her float out into the Gulf on a small metal fishing boat with a forty-horsepower Evinrude motor pushing the whitecaps. Such an eye for detail, I must've been a spook and a reporter sometime in my life.

I opened my eyes again and kept them from shutting, but it was a minute or five before I could sit up. There had been other dreams, too. Probably also about Ronnie, but I couldn't get them back. Or maybe they were about Rose. Either way, lots of bodies. Everything had become one long melding of awake, asleep, consciousness, oblivion, sober, drunk, hunter, prey, victim, killer, mourner of children, righteous revenger, knight of the sad body count.

I made a pot of motel coffee. Smelled worse than it tasted. Then a quick set of sit-ups and push-ups and shadow-punching. By five, I was showered and in fresh jeans and shirt and had regained a sense of where the hell I was. I was looking for my keys to go out and get breakfast when the phone rang. It was Elle. Again.

"He called. Blaine. He sounded strung out or drunk or both. I've been trying to reach you all night."

"I never heard it ring." My jaws had been set so hard when I was sleeping, I could barely get the words out. "Good morning."

"I called maybe six times."

"Sorry."

"We went over this. You need to get a lot better about taking calls. I mean it."

"Okay. Sorry. I'm just trying to wake up."

"This will get your attention."

I went to the window and peeked out the curtain. Not quite dawn, but it was coming. "Okay, I'm awake."

"He woke me up, too. That's why the hour."

I couldn't suppress a yawn.

"Come on, Jack. Wake up. You're still in Lake Charles?"

"I am. Hang on." I poured the dregs from the coffee pot into my cup and inhaled it. "Okay, keep going."

"Blaine. Blaine called me."

"Got it. I'm just a little slow because I wasn't sure he'd still be among us. But good. Call me any hour of the day."

I could hear an impatient exhale. "So he said he was sorry to call me in the middle of the night, but he said you told him that was the only way he could call me. If he had some kind of information. I guess you were right. I mean I didn't even have to call him. He called me. That sinking in?"

"Uh-huh."

"I mean even drunk or high or whatever he was on, he was sounding scared of you."

"Maybe not just me."

"Maybe."

"What was his news?"

"Topper had been there. He took Blaine's pickup, that was filled with dope. Marijuana, he said."

"And?"

"Don't gloat. He said Topper was taking it to his 'crew,' he called them, over in East Texas."

"Where?"

"It's called Uncertain. The town." She waited as if I'd say something and I didn't. "I mean it's a real town."

"I know. Caddo Lake. I've been there."

"Write this down, Jack. 27 Blue Cypress Road. I think it's just outside the actual town. Blaine wasn't exactly sure other than the address."

"Why did Topper tell him all this?"

"Blaine said it was in case Topper didn't call back by Tuesday morning."

"And Blaine was supposed to go looking for him?"

"Topper seemed to think so. But Blaine said Topper was taking a lot of pain pills and maybe some uppers. So he was talkative. But you know Blaine would never go there looking for Topper."

I thought about that. "Did Blaine say how any of this would lead to Rose?"

"No."

"But you think it will."

"You don't?"

"I do. But it's good that you think the same."

"So you can get to Uncertain?"

"I can. Can you still get the money?"

"I'll have it today, no matter where I have to take it."

"Don't go anywhere yet, though."

"I know. What about Red?"

"He's in."

"What should I do?"

"Just stay put. It's getting close. You're doing it right."

"You don't need to pump me up."

"I mean Red and I will get to Uncertain. If Rose is there, we'll set things up."

"What if they want to make the trade before I can get there?"

"They'll wait. Red says they're amateurs. They'll change the time and place just to act like they're in charge. But in the end, they'll wait for the money."

"If Red sees it that way."

"I do, too. Did Blaine say when Topper might have left Atlanta?"

"This morning, I think."

"So he could get there tonight. To Uncertain."

"For all I know he could already be there."

"It's a drive. But he's a walking drugstore. He won't stop."

"You know him better than I do."

"No."

"I didn't mean it that way."

"It's okay."

"But you won't go in . . . and get yourself . . . in trouble. I mean alone. You'll work with Red."

"He's on this. We'll handle it."

She was breathing hard into the phone again. "And Topper won't want Rose for himself?"

"No. Plus he'd have to figure a way to cover the million she'd bring in."

She was quiet a moment. "Jack, I'm barely sleeping."

"We'll get her out. It won't even be a fair fight."

"A fight?"

"I didn't mean it that way." But of course I did.

I pulled the curtains back all the way to let in the morning sunlight. In the process I half-tripped over an ottoman in front of a chair, stumbled and banged my knee against the corner of the metal bed frame. I murmured "fuck," and instantly the image of Blaine's face when I broke his ankle flashed up. It seemed cruel then, and even now. But it was also necessary, and deserved. Because I had hurt him, we now had an edge on whomever had taken Rose.

When I was doing intel, one of my COs used to say that we needed to stay focused on the op. To trust that our part was integral to something larger that we might never know. That what looked like a bad thing for us was a link to something good for many others. To assume that. Basically that was the entire military trip. It was also when I started questioning what I might call the difference between a good kill and a bad one. There wasn't an easy answer. It was bothering me again. So I decided to stay focused on the op. On the mission. At least I knew for a fact that this mission was righteous. I mean I assumed that.

~~~

29

Red was an early riser and was already up when I called with Elle's news. His voice broke up badly from static and I asked where he was, that it sounded like he was on the road. He said he'd gone into Biloxi to grab breakfast and was driving like a tourist on the shore highway to kill time until I called.

We agreed to meet no later than 6 p.m. in Uncertain. Barely a wide spot in the road, it was only a few hours north of Lake Charles. We would have plenty of time to make it and do a recon. We talked about how we might get into the house for the swap. If in fact Rose was there. Red said "deadline" in a way that sounded like it was in air quotes. He said he had figured it eventually would go down somewhere closer to Dallas, but if they really were in East Texas, so much the better. "It's in the fucking swamps, man. I mean there won't be anybody between them and us. Bad for them."

He told me how the family was looking at this. Usually he just grunted a few comments that he figured I needed to know. In this case maybe he just wanted me to know he had a motive other than being a do-gooder. He said his bosses turned out to be extremely interested in whatever Topper and his redneck militia in Texas might be up to. Grateful that he had called, in fact. It was more or less a jurisdictional thing, sort of regular business in the mob industry. The Mexicans didn't like hearing about them, either.

Red said bottom line was the family had given the militia a red card and designated him as the umpire to throw them out of the game. Topper, too, if needed. I forgot about his interest in soccer, which always seemed strange. But there were a lot of things about Red I had yet to learn.

I said I was positive the militia, not the Jovenes, had Rose. But I wasn't clear on how exactly Topper fit in. He said that was the way he saw it, but he always allowed for contingencies, and he said I ought to know that. I said I did.

We discussed what to tell Elle about getting there with the money and decided to leave her in Atlanta until we had a better feel for what, if anything, might be in Uncertain. Red's basic position was that we would get Rose back and no money would change hands. I agreed, but I didn't tell Elle that. I told her to just be ready to come on a moment's notice and I'd let her know. She said it was hard to just wait and maybe she should join me, like we'd done back when. I said this was different. Very different. She didn't need me to explain.

I got to Uncertain earlier than I wanted, but better than being late. I'd been to the swamps around Caddo a few times, always on some kind of assignment. CBS-7 and the other Dallas stations had a strong interest in the East Texas market, and we'd cover anything from a triple homicide in a fishing lodge to small-town Christmas parades. Once I'd stumbled on a catfish café that sold guns, ammo, and kid toys. I never liked going and usually wound up drinking on the way back to the city if it was a wrap and the camera guy didn't mind driving.

Uncertain and everything around it was carved out of cypress trees blanketed with Spanish moss half-floating atop still, dark waters teeming with snakes, gators, mosquitoes, ticks, and the constant presence of things unseen. Throwback country in every way. Most of them not good. Hard-core Klan-loving racists and gun-crazy backwoods misanthropes. A few back-to-nature hippies but they were nearly extinct.

It was anybody's guess why a dandy like Topper had chosen the location to meet his militia pals to tie off the drug deal that started unraveling in Atlanta at an abandoned house that still might have rotting corpses in the backyard. My guess was that this was and would be a psycho trip start to finish, because you play with what you get.

I stopped at an outdoor sports store on the way to buy a good flashlight, a pair of overpriced binoculars, some extra boxes of ammunition for the Remington and the Colt, and a few supplies if I had to spend the evening in my truck. And a lot of mosquito spray. The store had a detailed map of the area framed on the wall for visiting hunters and fishermen. It was an easy place to get lost. I took a few minutes to study the layout. The road the house was on was actually visible, including the dead end it made into a creek feeding into the lake. My biggest concern was finding a vantage point from which to recon without being seen.

The two-lane asphalt road into town from the store was a couple more miles of bars, restaurants, auto parts stores, real estate offices, and small business strips. Getting a sense of the physical layout made me feel better about our odds, and worse. Better because of the steady line of vacation cottages and fishing camps that had grown up helter-skelter. Zoning was not a concept that had infiltrated Uncertain.

Worse because it was Saturday, and the congestion of weekend vacation houses that made the stretch of road common and unremarkable also meant there wouldn't be any decent vantage points for a stakeout while I waited for Red. I'd have company no matter where I set up.

I drove past the house with the address Elle had given me. Three pickups were parked in the gravel drive and on a lawn beaten into dirt. The road ended abruptly a half-mile farther at a cul-de-sac, also lined with vacation houses. I made the turnaround and drove back past the target house again, careful not to appear interested.

A two-story cabin on a slight incline about a city block away looked like it had a decent view. I slowed past it and after a few hundred yards pulled over and took another look. What had caught my eye was how unkempt it was. Weeds in the yard, no cars, no lights on or signs of activity at all. The kind of place an absentee landlord might rent out or use as a vacation place. Perfect.

I couldn't linger so I drove back into what passed for a main street, stopped at a gas station to fill up, joked with the teenage attendant about the high price of gas, and then spent another half hour just cruising around.

When I figured I'd been gone long enough I made my way back to the deserted cabin. I backed up the incline of the weed-covered gravel driveway until I was nicely nestled between the cabin and a rusty metal storage shed. I could just see the front of the militia shack, and with my binocs it was a fairly decent overall view. I turned off the engine and gave it a pretty good look, couldn't make out anything, and settled back in my seat. It was hot and I lowered the windows. I may have dozed off for a few minutes.

I awoke with a start, sweating. Maybe another nightmare. I picked up the glasses and had another look. I must have missed it the first time, but the bumper and grill of the red F-150 pickup was very much like the kind Red drove last time I had seen him. It was parked on the far side of the cabin, backed up against a moss-covered cypress. I put the glasses down and thought on it. Then I called Red. Got his voicemail.

Nothing happened for an hour, and it wasn't getting any cooler. I got out, walked around to the far end of the lot to feel the slight breeze and pee. When I came back I rolled up the windows and cranked the engine for the a/c. There was enough ambient noise so no one would notice. A few cars came and went on the road. None seemed to take any special interest. Actually, I probably fit the profile of any number of city-dwelling "sportsmen" come down here to drink and fish and shoot and kill stuff and get fat with their sense of manly endeavors.

At 5:30, I tried Red again. In theory we were supposed to meet in a half-hour. But we hadn't firmed up a place and he'd have no idea where I was parked. So he had to be expecting my call. If he didn't answer, I needed to leave and come back. This time he picked up.

"You're here?" he said.

"I've been here for a while. How about you?"

"Where exactly are you?"

"Where I can have eyes on the house."

"Shut up . . . I'm on the damn phone . . . Sorry . . . talking to someone else." I could hear voices.

"Where are you? Who's that talking?"

"I saw you called. You didn't leave a message so I didn't call back. . . . Shut the fuck up I said . . . Just some assholes I'm lining up to help us."

"Red. Are you here? Am I looking at your truck?"

"Sorry Jack. I'm not going to bullshit you."

"What the fuck?"

"The fuck is that I got here about two. Hang on." It sounded like his hand went over the phone. I heard something like, " . . . not telling you again . . . "

"Say what?"

"Sorry about the fucking interruptions. Morons . . ."

"Fuck all that. You're here?"

"One of my guys works this part of town. He knows if something big is moving. And this guy from Atlanta, Topper, we had a good leak on him, too. From the Mexicans, turns out."

I held my phone away from my ear and breathed out a couple of times. "Jack? You still there?"

"I'm coming down there. Goddam."

"I was going to say that."

"Good." I hung the phone up, started the Jeep, didn't give a shit who saw me, and all but peeled out of the driveway. I pulled up in front of the house, right up against Red's pickup. I thought about bringing a gun with me. But somewhere along the way I'd learned not to let stupid manage anger.

<hr/>

30

I parked in the dirt in front of the house and marched in without knocking. Red greeted me legs apart in the entry foyer. Big was such the right adjective.

"It's messy. She's not one of them. How ya doin'?" He shook my hand at once, and managed a smile through his red, black, and increasingly silver beard. I'm in good shape, but damn, he had a grip.

I looked past him at the living room. He was right. It was bad. Blood spatter everywhere.

"Fuck, Red."

"I get it. But we had to move fast."

We looked each other over. I made no attempt to hide my pissed-off. "I figured we'd come into this together. You know. Like the whole fucking reason I called you."

His eyes narrowed. "Like I say, I get it. But things changed. I had to move. The family was real specific about this."

I held his gaze, which didn't waver, then decided to let it go. I was also aware that there were two other people, alive, on the other side of the bullet-riddled room.

"Po-Boy, Carlos, just roll 'em up and finish the cleaning. We been here long enough. Need to be gone." Red's big left arm did a half-sweep in their direction, giving me an invitation to look over the mayhem. Three bodies, lined up on a thick plastic mat, were bunched tight like steaks on a grill. Two had Nazi tattoos on their arms. One also sported an "HH," for Heil Hitler, on his bald head. Skinhead stuff. The third guy was harder to recognize. Probably a shotgun to the face and upper torso.

"Topper?"

Red shook his head. "He was gone. Before this last one died"—he indicated HH—"which took a little while, he said the perve, what he called him, had gone into town for cunt shit, what he called that, with the nigger cooz, what he called her. You know, that kind of guy. So neither one of them was here. One of the reasons we haven't left yet. Waiting to see if they'd come back. They didn't."

"And you just shot it out?"

"More or less." We exchanged looks, not nice ones. "We basically did the shooting. I think maybe they thought we were Topper and Rose coming back in, or something. They were just sitting here drinking beer, some kind of game on the TV." He pointed at what was left of it. "It only lasted a few seconds. Good thing HH was talkative."

"I'm sure he was happy to chat."

"Po-Boy told him we'd let him live if he did." The wiry Cajun was pulling plastic over the corpse. "But whadyya gonna do, you know?" Red said.

"The drugs?"

"We got them. Topper left his pickup. HH told us, before his demise, that Topper didn't want to drive it around no more, considering it was full of felony. So one of these dead dipshits loaned him a truck. We just don't know what kind. HH didn't get that part out before Po-Boy shot him."

"Well I fucking thought he was done," the Cajun called out, almost like a dog afraid of being beaten.

Red looked at me, closed his eyes for a second, and shook his head. "Don't matter, leave it. Just get all this done."

"So you have the drugs, but Topper and Rose, not so much."

This time Red's look was knife-sharp.

"It wasn't like that. Don't go smartass on me. I'm not in the mood."

"I just thought we'd nail it here."

"I did, too."

"So no idea where they're gone."

"Well, yeah, there's an idea. I mean I pretty much know exactly where."

"HH got that out, did he?"

Red set his jaw, turned away, and went over to Po-Boy and Carlos, snapped out a few clean-up instructions.

"So where?" I asked when Red finished his management duties.

"It's all headed for some West Texas shithole ranch out near Abilene. And yes, HH managed to get that out." Po-Boy started to say something but stopped when Red glared at him. The premature termination of their only source of intel would come up later in Red's after-action review. Or whatever the mob called it when there was a major fuck-up.

"He said for sure it was the same crowd out there, Salvation Brigade?"

"He didn't. But we found some of this shit lying around. Who gives a fuck." He pointed to some flyers and posters on a table.

"Same back at Topper's. Damn, Red."

He swatted one of the posters to the floor. "Fuck this, Jack. Let's move on. I got here before you did. Fuck difference does it make? You want a beer? I sure as hell wouldn't mind one."

I didn't say anything.

"They're in the fridge." He started talking to the goons.

I went into the kitchen. The choices were Corona and Dos Equis, which struck me as odd for a bunch of white racists. I grabbed one of each, gave the Corona to Red. We both drained about a half bottle in silence.

"About the Mexicans," he said. "That guy, Blaine something, you had a chat with. They did, too."

"How?"

"They just said they'd talked to him, didn't say how they came to have his acquaintance."

"So they also told you where Topper was headed."

"See, I always said you was smart."

"No, you didn't."

"Well, I must have thought it."

"Anyway."

"I don't get why you're pissed off."

"Give me a break."

"Goddamn, I did you a fucking favor, taking care of all this."

I finished the beer. "Really? We set up a plan. I tell you everything I know. I think everything is in synch between us. But hell. You already know. And you don't share. Leave me sitting out in my fucking Jeep for an hour."

"I told you I had to move. We couldn't be sure if these idiots would split right away, especially if your boy Topper showed. You couldn't of got here in time anyway."

"You don't know that."

"You need to get over this snit, brother. Fuck, I was TCB. End of fucking lament."

I looked around the room. He was probably right. But it didn't feel right. It didn't feel wrong—yeah, he did definitely TC'd the fuck out of B with these slimebags. But that didn't feel right, either.

I made a note in my head that Red would roll how he wanted to. I mean I knew all that from chasing down Trey Barnett back in New Orleans for killing Elle's brother. But here it was again. It wasn't that I didn't trust Red. He wasn't betraying me at all. He was just ignoring me when he needed to.

Po-Boy bumped into me while carrying something out to a pickup and I moved out of the way. "Sorry," he mumbled.

"So back to letting me know . . . the Mexicans . . . they gave you the okay to get here to take the dope. Time being a factor and all."

"You starting to figure it out?"

"Well, shit, I don't know. Why the hell would the Mexicans let you get all the dope?"

"Think on it some more." He was smiling a little.

"Jesus, a fucking game to you?"

"You think it's just about busting balls and taking assholes out?"

"They gave you the dope so you'd take out the Salvation Brigade."

"Because . . ."

"Because they don't like entrepreneurs any more than the family does."

"Fucking home run, amigo. I'll get the beers this time."

He did.

"It was all pretty straight up except the fucking Savannah asshole had to pick the wrong time to take a drive with our girl Rose out to the 7-11, or whatever they call them in swampville."

"Yeah, that was a drag. Him and Rose gone and all when you were shooting the place to shit."

His face reddened. "Yeah."

He said something under his breath probably best I didn't hear and turned his attention back to Po-Boy and Carlos. The bodies were all rolled up and wrapped inside black bags, sealed tight with generous strips of duct tape. Red pointed toward a stretch of brown tarp near the door and they used that to cover the bodies even more. Carlos was complaining, just a little, and wanted to just set the whole house on fire. Po-Boy knew to keep his mouth shut.

~~~

31

Red took another guzzle of his beer, went to the fridge, and leaned against the door. Looked at me like a teacher about one wisecrack shy of booting the clown out of class. "So moving on, whoever got here first, we have an address, even a map, courtesy of our late friends. Some old bankrupt farm or ranch in country so shitty no one wants to live there. Which is good. We're going to take them down."

"What makes you think Rose will be there?"

"Money, fuck else?"

"The ransom, you mean."

"Without the drugs, that's the only chit they got left. Another reason the Mexicans weighed in. They smell easy money. It's not like they'd do us favors. Shit, Jack, I think they know you, or somebody like you, is working with the mom."

"Really? That seems pretty remote."

"It does make me wonder how they're so plugged in. I mean other than your pal Blaine. Who seems to have talked. A lot."

"Is he?" I asked after a moment.

"Alive? No."

I wasn't even ready to compute how this might lead back to Elle, or if it had already, or how it might lead to Rose. Or where the hell Rose even might be. Only thing I knew for sure was that I always seemed to be arriving at places where a lot of people had died horrible deaths. I was starting to get a complex about showing up. Or maybe that was just the beer on an empty stomach. I got up to grab another. For us both. The choices were rapidly going downhill to Bud and Miller.

"So I assume we're headed west."

He snorted. "I think we have a few days. They'll be disorganized. Scared, probably, finding out what happened here. It'll be the first thing Topper spits out when he gets there. But they won't hurt Rose."

"I guess."

"I figure they'll all be daisy-chained together at that ranch or whatever tomorrow or Monday, outside." He looked around the room again. Po-Boy and Carlos were crisscrossing the floor.

"Half an hour. We'll be good. We just want to make real sure we got it all. It was a big fucking mess," Po-Boy called out, still trying to suck up.

"So fucking step on it."

"We ought to burn it. The whole damn house. You know," said Carlos.

Red glared at him. "I heard that the first thousand times, goddammit. Just do your fucking job. Speaking of which, anybody check that Toyota that he left here? See if it starts, has gas, any of that shit? And everything is tied down good?"

"It needs a fill-up but it's ready," Po-Boy said. "Do you think he meant to leave all that weight? Just haul ass with the chick?"

"He was coming back," Carlos snapped at him. "The bitch just went at the last minute because she was bored, is what she said."

"I didn't think she liked him."

"You're a fucking idiot and a dick."

They both laughed.

Red looked at me and shook his head. "This is why I wait to bring them in right before a job. And move them out right after."

"Still," I said, "not sure why she'd want to just take a convenience store ride. She probably knows him better than anyone in this whole mess."

Po-Boy and Carlos exchanged looks that Red couldn't see.

"Anyway, she went with him and they're gone. That's all we know for sure," Red said.

"Yeah," I said. "Too bad now we can't find out how she got here in the first place and why they let her get out of their sight with Topper, or why she was even alive, and generally what the fuck was going on." I got the sharp look I expected.

"You can't read that?" He was mocking me but I ignored it.

"If you mean she was here because Topper had her kidnapped, yeah. I mean yeah, and no."

"Meaning what?"

"Meaning if she was already in Savannah to see him, why would he go to all the trouble to have these idiots kidnap her, or pretend to kidnap her? This is a guy who cuts people up and sells the parts. He could've just disappeared her all by himself and gone for the ransom without any partners if he'd wanted to."

I could see Carlos and Po-Boy still trying to silently signal each other, and then they both retreated back to the farthest wall, as if this conversation were above their pay grade. Or as if the less they knew in their line of work the better.

Red gave them a fleeting glance that erased whatever composure had been on their faces. "Thing is," he said, "we got the weight, and we know where she's headed, and we know these guys are losers. Pretty soon we just tie up the last knot."

"Leaving Rose where?"

Carlos and Po-Boy fidgeted like they wanted permission to go outside.

"Once they get the ransom they either kill her or . . ."

A possible future flashed through my brain.

He put it into words. " . . . Or they find another use."

"You mean sell her."

"You asked me the play. I think that's where it's headed. He looked over at the nervous help. "For god's sake, you look like a couple of fucking schoolgirls."

"We just want to get on with our work. You know," said Po-Boy. Carlos rolled his eyes.

"Go check the damn rides again." They were out the door. Red watched longer than necessary.

"Well," I said. "That's pretty much where I come in."

"Where we come in."

"So this is still in your interest? In the family's interest? You already got the drugs back for them."

"It's not just this load. It's the future."

I looked around the room, still trying to get a sense of what had happened and been said in this swamp hole in the last day or so. What Rose had said. What Rose had done. What had been done to Rose.

"What do you think?" I asked. "They never came back, period?"

"Do I think a stone-cold killer like Topper would just cut out, leaving a truck full of drugs in his Toyota?" He laughed dismissively.

"So they came back and saw you were here."

"That'd be my guess."

I put my beer down and rubbed my face with my hands. "And you still think they're going to that ranch out in West Texas."

"I do."

"And she'll stay alive."

He finished his beer. "Look, hell with all that shit. Think going forward from right now. Frick and Frack here will finish cleaning up and haul ass in the Tundra with the drugs to the family. That's the end of concern with that. As for Rose, we hole up for tonight some place on the way to Dallas. Grab some zzz's and get back on it first thing in the morning. We should have better intel and you'll have better sense by then. Hell, you got raccoon eyes."

There was a sliver of dark humor in his smile but also a lot of truth about how this shit wore you out.

"I can get us some help if it's in Texas," I said. I hadn't known for sure until I got here that I wanted my old pal AK-47. I did. And not just to help find Rose.

"The Vietnam vet with the funny name?"

"He's solid."

"You trust him?"

"I do. He saved my life in Costa Rica one time. Took a bullet for me. And he knows people all around here."

Thoughts spun through Red's eyes and furrowed his brow. "Sure. Call him. I guess this part is your game. But if you need it, I got guys, too. Not necessarily them." He looked at Po-Boy and Carlos carrying out the last of the body bags.

"Roger that. I'll set it up. I know what I'm doing."

He returned a smile I had only ever seen on killers of men. "We're good then."

"I just said that."

We watched Po-Boy and Carlos finish loading the dead Nazis into a black Dodge Ram. It had Louisiana plates, but I knew not to ask anything about its home.

"You'd better get going. I'll be another half-hour with the geniuses. Call me wherever you get a hotel. Call Elle. I'll check in later, see you in the morning."

"Unless."

I left them to their work. The phrase "casualties of the war on drugs" flashed through my mind but not in a sympathetic way. It was pretty clear which side of the war everyone was on. We just had different chains of command.

Last thing I saw was Red going out to his own pickup and leaning over the back bed to pull out the plastic gasoline jerry can he kept for his fishing boat.

~~~

32

I found a chain hotel outside Tyler. I called Elle once I'd had time to think about what to say. I said Red had gotten to Uncertain early because he got a tip from some mob hustlers in Shreveport about a drug deal. I said he'd gone in to see if Rose was there, or Topper, but they'd come and gone and were headed out to somewhere around Abilene, which is kind of what we'd been thinking. I didn't go beyond that.

I said we'd be going to West Texas tomorrow, with the information from Uncertain and Blaine and my time with Topper, and I'd let her know what I heard and for her to do the same. I said she might want to make arrangements with a bank in Fort Worth. She said she had already drawn the cash and would just keep it at her house in a safe place. Pending. I said it might be a couple of days. I knew I had lied to her—had been lying to her, directly and by omission—and I would likely lie to her again. It was that way.

Red and I didn't talk until morning. He said he had slept like a log and to my surprise I had, too. I guess bone-grinding exhaustion can stifle even the worst of bad dreams.

We convoyed west. Traffic made getting around Dallas and Fort Worth slow even though we took the southern loop through suburbs spawned by white flight and tax dodges for businesses that'd left the Rust Belt for the Sun Belt, only to find their belts tightening again.

He still didn't completely believe anyone from the Salvation Brigade would be at the ranch. It was equally or more possible that the meth Nazis, or whatever was left of them, would have split up. The only binding factor to get the gang back together was their million-dollar asset. Red didn't put much stock in us knowing anything for sure. "They're just yanking our chain. Or Elle's," he'd said, wolfing down a breakfast taco before we left Tyler. "It's still greased pig time at the rodeo."

My greatest concern wasn't the run-around, but how the militia masterminds might be responding to the stress of being hunted. Not just by us, but also by the mob and a Mexican cartel. Most of the paramilitary scenes I'd ever encountered had to do with a lot of insecure head cases pontificating and posing and making threats toward people who couldn't fight back. Now they had to get used to being on the other end of that.

The spread we were looking for was somewhere off I-20 west of Fort Worth and north toward Quanah. Closest big city was Abilene, king of what was left of the oil patch towns. I knew we'd have to confront tweaker world sooner or later, and this was as likely as anywhere. The smack and the coke and some of the pot might be coming in through Mexico, or Afghanistan, or other foreign trade routes, but for the really nasty shit, meth and speed and X and their derivatives, it was hard to beat made-in-America. Cheaper and faster to produce, and no customs hold-ups.

For the wasted young who were growing up with zero promise in small towns, rural dead-ends, and busted-down suburbia, dealing meth was the top-earner fast-track that in higher levels of the American Dream came via expensive colleges and networked jobs. But regardless of the socioeconomic nuances, they were dealers of horrible prolonged death. After Ronnie, I just wanted to kill them all. I didn't care who sorted them out.

Red didn't like following close so he trailed a couple minutes behind. I kept my speed down because he wanted us to take our time. The drive was long and boring so I broke it up a little getting on my cell phone to fill in my new partners a little more about each other. We didn't have time to bond as battle buddies, but I knew that soldiers who knew even a little about each other were more likely to succeed in a mission and stay alive.

Telling Red about AK took up most of the way from Six Flags to the other side of Fort Worth, including extra time in the eternal traffic jam. I basically hit the highlights, although with AK that included a lot. It went more or less like this:

The big man was born in Las Palomas, a Mexican village just across the border from Weslaco in 1947, via a singular blend of fortune and fate. His grandfather, Hermann Kreutz, was a German army captain on loan to the Porfirio Díaz government. Hermann was killed by Pancho Villa's troops in 1910 for sleeping with Esperanza, a Villista who would become AK's grandmother.

I asked Red if he wanted to know more and he said he'd listen to anything but the fucking country radio stations or talk-show psychos. Also he'd never turn down intel. I recounted what I could remember.

Esperanza deserted her well-off family to serve the Revolution. She could have been shot next to Hermann for consorting with the enemy but was so beautiful and able to translate both English and German that Pancho himself intervened to spare her life. And she was pregnant. Before the year was out, she bore Kreutz's son, Walt, who married a gringa idealist, Sonia, who'd come down from Chicago to teach art.

Walt and Sonia begat Alvarado and two other Kreutz kids. They crossed into Texas and lived a modest life running a café and small inn, did a little smuggling as a sideline. When he was old enough, AK started college. Freshman year, he got into trouble fighting with the wrong kid, and according to the custom of the time, was given the option of joining the Army rather than go to county jail.

Which led to Vietnam. I told Red that's where he got the AK-47 nickname, and I could sort of hear an amused groan. I said how AK got back from the jungle alive was another long story, but when he did, he moved to San Antonio and took odd jobs. He also had a son, Benito, whose mother ran off to San Diego. Benito turned out to be gay, which didn't bother AK, but did catch the attention of some racist speed-freaks in McAllen one night. Benito, a teenager, had emerged from a locally known gay bar. They outnumbered him 3-to-1 and kicked him to death with their Doc Martens.

AK took months to crawl out of his booze hole. To everyone's surprise, he seemed to have reached some kind of peace. His heart wanted him to do something positive for Benito's legacy. He donated his free time to helping crime victims. But his soul was stuck on revenge. The murderers were in Huntsville on ten- or fifteen-year stretches. He couldn't take it out on them.

But plenty of other scum fit the bill. Doing good for victims was okay, but punishing perpetrators was better. He hired himself out for off-the-books collections, tune-ups of wife beaters, occasional skip-tracing, some black ops contract stuff. As long as it never involved selling or moving or recovering drugs. Hammering dealers was fine. Plenty of work came his way. It was profitable.

I didn't go into this part with Red, but the way I met AK was on the Costa Rican coast near Honduras, me with the Army, him with either the DEA or the spooks, he never said, looking for some especially bad guys smuggling drugs and guns. It was around the time I also met Annalisa. When I said I'd never told anyone about Ronnie, I was incorrect. AK knew her mom, and he met her as a little girl, and he knew how she had died. Both our kids dead long before their time was one of the other things that bound us, and maybe separated us from Red.

I finished the story telling Red that AK used the money he earned in his post-military specialty work to get a degree in sociology and philosophy from a state school. Never used it but said he owed it to himself, a promise he'd made if he lived through the war, something like that.

Red said he understood. He said I'd picked a good man. And that he wanted to meet him.

Calling AK to fill him in on Red didn't even get me much past Weatherford, west of Cowtown. I knew so little about his personal life, only picking up bits and pieces here and there. But I did know that he'd saved my life. AK liked that. He also liked that Red had smacked me around a little because of my mouth. And he liked the condensed version of how Red had helped me find and kill Elle's rapist half-brother, Trey, Rose's biological father who'd also run afoul of a big dog in the Dixie Mafia.

After I had told him about that and we hung up, AK called back, saying he'd given that some more thought and he was really glad to be a part of this, and working with Red. He said he just wanted to tell me that. Another difference between AK and Red. AK didn't hold much back. Red held back almost everything.

~~~

33

We joined forces at 1 p.m. at a busy interstate gas station and convenience store I knew of about sixty miles east of Abilene. The place was always filled with tourists, long-haul truckers, and high school or college athletic teams on road trips. They knew this was the only exit to refuel, eat, and pee for many miles of nothing. Three guys getting together to grab a beer and sit on the picnic tables next to the huge parking lot outside would attract zero attention. Zero attention was something we hadn't been too good at achieving to this point.

AK was waiting at the far end of the lot when we drove up, leaning against his sun-faded, dark blue Suburban, as old and busted-up as he was. Hadn't seen him since I left Dallas but he looked the same. Straight-up Vietnam vet, old school, with gray beard, VFW ball cap, and Army green fatigue shirt with the sleeves torn off. He wasn't like something in the movies. He was the something on which the movies were based. I parked my Cherokee on the gravel. Red's F-150 on my flank.

We got out for introductions. I shook AK's hand, then a quick old school hug. He and Red exchanged handshakes, and mutual once-overs. Looking at them together, I couldn't help but notice that, except for different fashion and hairstyle preferences, they were the same guy. Must have said something about my choice in friends. I was relieved to see the slight nods of male approval. I'm sure it helped that we all were vets. But I hadn't relaxed until now, when they met face-to-face in the parking lot.

We walked across the gravel lot to a row of wooden picnic tables under some scrub oak along a rainwater ditch. It was hot. I said I'd go in the store to grab some waters. They both wanted beers. By the time I got back they were talking easily.

I had a map in my back pocket and spread it on the table. I drew a circle around the place where the ranch most likely was. We didn't have a street address, and maybe there wasn't one. Our directions consisted of "about a mile down that asphalt county road to the left before you get to Haskell. Wildfire Road. Then turn at the dirt road with the gate and cattle guard. Can't miss it." Or so I'd written down Red's memory of Heil Hitler's last words.

We wouldn't know if it was isolated or in the middle of a drilling site or no-questions-asked trailer park for migrant workers until we actually got there, but our collective guess was that whoever chose it to cook meth had been careful to make sure the neighbors were scarce. Still, looking at the map, it wasn't too hard to see the squiggly line for Wildfire Road. Probably an hour, maybe two, from where we were.

We went over possible strategies as they finished their beers. Came up with a plan. Recon this afternoon, attack around midnight. There wasn't a plan B. Whatever we did, it had to be fast, and it had to be tonight. Every piece of intel we'd been getting had the life span of a moth. It was starting to feel like we were guerillas, attacking and moving on, always depending on chance, never a minute to rest, or to let the enemy rest. It was all about stamina, determination, persistence, adaptation. And luck.

Red and AK exchanged cell numbers and we ran through a quick inventory of our weapons—both of them were armed to the limits of the Second Amendment. Everyone took a turn at the toilets and gassed up. We agreed to find a cheap motel on the way to the ranch to sit out the remains of our day as if we were a bunch of oil patch contractors waiting on tomorrow's shift schedule.

Once the action began, we estimated time on target at two hours, three at most. By zero dark thirty we'd exit the site, split up, and head back on our own paths—Red to the Alabama coast, AK to South Texas, and me back to Atlanta with a young woman about whom I knew everything, and nothing.

What was the saying? Men plan, God laughs?

~~~

34

We passed an oil patch motel, $28 a night, free XXX cable, concrete block breakfast diner next door, about twenty miles out from the Wildfire turnoff, and checked in, staggering our arrivals just enough so we wouldn't appear to be traveling together. Roughnecks and tool pushers and service contractors already were pulling in for the night.

I'd volunteered for the recon—driving into the ranch to see, first, if it was even the right place, and two, what might or might not be going on there. So we would go in two vehicles—Red with me in my Jeep, and AK in the Suburban as a backup. Then we got to thinking that another backup might not be a bad idea and ended up all going in our own rides.

Given the crapshoot nature of everything until now, extra transportation caution on a fairly short drive wasn't a bad idea. All we knew was that some white-boy hoods—not even sure how many—were cooking meth, dealing, and kidnapping. And that they had made a connection with a deranged purveyor of human parts who masqueraded as an eccentric proprietor of an elite restaurant in an Old South city, and had now crossed paths with an aggressive new gang and a major cartel.

Despite our confidence, another way of assessing it was that we had as much chance as an infantry squad taking on a heavy weapons platoon at the top of a cliff. And we were happy to be doing it. That was the weird thing. That was the thing that was wrong with me.

We assembled along a wide space on the shoulder of the county-road asphalt a mile from where the map indicated we'd find Wildfire Road. Immediately got into an argument. AK said he'd thought it over and I couldn't do the recon. Nothing against me volunteering, but it would never work. He said he wished he'd brought it up before we left. I didn't like it.

"It's my op. I should take the risk," I said. "We went over this."

Red tilted his head at AK. "He's right, Jack. You go in, new black Grand Cherokee, Louisiana plates, and turns out Topper is there after all. It's fucking over."

"What I'm thinking," AK said. "Next thing you'll be hauling ass back here if they haven't dropped you on the spot. Then it gets nasty."

"Could be bad for whoever goes in. I can't ask you to do that."

"You're not asking, Captain Prine. I'm volunteering."

"Listen to your NCOs," Red said, and they shared a look at my expense.

"You know it's true," AK said, hitching up his jeans. "They'll figure I'm just another Mexican looking for a job in the oil patch."

As if on cue, a welder's rig clunked past us.

"Fuck, this place is crawling with Mexicans hunting for work."

"This isn't even your fight, AK."

"Sure it is."

I closed my eyes to let it play in my head for a second. Then I looked at him. "So you go in, have a quick look, say something in Spanish, like you were trying to find another place, had the wrong directions or whatever—kind of like what we said I was going to do—and come back out."

"Only better, because to them I'm just another wetback. Hell, I drive up in an old rattle-ass Suburban, they might not even come out to talk to me. I get a free look and leave. You think I'm taking a risk? You might be, but I'd just be an annoyance. You know how us Chicanos can be invisible to white people." He laughed. "Especially these white people."

"Something goes bad you get out and Red and I are here. They wanna play, we play right then."

"Jesus, Jack, down boy. You wanna storm in guns blazing in broad daylight? That'd be the fucking cat's ass, wouldn't it?" AK said, half-smiling but mostly looking at me like I was some kind of shavetail on his first patrol.

Red laughed a little, too. "Okay, back to reality. You ready to saddle up, AK? It's hot standing around in the sun for godsake."

"That's how it played out in Uncertain, right?" I said, turning on Red, for no good reason whatsoever, and regretting my words before they'd even cleared my tongue. "Just barged in and blasted everyone in sight?"

Red locked his eyes on mine. "We knew what we were laying into there. Fuck do you mean?"

"You know."

"Back off, brother." He was all but squaring around against me.

AK moved between us. Looked at Red, then me. "Something I'm missing? What the hell, Jack?"

Red spat onto the ground, his eyes never leaving mine. "Jack here is talking about how me and my crew took out the East Texas chapter of these Salvation boys back at Caddo Lake. He won't fucking let it go."

I knew I was an asshole and shut up.

AK spit off to one side. "There's bad blood here? Nobody said anything about that."

I raised a hand palm-out in submission. "Forget it." Red held up a hand in the same way, then turned around, back to me. I guess he was looking out at the horizon.

AK studied us for a moment, no telling what was he was thinking, then headed to his Suburban. "I'm going down there," was his only comment.

Red nodded, as if concluding an argument with himself, turned back around, and went to his Ford. I went to the Jeep. We pulled out, lethal little convoy that we were.

We'd barely turned onto Wildfire off the county road when Red stopped near a gravel-covered lane blocked by a rusty metal gate and two concrete posts. A cattle guard just inside the gate. After that the lane curved into a line of oak and juniper trees and thick brush. Had to be the place. I pulled in behind Red. AK behind me. I leaned out my window and gave a thumbs-up. Red and AK did the same.

After a moment, the Suburban stopped at the gate, AK got out and pushed it open, then rumbled slowly over the cattle guard. Protocol was always to shut a gate behind you, but we wouldn't be playing by the rules. I could see AK had rolled down his windows, and then I could hear a Mexican pop station playing loud *conjunto*. He was in character.

~~~

35

In less than five minutes, he was coming back. I could see the dust from the lane and hear the accordion before I saw the Suburban. It bounced across the cattle guard and turned up past me onto Wildfire, then kept going. I made a U-turn and followed.

Red peeled out, too. Within minutes we were back at our assembly point along the county two-lane. We got out and gathered in front of Red's Ford. The look on AK's face was the perfect frame for what poured out of his mouth.

"I don't like it. Old ranch house, seen better days. Stone and wood, tin roof, open front porch, maybe couple thousand square feet, looks like a couple of bedrooms added on toward the back, probably for when they had workers for ranching. Some kind of small barn in the back, about the same condition as the house. Two trailers up near the barn next to a line of oak and mesquite. One looks like it's been there, the other like it was just parked. Still on a wheel bed."

"Vehicles?" Red asked.

"Three big pickups, all macho-ed out, maybe another behind the barn, a couple of Harleys. One looked broke down for repair."

"So we don't know how many's there?" I asked.

"Hard to say. Can't be more than a half-dozen or so. Some guy, in his thirties, T-shirt and jeans, tats, shaved head, comes out from the barn and walks toward me. Carrying a friggin' AR-15, wearing a holster. I figure I need to talk to him rather than drive off."

Red nodded.

"So I get out and walk over his way—he was maybe fifty yards off—and do my humble Mexican thing. I say I'm looking for Senor Galindo. In Spanish."

"He answered?"

"He says, 'Speak English, greaser, or get the hell out.' So I keep talking in Spanish, asking for Senior Galindo. That pisses him off even more, and after a minute or so of me just standing there acting like I don't understand, he says 'fuck this' and calls back toward the barn.

"I can't make out what he says but this tiny young girl, looked very Mexican, she comes out and walks over to him. She's afraid. Really afraid—I can tell just from how she moves. He looks down at her and tells her to 'tell me what this fucker wants.' So she hollers across to me *'que quiere usted'* and then I repeat the Senor Galindo thing and she tells him in English.

"He looks at me funny and says something to her and she asks me in Spanish what do I want with him. I say he was running an ad for a long-haul driver and that's why I'm here. So she tells him that and he comes a little closer to me, gives me a look-over and goes back to her, speaks to her harshly I could tell even though I couldn't hear. She calls over to me, 'Ain't no Mr. Galindo there, you got the wrong place so get out.' Words to that effect.

"So I say, okay, *perdóname, señor*, and raise up my hand to wave goodbye and I hear him say, 'just get the fuck out of here, wetback,' and I go back to my truck. I pretend to take a while to get it started and look the place over again. The girl is already on the way back to the barn, the guy is looking over to the house like somebody is looking back at him and he calls out, 'fucking wetback looking for work.' Then he stands there a minute, like he's waiting for a signal or something. Then he goes back to the barn."

"They're running girls," I said.

We all exchanged looks.

AK continued, biting off each word now. "So I start it up and then the door on that older trailer opens and there it is. Straight-up tweaker, skinny, long hair, crazy-looking, peeps out like what the fuck is going on out here, has him a good look, and then back inside, trailer door closed. Thing is, he's wearing a plastic apron."

"Cooking."

"Cooking."

Red leaned back against his truck, looked at his watch. AK took several breaths, then went to his Suburban and grabbed a bottle of water.

"Those pickups. Any of them look different?" Red asked.

"Hard to say. Couldn't really see the one behind the barn, except it was green. The other three were black. Wait, one was camo. They had jacked-up tires. Why?"

"Topper and Rose took off with some kind of big rig back at Uncertain, but we don't know what."

"I don't know. Something felt weird, though."

"Best guess. Rose is there?" I said.

"If you want my gut, my gut says yeah."

"Any Confederate flags, signs, that kind of shit? Any people at all other than the freak and the girl?"

"I mean I knew more were there, they just didn't show." He stopped, his brow wrinkled.

"What?" I said.

AK looked at Red. "These nut jobs, I mean they normally have racist crap all over the place. They want people to see it."

"Right."

Red kicked at the dirt. "Fucking knew it."

"Meaning?" I said.

"Militia my ass. It's a fucking meth factory. My guys will want to know what I did about it. The girls, maybe, can slide. Not this."

AK and I looked at each other.

"Girls and drugs," he said. "Perfect. Motherfucker."

"It's not like I didn't figure something like this," I said.

"Yeah, well."

"I'm not arguing. Just taking it in."

Red looked at AK. "You still in? You didn't sign up for this."

AK nodded, glanced up at the late afternoon sun, then back at Red. "You know, I saw that girl and it was all I could do to get back in my truck and leave."

"So."

"So."

"Then we're all in," I said. "And it still definitely is about Rose."

Red's jaw set. "We got to talk more about who might be in there," he said to AK. "And when we want to move. I'm still for midnight. They'll be fucked up or tucked in or both. You get any sense of discipline at the place?"

"Fuck no."

"Right. So we hit the house first, then the barn. Then the cook trailers, if need be." He looked at me. "Watching for the girl all the way."

We went back to the motel. We set chow time at eight, giving us plenty of time to rehash final details and maybe catch a quick nap. At least I was going to. We might as well have been planning a Friday night outing to a ball game. I wasn't the only one for whom this kind of thing was becoming its own kind of jones.

~~~

36

We huddled in Red's room to down the BBQ sandwiches AK had gotten from a nearby place the motel clerk said was good, because the Egg Burger next door was closed. He told AK he wasn't missing anything. I brought the map and some paper. We talked out the options and obstacles several times. One of the main concerns was how to spot Rose. None of us had ever actually seen her. I pulled out the photos Elle had given me and we looked at them very closely, but if the barn actually was full of girls, could we tell her from the others?

And could we do that in enough time to save her if it got as nasty as we expected? AK said it would be okay, that we were going to free all those girls anyway, that they would come out alive and go back to wherever they had been before a black hole in the world opened up around them. Nobody objected.

We went over the weapons inventory yet again. We discussed whether to carry shotguns for when we got in close. I had the Remington, and they the short-muzzle police models. Then we decided we'd leave them in the trucks. The assault rifles AK brought were plenty, and we wanted to move light and fast. We had plenty of ammunition. Red and AK both had combat knives, which I didn't but I didn't have much skill with those and preferred my Colt if it got that close.

"You gonna help pay for this stuff I brought for you?" AK asked me. "I had to call some favors to get them so fast. Favors that aren't free."

"Well I was figuring to just borrow them."

"Funny."

"Rent, maybe."

AK rolled his eyes and looked at me and Red. "When we're done, we're gonna put all these weapons, yours or mine, in my truck and I'm gonna take 'em to a buddy who'll make 'em go away. So don't lose anything. Right?"

Red and I nodded.

"And that's when you done bought 'em."

I looked at AK a minute just to get the feel in my gut he wasn't joking around anymore. I nodded. Red shrugged but it meant the same.

"Right, then," AK said. "And in case we need it, I know some freelance medics in Dallas and San Antonio, maybe another in Houston if he's still alive."

"I know some guys, too," Red said. "Let's hope we don't need 'em."

I watched the cable news at ten mostly as a critic, noting what they covered well and what they screwed up. It passed the time and also gave me a little sense that the world was still turning out there, and not in a good way. Never anything about what we'd been doing, not even Uncertain.

AK mostly stayed outside, said he was looking at the stars because he knew he wouldn't be able to do that forever. The moon was just past full and even with the clouds, it hung like a big flashlight. Good for our plans.

Red went in and out, on the phone a few times to New Orleans or wherever he had to touch base with his "guys." At one point I heard him talking to AK, leaning against one of the trucks in the parking lot. I heard AK mention his son's name and figured he was telling Red more about what happened and why he was getting mixed up in something that had no real connection to his life at all.

After the news I walked outside to get acclimated to the warm air, not the a/c of the motel room. Red and AK were sitting on a concrete and therefore theft-resistant picnic table in a beat-down grassy patch near the office. AK was a smoker but Red had quit and I never started. Red was staring up at the moon and the sky now, too, maybe looking for what AK saw.

"Damn thing about the jungle," Red was saying, as if finishing up a conversation, barely noticing I'd joined them. "You'd be sitting around with some guys waiting to maybe go in the bush or maybe spend another week bored out of your skull and all hot and sweaty and maybe a little fucked up and mostly just miserable and then some kind of sky out of a painting would open up overhead and you'd forget everything for a little while staring at it." He stopped. "Damndest thing."

"You liked that war? I mean, thought it was right?" AK asked.

"Fuck no. You?"

"Fuck no. It was a goddamn nightmare."

"People don't usually get it. Hating it and doing it at the same time."

"Hardly anybody who wasn't in the shit."

"I finally just let it go," Red said. "'Course, I was really only there at the tail end, unless you count the shit in Laos and Thailand. All that never-happened kind of shit."

"It all counts," AK said. He turned to me, as if just noticing my presence. "You told me it was kind of fucked up in Honduras or Panama or wherever, and Korea, different kind of way."

"That would be accurate."

They both laughed.

"Can you fucking believe?" AK said, sweeping his arm over toward our trucks.

"It is kind of . . ." I didn't finish the sentence.

"Thing is," said Red. "It's the same for us, I mean your basic night attack on some fucking VC outpost, but now it's all different. I mean we all are." He looked at me and at AK and shrugged. "What it is."

"I never really let it go, I guess," AK said. "I mean I sort of did and then they killed Benito. Now, it's sort of set in. Hell, look at me. I'm a fucking comic strip of a bad joke." He finished his cigarette and flicked it down and crushed it. Shook his head. Looked at his watch. They both stood.

They were huge up close together. "Fuck it," Red said, and put his big hands on AK's big arms and then his big arms around AK's big shoulders and hugged him. Then stepped back.

I felt like I was looking at something beautiful and terrible and that I would never see anything like it again. It lasted about ten seconds.

AK stared at Red, and then turned away, heading for his room. "Mount up," he said.

We packed everything into AK's Suburban because it had the most room, and if they noticed us before we got to the cattle guard, we could pretend AK was still lost and looking for Señor Galindo. He could do stupid Mexican again.

If it got as far as answering those kinds of questions we'd probably already be under fire anyway so we didn't spend a lot of time rehearsing. We'd drive in as close as we could, dismount, fan out, and move forward. Like Red had said, that time of night they'd either be asleep or drunk or fucked up.

My concern was finding Rose. If she was there. AK's priority was to take the barn. Seeing that girl was not just eating at him, but consuming him. Red just wanted to tie up loose ends and give a body count to his bosses. We didn't intend to kill 'em all and let God sort them out, because God wouldn't want any part of this night.

～～

37

AK paused the Suburban just past the cattle guard and looked up the trail to the compound. "It's maybe half a klick, if that. You think we might just leave the rig here?"

"Good for me," I said. "Red?"

"Yeah. We can go quieter. What's that gravel lane like as we get closer?"

"Mostly open, uneven, scrub and rocks and a few mesquites, a couple small gullies for runoff. Pretty much like everything we've seen around here since we got off the interstate."

"Done, then," AK said.

I looked at the watch I'd brought for the occasion. "I got eleven forty-five. Wanna say a time to get back here if all goes to hell?"

"We ain't done in an hour, we got problems," Red said.

"Twelve forty-five, then."

"Twelve thirty," AK said. He pulled onto the beat-down grass about twenty yards from the opening to the trail and turned off the engine. We got out with our gear.

AK went to the front of the truck, leaned down at the left tire, and covered his keys with dirt and dry weeds. He made sure we saw.

"Just remember where you put them, 'cause you'll be leading us all out of here," Red said.

"Copy that, brother. But you know, just in case."

"Follow me," I said, walking off, then looking back to see if they got the joke. Hell, I was the officer among us. They got it. Not sure they thought it was funny. Nothing in the way of humor at all.

I took the left side of the lane, AK the right, and Red about ten steps behind AK. The moon was still doing its thing and within about two minutes of quiet advance we could spot the house and barn and outbuildings. A light shone from a room at the right rear of the house, and one of the two meth trailers was definitely lit up. Maybe a low light in the other one, hard to tell.

The lane broke up at the outer brown patch of a yard in front of the house. We formed an assault line as we had planned. We kneeled, gave ourselves a minute to let our eyes adjust and to get fully focused on how to move.

AK had the barn, Red and I would take the house, and I'd hook off for the meth lab if needed. If it was like your garden-variety speed factory, nobody inside would have a clue what was going on outside. I looked at my watch again. Eleven fifty. I raised my right arm, pointed forward.

"If that barn is as full of girls as I think, I'm going to kill whoever is keeping them there," AK whispered.

"Good with me." I glanced at them both.

"Main thing is that one girl," Red said, then looked at me. "And I would like a word with your close friend Topper. I mean after you've had a chat with him yourself."

"Move out," I said.

Red made the wooden plank steps to the small front porch first. I stayed a few yards back on his left flank, watching the trailers as I moved. Red paused, listening for something but apparently not hearing it. He tried the door. It swung up with barely a push. He looked back at me and shook his head. He didn't have to say "fucking morons" but I was pretty sure what he was thinking. Then he was inside.

I heard two pistol shots, then several more in return from assault rifles. Then a short burst. I stopped briefly at the door, nothing shot at me, and I went in. A kitchen light off to the left illuminated the big front room well enough. Two bodies lay on the floor.

Red was standing next to a small table to my right. He flashed a hand signal to get my attention and pointed toward the rest of the house. I flashed up my fist and shook it twice toward my face to indicate I was sorry for getting distracted. He pumped his fist back and kept looking and listening toward the back rooms. I could see, between me and him, a better view of the Salvation boys, one of them without most of his head. Both were wearing camo.

I could also see the deranged décor that hadn't been outside. Confederate flags, Nazi flags, a couple of Klan robes, and stretched across most of one wall, a huge black flag that said Salvation Brigade in bright red, with swastikas and crosses in each corner. Also on the wall were a silver-colored Christian crucifix and dozens of pinned-up photos of the boys posturing in militia gear. Boxes of what looked like assorted Brigade paraphernalia were in a corner, as if being sorted and repackaged. What struck me most of all was the U.S. flag hanging next to a window.

I began moving forward but Red immediately threw up one palm to tell me to halt. The other hand was gripping his M-16, the butt pressing into his shoulder. I could hear cursing and yelling and then two men, one in camo T-shirt and the other naked, ran forward holding a pistol and a rifle, respectively. Red fired a burst and so did I. Both men dropped. The naked one slammed against the hall wall and when he dropped his rifle it hit the floor, spitting out two rounds. One zipped past my right shoulder but barely creased skin.

Right after that came a scream, shuffling of feet, and a "Get the fuck out there, bitch." A young woman was being pushed in front of a sinewy little bare-chested guy with camo pants and desert boots, holding an Uzi.

"I'll kill this b—" camo pants started to say until his head exploded from Red's single shot. But he'd already pulled the trigger on the Uzi, and a round tore open the girl's neck, spinning her like a top and spraying blood everywhere.

It went quiet. Red and I crouched, waiting to see if there were any more. About a ten-count and he shook his head at me to indicate that was probably it. I went to check the girl but it was only a formality.

Red came over and pulled her eyelids down, seemed to say something under his breath. I watched the hall. Then we both moved down through the rest of the house. There were four bedrooms, like AK had guessed. All messes. Various cots and frame beds. Transient kinds of stuff.

"Clear," I said and then I heard Red call out the same from his half of the search. "I think the guy had the girl in that last room, looked like that kind of thing. Son of a bitch," he growled.

"We're missing a couple," I said, just as shots sounded from the outside. Likely from the barn.

"I'll go. Get on that fucking lab," Red said.

We rushed outside and split up. Flashes were still coming from the barn. Also screaming. Many voices. Female.

The trailers were close, and their lights helped me avoid holes and fallen tree limbs. I held up a few yards short, but couldn't see any movement. I opened the door to the one with all the lights and surprised two skinny freaks, both wearing plastic aprons, safety glasses, and big headphones. One was bopping to whatever he was hearing. The other just zoned out.

The ersatz lab was about as I'd imagined. A big stove festooned with pots and kettles and plastic wires connecting to various tanks, probably for ephedrine and whatever else they hell they were adding to the cook. Plus storage buckets and thick plastic sheets hanging from the ceiling to cordon off the cooking.

Even at this level of redneck production, I was impressed at the sloppiness
and danger. All I could assume was that the Salvation Brigade had come
across this revenue source somewhat recently and was relying on the local
labor pool at least for the start-up. And that was about five seconds more
of evaluation of the quality control of the operation than I had intended
to spend.

I didn't know if they were reaching for guns or tending to their cook, so
I shot them anyway. Before I really had a chance to think about the barrel
flash igniting a spark in the room. I'm still not sure why it didn't explode.
Maybe because I was near the open door, or maybe I was just stupid lucky.
But when the second chemist fell, he dragged down a length of plastic piping
leading from a copper pot to a metal keg. The collision caused a spark, and
that's what started the fire. Or that's how it seemed. It happened so fast I
couldn't be sure.

I jumped back through the door into the night as the fireball expanded, first slowly and then in a quick burst. Just as rapidly, it consumed the
oxygen in the trailer and flamed out, leaving a pool of low-burning flames.

"Fuck," I said to no one but me, and hurried to the other trailer. The
light I thought I had seen was still in one window, but no sounds. I figured
anyone in there would have heard the noise and seen the fire so I expected
nothing. But even if I had expected something, it wouldn't have been what
I saw when I opened the door.

It was mostly empty, not yet set up for a lab. Where the supply and
mixing counter would have been was Savannah's own Meredith Topwynn,
struggling to free himself from handcuffs fastened to a metal bar lining the
far wall of the trailer.

He saw me, and pulled harder at the cuffs. He was wearing sweatpants,
no shirt. I could see blood along his wrists. Also a criss-crossing of long
scratches or possibly knife cuts along his hairy back and chest and arms. I
didn't want to spend a lot of time looking but I had to at least have a moment.

"Jesus fuck. *You*?" he yelled. "What the fuck next?"

"Nice to see you."

"Get me out of this. There's a goddam fire next door. This whole fucking
place is a three-alarm waiting to happen."

"Maybe." I stepped back out the door, looking toward the barn, and listening. Still some screaming, but no more firefight in progress.

"Red!" I yelled.

"Clear! Five bad guys down. One civilian."

"AK?"

"Clear! Three bad guys down."

"Two bad guys here. And Topper. I'm heading over. Can you see me?"

"Roger that. Come on."

I looked at Topper again to be sure he was still bound to the bar.

By the time I reached the barn, Red was outside.

"It's secure," he said. "AK's good."

"Yeah."

"Before you go in, get ready."

"For what?"

"You'll see." He swept his free hand toward the open barn doors.

~~~

38

AK was standing in front of at least a dozen girls, mostly Mexican from the nervous Spanish chatter. All under twenty-five. Probably way under. Some brown, some black. No white. They were wearing shorts and T-shirts, in various states of dishevelment, and standing or sitting against the back corner amid a cluster of cheap cots, various piles of empty water bottles and fast-food wrappers. The smell was bad.

It took me a moment to see the one girl that didn't fit. Leaning against the rear barn wall, jeans and dark purple T-shirt, watching. Not in fear. More as an observer of the human condition. And considering her options.

"I think that's her," AK said.

I looked closer. It was. Not in the way of the photos Elle had given me—pretty and maybe a little delicate. This girl's stare and body language said nothing about delicate. It was like she didn't even notice the dead bodies, the funk and smoke of the shooting. Or even me studying her so hard. Then she gave me a head-nod of acknowledgment. I glanced at AK, who shrugged.

"We're getting them out of here," he said. "They're all in shock. At the least."

"Roger that."

"Red says the house is clear, too."

"It is."

He sniffed. "What's burning?"

"Meth trailer. We need to move."

"*Vamonos*," he said to the girls. "Get your shit and get out the door. It's gonna be okay. *Todo estará bien ahora*." A couple of them said something to some of the others, probably translating the English into Spanish.

They started to move. A few picked up small bags or loose scraps of clothes and whatever else they had been able to scrounge or keep with them. Most had nothing but what they wore, or nothing they wanted to bring. None of them were crying. Some looked harder than the others. But all their eyes were wide and mouths tight. They were looking everywhere, especially at AK and me.

They wanted to trust us, but they had been in a world where trust had turned into terror. As they passed, and I could see closer, I revised my age estimate of twenty-five. I doubted any of them was more than twenty. One small Mexican girl, hair braided in the indio way, was thirteen, tops.

I caught the look in AK's face as they passed. He might have seen the same on mine. We would have killed every asshole we had just shot all over again, into a hundred lifetimes.

Rose had fallen in at the end of the line. Still the observer, still calculating the odds. She stopped when she reached me. She was a carbon copy of her mom.

"You're Jack."

"You're Rose."

"Took your fucking time." She leaned forward, put her hands around my face, and kissed me on the cheek. "I don't know any words to say it." Then she walked outside with the other girls. At the door, she paused, looked back at me. "You got Topper?"

I cocked my head, as if trying to hear her.

"I mean, is he dead?"

I was outside next to her in four steps. "He's in one of the trailers. The one that's not burning. You want to fill me in?"

She took a step back, eyeing me but not afraid. "We need to get out of here."

"That's the plan. And Topper? Tell me." I took her arm and moved her along toward the rest of the girls as fast as I could.

AK and Red had them rounded up near the pickups. AK was talking about drivers. Two of the girls said they could but their licenses had been stolen by "*esos cabrones.*" Another said the licenses might be in the laundry bag full of cash the *cabrones* thought was in a secret place in the barn. It was under a floorboard covered with a gallon drum of paint. They'd planned to split it up for going-home money once they were free. AK looked at me, held up his free arm in a what-the-fuck wave, and pointed to the barn. The girls went back for the stash.

Meanwhile Red was kicking over the two Harleys, checking the saddlebags for guns or anything useful. He watched as I led Rose to the trailer where hoarse screams for help pierced through every other sound of the night. "Just be a second," I called out.

As we got closer I could see the fire was gaining traction, but still contained in the main trailer. And I could hear his yelling, to anyone who might be able to hear him, more clearly. "Fuck's sake get me out of here. I mean you have no idea, do you?"

Rose stepped into the narrow door frame. "I do. Have an idea."

I'll always regret I wasn't able to see his face. Although I could hear what was left of his voice. "Motherfucking son of a bitch. I thought you were gone. What the hell?"

"This must be quite a surprise." She went all the way in and sized up his predicament, turned to look at me with an extremely twisted smile.

I waited a beat, then followed her inside. "Anyone want to fill me in?"

They seemed to be trying to read each other. I could almost see a white-hot stream of bad energy. Neither answered my question.

"Fine. Don't tell me. But you have about two minutes. As soon as the girls are in the trucks, we're gone," I said, and coughed from the smoke as if on cue.

Topper dropped out of the staring match with Rose. "Then you'd better cut off these cuffs."

She turned to look at me. Her lips were closed tight, jaw muscles knotted. She didn't need words.

"Maybe you could give me a reason," I said, moving closer to Topper. "You may remember our first encounter."

"Oh, right. Fuck that, you're fine."

"Tell him," Rose said, finally speaking.

Contempt replaced the hatred in Topper's face. Then something like condescension as he tried another eye-lock with Rose. "Look, he wants to get you back to your momma. I can make that happen faster, get all these other problems out of the way. This can still work out, Carla dearest." He said it like I wasn't in the room.

"What problems?" I said. "Looks like 'Carla' is free and ready to go home."

Topper looked at me dismissively, then laughed. Then coughed.

"What do you want to do?" I asked Rose.

"I want to be a fire-starter. You know, like in the myths." She coughed, too, dabbed at her eyes. The fumes were manageable but not for much longer.

Topper made a sound something like a laugh but fell short.

"Why is he like this? Out of curiosity," I said.

She took a step back to get a better overall perspective. Shook her head. "Short story, I came here with him so he could keep the kidnap thing going and get the money, give me a share. Then he was going to kill these idiots somehow and we'd split. Or just split if he couldn't figure a way to kill them. They were stupid enough it could go either way, is how he put it." The words slicing out like blades between her teeth.

"Split? Where to?" I asked.

"Him, probably Savannah. Me, I have a friend over in Dallas."

"You'd move to Dallas?"

"Not move. Just get my bearings. This whole thing has gotten pretty out of hand."

I couldn't laugh but I wanted to.

"Should've kept to the plan, bitch."

She coughed and then snorted through her nose, kicked a crumpled cardboard box at him. "And then after we were gone I was going to kill him and take the money back to mom."

"As if."

"But of course I didn't mention that part to him."

"I like my idea better," he said.

"Right. No fucking doubt you did." She moved up to him again, dropped down into a squat just beyond his reach, like she wanted him to see her as close as possible.

"So once we got here he got greedy," she said, talking to me, looking at him, fanning the air to try to get the smell and eye-sting away. "The million wasn't enough. Basically, he decided he could just eliminate the downside risk—that would be me—altogether. So he gave me to these pigs."

I didn't tell her that was already the play Red had figured out back in Uncertain. Only thing I couldn't work out was how she never saw it coming.

Topper coughed some more, wriggled a little, as if he could get free. Then he stopped, did his best bravado. "They were incredibly happy, you know, these boys. I mean they had great plans for you. Primest of the prime meat. I guess if you were so fucking smart you'd have seen that, though. I mean before it happened, bitch."

She spat in his face. Twice. Second time, his tongue came out and he licked at the spittle on his cheek. Still the bravado thing. I just wanted to shoot him.

She pretended to spit a third time and he flinched. She looked over at me with a smile. "The truth is more along the lines that once this shitface 'gave' me to his militia buddies to sell with the other girls, the geniuses got to drinking and doing some lines and decided I'd be worth way more than a million to the cartel—maybe even twice that much. And then they had an even better idea. Just make me a gift. You know, special peace offering to start doing distribution business for them."

I looked at her, and him. "The girls in the barn go for that much?"

"They're all primo, but they don't. She does," he laughed. "Go ahead, finish up your story for your Texas rescue dog here." He coughed again. Sounded really bad.

She raised from her crouch and lightning-fast punched him hard in the face, taekwondo style. She saw that I noticed.

"I'm going to cut you into little pieces when this is all over," he yelled, trying to shake off the blow. "I'm gonna sell your tits to those Miami boys for dog-chews."

"I'll take the action on those odds," she said. Then, to me, dabbing at her eyes again to clear them. "It's a little more complicated, I guess. But that's the thumbnail, Jack Prine. I gather we're in a hurry."

"You fucking whore. I should have left you back in Savannah with your little friends. And your really special one, Elena."

She took a step, side-kicked him hard in his groin. He doubled over as much as the cuffs allowed. "Fucking bitch."

I waved a hand like I didn't know who he meant. I don't think she bought it.

"Oh, wait, you don't know about Elena?" he sputtered. "I guess you'll find out."

She squared off to kick him again but stopped herself.

"Look," I said, "We need to keep moving. For one thing it's too damn hard to breathe. But for the record I'm still not sure why he's all tied up here. Wasn't he the money man?"

He had retreated against the railing, his legs drawn together but contempt still all over his spit-coated face. She faked a kick and he came close to cringing.

"About the time the boys decided I'd be worth more to them as a tribute to the cartel," she said, "they also figured out they didn't need Topper here anymore, either. Not to mention they were still pretty pissed off about losing the drugs and their crew back at Caddo."

"We weren't done with all that yet," he snarled.

"They were," she glanced at me. "They'd put up with his rich boy shit as long as he had drugs for them. And they were stone racists, solid fact, but really all the white supremacy shit meant nothing to them compared to hard cash. They were already way ahead of his curveballs as far as all that goes. Travis Lee, guts blown out over there by the barn, told me I'd feel better knowing they were going to cut him up and feed the pieces to the wild dogs. They knew what the freak was all about."

Topper coughed, strained at the chains. "Fucking cooz, you have no fucking idea."

She started for him again, and then noticed a length of sawed-off PVC pipe on the floor among the other remodeling scraps. I knew what she was going to do and let her. His nose cracked loudly. This time he didn't have any smart-mouth. Just a yelp of pain. But now he was bleeding from the nose and mouth, barely able to breathe. She spat out something that had gotten into her throat, stood spread-legged over him like a boxer who'd just floored the favorite.

"At least get me my pills. They're over on that crate where the assholes left them so they could fuck with me. I've got that thing where I can't stop bleeding." His words were slurred and garbled by his broken nose and the effluent.

I heard Red yell out, "Jack, let's move."

I looked at Rose, the pipe tight in her hand. "We taking him? Your call."

She was breathing so heavily, from both the fumes and the emotion, I thought she might hit him again. Instead, she shook her head, exhaled. I could see she was trying to get back in the game. Which took discipline that comes from training. I realized she had a lot of cards I hadn't seen yet. She glared at Topper with a coldness years in the making, and walked out the door without another word.

"You got to be shitting me," he yelled, almost impossible to understand now.

"Best of luck," I said, and left. The wind had picked up and the fresh air outside was like a tonic. The pyscho inside would never smell anything again.

Rose was gathering dirty work rags from a pile of empty buckets, caulk tubes, and plywood. She walked over to the burning trailer, caught a flame from a window that had exploded out. I nodded and said nothing. She threw the burning cloth inside Topper's trailer against a bag of trash and sawdust and broken floor moldings. Kind of like a gargantuan Molotov cocktail.

"Get me out of this. I can pay you, you fucking freaks."

The trash bag started to smoke.

"I think the wind is shifting," she said to me. "Let's go." We started toward the barn. She paused. "Wait a second." Then she ran back to the trailer, leaned through the door before the flames picked up, and said something to him I couldn't hear. All I could hear was him yelling "you fucking whore" as she turned away, and then nothing but coughing.

She caught up with me without looking back. "Can I take his pickup, that big green Ram by the barn? Keys are under the mat. I've got stuff in it. We could use the extra ride, right?" It wasn't really a question.

When I turned to look at her she was silhouetted by the burning trailers like a mythical warrior in a world-ending battle. "Good idea. We need to get it out of here anyway. I'll go with you."

"Yes, it is a good idea," she said, more than a hint of sarcasm. Then, in a changed tone as she caught up with me, "There's some stuff in there you might want to see anyway."

"Okay, but we have to leave ASAP."

"It'll be fast. Something he had from mom. I just think you should see it."

"We're bringing that green Dodge dually out to the road," I called out to AK as we got closer. "You can give it to the girls if they need another truck."

He waved a thumbs-up while checking the other pickups for gas and keys. Of the three, two were wide-body with extended-cab passenger seats for crews of six, maybe eight girls. It would be tight, but they could cram in. The extras could stretch out under blankets in the cargo beds. Not unfamiliar to just about any kid either side of the border, and at night nobody would see them.

~~~

39

AK had just closed the door on the third truck, the GMC, which he decided not to use, when Red yelled for him to "wait up." Rose and I had stopped a moment outside the barn to look as the flames continued to swallow up everything inside. Because of the noise from the fire and fading shrieks from the burning meth trailer, I couldn't hear what my two buddies were saying to each other, but suddenly AK pulled back as if he'd been broadsided with a fence post.

With my free hand I took one of Rose's, not out of affection but of security, and moved closer. After a few steps I shifted my grip up to her wrist and fastened down a little tighter. "That hurts," she said, and we both knew she was lying.

Even in the flickering light I could see AK's eyes narrowed, his face gone deep red. Worse, he had raised his M-16 to port arms. "Not the girls," he said, loudly.

Red, in turn, was standing in a defensive posture, his eyes locked on AK in a way that could only lead to bad. A Glock was hanging down in his left hand. I moved closer with Rose, hoping that seeing us would defuse the tension.

It seemed like an eternity until Red breathed out, nodded his head slightly, let his body relax. "Fuck it. No time for this."

I heard a big exhale from AK, too, as he nodded back, and lowered his rifle.

"Only thing is we reevaluate if we have to," Red said. "You gotta be real."

AK stiffened.

"I mean, let's not assume. You know that, right?"

The redness in AK's face had lessened but not disappeared. Something was working through the muscles and veins in his forehead. "I copy all that, goddam it. I'm just saying they're coming out with us. We are not motherfucking leaving them."

"It's on you what happens to them. Just saying that again."

"Hell, yes, it's on me," AK growled. "What I've been saying."

I thought they were going back to the face-off again.

Red looked AK up and down, then turned away, toward the pickups. After a few strides he stopped, turned. "Thing is, brother, it's on me, too. I mean I got people who won't want any of this to spread. They'll want it buried. Fuck, they'll bury us, too, it goes sideways for any reason at all. You copy that?"

AK didn't move. "I said I'll take care of them. You don't have to be anywhere around me or them after tonight." He looked over at Rose, and me. "You have any goddamn thoughts on this, mister guy who started the whole fucking goatfuck?"

We looked at each other as if anticipating something that didn't need to happen but still could. Rose stayed put, because she had to, although shaking her arm intermittently let me know she didn't like it.

"You want to know what I think?" I said. "I think this. Stop this shit. You understand what Red is saying, right?"

AK gave me an odd look. "I fucking get it. That's not what I'm talking about."

I turned to Red. "You understand what AK is saying, right? I know it's not exactly what we came to do. But I mean, I'm with AK on this, about the girls."

Red gave us both a very long look, somewhere between impatience and resignation with fools. "Look, I'm done. My debt to Elle, that's all done. Maybe done with you, too." His voice a little grittier. "Just to be clear."

"I get it," I said. "But just to be clear. AK is gonna take the girls, get them out of this fucking disaster. Shit, Red, it's important to him."

"Like I said, it's on him." Red and AK locked eyes.

"I'm not disagreeing."

By now the girls were starting to squirm around inside the trucks and we all knew it was time. AK said the one named Lecia—he pointed to her—was driving one truck. Angelina—pointed to her—was driving the other. Red looked them over, inhaled deeply but said nothing. He gave AK a thumbs-up. An ugly truce, but solid.

AK hopped on the running board of Lecia's truck, and Red went with

Angelina. AK yelled over at me that they were going to make a final check when they got to the Suburban and then move out. I started with Rose for the green Ram, presumably the one Topper had liberated at Uncertain. I said I'd meet them out there.

I let go of my grip and she rushed ahead of me, went around to the driver's side, opened the door, and pulled the keys from under the floor mat. She came back around and met me at the passenger side, opened that door, and went immediately for the glove box. "It's this," she said. She stepped back, smiling. I could see the blue plastic folder she'd tossed on the seat. "It's what I wanted you to see."

I'd just put my rifle against the side of the truck and leaned into the cabin to open the zipper when something hard cracked against my skull. I fell across the seat, my first thought that somehow one of the militia goons had survived or sneaked up. My second thought was how much my head hurt. I pressed my hands against the passenger seat as I closed my eyes hard to try to get into focus.

I was trying to slide back on the seat and pull the Colt from my jeans when I felt her hands push me back just enough to cause me to lose my balance. Right away I felt a sharp pinprick through my T-shirt and into the flesh around my collarbone. I cursed, and straightened up so fast my head nicked the top of the doorframe, which stopped me again.

I regained my balance, gripped the pistol looking for whoever was doing this to me. But the pistol wavered and my hand dropped to my side. She had taken a couple of paces back.

"What the fuck?" I said, or tried to say. With my free hand, I reached up around my shoulder and felt a dart. I knew exactly what they felt like and in that split second I was back standing by my Jeep at Topper's compound in South Carolina. But already my mind was going fuzzy. I wasn't going to shoot her, and probably would have missed anyway. All I really wanted was to get the dart out of my hide. Which I did. But it already had unloaded the serum.

It was happening too fast. Maybe faster than before. I looked at the dart, and then at her. I took a couple of steps. My knees buckled, and I fumbled for the stability of the truck to brace myself. Too late. I dropped down on my butt, and felt my head hit the hard shell of Detroit iron.

I tried to get some words out like "What?" and "Why?" but it was like counting down under anesthesia before surgery. "Shit, not again," was about the last coherent thought my brain could manage. Or maybe that's what occurred to me much later when I woke up.

"Stay away from me," was the last coherent thing I heard her say as I fell over on my side, felt the dirt on my face, breathing it into my mouth and nose. Or she might not have said anything at all. I'll never know.

~~~

40

I let the water run full cold. That'll wake you up. Pretty much. Plus some hirsute giant shaking you like a rag doll and telling you it was time to get your ass up and moving. And then pulling you out of bed and pushing you toward the bathroom and throwing the first handful of water into your face. But that's the only thing that could have got me moving.

I managed a shower, put on fresh jeans and a black shirt, washed off my boots in the sink, and slammed down a cup of fast-heating motel coffee, which I guess the giant must have made while making sure I didn't go back to bed before he left. It was vile.

Then I drank another and looked through the blinds of the motel window and saw Red and AK waiting outside in the parking lot next to Red's truck. The outlines of a recollection of last night zipped through my synapses. They'd gotten me out of my clothes, but couldn't get me to clean up, so left me on the bed. Now I could smell the smoke and the chemicals and the blood in my cast-off jeans and socks and boots on the floor over against the cheap dresser and TV. I picked them up and stashed them in the plastic laundry bag from the closet. I put them on the bed so I'd remember to throw them away. Then I went outside.

AK was punching in numbers on his cell. At the time, I didn't know it was to the girls from the barn, but Red probably did. He didn't seem happy. Both of them looked me over and then looked at each other. Red said he was starving and I was, too, so we walked over to the Egg Burger. Red approached slowly, just to be sure it wasn't also a cop hangout. AK pulled the phone down from his ear as if angry at whatever he had heard, and followed. Red told me he'd watched the early news on the Abilene and Fort Worth stations and saw nothing, which was a good sign since once the fire died out, nobody'd have much reason to go up to the ranch. All we had to do was act normal and keep moving.

No one inside seemed to notice us, especially me. I knew I was wobbly but maybe it didn't show. Even if it did, the truckers and day laborers and construction crews chowing down for early lunch had enough on their minds. I had eggs and bacon and three more cups of coffee. It all went down good and I knew I had needed it. There was much to be said but Red wouldn't let us talk about anything of importance. He was right. We were in a grease-scented room full of hard-noses. But in truth a lot of them were lonely enough that they'd learned to eavesdrop like some people learn to watch soap operas.

We went back to the motel. On the way I said I wouldn't mind resting a little more, a notion that was immediately quashed. AK said I'd had eleven hours, from the time Rose had zonked me. He said it was twice as much as either of them had slept. I told him to fuck himself and he said the same, and then I said I needed more coffee. AK slapped me on the back and said something like, "knew we could count on you, you gringo pussy," I think, and turned back for the diner. He said he'd get more joe and meet us in my room. I could see him pulling out his cell phone as he walked away.

Red opened the door to the room and said they wouldn't leave me alone because we needed to move on and it'd be hell waking me up if I fell asleep. He knew I was in no shape for any kind of action, but he figured I could drive a few miles. He said the new plan was to get out of here right away—he gave me a hard clinical look—and check into a different motel nearby. We'd wait out the rest of the day there while I kicked out the trank, and also get in touch with Elle. To see if Rose had called. Or not.

I repacked my duffle, took a leak. Red stood by the window, peering through the blinds. AK showed up with two big Styrofoam cups and put them on a small table near the window. He told me to sit down and drink. Then he settled back against the wall behind the twin bed I hadn't slept in. Red left the blinds and took the chair on the opposite side of the table.

I pulled off the plastic top from the first cup and took a long swallow. It was damn hot.

Red looked over at AK, who nodded.

"We're gonna do the after-action report now," Red said, trying to judge if I really was tuned in. "Like I said, we need to leave, but you need to know shit before we take off." He looked at AK again. "In case." Then back at me. "Lots of shit happened after you took your nap back in the dirt." AK mouthed the word "pussy."

While I was considering that, Red suddenly jumped directly in front of me, clapped his hands together like lethal slaps in front of my face. I jerked back. "Okay, reflexes working. You still think you can drive?"

I nodded, probably made a sour face. Red went back to his chair.

"Say it aloud."

"Fuck yes I can drive, okay?"

They looked at each other a little longer. Red shrugged. AK looked up at the ceiling, then down. "He can do it."

Red gave me another cold diagnostic stare. Then he leaned back, breathed out. "Shit we gotta know, Shakespeare. You took a nasty drug."

"Tell me about it." I leaned across the table top. Like I could challenge the big guy. Both he and AK laughed.

"As long as you're done with that," he said, making wild crazy eyes, which I guess was to make fun of how I must have been post-dart.

I stared into the muddy-looking coffee. Almost got lost watching the swirls. I realized that, then sat up straight. "Can we fucking get on with this whatever you want to tell me?"

Another look between Red and AK. It was starting to piss me off.

"You don't have to keep up the fucking body scans. I told you I'm good."

"Let's cut him some slack, man," AK said. "Joke's over."

Red shot him a look. "It's not much of a joke."

"Anyway," AK said.

"Anyway," Red said, and leaned in toward me. "So first things first. What do you remember? All merriment aside."

I settled back into my chair, closed my eyes.

"You still with us, there, compadre?"

When I opened my eyes Red was slumped back into his chair, arms folded across his chest. I breathed in and out. I really did feel alert, but my body could betray me without warning. "I remember Rose looking down at me. It *was* her, right? I mean, it was the same fucking trank Topper hit me with back in South Carolina, right? I mean, that's how it felt. Still feels."

They looked at each other.

"Pretty sure it was the same, yeah," AK said.

"What's not pretty sure is how you're still alive," Red cut in. The look he gave me wasn't one of empathy. "So I'll be real interested to know what the fuck Rose was doing. I mean, if you have a clue."

That pissed me off, but he was right. "I don't know." I put some more hot coffee down my throat.

"*Basta, basta*," AK said. "You think he wanted to get knocked out on purpose?"

"I think there's a lot of shit that isn't adding up. But no. Not on purpose."

"*Bueno* then, okay." They looked at each other in a different way and I knew that something had definitely gone one-eighty between them yet again. And it wasn't just because of me getting ambushed by a girl. Then the fog lifted a little more and I remembered the run-in at the barn right before Rose nailed me. But they were the ones doing the briefing.

"So," AK said, "if we can get back on track. I'm going to tell you what happened, what went down after you checked out, then 'til now."

"He gets off track, I'll fill in the blanks," Red said. AK allowed a thin smile. Then he sat up on the edge of the bed and looked past Red out the window into the motel lot, past the pickups and bobtails, past the Egg Burger, past the frontage road and interstate and beyond that. To somewhere else that only he could see.

Then he laid out the story. Not a military-style after-action report. More like he was spinning a yarn for a bunch of old men in a South Texas dive bar, not much concerned with the chronological order, or sometimes even the facts. It was like they each saw what had happened at the ranch in different ways. I still don't know exactly how it was. But this was the way I heard it and stored it, as best I could, in my mostly recovered brain.

~~~

41

First up, AK said, was the mess we'd left. He and Red had pow-wowed about a clean-up after they'd gotten the pickups with the girls lined up behind the Suburban outside the compound gate. At that point they still thought I had Rose and would be driving out in a minute or two. All we had to do was leave with Rose when I showed up.

The problem was the girls. AK said once the battle was done, perspectives had changed. Ultimately nobody would care about the dead Salvation Brigade morons. Maybe a little about Topper, since he had some kind of money problems with the cartel, and also maybe with the mob. But someone would care about the girls. So they got into that again.

At that point the two of them exchanged a look. But they let it pass and AK went on with the story.

They agreed that, regardless of the girls, just cutting out and leaving the bodies and destruction wasn't an option. Red invoked Murphy's Law—if something could turn to shit, it would. Despite the remoteness and general uselessness of the ranch, there was a pretty good chance someone would check on or accidentally come across the place within a day or two at most. They considered calling one of the family's clean-up crews, but Red said it would take too long to get it there from Houston or Shreveport.

Red said the best option was to make it look like a cartel hit. We'd talked about it briefly once before. AK agreed. Fake and burn, the more careless in appearance, the better. The cartels would take a macho pride in showing the local Barneys they didn't give a shit what they left behind. What would they do, cry to the DEA?

Except we don't hurt the girls, AK had said. Red reminded him they'd already been over that. He said they could make the cartel ruse work without involving "extra bodies."

At that point Red interrupted AK to say that he hadn't said the words "extra bodies." AK shrugged and said he did, but anyway, that's what he meant. That he meant the girls. They bickered and cursed over language a minute. It was obviously a stupid argument, and I started to suspect that neither had slept a wink.

AK went back to his tale. Instead of hiding things, they would make them outrageous, taunting, horrific. AK would send the pickups with the girls to his cousin Renaldo's farm, up past Lubbock near Palo Duro Canyon. They'd worked together before. Red said again that once the girls left the militia property, they were AK's problem.

AK briefed the two drivers, Lecia and Angelina. Two other girls, one from each truck, joined them at the side of the road. Lecia, clearly the alpha, said they could help remember everything because there was too much going on and everyone was scared and it was night and she didn't want to get lost. Neither of the two extra girls spoke English, so Lecia translated until AK reminded her he spoke Spanish, too.

He gave stern warnings to Lecia and Angelina not to speed and not to stop for anything. It would take three hours. It was after midnight and the cops liked to look for drunks in the small towns on the way. Especially driving new pickups. Especially crammed with girls and young women. There was a risk but at least it was a weeknight. The bad nights for running into cops were always weekends.

He gave Lecia a cell phone liberated from one of the dead patriots but said not to use it unless they got lost or there was an emergency. And then to smash it and throw it away. He told them he'd be there in the morning and they'd figure out where to go from there.

He told them about Renaldo and that they would be welcome. They would be safe. It wasn't a hard sell. Only two of the girls from the barn were addicts, the rest basically just picked off the streets or from bars or even one from an airport. Anything at all was better than where they'd been. Lecia said something to Angelina about following but not too closely and if anybody had to pee to do it now. Which most of them did.

While the peeing was in progress, AK called Renaldo to set up the deal, about which so far Renaldo knew zero. It was bass-ackwards and risky but things were fucked up and you did what you could. But AK knew Renaldo would be home at the farm, and knew he would help. AK apologized and said it was an emergency.

Renaldo was five-by-five with the whole idea. And not just for the six hundred dollars a night that AK promised. There was plenty of room in the barn, filled with nothing more than a tractor he no longer owned and the ghost of an immaculate red and white '57 Chevy he'd had to sell. Also plenty of room in the old seasonal worker bunkhouse, and for that matter the spare bedroom and back porch. Hell, they could stay for a week. He said he could use the extra dough.

By the time the deal was done, the girls were ready to roll. AK said a prayer to the Virgin although he didn't especially believe anymore. Red just watched until the tail lights disappeared. Then they got in the Suburban and drove back into the compound.

AK said he was complaining that I had left with Rose without stopping to help with the girls or the cartel setup, and come to think of it, he hadn't even seen us leave. For that matter he wasn't even sure if I was headed up to Abilene or on to Fort Worth. Red was pissed off, too, and while they were driving back in to find me, called my cell to see where the fuck I was. There was no answer. Which pissed Red off even more.

AK glanced at Red, who was drilling lasers into my head as he remembered what came next.

They parked the Suburban around the back of the house and Red called again. Both he and AK heard my cell phone ringing at the same time, and also about the same time saw my body crumpled near the barn where the Ram had been parked. Red said it seemed like a longer sprint than it really was until they got to me, saw I was breathing, not to say gurgling a little in the dirt. Red rolled me over on my back and propped up my head while AK checked my throat for any blockages and pulled open my eyelids just to see the pupils move.

They dragged me a couple of yards and leaned me up against a scrawny oak. They watched me for a few minutes in the light from the open barn door, and decided I was okay. It was while they were making the assessment that a glint of metal caught AK's eye and he picked up a small, cigar-shaped metal cylinder and the syringe discarded next to it. So I was wrong about it being a dart but no point bringing that up now. AK inspected it, passed it to Red. They decided it had been loaded with trank instead of poison, mainly based on the remarkable medical diagnosis that I wasn't dead.

~~~

42

As I lay gasping, the flames from the meth trailer had settled into a thorough burn without any more explosions, and the one next to it had caught as well. Red and AK walked over to see if Topper was still inside. AK said he started coughing too much from the fumes and had to stop.

Red made it a little farther. A gust of wind parted the smoke enough so he could see a large, charred body slumped against the inside wall. He called it out to AK. Excellent, AK called back. It'd be his appetizer for roasting in the flames of hell, which AK emphasized were the exact words he had chosen.

AK said he watched the trailer burn another minute, which he acknowledged was kind of sick. The meth cooks already were roasted and might never be ID'd. From there, they worked nasty and fast. They policed up what brass they could find in the poor light. Red dragged the five Salvation bodies from the house over to the barn while AK pulled three from inside the barn. They left the dead girl in the house, so as not to have to mix with them. They lined up the thugs as if in formation. AK said maybe they should do them in a circle with their heads to the inside but Red said that would look like a cult, not a cartel.

They just improvised as they went on, AK said, as a way of framing what happened next. They were wondering if they needed to cut away some of my clothes to help me breathe and cool down while I was propped against the tree. The trank had spiked my temperature and when they tried giving me water, I spit it up.

AK was flipping his combat knife and catching it by the handle when the idea hit them. He said it almost made them laugh because they looked at each other at the same moment. It didn't need to be spoken, nor elaborated. Red pulled his knife from his belt, too.

They cut off the tongue of each of the corpses, then undid the zippers on their pants and stuck each guy's tongue into his crotch. For some reason the cartels were very big on putting mouth parts where dicks were and vice versa. It didn't take as long as you'd think, AK said. Which even in my hazy state struck me as an odd observation.

Reflecting on that seemed to make AK slow down the storytelling, so Red picked up the thread and bulled his way through what details he felt I should know. He said I deserved to have to listen since I had been such a stooge with Rose.

Then he paused, looked at AK, who shrugged as if to say to go ahead. Red took a breath and said once the tongue-cutting was done, they decided there needed to be another message. This time more about the girls. Or maybe for the girls. I might have gotten the words confused. He said it was AK's idea. Red said he hadn't wanted to do it. He added an editorial comment that AK was actually kind of into it, that AK's whole demeanor around the thugs was "kind of psycho." And if Red said something was psycho, it was.

AK didn't object to the characterization. Then he took over from Red to explain how he had gone around to all the bodies and cut off the dicks. Then he started putting the severed dicks into the mouths where the tongues had been. He said it was kind of an "inspiration," which drew a quick eye-roll from Red, although he nodded when AK pointed out that Red had helped out on the last few to speed things up. Red said that he had to admit it was exactly the kind of thing Mexican *sicarios* might have done. Maybe even Colombians.

The only thing left was the fire, AK said. The wooden barn was easy—full of bedding, hay bales, assorted trash from the captive girls, and a mound of cardboard boxes, probably from the drugs and equipment needed for the cook trailers. The bodies were different. They absolutely had to burn to crisps. They needed gasoline or paint or maybe something from one of the trailers if it wasn't already burning.

Red said the bed of the GMC, the truck they were leaving, was full of crap and maybe a gas or oil can. Sure enough it was strewn with welding tools and propane cylinders, a lawn mower engine, cast iron pipes, big garden hose reels, and two ten-gallon red plastic gasoline tanks. Red said who knew what the hell those idiots were actually up to out there in the middle of nowhere.

AK used one gas tank to drench the bodies in the barn. Red used the other for the house. He said he hated pouring it on the girl. At the barn, AK made a fuse trail with the gasoline and sparked it with the Zippo lighter he always carried, hand-etched with "B Co/3rd Bn." He did the same at the house.

They loaded me into the Suburban and drove out of the compound to get Red to his pickup. Because the trail bent hard to the right, about halfway down was the last time they could really see the whole bonfire as it grew among the buildings and fed on corpses.

There was more to all that they had done, like leap-frogging my Jeep and Red's pickup from the assembly point back to the motel, and I would hear more in the coming days, but I had the essentials. If they had wanted me to know that it had been pretty bad, they succeeded.

"I owe you," I said. They both nodded like it wasn't worth mentioning. Red got up to stretch, and then AK and I did the same.

Red paused by the window as we were leaving and looked out again. The fingers of his left hand thumbed the cheap blinds. "The weird thing after all that was when AK and I was looking back at the fire," he said. "All you could see was the trees up against the skyline and yellow fire and black smoke. The moon kept going in and out of the clouds so it almost looked like a slide show. You'd think it was some kind of wildfire, like the name of that road, or maybe a brush clearing or dumbass redneck tire dump arson. I mean, you'd never have a fucking clue."

He turned to look at me. "We got to get this job finished, Shakespeare.

You know?" He walked out the door, AK behind him.

I said I did as I followed them out and locked the door, but he probably didn't hear me. But I didn't know. I was starting to think I never would.

~~~

43

I'd said I could drive to Abilene and now I had to prove it. We checked out of the dump and hit the diner for twenty-ounce cups of industrial brew. We took to the interstate and split off one by one to faceless hotel chains. Cops would be less likely to look in those places for the drifters and grifters that assembled around any squatter camps.

Two questions remained. First, where did Rose go? Second, why should I keep looking for her?

She had said she had a friend in Dallas, but that could have meant nothing or the opposite of nothing—another false trail. I was putting off the check-in with Elle until my head cleared a little more. I needed to be careful what I said. I was going to keep my promise to find Rose. But now I had my own reason, too. She had drugged me and I had to know why. I didn't know how to wade into all that with her mom.

If we still knew nothing by morning, we'd head to Dallas. It could be our last stop. Maybe they'd stay with me on the hunt, maybe not. This search and rescue was more like a search and destroy, or a rescue and revenge, all but losing any sense of purpose.

AK wheeled in behind me at a La Quinta to get me registered and handle the details. I was still a little shaky. He told the clerk I'd been hurt on one of the rigs and had misplaced my wallet and so he was helping me get a room to rest up. The clerk may or may not have bought it, but mostly didn't care.

Room 168 was at the end of the front wing of the building. AK walked me there, then took off to get his own room at the Marriott at the next exit. We would connect by phone no later than 3 p.m. My job in the meantime was to get in touch with Elle "no matter how many fucking times you have to try."

I turned on the TV to help keep me awake. I did some push-ups and crunches. To be safe, I set my phone alarm for three. I walked outside for a while around the parking lot. But I forgot my phone and hurried back to the room. The armchair was uncomfortable so I sat in it. Clicked through TV channels again. Nothing about a sadistic mob hit, a meth lab, or homegrown Nazis. The usual drivel. It was irritating, but that was good. Irritation was my stay-upright regimen for the day.

Even so, I almost fell asleep. I was saved by the cell. The ringer was on high volume and it served its function. I'm sure my voice was slurred when I said hello. I hoped it was Elle.

It was AK. Gravel-voiced and edgy.

"Fuck, man, Renaldo never called in like we planned, and he doesn't answer his phone. It's been way too long. I think I need to go up there."

"Shit." Trying to snap into clarity. "Really?"

"Are you awake?"

"Yes."

"You sound fucked up."

"I'm okay. Just a little slow. Look, it's not even two o'clock. I thought you said three."

"Fuck all that. Jesus Christ, Jack. It's Renaldo. Something's wrong. I can feel it, man."

"When was he supposed to call?"

"Last night. Whenever they got in."

"And didn't."

"What I just said. And then also he was supposed to call at 0700, and if I missed it, at nine."

"You didn't say anything."

"I figured he was, you know, busy getting them settled. I wasn't worried at first. I trust him. He's smart."

"Shit."

"I called again from the diner and then again right after I checked you in. It just goes to his voicemail."

"Not good."

"Look, I want to go up there. You heard from your woman?"

"No."

"Well fucking call her. I thought you already did. I mean that's your only goddam job."

I let his anger slide. "Sorry. I kind of zoned out. I mean, that's why we're here, right? So I can get this shit out of my system before we move."

"Well, get it out enough to call her now. See if she knows anything about where the girl is headed. If not, I'm going up to Post right now."

"I'll call her. But wait."

"I'll give you an hour, max. Then I have to go. I don't like this." He paused. "You shouldn't, either."

"I'll call her now. Then I'll call you back."

"Do it. Something bad has happened, man."

~~~

44

I called Elle immediately, but it went straight to voicemail. I called again and same result. I'd already left a few messages so I just hung up. I'd just keep calling. So I tried two more times and then went down to the lobby for stronger coffee. The place was crowded with suits and pantsuits. I felt like I stood out in my T-shirt and jeans but probably I didn't. Usually we think people pay more attention to us than they actually do. I'd learned that in intelligence. It was a common failing for people who were up to something, and weren't trained, to exhibit overly defensive behaviors. In trying to look normal, they inevitably demonstrated that they were not.

The coffee made me hungry so I raided one of the vending machines for a granola bar and chips. I tried one more call, then headed back to my room with a refill of coffee, an "*hola*" to the cleaning ladies along the way.

I was at the door to my room swiping my card key for the third time when my cell went off. The lock light on the door also finally went green and I fumbled to push the handle, answer the phone, and not drop my cup.

I failed at the latter, and had to look around like a little kid to make sure no one had seen me, or the brown stain spreading on the carpet into the hall. Like I said, still a little off my game. But I managed to get inside before she hung up.

"Jack? . . . Jack?"

"Sorry, wasn't able to talk for a second." I noticed the stain now spreading inside the room. I went over to the window. My view was a row of hedges, a retail strip, and the interstate.

"You can now?"

"Definitely."

"Where are you? Have you found Rose?" Her voice was eerily professional, cold.

"I'm in West Texas. And yes. And she's alive."

I could hear the sharp inhalation. "She's safe. She's safe." Then slow, labored breathing. Maybe some kind of muted crying. "Do you have her with you? Can I talk to her?"

That question was the reason I had avoided the call.

"She's okay. But I don't have her with me."

She was barely able to get out the next word. "What?"

It took about ten minutes, mostly me talking, sometimes her asking questions, the kind an attorney might pose in a deposition. It probably sounded like I was narrating a documentary for the news. My head hurt just laying it out to someone who hadn't been directly immersed in the savagery. But on whose behalf the savagery had been carried out. The worse part was the un-Hollywood ending.

"We were getting into the truck, to get away"—there was no good way to say it—"out of nowhere, she . . . whacked me on the head with something. A blackjack or something, knocked me out. Before I could come around, she was driving away. We couldn't catch her."

"What?"

"She waylaid me, Elle. Left. On her own."

"What are you saying?"

"She was fine. No injuries or anything. But she didn't want to come with me."

"I don't understand."

"Me, either. Have you heard from her?"

"Of course not. So again, what are you saying? What the hell are you saying?"

"I'm saying Rose cold-cocked me and ran away."

"Hnnnh. Just like that?"

"Exactly like that."

This time I wasn't lying about details to spare Elle's feelings. More like I couldn't be sure whether even she was telling the truth. Pretty fucked up to be that suspicious, but by now everything was pretty fucked up.

"Jack, I don't know. I don't know."

"I know I don't."

"You have no idea where she might have gone?"

"Not really. She said something about some friends in Dallas."

Silence at Elle's end. "I'm sorry. I'm just trying to think."

"Right."

"What do you think?"

"I think that if we don't get some kind of direction from somebody by tomorrow, I'm going to lose AK and Red."

"And I'll lose you?"

"I could hang a little longer, but, yeah, maybe."

"That's so cold."

"I don't know. We just don't seem to be getting anywhere."

I wasn't going into the full dark side, but she had no trouble sensing where I was. Where we were. I could hear her phone rubbing against something, like her head or her face.

"I don't know how to call her," she finally said, in a voice I barely recognized. "None of the numbers I had work anymore. And I don't even know how to reach Blaine."

"Damn."

I didn't tell her she never would.

"I mean it, Jack. I don't know what to do."

"What about the money?"

"What?"

"The money? You have that set up with the bank? To pick up like we talked about?"

"The money, Jack? That's what you're thinking about?"

"As long as she's alive, someone will want the so-called ransom. Even her friends will want it. Maybe especially her friends. Whoever she's with. She doesn't seem to run with a good crowd."

"You don't have to say it that way."

"Right now, I do."

Silence. Then, "Yes, the people at the bank have it set up. For wherever."

"I'm going to Dallas tomorrow. Wait it out there."

"That's where she told you, right?"

"Yeah, before she tried to kill me."

"Jack, don't."

"Forget it. My theory is that you'll hear before I even get there. She's got incentive."

"The money again. Jesus. "

"So we'll see where it goes. You'll call me immediately."

"Of course. You really think she's in Dallas?"

"I do. I don't think she mentioned it by accident. I think she knows exactly what she's doing."

"Meaning?

"Meaning you need to get ready for a side to her you don't know."

"I'm not a fool."

"You're her mom. You think it's about coming home."

"I'm not going into this. I don't want to. I get it."

"Okay."

"Jack?"

"Yeah."

"I'm so sorry you got hurt and so glad it wasn't worse. I should have said that right away."

45

AK's interest in Elle's call was minimal. "So nothing new. I get the feeling that girl doesn't want to be 'saved.' You know?"

"That's what I told Elle. She doesn't want to know."

"So no reason for me not to head up to Post right now. This could drag out forever. If you're coming with me, you got thirty minutes to get your shit together."

"Didn't we talk about waiting until tomorrow? Head over to Dallas?"

"So?"

"So you're leaving now?"

"So I got a bad feeling. Told you that. I'm not waiting."

"Damn, AK."

"So you coming?"

Only one answer was possible. "Fuck it. But I need to call Red first."

I heard an odd grinding sound from deep in his throat. "It don't matter what Red thinks. *Comprende*? Renaldo's missed three check-ins and a dozen of my calls."

"Whatever you want, but I'm letting Red know anyway."

"Just meet me at my truck in thirty or I'm gone without you."

"I heard you."

"Good." He hung up.

Red was in 427 at a Holiday Inn about three exits down. I drove over. I needed to see his reaction in person. This business with AK wasn't getting better.

The coffee was made and he got me a cup, added two sugars. "It'll push you along," he said. It was like drinking candy. I set the cup on the window sill and leaned against the wall. He pulled out a chair from the desk. I told him I was going to Post.

"When?"

"Now. He's waiting for me."

"You're not coming back here."

"Negative."

He let that settle, looked around the room at his own travel bag. "I got no reason to stay in this shithole tonight, then. There's something I can do for the family in Dallas. Or I can just go back to Biloxi."

We looked at each other but it was what it was.

"You thought it'd be a quick snatch and run."

"More or less."

Muscles rippled in his jaw. "You deal with these kinds, you never know. Me, I should've emphasized that more."

"Wouldn't have changed anything."

He let his head fall back, looked up at the ceiling. "I do like Elle, you know."

"You've paid the debt."

"Maybe."

I nodded. "The way she said 'leave me alone.' I was about to pass out but I feel like she didn't say it with much love, you know?"

"You expected?"

He got up and started stuffing clothes into his bag.

"Elle is about to lose it," I said.

"Doesn't mean you have to."

"No." I started walking toward the door. He pulled a Glock from his bag, showed it to me, I don't know why, stuffed it back in under his clothes.

"Next twenty-four hours you have some decisions to make, my brother."

I stopped at the door, leaning against it, fiddling with the do-not-disturb card. "I know."

"I can't say I respect a man for being stupid. But I do respect loyalty." Pause. "Even when it's stupid." Another pause. "Even for a woman."

"Thanks?"

"But, fuck, Jack."

"I know."

"And you know, AK's a solid brother, but man's got some obsessions. Don't get caught up in that shit."

"He just wants to get the girls to their families or whatever. Safe."

"Yeah, but it's like when we started. You think one thing will happen, then something else does."

~~~

46

I was fifteen minutes late getting back to AK. He was sitting in his Suburban in the parking lot. Engine idling, a/c running.

"So?" he said, lowering a window as I pulled alongside.

"So."

We headed west. He mostly had to go the speed limit since the metal tool bin in the cargo bed of his pickup was filled with highly felonious weapons and ammo bound for his friend in the disposal business. As we got closer to Renaldo's spread, the arid landscape edged into sparse, pristine high plains of mesquite, scrub brush, juniper, and live oak.

The turn-in was nothing more than a narrow dirt and gravel lane next to a black mailbox nailed atop a mesquite stump. I followed the Suburban past weed-covered fields, a rusty plow and flat-bed trailer with its tongue propped up on rocks. We ended up at the predictable cluster of a house, barn, garage, tool shed, old cars and pickups. In the back was what looked like the bunkhouse and a tin-roofed shed housing what looked like a generator and some kind of water pump. In my experience, small farms and ranches everywhere more or less looked alike, probably out of common necessities. But I could tell this one was going to be different.

AK stopped abruptly, fifty yards short of the house, gravel crunching under his tires. I stepped hard on my brakes to keep from running up his ass. Then an arm extended from his window, palm toward me, then slightly down. He moved ahead slowly. I figured he was going to give Renaldo plenty of time to see us so as not to startle anyone.

When he got close to the sagging wooden fence in front of the house, he shut off his engine and got out. I pulled in behind. I think we were both wondering the same thing: Why was it so quiet? Where was everyone? Even back at the militia compound, where the girls were prisoners, some of them had peeped out to see AK when he had done his looking-for-Mr. Galindo act.

He glanced back at me, shook his head as if to say what the hell, then walked to the back of his truck and unlocked the tool case. I turned off my engine and joined him. He gave me an M-16 and a clip and took one of the shotguns for himself. Neither of us spoke. I'd forgotten how quiet the country could get.

He turned toward the house. "Rey. Hey, it's AK. You here?"

Nothing.

He called again.

"Something's fucked up. What do you think?"

"I don't think anybody's here. "

"Shit. I knew it."

"You want to move up and see?"

"I'll go first," he said, pulling his shotgun to the ready. "Wait a few, then head off to the right where you can see the back."

He was almost at the front porch when the compressor on a window a/c unit kicked in. AK dropped down to a crouch and might have been within a couple seconds of shooting the front door into splinters, but he caught himself in time. I also dropped down to a crouch but the noise hadn't startled me as much.

AK looked at me. I could see his mouth form the words, "Motherfucker." Then he moved to the front door.

"Rey? AK. You in there, man?"

He waited a ten-beat and tried the door handle. It wasn't locked. Not even completely shut.

"Rey? Coming in."

I continued my sweep. I was just getting to the back door when he came out of it.

"Fucking nobody, man. Nobody. But somebody was here. Shit's all knocked over. Cots and sleeping pallets in the front room and the two bedrooms. Whoever was here, they're gone."

We looked at each other.

"Maybe they went to buy clothes and stuff at Wal-Mart."

"He might. But he wouldn't take them with him."

"Well, yeah."

"It ain't right."

"Where would he have bunked up the girls?"

"Some in the house. The rest probably over there, where they used to rent out to roughnecks and ranch hands." We both looked at the old bunkhouse, weather-battered concrete blocks and tin roof, to the right of the barn. Reminded me of an Army barracks. He headed that way.

I stayed a few feet to one side. I carried the rifle with the butt on my hip, not really expecting to use it.

We got to the bunkhouse and AK opened the door at the end. "Son of a bitch. Son of a bitch," he roared. No longer trying to stay quiet.

Inside were a dozen single beds, one actual bunk at the far end. All with sheets and blankets, and all disheveled. One bed was leaning on its side. The things the girls had brought with them from the Salvation Brigade barn were scattered across the concrete floor.

Now I saw what AK had. Blood splotches on the floor and one of the walls. But no bodies. No bullet holes. Just evidence of people who had left in a hurry. Not of their own choice.

"Rey wouldn't have done this."

"No."

"I'll go look in the barn, but he never used it," AK said. "You go over to the pump station, see if there's anything. We can look around the whole perimeter and then maybe up into the hills around here. I mean I don't think anyone would go up there, it's all brush and rocks." He stopped, looked across the grounds where his friend had lived for so long. "I mean, what the hell, Jack."

"Let's keep looking," I said, and stepped off.

I wish I'd gone to the barn.

I didn't know Renaldo, but it was a good guess I'd found him. They didn't bury him, or burn him, or even cart him away to the brush after indulging their stupid and vicious cartel sadism. They just left the remains next to the pump for the coyotes and dogs. The remains consisted primarily of a body without a head or hands. The missing parts were there, just no longer attached. Tossed to one side. Only potentially merciful thing was his right eye. A bullet had gone through it. With any luck it had happened before the chopping up. It was work Topper would have admired.

"Over here," I called out, pushing down an urge to vomit from the stench.

AK double-timed, then slowed to a halting walk and then stopped dead still. I held up a hand to try to warn him but it was too late.

"Fucking hell." He came up beside me.

"Sorry, man." I didn't know what else to say.

"*Animales.* These people are all fucking animals." He knelt, touched Renaldo's chest, and then patted it as if to reassure his friend that everything was okay. Then he stood. Anguish contorted his face into something awful and sad.

"They got them," he said. "I don't know how. But they got them."

"Yeah." We both just looked at the remains, like you do when everything becomes the opposite of what you had expected. AK looked out over the rest of the area. "There's some tools in that shed by the barn. Probably some shovels. We'll bury him up on the hill. It's his place. That's what he'd want." His voice had gone flat, the monotone of shock.

"Whatever you say."

"It's what he'd want." He was holding it in with a vise grip. I knew he'd done that a lot in his life.

"Sure."

"And then I want to find the girls. And I want to kill the filth that took them."

Rose wasn't even on his radar anymore. I knew that what Red had told me about AK was right, and I was forcing myself to see it that way. I just didn't want to at the moment.

He found shovels and a pick-axe and we dug a hole at a good place on the hill, next to an oak. AK went back to the house for Mexican blankets and we used those to wrap up the body and its pieces, in roughly the places they would have been. It was one of the worst things I've ever had to do. Even when you put the head where it belongs, and the hands, they don't stay in place like they do when the muscles and bones hold them together. If Hamlet had found Yorick like this there would've been no oration.

We covered the body and filled the grave with dirt and put rocks on top so the buzzards wouldn't find it and the coyotes wouldn't dig it up. Although they might anyway. We found a chunk of stone and put it at the head of the grave. AK used his combat knife to start carving an inscription. I sat on the ground next to him. Nothing to say. Just to be there while he worked.

He started talking, as much to himself as to me, about how Renaldo had done his best to lead a decent life and keep his family together. He said the boot-making and cobbler business gradually had lost steam. Renaldo'd made do with VA healthcare, odd jobs, some work at the local private prison until he couldn't stand going in there anymore. He took in custom gigs here and there but they didn't come often enough. One summer and fall he even did field work with the Mexican migrants. Which hurt his back so much he could never do it again even if he wanted to, which he did not. To keep out of foreclosure, Renaldo started growing pot in the back of the acreage, and went to Dallas a few times a year to sell to a guy he'd grown up with. AK smiled a little, then dug in harder with the knife.

When the carving was done, he dusted it off with his hands, made sure the stone was set well on the grave, and stood up. He said, as if to the wind, that his friend had died trying to help people who had been thrown onto the fires of hell. He seemed about to amplify on that but instead bent down to scoop up a handful of dirt. I did the same. "Ashes to ashes, dust to dust, my old friend," he said, and we threw the dirt onto the protective rocks. He bowed his head and said something I couldn't hear. It was probably a prayer. I tried one in my own head but my spiritual side was nowhere I could access. I read the lines he'd sculpted: "Renaldo de Vuela, 2003. A brave and good man."

We started walking back to the house. Silent at first, then AK said he should decide if he needed to notify Rey's kids, who'd all moved to Amarillo, or his ex, who had left years ago for Tulsa. Then he said fuck her, she was a cheater, and the kids would find the grave if they ever bothered to visit their dad.

To change the subject, because hard as this was we couldn't spend any more time mourning, I said maybe we could look around a little for any clues as to what had happened. He clapped me on the back and nodded. He knew what I meant. This was a long way from over.

We were almost at the door when a quavering female voice came down from somewhere up in the brush, not far from where Renaldo now resided: "*Señores, por favor! Señores! Ayúdame!*"

~~~

47

The girl stepped out from behind a thick, gnarled oak.

"Fucking kidding me?"

AK and I watched as she came slowly down the hill toward us.

She wore cut-offs and a "Dallas Cowboys" T-shirt that was maybe three sizes too large. She raised her arms and walked forward. Whatever fear inside was pushed down. We could tell she recognized us, but she wasn't sure what to do. She probably knew we were her only chance and she had to take it.

"*Alto,*" AK called out, still not sure what we were looking at. She stopped.

"*Dónde están los otros?*" he called out.

"They take them," she said. "I can speak English."

"Where? Who?"

"I don't know. Please help me."

"Why didn't they take you?"

"I was up there. I was just walking around, and you know, having to pee."

"Just you?" He looked at me. I shook my head. Neither of us recognized her, but we hadn't really gotten a good look at the girls in the barn.

"Can you help me?"

He beckoned with his free hand for her to approach.

She started to run to us but he leveled his shotgun and she slowed.

"Please, please. Don't kill me."

AK looked at me, rolled his eyes.

"How long were you there?" He pointed up to the hill.

"It was this morning. I am up there all day. I am afraid to come down."

"And now?"

"I see you. You were back there. You helped us."

"What's your name?"

She stopped a few yards in front of AK. She was probably fourteen or fifteen, tiny, covered in dirt. She looked badly sunburned and dehydrated. AK lowered his weapon.

"Do you have any water?"

Up close, you could hear the dryness in her throat.

"Yeah. Lots of water. First, we need to know if they're all gone. The girls. The people who took them."

She nodded, shifting her weight from foot to foot, trying to see what the big guy with the shotgun had in mind now.

"They killed my friend," he said.

"Mr. Rey?" Her face screwed up at the news.

"You didn't know that?"

"I ran far back up there and hid in some rocks. I almost got stung by a scorpion."

"You didn't see anything?"

"I didn't see anything. I just heard things. I heard the girls yelling and screaming and some men screaming back and then I heard some guns. I just hid and closed my eyes and didn't move a muscle."

"How long?"

"I don't know. I heard some men coming up near me and I could hear them say things like 'just let the bitch die' and 'we got no time for this,' and things like that but I thought they would get me but they didn't, and I could hear them going back down the hill and away. They were speaking Spanish, but I also heard a little English."

"And then you came out?"

"I waited a long time. I know the sun came up over my head but I was still afraid and I thought I would stay until dark. And then, you know, here you are."

"So you came out."

"I waited until I could see you but I still didn't want to. But then I saw you were leaving. So, I . . . so I took this chance. Are you going to help me?"

"Sit over there," AK said, indicating a green plastic chair near the back of the house.

"What do you think?" he asked.

"Sounds true enough. I mean what else has she got?"

"Agree. Fuck. This is just getting worse."

"Well at least she'll know something more than what we do now."

"It was those fucking Mexicans, no doubt."

"No doubt."

"But how, man, how could they have known?"

"No idea."

"And why aren't they all dead, with Rey?"

I glanced at the girl. "My guess, they're worth more alive. These kind of guys just see girls like her as cash cows."

"Also witnesses."

"Maybe. But money first. And who would believe them anyway. Ask her where she's from."

"*De dónde?* Where you from?" he called out.

"Reynosa."

"You learned English there."

"Sure."

"And how did they get you?"

"Coming across. Same as the others. The coyotes sold us, the ones who came without their families. My parents paid to get me across, so I could go to school."

"They were all like that?"

"Some already got over here, got picked up by, what you say, criminals. Drug dealers. They told us we would all be dead if we did anything. They even killed Seloria back at that other place because she tried getting away." She stopped. "Some gringo was there and he cut her up in front of us. I think they put her body in a freezer or something. We were too scared."

"Topper," I said. "Never checked the damn freezers back there. Fuck."

The girl's face registered uncensored terror so I shut up about that.

"One of the girls, she was black, American, her name was Rosa or maybe Rose. She knew the guy and said we need to try to get away because he was crazy and would kill us all if he could. Even if they wanted to sell us to that cartel, he didn't care. She said he was crazy and liked to chop people up. That he was going to do that to her."

"When did she tell you that?"

"It was right before you came. She and that gringo just showed up and I thought they were together but next thing she was all tied up and they threw her into the barn with us. I mean we untied her but she was in there with us. That's when she told us what would happen. And then they got Seloria and did that to her."

She stared to sob. AK knelt next to her. She put her head against his shoulder and sobbed even harder. He looked at me. I had completely forgotten. I went into the house, found a plastic glass, and filled it with water.

She drank it. Then she just sat in the chair, looking toward the hills. There was more to say, probably, but not then.

"Your name," AK said. "Tell me."

"Maria Christina."

"I'm AK."

"I wish my English was better."

"It's as good as mine, maybe better."

"We had good teachers."

"I'm sorry," he said. "About all this."

She leaned forward, the empty water glass in her hand. She held it out to me. "I'm thirsty. Sorry."

I took the glass and refilled it.

AK put his arm around her and held her against him.

Maria Christina drank that glass dry too. Then asked for another. I got it. I would have brought her water until the end of time. It was lucky she didn't die from heatstroke. Lucky as a relative term.

We all sat in silence for fifteen minutes, each in our own thoughts. There was nothing else to do.

~~~

48

The evening light was still good, so we took another half hour to go through the house and the buildings one more time, looking for anything, finding nothing. Maria Christina stuck to AK's side, afraid even to go into the bathroom in the dorm house, and had to be persuaded that he'd still be waiting on the outside when she was done.

She told us a little more about how they'd arrived at Renaldo's the night of the rescue, so late that most of the girls either fell asleep or kept nodding off. The others, like herself, were too scared and kept up talk with the drivers about what had happened and what they wanted to do when it was all over. Bebe and Pietra, the youngest, just wanted to go home. The others wanted to find somewhere in Texas or California. They didn't tell Bebe and Pietra that home no longer existed.

Maria Christina said Renaldo was "about the nicest man we ever met." He had their beds already set up and bottles of water and some cheese and meat sandwiches and snacks so they could eat before going to sleep. He gathered them on the dry grass outside the bunkhouse so they could be under the stars and "learn to breathe again." Lecia and Angelina wanted to know where they would be leaving, but Renaldo said to sleep first, plan it out tomorrow morning. He said they would be safe, that he would stay up on guard all night. That his friend AK-47, which made them laugh, would be there soon and get everyone where they wanted to go.

She said they were all so tired, and so happy not to be slaves, that they believed him. And they all went to bed. Maria Christina said she fell asleep almost right away, but had woken up just after dawn needing to go pee. That's when she decided to grab a leftover sandwich and a bottle of water and walk up the hill to see the birds singing and just sit and watch the sun come up and feel free. The other girls never even knew she'd left. She said that was the only thing that saved her.

She'd only been up the hill an hour or so, but she didn't have a watch, when the line of black pickups appeared on the road. They stopped in front of the house and she couldn't really see anything from where she was. But then there was yelling and after that shots and then more yelling. Then she could hear people running toward the dorm and more yelling and then terrible screaming and that's when she ran into the hills.

Then she went silent again, like she'd emptied her lungs completely. She remained as close to AK as a loyal dog. He said he wanted to go with me to Dallas but didn't know what to do with Maria Christina if he did, that he wouldn't leave her. I said it was okay, that Red would be in Dallas. I saw a cloud pass across AK's face. I didn't want to press it but I should have.

I put the M-16 back in AK's tool case in the truck bed and got my Remington and Colt that they'd rescued for me from the barn. I also picked out Red's Glock. AK said that was okay and that I could take the M-16, too, if I needed it, but I'd have to be sure to ditch it safely, since it could potentially be matched to casings. I said I was good with what I had. I'd never fired my own weapons so they were clean, and so was the Glock. As for Red's own M-16, I assumed he'd know how to make it go away.

AK gave me the standard vet-to-vet hug you've seen guys do a thousand times at the Vietnam Wall or in movies. Guy stuff for things they can't or won't express. It seemed a little more personal this time.

Maria Christina rushed up to hug me as well. She couldn't have known that to me, at that instant, she was someone else. All she could have known was that I hugged her back more than you might expect from a guy you'd just met under the worst of circumstances. But in that embrace I was with Ronnie. And then I was listening to Annalisa tell me our daughter was dead and then I was on the beach at Biloxi and then I was in some kind of black, cold celestial space. Then it was gone. Ronnie slipped from my arms, Maria Christina in her place.

We saved at least one.

I left. I drove on. I wanted to sleep but the adrenaline said no. If I stopped I'd just lie awake in a motel bed. Might as well put away the miles.

I was at the edge of Fort Worth, night having overtaken dusk, when my cell rang. I made damn sure to answer. It was Elle. Rose had called. She was okay. They'd given her only sixty seconds to talk. She was with someone named Javier. Javier was with Los Jovenes. They were in Dallas. They wanted the million if she wanted Rose. She did. They said they'd be back in touch in twenty-four hours and to be ready, and then hung up. They liked being dramatic that way. So she had set up a flight and gave me details to meet her in Dallas in the morning. I said they'd probably change the time again and she said she didn't care. She wasn't going to sit at home anymore. It was killing her.

~~~

49

La Playa anchored a corner on Jefferson Avenue in North Oak Cliff, not far from the old Texas Theatre where Lee Harvey Oswald was arrested after killing a cop. Most of the customers were Mexican national or Mexican-American and spoke Spanish to the waiters when ordering. The old-school diner was a favorite of the local business and city worker crowd. A regular core of *viejos* gathered every morning at the same table to talk local politics and sports. Places like La Playa were generators of quotidian meaning in the towns in which they evolved. In New Orleans, they were the fabric of life. Here, in the city with no time to waste, they were throwback oases in a concrete barren.

I got there at nine, as Red and I had agreed when I called him last night from the tourist motel I sheltered in near the Texas Rangers ballpark in Arlington. He was at a safe house in Oak Cliff the family had acquired following the untimely death of a dealer who had fallen behind in his payments. I went over what Elle had told me, thin as it was, and said I'd call back if I heard more from her. I hadn't.

He signaled me over to a two-top by a window. He was wearing a loose blue-and-green Hawaiian shirt and looked as solid as a concrete tackling sled. His wet hair was slicked back and his beard a little damp.

I must have cracked a smile at his post-shower look when I sat down. He said he'd gone for a run, which surprised me even more because I never thought of him as a fitness type. On the other hand, he didn't stay strong by just lying around all day eating bon-bons.

A waitress in a fresh uniform who looked like she had come with the original building brought a glass of water and a menu. A bus boy who looked like he was ditching high school was right behind her and poured a cup of coffee for me and a refill for Red.

As soon as they left he asked if I had anything new. I still didn't and he still didn't like it. So I went over the plan from last night again, but with the details I'd skipped over. Elle was coming in at 11:15 at the private airport next to Love Field. She was bringing the money. The banker friend in Atlanta who had been helping her set that up also got her a seat on one of the company jets to Dallas. He said I might have mentioned that about the Atlanta banker before. I said I was sorry, that last night I was exhausted when I called. He asked if I'd forgotten anything else. I said I hadn't. He said forgetting things could get people killed. I apologized again, although I didn't like the grilling, and said I trusted Elle on it. He gave me a hard eye and drank some of his coffee, and then let it go.

The waitress came by again for our orders.

Now he wanted more details. Like where and when. I said she didn't know, that the Jovenes were supposed to call with all that after she got here. I said I'd told him that last night. He didn't respond. I said I'd also told him we just had to wait for the call. That's why we were having breakfast at nine, instead of seven.

He looked out the window at the cars and people on the street for what seemed a couple of days. An orange Chevy pickup loaded with a half-dozen clowns holding balloons passed by, honking. A party, a convention, I had no idea why. We watched it go by and then he looked at me, closed his eyes, shook his head. I knew the continuing horseshit about meeting times and places would get to him and it did.

The food came out quick and was good and I ate it crazy fast. I'd been living on snack bars since the Egg Burger. Red looked at me with something resembling a smile, but took care of his plate pretty efficiently, too. We didn't talk. He left a twenty for the grub and a ten for tip on our way out.

His pickup was on a side street a block away. As we walked he said he would leave town by day's end. Regardless. It was already steamy hot, like breathing warm water.

At his truck, he opened the passenger door and showed me a canvas bag on the back floor holding his M-16. I told him I had my 12-gauge and Colt in my trunk. And his Glock, which AK had given me to return. He said I should just hang onto it for now. I said I brought it because I thought he would want it and he said, yeah, and thanks, but not here, not now. He looked at me in an odd way, at least I thought it was. Maybe I was getting paranoid.

He said I should know he'd also sent for Po-Boy and Carlos. They were coming in from Shreveport and would be in Dallas by about 2 p.m., if we needed them. He said there were family contract guys in Dallas but he didn't know them well and would rather work with half-wits he could trust than with hotshots he didn't know. I told him I didn't think we would need them. He said he thought we might. Either way, they were coming. I was in no position to turn down backup.

He said he was going back to the family house to wait for my call from the airport. No point going with me since the timeline was "fucked as usual." He had some calls he could make. He said I should get ready for a lot of driving because, like he always said, it didn't matter where the first call gave as a meeting spot because they'd change it. He said he just wanted to be sure I remembered that. I may have rolled my eyes but he must not have seen it.

I started walking to my Jeep when he called out. I turned, put my hand up over my brow to block out the sun that just came out from clouds. He was leaning against the door of the pickup. "Something else you wanted to tell me?"

I squinted, as though just seeing him standing there, and ran the question through my brain. Maybe he did see me roll my eyes. "You mean about meeting Elle? I think I pretty much covered it."

He didn't answer or move so I walked back toward him. I wasn't really sure where he was going with this. I didn't really even know why he wanted to show me his firearms. Or maybe he wanted his Glock after all. When I got close I could see anger. Almost as quickly, the expression downgraded to a world-weary exasperation. He knew I was clueless.

"The girls, Shakespeare. AK. You know, the guy who gave you your guns back? My Glock? Took you to see his pal Renaldo. To put the girls up? How'd that go? Jesus."

I stopped like I'd been hit by a cement truck. The primary phrase that formed in my mind was "fuck me." Had I not told him? All I could do was look at him, trying to form any kind of coherent reply. Was the trank still doing Swiss cheese on my memory? Was I subconsciously choosing when, where, and what I wanted to remember? Not a good sign. Bottom line was I hadn't said a damn thing about Renaldo's farm and Red was calling me out for it.

"Sorry. Jesus. I keep losing track."

"No shit."

I rubbed sweat from my brow, closed my eyes, and leaned back against Red's truck. I apologized again, which I realized was getting old, and summed up the trip to Post in an excruciating ten minutes. I didn't look at him when I was talking. I don't know how I expected him to react, but when I was finished, he put a hand on my shoulder, said, "Sorry, that's rough, amigo." He opened the door to his truck. "Call me soon as you pick her up." I stood halfway out in the street and watched until he was around the corner and out of sight.

I checked my watch. It really wasn't that long a wait. I would meet her in an hour. By noon we would know where we were going. By six we would have Rose or we would all be dead.

~~~

50

I drove back across the river and north around downtown Dallas on I-35. Traffic was light. I'd made runs to Love Field countless times over the years. But I'd forgotten the surrounding state of decay in which it operated. Bars, cheap motels, car rental lots, liquor stores, apartments where nobody'd want to live who didn't have to. All swathed in the ceaseless din of the jets.

The private field was next to the public airport. If you didn't have to fly commercial in and out of town, this was your choice. I parked near the passenger terminal, gateway for the hangars and planes ranging from small props to corporate jets that could've shamed a third world air force. Impressive, but not exactly the point of my visit.

I entered the terminal, felt the sweat dissolve in the frigid air-conditioning, and took a seat with a good view of the gates and tarmac. But what I was mostly seeing was the opaque swirl of the immediate past. I had no more idea why Rose betrayed me than why she hadn't killed me. The Buddhists had taught me that the only way to get a grip on the unknown was to let your perception of it go. Let everything go. See nothing. They call it "no mind." I tried to let everything go by watching a Lear Jet in a big hangar across the runway being prepped by its ground crew. But I couldn't see the nothing. Only the people and their equipment trucks and a spotless fuselage.

Elle's plane was a Gulfstream, now taxiing up to a hangar, almost exactly on time at eleven-fifteen. My view was blocked briefly by a catering truck, but then she came walking in through the terminal doors, pulling a black roller-board suitcase, a slender handbag over her left shoulder. She wore sunglasses, dark slacks, flats, and a light blue blouse. It would have been easy to tag her for a corporate executive prepped-up for her important presentation to the board. She saw me at once.

A few steps behind her was a tall black man in a business suit, pulling his own luggage. He joined a young Latina woman also in a dark business suit and they began talking right away in what seemed serious mode and headed toward the exit. But he shot a quick glance at Elle that you'd give to someone you knew better than you were letting on.

The expression on Elle's face told me the money was in the suitcase and that there hadn't been any problems. We hugged, holding each other longer than the situation warranted. But it felt good. I pulled the suitcase behind me as we went out to the parking lot and my Jeep.

The transition from the inside of a building to the bright Texas sun made me squint and I heard Elle sneeze, which I had always heard was an indication of good reflexes. She would need them. I told her we would be heading south into Oak Cliff.

I was just guessing but it seemed to me a reckless Mexican gang kid looking to shake down his girlfriend's mother might just stick with the kind of neighborhood where he wouldn't stand out because of his look or his accent. There were other places in Dallas that would also do, but my gut said the Cliff. Sounds less impressive when you know Oak Cliff is basically just the lower half of Dallas. Lots of room to move around, jump strangers, do deals, get killed.

I suggested stopping for coffee and a bite. We had to use up a little time in an inconspicuous space. Or we could fade into the crowd in a mall south of the river. Elle said she'd had breakfast on the flight and wasn't hungry. And she didn't want to get stuck inside anywhere in case Rose called early. She said maybe we could just stop at a park. There'd be no delay if we had to leave fast. She had a point.

North Oak Cliff, around where I'd had breakfast with Red, had neighborhood parks, but the first two we drove by were full of kids. I went on a few more blocks and stopped on a wide, quiet street in front of a house with a for-sale sign. It would get snapped up fast. This was a neighborhood of sensible refurbished cottages, light traffic, and lots of trees. Schools where your kids had less of a chance of getting shot or beat up.

I tuned to a station playing a mix of jazz and blues and thought maybe music would help pass the hour until the scheduled call. It didn't. We ended up talking about what had happened to us since that call to come to Atlanta two weeks ago. Or was it two centuries? Two light-years? There were details on both ends that needed filling in. Nothing shocking. What could shock anyone in our positions? We were both so numb that the airport hug was the only physical contact we'd made.

I told her a little more about my stay with William, but she already knew most of that from Lenora. She gave me a little more about the way Rose had finally found her and moved to Atlanta. I told her a little more about AK, which seemed to both amuse and disturb her. Ditto about the woman named Ginger/Simone/Brick who had connected me to the nightmare that was Topper. I told her more about Rose in Savannah, and the bartender Elena that had become her friend. I didn't tell her Elena's fate, and just enough about Topper and his treatment of Rose and others to help her understand his role in where we were now.

I told her that a dozen people, give or take, had died as a result of what Red, AK, and I had been doing. I reviewed the main battles, especially the one where we found Rose. I said I could make a good case that each of the departed deserved it and the world was a better place without them. Including Blaine. And that Rose was safer as the main consequence. I don't know if she bought into the ethics of wrongs making rights. She did know I had done what I had to and she left it at that.

She slumped back against the seat, mostly staring ahead through the windshield of the Jeep, looking at me only occasionally, trying when possible to let the background of Miles or Wynton or Muddy or Etta take her somewhere she never could truly go again. Her eyes were as wide as I had ever seen. Her mouth as tight. Her jaw muscles as active. I couldn't see into her brain but I had a pretty good idea of the landscape.

I was aware that she had let me do most of the talking. It was my experience that women often did that, and men were stupid or vain enough to let them. When I finally did shut up I knew she'd never look at me the same way again.

I turned the music down, turned in the seat to face her better. I said I'd run through the highlight reel because I was at the end-of-my-rope kind of mindset. I had no idea what would await us when we met Rose and the guy we assumed to be Javier. Javier of the Jovenes. Then I found myself doing all the talking again—why the Jovenes and the cartel weren't on the same page at all, how the Salvation Brigade complicated everything with the mob. Why Red and AK were at odds. It was clear enough but her eyes started to glaze over because for Elle the only thing that she cared about in any way now was her daughter.

"I get all that, I do," she said, shifting a little in her seat to look out her window. "But it's like this is now, all that was before. It's like nothing back there exists. It's like this is the real thing. The only thing. What we're doing right now. Today. The second my damn phone rings. This is it. It's the real thing." She didn't realize she was repeating herself. She finally looked at me full on for the first time since the airport. "It's the real thing, Jack. All this. Now."

"It is," I said, lost in the sorrow of those eyes.

She turned away again, rocking slightly, something I hadn't seen her do since we were in the Mississippi Delta and her brother Terrell's unavenged death at the hands of her half-brother Trey was poisoning her soul. "Rose will be there," she said. "I know you don't think so. But I know. This is where she'll be. She'll be there. This is the real thing. I'm taking her home. You know?" She wasn't even talking to me anymore.

~~~

51

I drove deeper into the Cliff in no particular route, just to stay moving and lessen the weight of the wait. Exactly at noon, Elle's phone rang. I was just approaching a discount supermarket and turned sharply into its parking lot. I told her to put it on speaker so we could both listen. She shook her head, said that Rose would know. Or they would. That it might spook them.

"Just hold it where I can hear, then."

She pressed the answer button and tipped the phone receiver my way.

"Carla?"

"Mom?"

"It's me. You can say Rose now."

Elle and I exchanged looks.

"You're here? In Dallas?"

"I am."

"She's here," Rose said to someone else. Then, "Okay, look, I'm going to give you an address. You need to be there in an hour. Can you do that? This is a big city."

"Where are you? I'm waiting in a place called Kessler Park."

"Who's with you?"

"Jack. You know that."

We could hear Rose's hand go over her phone and something mumbled. Then, "Does he have that mob guy with him?"

Elle looked at me. I nodded.

"He's not with me now, but, yes, he's here."

More muffled conversation.

"That's good. Bring him."

"Are you okay?"

"I'm okay. I told you that before."

"Are you mixed up in this somehow?"

I was surprised at her directness, but not as surprised as Rose.

"You mean other than being kidnapped and jerked around for two weeks by people who want to kill me? Sure, Mom. I'm mixed up as hell in this."

"I'm just trying to understand what's happening, you know?"

"What's happening is like we said. You come here, bring the money, they'll let me go."

"But who is 'they'?"

More muffling. "I can't say anything about that. But you probably have a good idea. I mean you already know. They don't want me to talk any more on the phone."

"Well, I need to know if you are coming with me. Home."

"Of course I am. I mean, that's the whole fucking point, right?"

"You're angry."

"Mom, I can't stay on the phone. Just come, bring that mob guy."

"Jack is coming, too."

Short pause. "Sure, why the hell not. Make it a party."

"Just so they know who will be there." Elle shot a glance at me as if to say, yeah, I got this shit down.

"Well then you'd better get started. Write this down."

I had a notepad and pen ready and nodded at Elle. She read off the address as Rose gave it to her. It was on the east side of I-35, which surprised me, since that was mostly a black area rather than Latino. But it would meet the other benchmarks of abduction—a blighted and neglected neighborhood where survival means not daring to care about who comes and goes, or what they do, or what they might hear.

Elle said we'd be there at 1 p.m. sharp, and I could hear the click of a disconnect. I looked at Elle, put it in drive, and eased out of the parking lot. I called Red. I told him about the special request for his presence. He said we might as well go to the address, but that there was zero chance in hell they'd be there.

"I get the feeling it's just Rose and the boyfriend," I said.

"Why?"

"There were just two voices, again. And she's going by Rose, not Carla."

"Huh."

"Kinda says something. Felt that way. Maybe it'll be easier to sort out." I looked at Elle and she nodded.

"Let's hope. But plan for the worst, you know."

"Any chance Po-Boy and Carlos will be in Dallas by then?"

"They said two at the earliest, but I'll see if they can speed it up."

"So no backup for us."

"Not at this first stop. What's the point?"

"I hope you're right."

"A six-pack and a steak back in Biloxi says I am."

It was the most optimistic thing I'd heard in days. "Deal."

"How's Elle holding up?"

"She's okay. She's with me."

"Hey, Red." She leaned in and I gave her the phone.

"Hey, darlin'. We're going to get this done today."

His voice was plenty loud, but she put it on speaker anyway. "I sure hope so."

"We will."

"And I need to tell you how much . . ."

"We're good."

She was quiet a moment, balancing the phone in her hand.

"Red?"

"Yeah."

"Why do you think that boy wants to see you?"

"I have a couple of ideas but they might be wrong so I'd rather just wait and see."

"You think it's good that he does? Want to see you?"

"Means there's something else they want. Other than the money."

"So that might be good? I mean for getting Rose back."

"Could be. Main thing is it gives me the right to show up. I was trying to figure that part out. So, yeah, this is good."

Elle made an odd face and gave the phone back to me, turning off the speaker.

"It's me again," I said, looking for an exit to cross I-35. "You think we can go in carrying?"

"Glock in the back of my belt all the way. I expect you'll want to do the same."

"Worse thing is they can ask for the guns."

"I don't see them asking. Anyway, I have a .32 snubnose in my boot. Nobody takes that one."

"I'm sure this guy Javier will be armed."

"Even so, he's not inviting me there to kill me."

"True."

"So like I said, I don't think this will be a problem."

"You mean we can just leave the money, take Rose, and go."

A silence like he was trying to keep it friendly. "Truth, buddy? Is Elle listening?"

I looked at her, hoping she'd turn her head. She didn't.

"Afraid so. Your voice carries."

"Doesn't matter. She might as well know."

"What?" I had to stop for a light that changed fast.

"The truth is I don't know what the fuck we're going to find. This is the damndest job I've ever been on. And I've been on a couple."

I breathed out louder than I intended.

"What I do know is that when it's done, the three of us are walking back out of that house, no matter what. Me, you, Elle. I know that."

Elle stared at me, pupils wide and dark.

"See you there," I said.

"Copy that." He clicked off.

I drove in silence.

We were at the address with ten minutes to spare and pulled to the side of the street a few houses down. Red's pickup showed maybe two minutes later and pulled in behind me.

The house was wood and white brick, now badly discolored. Maybe two bedrooms. The lawn was only a little overgrown, mostly brown from the rain-scarce summer. One of the windows was broken, patched with cardboard and duct tape. The front screen door was kicked in and the mailbox was overflowing with what looked like junk mail flyers. The surrounding houses, about the same size, also were in various shades of disrepair—driveways filled with old cars or trucks, yards with plastic kids' toys, half-filled wading pools. Nobody walking around, although maybe because of the heat. Hard to tell if everyone was at work or just holed up inside. It reminded me of the place in Savannah where this started, only worse.

I got out, walked up. I figured I had least had to go through the motions. I knocked, waited. No response. I looked down at the frayed rubber "Welcome" mat on the concrete slab in front of the door. I turned and gave a hand signal to Elle and Red indicating nobody home.

Then I sensed something moving down the block. Three dogs, those feral brown mixed breeds common to every rundown backwater around the globe, were walking up slowly and territorially. They sensed my outsider status instantly, and changed their gait, not quite running but very close to it.

My Colt was tucked into my belt but shooting wasn't an option. I could make it to the Jeep if I hurried, but it would be tight. Then I noticed a four-foot length of rebar leaning against the house a few feet from the door, next to a water spigot. I grabbed it and faced the animals straight on, taking an aggressive step toward them.

The dogs paused, the big one on the right sniffing the wind and watching me. He must have done the mental math that I wasn't a good chase-down option, or maybe had learned the hard way not to get too close to people he couldn't easily cow. They circled around each other a couple of times, started my way, and then turned back and trotted down the street in the other direction. I eased back to the Jeep, still holding the rebar. As I got closer I could see Elle with a cell phone to her ear, reaching into the console between the seats. She hadn't seen any of this.

When I opened the door she looked at me quickly to indicate she was on the phone. With her free hand she was writing on the note pad I'd just used. When finished she dropped the pen and held the pad up for me to see. I read the new address she had written. She raised her eyebrows, and continued her conversation on the phone. "Well, let's just make sure this is the right place this time. The guys I'm with aren't going to want to do this game anymore . . . Well, that's the truth. Why make this any more insane than it already is? . . . I know it's not you, but . . ." She held the phone away from her ear and looked at me. "She hung up."

"That's the next meeting place?"

"You know it? She said it's on the other side of Oak Cliff, way southwest of here. I said you used to live in Dallas. We could find it. We have to be there at two."

"Huhhn."

"She said they'd actually be there."

"Did she say anything about this bogus shit we just had to do?"

"No. She just said they had to be careful."

"So they're not even around here to see us."

"I don't think so."

"How do they know we came?"

"I had to describe the house while you were up there."

I looked off in the direction of the dogs, wiped sweat from my forehead and out of my eyes. "So anyway, now we're headed to the final destination."

"It's not a joke."

"I didn't mean it that way."

"Final destination, you said."

"In a good way."

She looked back at Red's F-150. "You'd better go tell him."

I could see the sarcastic turn of his expression before I got there. I gave him the address anyway. He had a Dallas map and we took a minute to be sure we synched on the right place.

It was southwest all right, deep into a nether part of the city that was almost completely Mexican and Central American. All the fun spots of the Reagan years—Guatemala, El Salvador, Honduras, Nicaragua. It looked working-class suburban, full of three- and four-bedroom ranch-style brick; over the years it had succumbed to the relentlessly predatory infrastructure upon which the Dallas skyline really had been built. I'd covered a gruesome murder down there. Cartel vengeance on a cop from Reynosa, across the river from McAllen. For our purposes, it would be fine.

We looked at our watches to be sure we could make it cross-town and then I headed back to the Jeep. And there were the dogs, snarling up the street toward me in attack formation. Type A behavior wouldn't stop them this time.

I got to the door just in time. One of the mutts hit the metal a second after I got in, plastering his paws on the window. He didn't bark. Just stared at me with cold black eyes. I could hear claws scraping as he dropped down slowly, gave me the parting sneer you can only get from natural killers, then turned and followed his pals on down the asphalt to whatever mayhem they had yet to find. Elle still was staring at the phone in her lap.

Red pulled up next to me. He lowered a window, looked at her, and me, and nodded. Then he drove off. I followed him to the interstate. We had ample time to make the next meeting site. If in fact that's where it would happen.

Elle put her phone down and climbed into the back seat just behind me. She pulled the suitcase up next to her and I heard zippers and flaps opening and closing and through the rearview mirror could see her looking at the bundles of hundreds, thumbing through a couple of them.

"It's all there, right?"

She didn't answer, just closed the bag. More zipper sounds. After that whenever I glanced at her she was staring out the side window. Even in the mirror I could see blood-filled cheeks in that immaculate caramel face.

～～～

52

We were so deep into southwest Dallas I wasn't even sure if it could still be called Oak Cliff. Between my musing and Elle's silence I damn near missed Evergreen Circle. I braked hard and pulled over to the curb just before the turn-in. Red did the same, stopping just short of banging into my back bumper.

I put the Jeep in neutral and told Elle to hang tight. As if she was doing anything loose at all. She nodded, still lost wherever she was. I walked to Red's truck and slid in on the passenger side.

"Want to go up in my Jeep from here?"

"Close fucking stop, buddy," he grumbled.

I didn't answer, but followed his line of sight to Evergreen Circle. It was really more a short street that ran about a hundred yards before opening to a half-moon cul-de-sac with five houses spread around. No. 10279, the one we wanted, was on the right edge. It was the kind of configuration where you could get bottled up easily.

"I'll leave my truck here. We're facing out if we need to leave in a hurry," he said. "Elle still okay?"

"Wrapped pretty tight."

"Can she go in with us?"

"I think she has to. But, yeah."

"What are you carrying?"

"I have the Colt. I could take the shotgun. You?"

"Same as before. Glock. Better leave the scattergun. It'll spook them. Something they can see."

I looked toward 10279. "I don't see any cars in the driveway."

"There's a garage, right?"

"Right."

Red nodded. "I was thinking on this. Our boy Javier wants this to go all thumbs up."

"Agreed."

"Like I told Elle, I've got a few thoughts on why, but I don't want to lock myself in."

"But what's your main thought?"

"I think he wants protection. From the Mexicans."

"Huhhn."

"You don't?"

"Maybe. I mean, sure. But something else is going on. It's eating at Elle and she won't talk about it. She just thinks we'll give them the money and go."

"I know."

"This whole thing has been off the level all the way."

"Roger that shit."

"You think Rose is bent, too?"

"Hell, you know she is."

"I know."

"Closing time," he said. "Let's find out." We went back to the Jeep. Red saw Elle was in back and got in the front. They exchanged hellos. He turned around, as much as his bulk would permit, to take her hand. I guess to give it a squeeze of confidence. She barely responded.

He looked at me, shook his head slightly. I put the transmission in drive and made our way up the street to the house. I pulled along the curb in front of it.

"They'll be looking at us," Red said.

"Should we bring the suitcase?" It was the first time Elle had said more than a few words since leaving the phony meeting site.

"Not yet." He looked at me, turned toward her again. "Truth. You up to this?"

She was sitting bolt upright, staring directly at him. "More than you can imagine." The abrupt transformation in her eyes was stunning. Ophelia mode vanished in a snap. A toughness back in her voice. "They won't care about the money?"

Red side-glanced at me with something like appreciation or amusement. Or surprise. "If I were them, I wouldn't expect to see the money right away. You know."

"Until we see that Rose is okay."

"Exactly."

"I agree," I said. "Otherwise we're just there to get shot."

Red gave me a warning look.

"I mean it's our bargaining chip is all."

"Okay," she said. I was afraid I'd sent her spirits south again, but she rebounded. "So back to your question, Red. Yeah, I'm good. Let's go."

Red leaned over to pull up the jeans over his right boot and pulled out his snubnose. He turned it over in his hand, then held it out to Elle. "This might be the real deal. No reason you shouldn't have your own."

She looked at him with silent gratitude and slipped it into her carry-on bag. "My dad had one of these."

"You know guns."

"I know guns."

"You're good with this?" I asked her.

"I'm not good with any of this, but, yes, I will take care of myself if it comes to that."

"Probably it won't," I said.

"Probably. Sure," she said, and looked out the back window.

"Saddle up," Red said, and got out.

He was halfway up the cracked sidewalk before Elle and I caught up. As soon as we got to the porch slab, the front door opened. It was her.

"Rose," Elle called out, rushed forward, throwing off Red's cautionary hand. He might have held her, but didn't. I could almost hear Elle's heart break. Rose not only pulled back from the attempted hug, but pushed her mother away like a running back stiff-arming a tackler.

Her face was contorted with revulsion. She looked well and strong in black T-shirt, jeans, sandals. A long way from the last time I'd seen her. Truly a beautiful young woman. With nothing in her gaze, or from her lips, that said she was happy to see her mother.

"Come in. But don't do anything funny," she said, looking past Elle, who seemed frozen in disbelief, hands interlocked and tight across her abdomen, not knowing how to move or why or where. "There are people in here. They have guns."

Red snorted derisively and stepped inside, slightly in front of Elle's left side. No one would get past him. "Well, fuck yeah we'll come in, darlin'. Good to see you again. Looking forward to meeting all these 'people.' And don't worry about 'funny.'"

Rose took a couple of steps back, well out of his reach. At the same time I was also coming in. I reached back for the Colt in my belt, but, like Red, didn't draw it. I kicked the door shut behind me. I think we all knew that not everyone inside was going out again.

~~~

53

Red squared off with his legs spread and knees slightly bent, the way a martial arts fighter might position. His right arm was crooked near his side in a way that he could grab his Glock in a heartbeat. I came up on Elle's right side, flanking her. Her hand was on her bag. I had all but drawn my Colt.

Rose continued to retreat until she was halfway across the room and poised like a tethered wolf at the side of the person Red had been looking at all along. I figured him for Javier. Tall, sinewy Latino with peroxide dreadlocks and clad in a black wife-beater T-shirt, green fatigue pants, and desert boots. In his left hand he held an M-4 carbine, although not pointing it at us. I would describe the overall effect as menacing but not immediately threatening. He nodded his head in what I guess was his version of a tough-guy greeting.

Two expensive-looking blue sleeping bags lay on the soiled gray carpet along the far wall. The rest of the place that I could see was a litter dump of grocery bags, pizza boxes, water bottles, and take-out containers. They'd been there one or two nights, but maybe not much more. If we were chasing, they were definitely running.

Rose stood on her toes to whisper something to Javier. I could see a Beretta tucked into her waistband just behind her hip. She gave me a head nod, which at first I thought was a clumsy way of acknowledging my continued existence, but from the way Javier looked at me as he bent down so she could reach his ear, was simply to identify me. I looked at her with the coldness she deserved.

Finally she shifted her eyes to Elle, who had started to move forward again. This time Red held her in place. "Wait," he said, as gently as he could.

Rose shot her mother another contemptuous glance, then, glancing back at Javier, came forward to about where she had stood before, just beyond Red's reach. She stared at him, like no one else was in the room. "They just want to make the trade. No fuss, no muss. This is Javier. He also wants to talk to you."

"To Red?" Elle interrupted, as if not comprehending that Rose wasn't talking to her.

"*Pero primero . . .*" It was Javier. His voice firm, but nervous.

"First," Rose said, picking it up, "they want to know you have the money. You're not carrying anything with you. Unless it's all in your little handbag, Mom. Very corporate look, by the way. How perfect."

"Are you okay?" Elle asked.

Rose shrugged.

"Do I know you?" Elle faced Javier.

It seemed to take him off guard. "Maybe. It was a while." So he spoke English. Without an accent. Rose glared at him as if he had done something stupid. He didn't say anything else.

"He tries to speak Spanish as much as possible," Rose said. "You know. For the Mexicans."

I looked at Red quickly. I could see he was already there. "Who's 'they'?"

"You know, don't you?" Rose shot a shut-up look at her companion.

"I just see one guy."

"Well, they're not all here." Her voice was a half-octave too sharp. Red could smell the nerves like a shark sniffing blood.

I kept scanning the house. Something wasn't right. The carpet gave way to faded linoleum as it reached the back door. That's where I saw a third sleeping bag, rolled up next to a gallon water jug. I head-signaled Red.

"The fuck's going on?" he said.

Javier held up his right hand as a disclaimer, the carbine still ready at his left side. Rose gave him another glare. Just then a beam of sunlight shot through a broken slat in the blinds and illuminated her face. We could all see the black-and-green bruise across the top of her left cheek.

Elle looked at me. I shook my head.

"I was wanting to talk to you, Mr. Red," Javier said, now moving forward just a little, until he saw Red's expression. "But we also need the money." He paused, as if trying to get the words he wanted. "It's not just for us, you know."

"Talk about what?"

"I might have something for you, for the people you work for."

"What people would that be?"

"I mean, you know. From New Orleans."

Red's glare had the desired effect on the kid.

Rose saw it and stepped in. "Can we just do this? I'm right here." Turning to Elle, "Mom, give him the money and we can go, or they can talk or whatever. But I can go. That's the deal, right?" She shifted her glance to me, then Red, then back at Javier.

"I can do that," Elle said. It was one of the saddest things I'd ever heard a mother say to a child.

"Then where is it?" And that, the most cruel from a child to its mother.

"I just need to know you're okay."

"I just need to know what the fuck this is about," Red said.

No one spoke as Elle and Rose stared at each other. Then Elle broke off to look at Javier again. She tried to approach him but Red held her arm tighter. "Part of your right ear is clipped off," she said. "There's a burn mark on your neck, maybe your back, too. And you're tall, handsome. You're the one Rose told me about. Berto. I remember who you are. You saved her life. Am I right?"

Javier tried to look indifferent but he was obviously perplexed. He looked to Rose, who shrugged, and for the first time truly fixed her eyes on Elle. "So you remember," she said. "Good for you."

Elle's face seemed to drain.

Rose knew the buttons. "Good eye for the detail. But Berto is Javier now. Been that way for a while. Roots, you know. Oh, wait, you wouldn't know."

Javier smiled, proud of the attention and oblivious to the context. "Only look, Mrs. M., she saved my hide, too, if she didn't tell you. I got her out of the fire at that foster home but then later on she popped the guy that wanted to throw me out of that window up in Charleston. I mean, it was pretty fucking awesome."

Elle stared at them both.

Red never took his eyes off Javier.

"Rose, why didn't you ever—" Elle began.

"—Tell you about all that? You really want to know about everything that happened after you abandoned my ass?"

"Oh, Rose . . ."

"Look, Mom, we can catch up on old times later. I mean, how's Dad? Such a sweet perve. Oh, yeah, you killed him." Elle didn't move. "For now, though, how about getting on with getting the money for Javier so I can get on with getting the fuck out of here."

"He hit you," I interjected. "Why?"

She touched the bruise involuntarily. "Fuck you."

I looked at Javier. His mouth twisted in a sneer.

"Hang on," Red said. "I'm going to say this for the last time. Before we give you any money, let's back up again. I need to know what you have to say about why you wanted to fucking meet me, son."

"Tell him," Rose said.

They exchanged some kind of silent message, then Javier drew a long breath. "Thing is, Los Jovenes, that's the ones we are with—" He stopped to correct himself but knew it was too late. "I mean that I work with. Me." He looked at Rose but she rolled her eyes. "I mean we. I mean Los Jovenes don't get along so great with the cartel, the Gulf one." Perspiration formed on his forehead.

"I know which cartel," Red said.

"Well, we were trying to make things right, wanting to get those drugs from that guy Topper and give it to them, you know, to smooth out stuff, so they'd give us a little space. Then you got the drugs yourself and I think you sent them to the cartel. You know, for your guys." Now obviously sweating.

"I'm listening." Red was, but something else, too. He let go of Elle's arm, with a glance to stay put. She did. The more Javier talked, the more her posture straightened.

"So anyway now," Javier said, shifting from one leg to the other, "the other Jovenes, you know, thought maybe we could work out something with the New Orleans and Memphis people, like, you know, being allies. We can do a lot, you know? We know a lot of people, can move a lot of weight. I mean, if the people already in the game will let us. We're real willing to cut deals, do whatever it takes, you know."

It was almost sad to watch his face affect gangster bonhomie.

"So. You want me to take this, what, proposal, back to my bosses."

"That and the million for Rosie. You know, kind of a gift to get a meeting."

Red looked at me. Elle and Rose were focused completely on each other.

"Or, you know. You can take Rosie to them, too." He smiled like he'd just put the icing on an already sweet deal.

Red's face went solid granite. "That's what I was waiting for."

Javier's cockiness fell along with the muscles around his eyes and mouth.

Rose's head snapped toward the friend who presumably had drawn her into the Jovenes and had just offered her up as a trophy to their enemies. For a moment she was silent, almost dumbstruck, as if it were impossible for him to have just said that. But it wasn't, and he had.

Something too deep to comprehend seemed to explode inside her small torso and flare out in the fury of her eyes. Panic, betrayal, primal abandonment. The kind of stuff shrinks knew about. Maybe what Elle had been fearing all along.

"What the fuck, you motherfucker!" she screamed. Javier stared at her, as if not quite understanding what he had done.

"And fuck you, mommy dearest," turning from him to Elle, like a child unsure who to confront. Then back to Javier, "Jesus fucking Christ you fucking asshole, you're going to fucking try to sell me, you fucking airhead moron. Have you got a fucking clue?" She reached back to pull the pistol from her jeans.

Javier backhanded her hard across the face before she could clear the weapon. She reeled back.

He watched her stumble for two or three seconds too long. By the count of two, Red's Glock was already in his right hand. By three he had put a round into Javier's throat, sending him spinning to the wall, flailing for Rose like a broken windmill. He caught her with one arm and the momentum carried her with him to the floor. She broke free as he went into spasms, writhing, gushing blood, his M-4 gone from his grip and loose on the carpet.

With the sound of the shots, the mystery of the possible third occupant of the house resolved itself into a hard-looking young *indio* in black boxer shorts rushing from one of the bedrooms working at the safety or maybe a clip jam on an Uzi. He got off several rounds. One caught Red in the left side, one whizzed past my head, and another caught me in the upper left arm at just the moment I stopped him with two .45 slugs, one in his chest and the other in his mouth.

Meanwhile Rose was getting to her feet, her Beretta pointed unsteadily our way. She got off one shot when she suddenly yelped in pain, dropped the weapon, and clutched at her right wrist. "You bitch," she said, reaching with her left hand for Javier's carbine a few feet away.

Elle was still pointing Red's snubnose at her daughter, but then her hand dropped. She sagged, stumbled, and fell back onto the floor.

Rose got to the carbine after all—maybe from anger, maybe simple toughness—and was trying to point it at her mother when two rounds from Red's Glock smashed into her chest. Simultaneously, I hit her right arm with a .45 slug, all but severing it. Javier's M-4 tumbled back against his still-twitching right foot. Rose was dead before her head hit the floor.

The house went quiet. Smoke and the smell of gunpowder made it hard to see or breathe.

~~~

54

I waved a hand signal to Red and hurried through the rest of the house to see if there were more surprises. When I came back, he was looking outside through the dirty blinds. No reaction to the noise. Probably wouldn't be in this neighborhood, but Red's look told me we needed to be gone.

The only sound was Elle, groaning as she pulled herself across the floor, her hand on her left thigh. She got to Rose's body, collapsed, and then raised herself a little, looking at the death grimace. She stroked Rose's cheeks. She was trying to say something but no words came out. She would never know what had happened to bring Rose to this place. She sank to the floor, blood of mother and child mingling on the carpet.

"Get shitbag boyfriend's belt or cut off his shirt. Use that to tie off Elle's leg," Red said. "I'm going to pick up the brass. We can't leave it like we did before." He saw me looking at his side. "Don't worry. It's not that bad." Then he winced. "Son of a bitch. And tear me off some cloth, too."

I needed Javier's shirt as well as his belt to make a decent field compress on Elle's wound. I was pretty sure there was no bullet. I took off her shoes and propped her head on her handbag. I gave the rest of the shirt to Red, who held it against his side as he searched out the casings we had used. I looked at my arm but I was too wired to feel any pain and it wasn't bleeding much. It could wait.

"Who is he?" I said, nodding toward the one I had shot.

"Looks like a pro. Cartel'd be my guess. We probably caught him taking a shit or something. Lucked out."

"Maybe."

"Go have a look."

I did. Nothing at all except a pile of clothes near the shower and a Glock under his sleeping bag. A plastic billfold with several hundred dollars, and no ID.

"This thing is fucked twelve ways from Sunday," Red said. "Why would the Mexicans have anybody in this mix."

"Could be a Jovenes. Except he's not exactly young."

"Maybe."

"Shit."

"Yeah, shit." He picked up a plastic bag from the pile of litter and dropped the brass into it. "Let's just get out of here. How's she doing?"

We'd both kept an eye on Elle. She was awake and not moaning—holding her own. I walked over to check her vitals again. She tried to raise herself up on one arm, maybe to see Rose's body better, but couldn't, and dropped on an elbow, then her side.

"I can't leave her," she said.

I rolled her on her back and propped her head again. I was worried she might cough up blood and choke. I stroked her forehead. It was warm, not cool and clammy. I looked into her eyes, touched her lips with my finger. They were dry. "I'll get you some water from the Jeep. We're leaving in a couple of minutes. You'll be okay."

I looked at Red, tilted my head toward Rose. "Can we?"

"She, her body, it shouldn't be in the truck with you."

"I can't leave her," Elle said again, her voice now almost too faint to hear. I checked the compress. It already needed changing. Red held out his watch.

"Go," I said. "I'll take her from here. Rose, too. I can do it."

He looked at me like I'd just said I could cross the desert without water.

"Just help me get her into the Jeep."

Elle coughed and I felt inside her mouth for blood or phlegm but it was fine.

Red looked at her. Not with confidence. "How?"

"My problem. Your guys, they can take care of all this other when they get here, right?"

"Like before." He walked over to the blue sleeping bags by the wall, then looked at what was left of Rose. He picked up one of the bags and unzipped it to see how long and wide it was.

"It'll work," I said. He brought it over and put it on a patch of carpet that wasn't bloody. We picked her up carefully as possible and laid her inside. I closed her eyelids. Red zipped up the bag. Elle watched us in silence, except for a faint "my baby."

"Go bring your truck up here. Can't carry this out to the street," Red said, looking at the bag, then Elle, then me.

"Right." I left and walked out as normally as possible to the Jeep. I had blood of my own and blood spatter all over my clothes but they were dark and not that easy to see from a distance. Halfway down the drive I noticed that one of the double garage doors to the house was partly open. Hadn't even thought of that.

I went back to see if it would raise up all the way. It did, squeaking and rattling because it was off its tracks, probably why it wouldn't close. Nothing was inside except piles of torn black trash bags, empty boxes, and what smelled like cat shit in one corner. I backed in the Jeep, and pulled the garage door back down. It was like an oven inside.

We carried Rose through a door to the garage from the patio. She was small but carrying her still put a twinge in the sliver of a wound in my arm. I could tell Red's side was hurting more than he let on. We eased the bag into the left side of the trunk, bending it to a near-fetal position. Biology would freeze it in that pose but we had no choice. It wouldn't matter anyway. Elle would want her cremated, same as Terrell had been, although we wouldn't be scattering her ashes in the Mississippi. I pushed my stuff as far away on the other side of the trunk as I could.

I got the suitcase from the back seat, jammed it into my part of the trunk, and cleared out the rest of my own things from the seat so Elle could stretch out. Red grabbed my duffel bag and an old Mexican blanket I'd crammed under the passenger seat so we could elevate her leg and keep her warm. Then we went back to have another look at the cargo hold, like movers assessing a load in their van. He leaned in to pat down the sleeping bag, either as some kind of goodbye to the girl we had killed, or to be sure her body wouldn't shift.

"Back to how you gonna do this, who's gonna take care of this and when?"

"I'll figure it out. There's people in Atlanta."

We both knew I was making that up. He reached for the trunk lid.

"Wait," I said, holding his arm. I remembered my Army poncho, half-hidden under my Remington bag and ammo. Red stepped back while I unrolled it and draped it over the sleeping bag. I pulled the cargo cover

over it all and secured it. The Jeep windows were tinted so nobody would be able to see anything easily. And I would be driving mostly at night.

Red pulled down the lid. It felt exactly like closing a coffin.

We were both sweating and went back to the house. It was still smoky but the a/c was cool and clearing the air. I stopped to have another look at the dead cartel guy and then started for Elle when Red asked me to hold up. He looked over at her and lowered his voice.

"Just to be clear, Shakespeare. You're gonna go out that driveway, go on the road for, what, twelve or fifteen hours with a dead body in your car and a woman with a fresh wound in her leg, you white, them black, and a million bucks in a suitcase and you think that's the best way to handle this? Just 'figure it out'?"

"Do I have a choice?"

"You do. Leave Rose here. My guys will take care of it. However Elle wants."

I looked around at what we'd left in the room. "I don't say you're wrong. And I appreciate it. But Elle wants to bring Rose home herself. I mean, who else gets a say?" I reached back to rub the sore crease in my arm and then started toward Elle.

He stood in my path just to let me know he could, then stepped aside. He held up his hands, breathed out. "You leave with her, and the girl, you're on your own. You got that, right? I mean for chrissake she needs a doctor."

We went to Elle, but after a step I put my hand on his arm. "I'll get a doc. AK said he knows people. I got it. I do."

He drew his arm away. "Say he doesn't answer?"

"He will."

Then we were looking down at Elle, who was looking up at us like we were from outer space. This time it was Red who grabbed my arm, not in empathy. "Let's say that happens. So then say you have a flat tire or get stopped for a broken tail light or a deer jumps into your windshield or anything at all and they find all this . . . And it comes back to me, to you, to the family . . . They'll kill you. Her. Me, too, likely as not."

I dropped to one knee next to Elle, looked up at him. "Shit, Red. I have to do this. I mean, fuck, man . . ."

Her eyes were so glassy I wasn't sure she had heard or comprehended anything that was being said.

Then she seemed to see me. "She's coming with us?"

Red knelt on her other side, stroked her forehead, tried not to show how he really felt. She smiled for a second until it turned into a grimace. He pulled back, looked at me.

"We're going to lift you," I said. "We'll put you on the back seat and we'll go. We'll get you to a doctor. You'll be fine."

"She's coming with us?" She turned her head to look for Rose's body, seemed confused, and lay back flat.

"She is."

Red slid his arms underneath and picked her up by himself, despite his wound. I could see his jaw clench, but he waved off my offer to help. I went ahead to open the doors and then helped him ease her onto the rear seat. I turned on the engine to get the a/c going and grabbed a water bottle from the console. She was able to take a few sips as she tried to get comfortable.

I remembered her handbag and shoes and went back for them. Red followed me to do another quick scan around the house. After a minute or so I told Red I needed to check on Elle. He said go.

When I got back to the Jeep, she was squirming to find a position that didn't hurt. I propped her head on her bag and made sure her left leg was raised and secure on my duffel. I offered her more water but she pushed it away.

I closed the rear doors and was in the driver's seat ready to back out when Red returned from the house. I lowered my window, said we were ready, and that I'd call him from the road.

He said wait, he wanted to say goodbye. I was pretty sure it was more to see if Elle was going to make it but it didn't matter. He opened the passenger door and leaned in to look at her. I had forgotten the blanket and he spread it over her after checking the compress. "It's holding. Not sure for how long," he said.

I turned in my seat to look at them. He tried to squeeze her hand in sympathy, but she pulled it back and pointed to him with a finger almost too weak to stay up. But her voice was steady enough. "What did you mean back there when you said you were waiting for that, when Javier said that about giving them Rose?"

～～

55

"Tell her," I said. "She deserves to know."

"Tell me, Red."

He backed out of the rear door frame, looked at me.

"She should know."

"Just tell me. She was my girl."

He leaned in again to see her. "It's complicated. And it's hot in here. Plus we got two damn doors open."

I raised a hand in acknowledgment and turned the a/c up to full blast. It was still hot as hell.

"I don't care about the weather," she said.

He checked his watch. "Fuck, Jack. This is in real time."

"It's a long trip. Just tell her. It'll keep her awake. I need that."

He looked at her again, then me. "Two minutes. I need to check in and Po-Boy just tried to call."

"Make it twenty seconds, Red. Anything. Please." She tried to prop herself up but her leg wouldn't let her.

"Okay fuck it," he said, angry, maybe at himself. "You want to know? It's like this. Rose worked for the cartel."

I wasn't surprised, but I didn't like hearing it. Elle's eyes darted around the Jeep and the windows as if she might see something to make what he said sound different.

"I didn't know until yesterday. Not for sure. My guys told me. After we left the militia place."

Now that surprised me. "You told them about the ranch."

He didn't flinch. "Of course. I tell them what's going on, they help me make it happen. And maybe they got their own agenda, you know. They don't always have to tell me what it is, or get my approval. Or yours. We talked about that, me and you."

"Huhhnn."

"What?"

"Something AK said. About the girls. About the cartel taking them from Renaldo's."

"What did he say?"

"He said he didn't want you to be around him anymore."

"Goddamn." Red backed his head out, bumped it on the frame, then twisted his waist slightly while moving. "Goddamn," he said touching his side, and looking away. He took a long breath. His wound hurt more than he was letting on, and I'm sure it added to his short temper.

After a moment he leaned into the door again, his forearm crooked against the roof so he wouldn't dent his skull anymore. He spoke to her, not me. "I had to call it in. It's part of the arrangement. That's when they told me who the cartel really wanted."

The blood had drained again from her face.

"She'd been working Topper, and then her old pal Javier, all along. Getting rid of the militia was easy. The real target was the Jovenes. The cartel is way more worried about them. They're better, they move a lot more stuff, they're ambitious, like Javier said. Only the cartel don't want them as partners. And then Javier played it all wrong. So . . ."

"Rose was working for them all this time?"

"I don't know exactly. Long enough. That one, Elena, too. That's why Rose was in Savannah."

"All this time." Her gaze shifted. "Why?" She no longer seemed to be present.

"I don't know any of that. Elena'd been with them awhile, I think, one of their soldiers or spies. Maybe she brought Rose in. I don't know. Something like that."

"My Rose, my poor girl . . ."

"We need to get moving," Red said, glancing at me.

I settled into my seat and pulled the door shut. He closed the rear door and stepped clear. Elle had slumped down, her eyes closed. She might have passed out but her breathing sounded normal. Her legs were still on the seat and she wasn't moaning in pain and that was the best I could hope for.

Red leaned into my still-open window.

"The militia was gonna give those girls to the cartel anyway. They didn't have much chance either way. We couldn't have stopped it. You get that, right?"

"I doubt AK would see it that way."

"It wasn't AK's call."

"I gotta go. Can you get that door?"

His body stiffened. "The Francosis run a business, dammit. So now the Mexicans owe them one. It's not complicated." He touched his side again. "We can talk some other time." He looked through the rear door window. "Anyway, tell her I'm sorry it went like this. Damn."

He breathed out hard and walked to the garage door to pull it up. I started backing out.

"Call AK," he said.

"I will."

"He can't come through, call. I have a guy in Shreveport."

I stopped. "What about you?"

"There's a place about halfway to Houston. If I need a couple stitches they'll do it there. Couple dozen Advil oughta hold me 'til then."

"Coulda been worse," I said, and eased down the drive to the street.

He stared at me as I rolled up the window and I thought we both might laugh. But we didn't.

~~~

56

I called AK before I got out of the neighborhood, got his voicemail, and picked up the interstate loop east past Dallas and then on toward Atlanta. I wasn't sure just how far to go until I heard back, in case his guy was west or south of the city. But the call came quickly, as I was approaching the suburb of Mesquite on Dallas's eastern edge.

He apologized for missing me but said he'd been at the store with Maria Christina and left his phone in his truck. Yeah, he had a medic buddy, Karo, over near Tyler. The one in San Antonio was a little better, but it was too far. I told him everything I could about the gunshot, and he said Karo could treat it no problem. It would hold until we reached an actual doc in Atlanta.

I didn't mention the body. So far, Elle barely even knew her daughter was in my SUV, let alone in a sleeping bag just behind the back seat.

AK said he'd set it up. Karo'd been a combat medic. His day job now was at a county hospital clinic. His off-the-book work was mostly for veterans, including getting them black-market meds that were otherwise too expensive.

We met near a gas stop not far from the clinic. He had a more cleaned-up look than AK or Red, or for that matter me, but probably because of his day job. In his eyes I could see the common thread, though. I followed him to his double-wide in the woods, all very "Copperhead Road." By then Elle was pale and in considerable pain, in and out of consciousness. I was worried she might finally be going into shock.

She thought we were at a hospital and I didn't correct her. Karo cut away the rest of her trousers to have a better look. He wanted to start an IV right away but I didn't know her blood type and she was incoherent when we asked. I went back to the Jeep to find her handbag. She was the kind who'd keep her emergency info cards up-to-date.

While I looked, he gave her injections for the pain and for infection, then cleaned and tended the wound. It had torn through muscle but not critical veins or arteries and the compress had stopped the bleeding. I came back and told him it was A-Pos, same as mine, and he said that was good, because he had plasma. I said she could have some of mine if he'd rather.

He looked me over and said he'd use his own stock, so we wouldn't have to go through sterilization. He said I could leave some extra money. He said she was lucky to be alive. Like Red, he was surprised I'd handled an effective field dressing.

Her eyes fluttered open as he worked. To distract her, he told a story about how he got his nickname, because a triage nurse had called him "sweet as syrup," which he wasn't, but it stuck. His real name was Travis, which he never liked anyway. I'm not sure if she heard any of it.

He muttered something to himself about trying not to fuck it up and it would never pass muster in the clinic. While the IV was emptying, he made extra compresses for the trip, told me how to change and clean the wound with each one. I already knew, but didn't get into that. He also peroxided my own scratch and taped it up with a gauze pad. Like every medic in the world, he gave me a quick sermon on the dangers of ignoring flesh wounds because they could go septic and kill you. I was running low on cash and he was okay with me giving him a thousand now and wiring the rest in a week.

I went out to the Jeep to get a change of clothes from my duffel and to see if Elle had anything in her carry-on bag that could do for the trip. I found a blouse and some light sweatpants and a hairbrush, but she hadn't been planning an overnight stay. When I came back he had disconnected the drip and said one pint would be enough. He gave me a bottle of Advil and enough black-market meds to keep Elle asleep or too fogged out to know what was going on. He said he had a light blue cotton robe he'd "liberated" from a casino hotel and we helped her to stand to get dressed and to pee. It was as awkward as it sounds, but Karo said it was important to get her to move and "empty her bladder" as often as needed, especially on the trip.

Making her walk just a few dozen steps had the fortunate side effect of pushing her into lucidity just long enough to give me the cell phone number for Lenora, who happened to be working in Huntsville, Alabama, at the time. I had asked Elle for it on the way to Karo's, but whatever she said was too slurred to understand. This time the numbers were correct.

I called Lenora immediately. I expected anger, and she delivered. She also was tough-minded enough to hold it in check under the circumstances. After some awkward q&a, we agreed she'd meet me at Elle's house in Atlanta tomorrow morning and stay with her as long as necessary. Which clearly didn't involve me as one of the necessities. The way she put it was, "Goddamn, Jack, you've done enough for our family, don't you think?"

She asked me about Rose's body and I told her that Red was taking care of it as Elle had requested and that I'd get the details to her as soon as I knew. That was a lie, but in this case the truth could wait. Somewhere between here and Atlanta, I'd have a workable plan to deliver the ashes of the girl whose mother had given her up, found her again, and lost her forever.

~~~

57

Driving to Atlanta was a blur of traffic, gas stations, coffee, and fast food. Elle stayed in deep sleep from the painkillers for all but an hour or two. I had doubled up her dosage just to be sure.

I passed the night listening to constantly changing radio stations—shock jocks, preachers, the occasional jazz or classical station on NPR affiliates. Sometimes there was news about the Mideast or Washington or somebody getting killed in an accident or plane crash or shooting. None of it meant anything. Never anything about us.

I had to stop twice to refuel and grab fast food and triple orders of large coffees, and to help Elle use restrooms. I had been giving her water and Gatorade to keep from dehydrating and that meant extra stops. It was harder than you might think to find places with outside restroom doors so other women couldn't barge in. Among them was a state-run trucker rest area, where nobody much cared if a white guy was helping a zonked-out black woman in a bath robe into the public toilets. A road hooker in dirty jeans and a rock band T-shirt gave me a nasty look, but when I explained that my friend was really sick, she let it slide.

Dawn and proximity to Georgia brought more country stations and classic rock, less talk-show ranting. I got better at the gas stops and fast food drive-thrus. Protein blasts of burgers and eggs and an ultra-high caffeine regimen kept me moving and grooving. I'd have grooved a little more if I'd hit up Doc Karo for some amphetamines but was glad I hadn't. Not that I could have slept if I wanted—deprivation and its consequences had become a theme of this entire hellish odyssey.

You'd think I would have pondered more often the presence of a dead body. And I won't say I didn't, but less from associations with morbid or nightmarish visions and more with wondering every time I hit a bumpy patch or had to slam the brakes hard whether or not the other gear, including Elle's million-dollar suitcase, would fall on top of it.

Sometimes I did think about the timeline of odor, though more in terms of basic science. Inside the zipped-up bag, and under the Army poncho, any kind of smell would stay trapped fairly well. Opening it later would be the issue. No ice, no dry ice, no preservatives of any kind. And although the Jeep a/c was full-blast full-time to help me keep awake, and to somewhat chill the body, outside it was summer in the South.

I made a game of guessing the time of noticeable ripening. I can only attribute that to my former life as a reporter. If you didn't make bad jokes about tragedy and horror, you couldn't stay in the business very long.

Major flaw in all this: I still hadn't figured out what to do with the body. Sure, I'd talked smack with Red about "figuring it out." He had busted me for it rightfully. My only real "figuring" at the time had been turning it over to Lenora to find the kinds of people that I knew she could tap for just this kind of situation. After our unpleasant phone call, that wasn't an option.

I drove, hoping something would come to me, not at all sure it would. At some point, though, thinking of Lenora led me to thinking of another person who might have strange friends in low places. It was more than a stretch, but all I had.

I got Brick on the second ring, which was unusual both because of the late hour and because she had told me she always let her voicemail be her secretary and answering service. I apologized for the timing, but she said she wasn't asleep anyway. I said I was calling because I wanted to see her. She said that was good. I said I also needed some information and help. She was a good sport about knowing I had another motive.

I cut to the chase because that was her way. I just hit the main points, because she shouldn't have to hear it all, but even the summary was hard to get out, and I could tell it was hard to hear. Except about Topper. "Oh . . . well" was all she said to that. When I was done, she said something like, good God, Jack, and asked if I was okay and I said yes, just exhausted and if she wanted, I'd tell her the whole story later but right now I had to take care of the body.

Because I had it with me. In my Jeep. Along with the body's mom, who was unconscious in the back seat. Brick was quiet a moment, stunned might be a better word, and then said of course she would help. I loved the sound of her voice. I loved that it didn't expect me to make explanations that wouldn't make any rational sense but that were true and binding. It was a good voice. It was strong and empathetic and also soothing and it was like talking to an angel. I came close to saying that but didn't. I was completely aware of how fucked up the situation was.

What I did tell Brick was that given her time with Topper, maybe she would know if he ever had to use someone to dispose of bodies. Rose had to be cremated, I said, but a regular undertaker would ask too many questions. Maybe she could help me find someone who didn't? From around there. Someone Topper had used?

I wasn't making the fucked-up situation any better, but I also knew she had saved Topper's life after I had left him for dead. That implied a connection between them beyond what I had observed or been told. It was a coldhearted way to put it to her, but I had used people in worse ways when I was an Army spook. But not much worse. And never this personal.

I must have sounded more unhinged than callous, because she talked to me the way volunteers do on suicide prevention hotlines. She said that maybe she did know people, or people who knew people, but that the person I really wanted to call was William. Then her tone hardened a little. She said the other thing was that she didn't ever want any dealings with Topper's "crowd of creeps" again, and anyway, even if they could burn Rose's remains they'd probably try to double-cross me or blackmail me somehow. So she wouldn't be contacting any of them.

I could hear her take some breaths and then her voice was back in angel mode and she said that on the other hand, the Chief was a good man. One of the best. She said I could trust him, but I already knew that. The way she said it made me wonder if she knew more about my stay with him than I'd told her myself. I hoped it hadn't come from Topper. Luckily I felt the crazy train pulling out of the station and chased the paranoia out of my head instantly. After all, she could hang up on me at will.

I said William would be perfect, if he could handle it. Or would handle it. She said she had gotten to know him over the years and that he some-times did things for money so that he could keep his spiritual work going. His line was, "Sometimes it's bad for good, you know?" She said she'd call him for me. That he'd be calling me right away after that and to keep my cell turned on.

We talked a few more minutes. She said she was leaving Savannah soon and it was lucky I caught her. I agreed it was, and asked if I might stop by on my way back to New Orleans, if it worked out that way. She said to let her know. Before we hung up she said to remember that William knew her as "Simone," that most people still did.

A few seconds later I had to hit the brakes for an overweight logging truck without tail lights in the wrong lane. I heard Rose's body bag shift against the back of the seat but it didn't wake her mom.

~~~

58

The sun came full up at the Atlanta outskirts and all but blinded me in the early rush hour traffic. On the plus side, the incoming lanes flowed well enough and I was at Elle's house in what seemed like no time. By the clock, a little before seven. I wondered if Lenora was up, never having gotten around to calling her from the road with my ETA. I got my answer when she flew out the door and down the porch to my Jeep before I could even turn off the engine. She could see Elle through the back window and had the rear door open before I could get out from my own. Elle was still in deep sleep, knotted up in the Mexican blanket. I said, "Hello, Lenora, I'm so sorry," but she didn't answer. Her expression was memorable.

I didn't have to ask what to do next so I stretched to loosen my back and helped Elle out of the rear seat, much as I had at all the pit stops. We were getting pretty good at it. But this time she couldn't stand. I took her in my arms and carried her up the porch and into the house. She awoke as I climbed the stairs, looked at me woozily, almost sensually, and I knew she had no idea where she was. Lenora squeezed beside us and held Elle's hand as we ascended. She said some things like I am so glad to see you, dear Ellie and you're safe now and so on, but Elle had zoned out again. She may have smiled, which seemed only to make Lenora angrier at me.

I got Elle into her room and eased her onto her bed. Lenora all but shooed me away while she adjusted Elle's head on a pillow and looked at the bulge from the compress on her leg. Then at me. I told her we'd seen a doctor and she'd had a pint of blood and was basically okay. She took the information with something like a professional sneer, as if it were being forced into her head, and didn't so much as ask a question about changing the compress. She pulled a cotton blanket up over Elle and told me to get out and wait outside and she'd call me when I was needed.

I took a chair on the porch. Maybe an hour passed. I almost dozed off in the morning sun. I could've used some coffee but I didn't want to ask, or go back in the house to make it myself. I went to the Jeep and got out Elle's suitcase and shoes and bags, all that we'd brought from Dallas, and arranged them on the porch. Except that one thing.

I sat in the sun a little longer. I wondered if decomposition would accelerate with the Georgia heat and without the Detroit a/c. I revisited my calculations about how long it would take. I wondered who would be the first to smell it. I was in a bad place in my head. I didn't wonder about that.

Lenora finally summoned me and I carried everything in. Elle had been cleaned up. She was wearing a green silk nightgown, sitting up against the backboard of her bed. She looked at me but said nothing. Then her head dropped down like she had narcolepsy. She raised it again, and then it dropped again. I knew exactly how that felt.

Lenora said she had called Dr. Finn, who would be arriving at any moment. Lenora knew him from Morehouse. She was plugged into a circle of colleagues who could work with standard procedures or clandestine. Sounded like AK. Turned out Dr. Finn knew of Elle anyway. He could handle the re-stitching and recovery and more blood if needed with no problem and no questions asked. Lenora said it was pricey, and looked at me like that was my fault, too. But price was no longer an issue for Elle. Not much of anything was.

I told Lenora I would be leaving but just then Elle woke up again. This time I could see her expression and her jaw set like she was determined to kick out of the painkillers. She adjusted herself on the bed as best she could and told me to bring in the suitcase. Her voice was less slurred than I expected. I pointed to it sitting on the armchair next to her bed.

Her eyes flashed with the power and brevity of lightning and she told me to take out whatever I thought I needed, or Red needed. For expenses. I said we didn't need any. She said to take something, dammit Jack, that this was a business matter and she wanted it to be finished. So I had to I say again I couldn't take the money. She stared at me, like the energy blast was peaking.

Lenora stepped in. She dropped the suitcase at the foot of the bed. She clicked the latches and when it opened it really was crammed with money. All in bundles of $10,000. Elle said $100,000 for me, and the same for

Red. Lenora shook her head and pulled out enough packets to make ten in one pile and ten in another, dropping them across the bedspread like dog shit needing to be scooped up. She was even more insistent than Elle that I take the money and run. Or die. She didn't actually say that, or that my services were no longer required, but I knew what she meant.

While I was looking, Elle pulled off the covers off two of her pillows and tossed them to me. "Go," she said. "Go."

I caught them like toys in a game and bagged up the bills. I tried to look her in the eye the entire time, and she returned the look full tilt, but it was as if she didn't see me at all. I knotted the tops of the bags and turned to go.

"Stop. Wait," she said. Then, to Lenora, "Auntie, we need a moment. Please."

Lenora looked at her, at me. "I don't think that's a good idea."

"I'm okay. I need to talk to Jack. Please."

Lenora looked at me even uglier than previously. Then, to Elle, "I'll go downstairs and get you some water, some juice."

"Thank you."

More stink eye from Lenora as she left the room. Elle pointed to the door and I shut it. We waited for the clumping down the stairs to finish.

"I know Rose is in the Jeep. You know that."

I sat on the bed. I wanted to make sure we could see each other clearly. I took her hand. She started to pull it away, but didn't.

"What are you going to do?"

"I'm working on it."

"I'm not mad. It's what I asked you to do."

"The money just now?"

"I mean that but not the way I said it. I keep zoning in and out."

"It's okay. But I still don't want it . . ."

" . . . Just take it, please. That's not what I want to talk about."

"About Rose. Dealing with it."

"I want what I said. The other thing."

"I know."

"Didn't Red say he could do it? And you wouldn't let him? I only half-heard you back . . ." Her voice drifted away with her eyes.

"We worked it out. That's why we brought her with us. Rose."

"Shit." She dropped my hand and reached for her leg after leaning forward on it too much.

"It'll hurt for awhile. We just need to get you to a real doctor. Today."

"Lenora will take care of that."

"I know."

"But not Rose."

"No. It would just jam everything up. I already told her Red was handling it. We should leave it that way."

"I love Auntie, but you do this, Jack. You promised."

"I am."

"That's what I wanted to tell you." She reached for my hand again, but winced at the movement and lay back against the pillows.

"I already called William," I said. Technically, that was half true.

Her eyes widened to saucers again. Moisture in them. "Then it will all be okay."

"It will."

"One more notch for terrible mom."

"We've brought her all this way. It's almost done now."

"I mean not as terrible a mom as if I'd shot my only daughter."

"Stop saying that."

"You promised." Her words were starting to slur again and her eyes were headed back to dreamland.

I touched her wounded leg, gently.

She snapped to. "Shit, Jack."

"Sorry, sorry. I need to go. I want you to be awake until I do."

"Don't do that again."

"I won't. I have to go now, Elle."

"Oh, Jack . . ." She hit the edge of almost losing it, but stopped short. All things considered, it was a hell of an accomplishment. I can't say I'd managed the same handling the flash memory of Ronnie.

"I'll take care of it."

"I love you."

"I love you, too."

Sad words. Because true. Because pointless.

"Go," she said. "Go."

"Lenora?"

"I'll take care of her. Now go."

I leaned forward to kiss her, and did, but on the forehead. She touched my cheek with her fingers. It was our goodbye.

THE LONG WALK DOWNSTAIRS took me past a glaring and silent Lenora and out the front door. I backed out of the driveway and sped away, catching a little rubber for good measure. For stupidity. For anguish. A dark gray sedan passed me on the next street headed in Elle's direction. I thought it might be Dr. Finn. At least he looked like a doctor.

I took streets and roads and highways vaguely in the direction of Savannah and Beaufort. To say I had lost touch with the reality and perils of sojourning through the Deep South on something between a doomed rescue mission and a righteous killing spree would be an understatement. And I wasn't done. If for some reason William couldn't take care of Rose, I'd have to keep the body until a backup crew that Red knew in Atlanta could meet me somewhere, somehow. I didn't want to have to make that call. Red wouldn't gloat that he had been right. It wasn't that kind of thing. It was the kind of thing that didn't need any more goat-fucks.

At some point, I saw the light blinking on my cell and realized I had a voicemail. William had left a message when I was inside with Elle. He said Simone had called him, told him what I needed. He could do it, no problem. He hoped I was well. He said to call him by 9 a.m., that arrangements might be a little different than usual.

~~~

59

I was late with the callback, but I wanted to clear the extended rush-hour traffic. I shouldn't have put it off. By then I had merged onto I-20, the fastest route to Beaufort, and to William's farm. Thinking that's where I would be going. Now I had to change course, drop down on a state highway to get to I-16, which took me directly into Savannah. I was going to Brick's.

"Thing is, lots of rumors going on about Topper," William said. "People know I did some work for him in the past, so a white man with Louisiana plates showing up at my farm right now might get attention."

"Even just for a delivery?" Red would have cuffed me. William held his reply a moment.

"It's more like you've been here before. And not that long ago."

"You're being watched?"

"Remember this is country. Out here people know who comes and goes. It's just that way. Especially they know when a white man visits a black man who's running an African religion business. You know how people think."

"Didn't mean to sound stupid."

"I just want to play it safe."

"So can we do this?" I hated to even ask.

"That's not what I mean."

I waited a moment, accelerating into the passing lane. "Okay. Good. I'm just, you know . . . I have a body in the back of my Jeep going into the third day now."

"It's all good, man. Look, just go to Simone's. She knows you'll be there. It's all set up."

"What, I mean, how?"

"One of my friends will meet you. I trust him completely. You'll give him the body. He'll bring it here. You'll never even be in South Carolina."

I hadn't expected any kind of help like this. Probably it was the exhaustion, but I felt my eyes water up. "That would be about perfect. I didn't want to put you out that much."

"You're not. This is how I stay in business, you know?"

"When you say Simone"—I almost said Brick—"knows I'll be there, you mean it's because you've set it up with her, right?"

"Right."

"Okay. I didn't know if I needed to call her."

"You do. Tell her the time. Then tell me or she can call and tell me."

"Are you coming with your friend?"

"No, no. That would kind of defeat the whole point."

"And you can handle this sort of thing at your farm?"

"It's not like a professional operation, but, yeah, I have a setup back in the woods where I can do a burn. Only it's with real caring. We bless the girl, we pray for her spirit, we watch over everything until it's done and then we gather up the ashes and put them in an urn and sprinkle the urn with sacred water."

"You do this a lot?"

"No. Just mostly with people in the faith. They come through Alafia or maybe just heard of me through the grapevine. I just have to be careful. State thinks you need a license to return bodies to the creator and the elements. Me, I think the way they do it is a desecration. So I started doing this."

"Simone said you might have done some things for Topper. I have to ask."

"I wouldn't lie. And yes. All he ever wanted was some body parts burned up. He didn't want any ashes. But I burned them with respect anyway and took them down to Hunting Island and put them in the ocean. It's been a while."

"Okay."

"He paid good money, and it helped me build the barn and clear some of the land. I converted it from evil to good. After I learned more about what he did, though, I thought the evil was too strong to change. I mean, since you ask."

I thought on it. The Buddhists say when you are ready for a teacher, the teacher appears. I had dual tutelage: Buddha in one ear, William in the other. Had I not just returned from my own personal killing fields I might have felt blessed.

"It's fine," I said. "I'm extremely grateful."

"I'll take care of Elle's daughter."

"I told Elle I'd been in touch with you. She was glad."

He was silent for a beat. "That's good."

"And you can get the ashes to her in Atlanta?"

"Of course. Tomorrow, maybe."

"So you'll be calling her."

"I will."

"That's best."

"Does Lenora know?"

"No."

"Seems like she would."

"She will. But Elle wanted me to get this done. Lenora would complicate it."

He paused a moment. "She's right."

"And Elle is still not thinking straight from everything. But she'll tell her aunt when she thinks the time is right."

He paused again. "Actually, Lenora already knows."

"What?"

"Nobody has to tell her."

"Shit."

"It's okay. It'll work out. It's the way their family is. Even secrets aren't secrets. They all have second sight."

"Except Rose."

"She did, too."

"I don't know what any of this means, William."

"I know you've had a bad time, but you did what you had to. You found her daughter."

"Yeah, worked out perfectly."

"You found her. You brought her back. What happened along the way wasn't about you."

"Hhhnn."

"You need to think on that."

"Okay. Look, I should get on the phone to Brick." I said it before I knew. "I mean Simone."

"It's okay. I know all her names."

"I owe you again, Chief."

"We're good."

"Okay. Well, goodbye."

"I'll just say until we meet again. Because we will, Jack Prine. And you're always welcome."

"I'd like that."

"Until then."

MORE BILLBOARDS, TRAFFIC, WHITE lines, eighteen-wheelers, cars full of people whose arcs of life I would never cross. More coffee. One more execrable fast-food breakfast. And then I was in Savannah. Brick didn't live far from Topper's house, at least in the same part of town. I had called to let her know I'd be there by one, and then again now because I was a little early. I guess having a lighter load had let me go faster and use less gas. And as soon as that pathetic joke formed in my head I could only think of Rose lying in the same blood as her mother's at the house in Oak Cliff. And then of Ronnie. And for the smallest of split-seconds I almost lost it. But I had no time for that. I just drove. After a while I realized the headache I felt coming on was from gritting my teeth.

But that was good. I used the ache to make myself think of what I needed to find out from Brick, not keep churning up unsolvable nightmares. It's a blunt psychological mind trick, but it had worked for me many times in the past, especially in the Army and in the media. It was a zen thing, for that matter. Be in the present. There is no past, only the path to the future, which only exists as you tread it.

My present was that Rose was where she needed to be, and my past was that Ronnie was long beyond my reach. My path now was to find out what had gone down between Brick and Topper. The hanging out at Topper's restaurant. The hundred thousand that she loaned him. The fact that she had saved his life after I left him for dead. The fact that many people died because she did. That one of them was Rose. That Rose died the way she did.

I knew I'd never figure out Topper himself, because, as Brick had said, he was insane and full of drugs and whatever came of that state of mind couldn't be pinned down by ordinary analysis. Brick was different. My mind wouldn't let it go. Maybe I wanted something that would leave room for seeing her again. But it wasn't about desire. It was about math. Something didn't add up.

I slowed as I approached her house, a gray- and blue-trim bungalow that would've fit in perfectly in parts of LA. A white panel truck was parked at the curb. A painted sign on the back doors said LOWCOUNTRY HANDY-MAN. YOU BROKE IT. LET ME FIX IT. A phone number underneath in red appeared to have been painted over a previous one.

I pulled behind it and stopped. A young black man in a denim work suit got out, gave me a good look. I did the same. We both passed inspection and he came forward to meet me halfway. I realized it was André, who had carried me out of Topper's butcher basement. He was wearing a thick leather tool belt and carrying a dappled length of painter's cloth. Nice touch, I thought. He didn't extend his hand, but simply nodded and asked did I have something for him to pick up.

I led him around to the back of the Jeep, opened the trunk lid, and pulled back the poncho. He looked at me, breathed out what sounded like a whisper of a blessing, and touched the bag gently. Then he dropped the cloth over it. We carried it to his truck and loaded it inside as if we were transferring a bulky antique.

"Okay then," he said.

"Thanks." I reached out to shake his hand.

"No problem."

"And for the other, too."

He just nodded again in acknowledgment, let go of my hand, and closed the panel doors. "Good luck, man," he said.

I gave him a thumbs-up, which was probably stupid but what words could I possibly have said?

He drove away. When I looked at Brick's house I could see her watching through a bay window overlooking a bed of purple and yellow flowers.

~~~

60

She was barefoot in cream-colored loose cotton slacks and a deep green scoop-neck shirt that tried but failed to rival her eyes. She'd cut her hair and swept it back in Elvis-style ducks, bangs in front. I had trouble remembering the real reason I wanted to see her. Or maybe it gave me a chance to forget why. Or maybe that was why I had come after all. Or maybe I was just running on fumes; it had been so long since I'd slept. Or sometimes you know what you're doing and you don't like it but you do it anyway because deep down inside something is wrong with you.

She pulled the door open wide so I could step inside.

"Hello, Jack."

We looked at each other an awkward moment or two and then she came forward, put her hands on my cheeks, and kissed me. Despite how I must have looked or smelled. "So," she said.

"So."

"Damn, Texas, you need a drink."

I tried to work up a smile, but I was badly disoriented and I'm pretty sure she had sensed that right away.

"And a shower. But we can get to that later."

She turned on the ball of her left foot and walked down the hall into her living room, a restrained mix of modern and Southern traditional. It looked comfortable and cold at the same time.

"Wine, beer, or whiskey?"

"Jack, if you have it," I said. "Daniel's. I mean, you know."

She'd converted an antique wooden table into a bar with all the right bottles, and lots of them. She poured a Jack, added water, which I was surprised she had remembered, and brought it to me. "Sit down," she said, indicating a dark leather couch. "Like I said, you look like hell."

I sat, and drank about half the glass.

She perched next to me. From the clearness of the liquid in her glass I assumed it was vodka.

"That's a lot on an empty stomach. Or have you eaten?"

"I ate. I'm not hungry."

She rolled her eyes. "Let me know if that changes."

"This is what I need right now, trust me."

She raised her glass to me and set it down. "So, you want to fill me in? I mean, about the trip. The trippy trip." She laughed. "Sometimes I can't help myself. You know, men like it when I flirt. They kind of expect it." She laughed again but then something else came across her face and she let it go.

I looked around the room. Photos of a younger Brick. Quite a babe. The years had been kind to her.

I let my head rest against the back of the couch, but not too much because I would fall asleep. "You want to talk about this?"

"That's not why you drove all the way here?"

"It is."

"Then, yes, Jack, I want to talk about it." She looked me over closely. "Do you need a doctor?"

I straightened up, drained my glass.

"I'll get you a refill."

"Okay."

"Then ask me what you want to. Whatever it is."

The whiskey was waking me up, although I knew it wouldn't last. I had already slumped back down, so I sat up straight again, cracking my neck, working my shoulders to get out the road cramps. I cradled the tumbler in my hands, looking down at the Mexican tile floor and expensive-looking woven rug.

I dug straight in, as I had in our phone call from the road, except this was the extended play version. What had happened since I last saw her, from Uncertain to West Texas to Dallas. Chased some people here, killed some people there, then some more here and there. And then Rose. When I finished, all the flirty muscles in her face had disappeared, as had most of the color. *Her face, at first just ghostly, turned a whiter shade of pale.*

She went to her bar, turning her back to me. Finally she reached for the Smirnoff and poured it. When she returned, she didn't sit next to me on the couch, but on the two-cushion matching sofa next to it. She took a drink, put the glass on an end table. She didn't say anything. This was my party.

"So the thing is, I was going home. Just going home. I mean to New Orleans."

"Jack. Stop."

"No. I'm not done." I looked at the door. "And I may still keep going home tonight."

I'd never seen her look at me with caution before, but I was now.

"So I was going home and this thing kept coming back into my head. You know how things do that? Come into your head, uninvited? You're thinking one thing, like, I just killed the daughter of the woman I used to love, and what am I going to do now, and then this other thing comes in. Like this other place, this restaurant under all the Spanish moss, and this va-va-voom blond telling me about this freak that she knows . . . you know?"

She stiffened even further if that was possible.

"And then all this last business of killing daughters gives way to all these other killings, and then being tied up on this table waiting to get my dick chopped off and heart and eyes gouged out or whatever and then being at a table in this restaurant with this woman who knows this freak. Like, a lot knows him."

I took a major swallow of Jack. Brick didn't move, didn't even reach for her drink. She wasn't hiding, not running, just looking. Like she knew what was coming.

I stood, walked a little away, turned to face her.

"So the thing is, Ginger Simone Brick, I just can't get out of my head. How is it that you went back to Topper's house, after all that, and decided to . . ." I paused ". . . *save his fucking life*? I mean, how do you do that?"

Even from where I stood I could see the pupils grow dark inside the green, and then the lids lower into slits as her lips tightened. She stood and smoothed down the sides of her shirt with her hands. Then her lips curved into a narrow smile, not the friendly kind. I wasn't in the mood to play nice so I just let the question hang in the air.

She walked over to a window on the far side of the room where big windows opened onto her small back yard. She looked out. I could hear a heavy exhalation and saw her head shake. Then she turned and walked back to me.

A dozen or so feet away she stopped and looked at the bookshelf on another wall. "Behind that second row of books, about where Flannery O'Connor and Walker Percy are, there's a Smith & Wesson .38. I've actually used it. I can get to it before you can."

"What?"

"Is that what you came back for?"

My eyes locked on hers.

She took a step toward the bookshelf. "I mean, he's dead. Elena's dead. Rose is dead. I'm sort of the loose end in Savannah." She laughed like a horse snorts. "Maybe that's what you think of me anyway."

"I just want to know why you went back for him."

"I told you already. Curiosity. And money."

"No."

She moved closer to the hidden weapon, never taking her eyes from me. "This isn't what I mean. I only want to know why. Jesus, Brick."

"Don't Jesus me. We barely know each other and what we know isn't reassuring."

Neither of us moved. "I'll leave," I said. "You'll never see me again. I just have to know why. What was really between you and Topper?"

"You're jealous?" I could see that her right arm was trembling slightly and her face was in agony. But she wasn't going to give me a break.

So I gave her one. I put up my hands in a gesture of surrender, turned away, and returned to the couch. Leaned back against the thick padding. "Stop. I'm tired and I'm out of sorts and I'm running on nothing and whiskey."

She moved up behind me. Then she was in front of me, ramrod straight and staring through my bones. Never shifting her eyes, she reached down for my glass on the table. "This needs a refill. Mine, too. I'll get us a drink." Before she reached the bar she turned, held out my glass like a casual toast. "You want to know? I'll tell you."

I made a return pretend toast. "To us."

She got our drinks. The pours were generous. We both took long pulls when she came back. She stayed with the sofa instead of the couch. My head was definitely buzzing. She put her glass on an end table, let her head fall back, too. She studied the ceiling, then her gaze shifted to the back yard, around the room, around the framed photos of her youth and her travels.

I followed her line of sight. It occurred to me that there was nothing in the photos or ornaments that resembled family.

~~~

61

"It's like this, cowboy," she said after a while. Her breasts rose and fell under the shirt as she breathed and she picked me off for looking at them. "When your eyes get tired," she said.

I changed my view to scanning the bookshelf.

"A long time ago, I mean back in the late eighties, when the music was godawful and the recession was going on and everything just seemed drugged out and superficial to the core, that's about when I first met Topper." She crossed her legs to sit like a Buddha statue, looking straight ahead. A smile flickered across her face. "He was different then. I mean a little. Before long I was practically living at his place and he was opening his first restaurant in Savannah, up by the art school, but he didn't have the knack and it folded. Over the years I was with a PR agency and then a hotel and then some developers. Topper tried a bar and I took a little career break and got involved managing that—he's always been terrible at business. That would fold, too, but I wasn't around. I mean I almost wasn't around, period. Something was wrong with a kidney. Not cancer, something else. It was just closing down."

She paused for another long drink. The sunset light from the window was catching her with disconcerting splendor.

"So I told him about it. By then he'd been getting into what would become his true calling—running a drug ring for rich people, which also let him get into real estate deals, which also let him launder money and pick up a fair amount of money just doing that. For a while. And that's when he started sampling his own wares. I mean he'd been doing the normal stuff, weed and coke, but he got into other things and became very much a home chemist, always experimenting. On himself and others. But I digress."

I leaned forward for my glass. She adjusted her body a little. She was trying to decide where to go with the rest of it.

"Long story short, I needed a kidney transplant and the list was too long. So one day to my surprise I got a call from a doctor saying they had a kidney for me and to show up the next day in Atlanta. I tried to find out what happened but all he said was that they had found a donor and it was taken care of. So I asked Topper and he said he'd made some calls and someone owed him a favor and it was his gift to the woman he loved."

Again her facial expression went through several changes.

"So, and I'm trying to spare all the details, but basically I got the new kidney, and it's a doozy, never a problem at all. So he saved my life. Straight up. No way around it. So that kept us together maybe another year and by then he'd cheated on me several times and was moving into the kind of person you came across. But honestly, there was a time when he was merely eccentric, not pathologically psychotic."

She stared out at something no one else could see.

"So you owed him."

Long pause. She turned toward me. "So here's the main thing. There's no simple way to put this. Getting the kidney opened the door for him to the whole body parts business. Quite a black market, as it turns out, and often pretty hooked up with selling drugs and rich people. In this case, very fucked-up rich people. Also rich drug lords and all their fun friends. I wasn't with him anymore but we did see each other a little over the years. He got crazier. A lot. I don't know how he put his restaurant together but he did, and got all the right sorts to go there. You know, you saw it."

"What do you mean by 'saw each other a little'?"

Her lips tightened. She shook her head slightly, then seemed to get a second wind. "What it sounds like, Jack. Jesus. Really?"

"I didn't mean . . ." I lied.

"Of course you did . . ." Now her eyes rolled and then that smile emerged that was completely indecipherable. "I can't say why. Truth is, I never really caught on with anyone else, and I was getting, you know, older. Sometimes I just needed to be with somebody. With him, it was no questions, no complications."

"Just tell me. That's why I'm here. I don't need the vague references. You know? I mean I knew this was a small town but not that small."

I knew my voice showed anger. Her voice sharpened to match. For the smallest fraction of a second, it was in the air that I might get thrown out after all. But she wanted to spill it as much as I wanted to hear it. I guess our eyes made a bitter pact to see it through.

"Small enough that people knew. The notoriety maybe even helped me a little when I also started selling real estate. But I did a lot better at it than he did and actually made some major bucks. Then I got a nice kicker when my dad passed away. He was a petroleum engineer. Good at finding oil. Bad at family. Bad at life in general. They found him naked and bloody on the balcony of a five-star in Macau." She looked off again. "He left me enough so I wouldn't have to work if I didn't want to."

"I see."

"Probably you don't. Couple more things happened. I made Topper two loans, one to get that place up in South Carolina where he nearly chopped you up, and the other for his restaurant."

"You said he owed you."

"He did. But that wasn't really why I asked you to come to this little meeting, right?"

I smiled, a little.

"You want the full confession? That'll make you feel all better going to all the trouble to come and see me? Fuckin' A. Here it is all wrapped up with a noose. Topper kept selling the drugs, and then he got mixed up with these Texas freaks, whom I believe you met . . . and killed . . . but also with some really strange people. I never knew who they were. But they had a constant demand for organ transplants and cadavers. Oh, yeah, and they also fed into some kind of crowd in Miami with an appetite, sorry, for bodies and bones. Especially skulls. Damn they were always wanting skulls. Did you know there's a way to soak them in acid so everything falls off and then you can clean them and dry them so they're all pretty? So that's what he started doing back there on his little wooded estate."

She looked away.

"This keeps circling back to my original question."

"Wait for it, handsome."

"Come on. You're telling me you were a part of all that?"

"I'm telling you just that."

"You helped him butcher people?"

"I did not. But I knew what he was doing and I never said anything." She laughed. "Is that weird or what?"

"Because he owed you money?"

She looked up at the ceiling. "No, goddamit Jack. Because if I didn't play nice with him I would have been one of his sales items." She flicked her hand across her chest. "Any idea what these would be worth to help some drug king get a hard-on? Shit, I mean you think tiger balls are worth something?"

She sat back, stretched her legs. Some time passed where all we did was finish our drinks, and then sit some more.

"Thing is," she finally said, "I went back to see him that morning because I was going to get my money or kill him."

"What?"

"I guess you got me going about everything."

"Jesus, Brick."

"But I got in there, and saw Elena dead on the floor, and him, and all that hot anger went cold inside. Like water dumped on a fire. You know? I finally saw it for what it was."

She leaned toward me. "He was just an animal, something that needed to go to the vet. And I did. I took him to the vet and they patched him up and on the way I got him to give me some money. The thing is he was so dead to me that nothing I did mattered one way or the other. But hey, you know, I got seventy-five grand for being a good fucking Samaritan . . ."

Her eyes were wet. Damned if she would cry. Instead, she sniffed, wiped her cheeks clean of any moisture, and picked up her empty glass. "So, what the fuck, how's that for a story, Mr. Retired TV Reporter with the battle scar on his cheek? I mean, you ran into some changes last week or two yourself, huh? Mr. Southern Fucking Revenge Killing Spree? Right?"

Her body was clearly shaking. I went over to the sofa, kneeled in front of her, took her hands, and held them tight as I could. She wouldn't look at me at first. Then she did.

"It's over," I said.

She breathed out through smirking lips, rolled her far-away eyes.

"I'm sorry. You didn't have to say any of that," I said.

She leaned forward and kissed me. Not sexually. More as just a simple connection with another human being. As if she hadn't had that connection in so long she had forgotten. As if she didn't believe she'd ever have it again. Or deserved to.

"No, I did," she said.

I turned to sit with my back against the sofa and her legs. I felt her hand atop my head, and across my cheek, like you'd touch a child. We stayed like that a little longer until I felt myself almost fall asleep. I stretched my legs and looked back at her. She was still focused on a universe far beyond ordinary telescopic technology.

"You must be tired. I know I am."

"I can go now," I said. "It's still early. I can drive."

"Stay. Then go."

She fixed me a sandwich and gave me some water and put me in the shower and went out to my Jeep to bring in my bag so I could change clothes. If she smelled anything in the SUV she didn't say. Or maybe there wasn't any scent. It had seemed to get thicker in the air around me all the way to Georgia. I asked her if she'd seen or read anything about Topper, specifically his demise, and she said no, just some gossip, but there was always that about him. I think we talked a little more while sitting in her bed. I know we had a couple more drinks.

I woke up about four. She knew I would leave early and I knew she didn't want me to wake her. I don't know how long I'd been out but it was like emerging from a coma. She was sleeping on her back and I reached across to lightly caress her breasts, then down her stomach to feel the lush thickness of her hair and then the smoothness of her thighs. I remembered what we had done before falling asleep. She had held me to her, pushing her groin against mine, her chest against mine, her legs against mine, and her lips against mine and kissed me with that same sense of someone only seeking a human connection. "I will miss you, Jack Prine," she had whispered, and lay back on her pillow. Then came sleep.

I pulled on my shirt and jeans, gathered my things in dim light from the bathroom. I looked at her a last time. A lot of me wanted to stay. But more of me knew I couldn't.

~~~

62

I inhaled eggs and bacon and grits and three refills of coffee at a window booth in an all-night truck stop and was on the interstate out of Savannah just ahead of dawn. I fiddled endlessly with the radio before finding Tom Petty's "Refugee," and stayed with that station.

I planned to cut across to Columbus and then down to Mobile and so to New Orleans, but my mind wouldn't let go of where it had been and I ended up blasting past Macon and then was so close to Atlanta I decided to just take the loop around to Birmingham, and down to the Big Easy that way. It was only a little longer, but I didn't have any place to be and no deadline to be there.

I had just crossed into Alabama when my cell rang and startled me. I'd forgotten I even had a phone. Not a good sign of coherence. A man with a foreign accent thought I needed to "switch my service provider." I hung up, and then noticed I had two missed messages.

The first was from AK, his voice thick with something, maybe tequila or maybe anger. Maybe both. He wanted to know if Elle was okay, and for me to know that he'd found a safe home for Maria Christina, with some of his relatives. But "I'll damn sure be watching for the fucking duration."

He also said if he ever saw Red again he might kill him.

The second was from Red: "Call me goddammit as soon as you hear this. You're in New Orleans by now, right? Get yourself rested up or whatever and fucking come over here this week. Got some shit to go over."

I tapped in Red's digits first. There wasn't anything I could do about AK's anger, and I didn't want to talk with him if he was drunk anyway. Sometimes it took him a couple of days to get out of it. I didn't really want to talk to Red, either, but I knew I had to. For a start, I had the money from Elle. How much I owed him beyond that was impossible to quantify. But that wasn't the issue. The residue from Renaldo's place couldn't lie between us without permanent damage. We had to deal with it.

I got his voicemail. Phone tag had never worked with us so I just said everything went okay and that I had to be going through Biloxi sometime late afternoon, and sure, I'd come by his place. I said I'd call back when I got close enough to give him a time and get the address, which I reminded him he'd never given me. I said he could call me back before then if he wanted. He didn't.

The drive was long. Not as long as from Dallas to Atlanta, but close. And I was tired of being on the road. Especially the road I had chosen. I had to start thinking of it that way. It was the only way.

Except for the cities, this part of the road was mostly lush green farmland, big rivers, and tree-covered hills that could calm the most troubled soul or scare the wits out of the most innocent. For a change, nobody knew where I was. Nobody was wounded or dead in the back of the Jeep. Already Brick seemed a surreal memory, maybe even a dream.

I thought back to looking at myself in her bathroom mirror before showering and climbing into her bed. Being startled at the man with the bloodshot eyes in the dark circles and three-day-old stubble and pale complexion and wondering how I could possibly expect anyone to want to fuck me. Or touch me. And then I wondered how I smelled, and I sniffed against my arm and held my palm to my mouth to smell my own breath and then I put my hands on the sink. There was a tube of Crest along the side, so I smeared some of that across my teeth and splashed my face. I looked at the crease on my arm. The water had loosened the scab but it was healing normally. Then I was tired of looking at myself. When I went to her, she touched the wound and I just said it was okay. She looked about as deeply into my eyes as anyone ever had and kissed me without saying anything.

There's no way to know what makes one person want another. Whatever made us want each other at that particular time was just at the outer reaches of what I could consider without also thinking of being strapped down on a table in South Carolina waiting for Topper and a redneck to slice me into prime chunks for a market of madmen. Now I was alone, crossing a river outside Mobile, just another killer in Alabama.

~~~

63

I hit Biloxi just past three, after stopping for gas in Ocean Springs and trying Red. He answered this time, like I was an old fishing buddy dropping by. It caught me off guard. He told me how to find his house, just past the casinos and before Gulfport. He said it would be easy to spot—dark green with a new tin roof, on high stilts. About two football fields back from the road, the vacant land in front all scrub brush and live oak. I should watch for an upturned rusty plow in the front of the house, which the previous owner had considered some kind of work of art and Red hadn't quite decided about. "It was you got me into all this art appreciation shit, Shakespeare, fuck you very much," he said, and then hung up.

I got there and parked next to the plow. He was standing on the wrap-around wooden porch above the stilts. Hawaiian shirt and shorts, leather sandals. It would have been possible to consider him another beach bum refugee from New Jersey and maybe that was what he wanted.

I got out, waved. I was actually surprised to see him up and about. Barely two days since he'd taken a bullet to his side. I guess it was like he said, looked worse than it was. He held up a beer bottle and tossed his head in the direction of the stairs. I vaguely remembered the first time we'd met, atop an observation tower in the Delta at Rosedale just before he gave me a beating for shooting some of the family's help.

When I got up to the porch I didn't know what to do but he offered a hand and I took it and he shook it.

"Good to see you," I said.

"You look like shit. There's a beer over in the cooler."

"I'm okay."

"No you're not. Get a beer."

"And you?" I found myself a Dos Equis.

He pulled up his shirt. The stitches were red and raw but he'd been taken care of. "Yours?"

"I fixed mine with Band-Aids and peroxide. If I have a scar it'll be cute. Not sexy like yours."

He pointed to a couple of deck chairs, one red, one green. "Clouds are keeping the sun away. Might storm up later. Breezy enough to be outside. Let's sit."

"It's okay. Heat feels good after being in the car all day."

"Breeze helps, though."

"Sure." It occurred to me he was a little house-proud. "Nice place. Great view."

He looked out, nodding. "I guess that was part of the reason I bought it. Other was what will make that view go away. Next five years they're gonna develop the hell out of this stretch, all the way over to Pass Christian. That vacant lot and this one with the house—I bought 'em both—easily will go for a couple mil. So I'm told."

"You're into real estate now?"

"Not really. Just this."

He adjusted himself in his chair, favoring his left side a little. The wood was hot from the sun.

I did the same. We were quiet a moment.

"Motherfucker," I said.

"Motherfucker."

"So you wanted to talk?"

"You in a rush?"

"No."

"Seen anything in the papers or TV? Abilene especially?"

"Nothing yet. I need to check the Dallas paper. You?"

"Nah. Sooner or later somebody'll go in there, though."

"Yeah."

"Then we'll see. You're the TV guy. What'll happen?"

"Depends on what the cops let them see. Might blow over, might turn into something for a few days. Then no one will give a shit."

"Still, we got to play it cool. One of the reasons I wanted to see you."

"Yeah?"

"Not a big deal. You know, precautions. That kind of shit."

"Whaddya wanna know?"

"It ain't like that," he said.

"Never mind." I took a long sip. He did, too.

"So fuck you going anyway? I figured you'd be holed up at least a day or two once you got home. You headed back to Atlanta already?"

I looked at the label on my bottle and then out at the beach on the other side of the highway. Same beach I'd been on when Ronnie showed up.

"No and no."

He beheld the same view. "Get it out. What the fuck happened after Dallas?"

I told him. It took the rest of my beer.

He listened without interrupting, neither approving nor disapproving.

"You were goddam lucky."

"Maybe."

"Maybe?"

"You'll think this is weird, but I think I took Rose with me for a reason. Maybe the reason was getting her to William. You know, instead of to the bottom of the Gulf."

He studied me like I had finally gone off the deep end myself.

"I gotta tell you, I wasn't sure I'd ever see you again."

"But here I am."

"Here you are."

We clinked bottles. We looked out at the Gulf some more. That's what it was there for.

"What do you see happening with Elle now?"

"I don't know. She barely talked to me."

"She should be damn glad what you did."

"Doesn't matter. It was her daughter."

"Hell of a thing."

"Hell of a thing."

He shifted a little to look at me full on. "What about you?"

"Pretty much as you see." I laughed a little.

"Walking wounded."

"You couldn't have known Rose worked for the cartel. I mean, no one did. Never would have, maybe."

"Lucky I butted in, huh?"

"All I know is what the Francosis told me. Who by the way are once again impressed with your talent for digging up shit they didn't even know was buried. I mean for a wild card and a civilian, kudos don't get much better from them."

He chuckled oddly, stopped, got up and grabbed two more beers. The coldness felt good sliding down.

"I'll never see Elle again," I said, not really to him.

"You never know."

"I know."

"If you say."

"Makes seeing Brick seem even stranger than it was."

"You did what you did. Don't beat yourself up. Trust me on that." He eyed me closely.

I stood, walked to the porch railing. I could see why he liked the place. A few minutes passed. He leaned against the railing next to me.

"We got her back. We just didn't know what we got," he said.

"Yeah."

"Everyone was a bad guy, Rose included."

"I didn't mind taking out the dealers. I think I liked it." I shot him a quick side glance but he was watching the water.

"They were all dealers."

I moved down the railing a few steps. Nobody talked. It was okay. My fingers cramped and I realized I was putting a death grip on the wood.

"And Rose, she tried to kill her own mother," he said.

Something opaque, dark as a line of tornado clouds, obscured my vision of the Gulf and then it passed.

"Still, I killed her."

"We both did."

I nodded like I was listening, but my mind zipped into the void. It said you can't save the dead, even when they're still alive. That's the deal with the universe.

I zoned back in and looked at Red. He was laboring with something himself. I was standing there making it all about me but it wasn't. We had to talk about it, now, or we never would.

"I understand why you made the call about those girls," I said. "You were on the family dime. The dime got dropped into a bad slot. You did what you had to do."

"It is what it is. All this is what it is."

"I get it."

"Do you?"

"Yeah, only in his case, *it* was AK's friend. Hell, they did to Renaldo what Topper might've done to me."

"Let it go."

"AK's never going to let it go. I called him and he's drinking and pissed off."

"Meaning?"

"Meaning nothing. And god knows where those girls are."

"We went over that."

"Only I keep thinking about it. Like with my daughter. You know. You can't control your memories. They just come at you."

"You have to."

I nodded. This was all going way down in the deep freeze until I could take it out years later and see the monster full size and dead and cold.

He looked out somewhere, the way AK sometimes did. "You know?"

It was so quiet at his place. I liked it. It seemed like nowhere. "I might."

"There it is."

"Fucking A."

"Fucking A."

"There's no right thing, you know."

"I used to think there was."

"You're not that guy anymore. None of us are."

Movies were playing in both our heads, but it was a multiplex and we couldn't share screens.

He stayed at the rail, while I went for the beers.

~~~

64

"You can drive to the city with a few brews in you?"

"Sure."

"And that's where you're going? I mean not back to Savannah or anything really brilliant like that again."

"Home sweet home for me."

"I'll drop by sometime, later on."

He clinked his bottle against mine.

"I meant to say a minute ago, but I got distracted. I brought something for you from Elle. Come with me down to the Jeep."

He asked what it was and I said he'd have to see it himself. It wasn't a secret, just hard to explain until he saw it.

We went down the wooden staircase.

"Still have that Colt from Dallas?" he asked as we walked along.

"I do."

"Leave it with me. That's something I meant to say earlier. Except for the distraction." He looked at me with a mild eye-roll. "Another reason I wanted you to come by soon as you could."

"I was going to drop it in the Gulf or maybe the river."

"Let me handle it. You never used that Remington, right?"

"Right.

"Okay."

We stopped at the back of the Jeep and I opened the hatch. I reached in for the bag with the pistol and gave it to him.

"So what was the thing from Elle? I already got the snubnose from back there."

I reached in for one of the pillowcases. I undid the knot and held it open so he could see inside. "It's yours."

He looked at the piles of money inside a long time, then at me.

"What the hell?"

"That other one right there, it's for me. Same thing. A hundred thou."

"Fuck you say."

"I didn't want it. Elle insisted. So did Lenora. It's not a gift. More a stay-the-fuck-away-from-me."

"Damn."

"Lenora said to take the money and get out. Never come back."

"Son of a bitch. Both of us?"

"Yeah. Me especially."

"And you took it."

"Wasn't much choice."

"Son of a bitch."

"Well . . ."

"This wasn't a job."

"I know. But there it is."

The late sun put his red-and-black beard in a good light. He didn't look like a person who had just gone through a river of blood from Georgia to Texas. Then his brow furrowed and he looked exactly like that person. "Goddam."

"Yeah."

I tied up the pillowcase again and handed it to him. He felt the heft, shook his head again. "Goddam, Jack." Then he pushed it back to me. "Keep it."

I pushed it right back to him.

He put his hands into fists and refused it.

I dropped it on the ground. We stared at it like it was radioactive. He kicked it lightly, looked off into the tree line, then at me.

"You might go back to Texas sometime?"

"Most likely."

"Give it to AK."

He bent down, picked up the money, tossed it into the Jeep. "That girl, the one he found. He took her back to his family, something like that, right?"

"Something like that."

"Well maybe she needs things. Kids are expensive."

"She's all grown up."

"Still."

"Yeah, still."

"You think he'd take it?"

I knew what he meant.

"I do."

"Okay then."

"Hell, there might be lots of girls like that one, need some things to get back on their feet."

"Probably there are." I pushed his pillowcase and mine back under the poncho. "So they'll need all of it."

"Yeah, probably they will."

I pulled down the trunk hatch. Red walked a few steps toward his house. Then stopped, turned. "I liked AK. I didn't want it that way."

"I know."

"Yeah." He turned back toward his house, calling out, "Watch for the cops up around Slidell." He started to wave goodbye but suddenly jerked his hand to his left side, and for the first time I noticed a limp.

It would have been nice to just stop somewhere across the highway and sit on the beach and get shit-faced watching the Gulf slide into a stormy night. But I'd done that.

~~~

65

June rolled into July and it just got hotter. Nothing you could do about that. Rain helped. At some point in the South you just realize it will never be cool again and there you are, like you get a vote about it. That pretty much sums up how the weeks went.

Not at first. At first I was jumpy as the cat on Tennessee's tin roof. I woke up in the middle of the night, twice, packed up my bags and drove off in case someone was looking for me. First to Memphis for a few days. The second time over to Dauphin Island so I could stand in the Gulf somewhere that wasn't Biloxi.

I heard zero from Elle, which I expected. William phoned the day after I got home to let me know that he delivered the ashes as promised. He said Elle wanted them scattered in the Atlantic, because Rose was a child of the water. Elle and Lenora met him off Hunting Island at dawn. William assured me that they had been more at peace because he had handled it. He said I had "done the right thing." Not quite the way Red had put it. The phrase hung in my head for the next couple of days. It never found traction.

I took to calling Red every so often. First was to make sure the house in Dallas had been cleaned up right, if there'd been any blowback from the militia compound or from Uncertain, and just generally whether or not he'd heard anything about anyone looking for us. I bought the Dallas paper several times a week from a bookstore on Magazine and saw one story about finding bodies and burned-out buildings in West Texas. It said it looked like a drug deal and the feds and cops were investigating. But I never saw any follow-ups, although it was probably on the local TV stations. I called to tell Red and he said Po-Boy already called and said he'd see it on a cable channel, but only for one day. Nothing, ever, about Uncertain or Oak Cliff. Probably never would be. Red's hoods at least were good at clean-up.

He told me it was a wrap. Unless somebody ratted or talked too much it would "be like it never fucking happened." He said I needed to cut way back on the drinking. He said if I couldn't chill, I should probably leave the country for awhile. Not Mexico. Ever. Somewhere else. China, maybe, or Japan since I was "into all that weird Asian stuff." He didn't care. He just said I had to get better.

After the fourth or fifth time I called, he asked if I wanted him to drive over to the city and talk in person, or if I'd rather come over to his place and stay a few days. He said he was mostly just fishing and lying low. So he didn't need any trouble. I think there was just the hint of a warning—not really a threat—about my passing bouts of paranoia or anxiety or whatever they were. The phrase "suck it up, buddy," came up more than once. But I didn't go to his house, or have him come to mine.

In our last conversation he said he wanted me to get rid of the Cherokee, that we should've done it weeks ago but now with all my random trips and "mental condition" that we couldn't chance me getting pulled over or just ticketed for parking. He said to clean out all my personal things, except for the registration, and park the Jeep in front of my house. I asked if I should leave it unlocked with the keys inside and he laughed and said "they don't need no stinking keys." I was impressed that he made the reference and when I said so, he barked at me for acting like he was "some kind of illiterate redneck trash."

I parked the car on the curb and the next morning it was gone. Since I only carried liability I didn't get any insurance money, or hassle. Since it was New Orleans, I didn't even report it to the police. Since it was Red, I knew no one could ever track it.

I thought about getting a replacement right away, a vintage Mustang that my lawyer friend Ray Oubre had acquired, but I passed. I hadn't told Ray anything about going after Rose and didn't plan to. For his sake as much as mine. I figured it best not to do any business through him. Then I figured I didn't even want a car. I was tired of driving. I had cabs, and could rent something if I needed a longer trip for any reason. None came to mind. It felt better than I had expected, and New Orleans was a constant validation that not having a car is a good way to live.

ALTOGETHER IT TOOK A couple of months for me to drop the weight of what we had done—at least what I had done—or at least put it down. I walked around the town a lot, especially along the river levees, sometimes the Quarter or Audubon Park. My only conversations were with strangers I chanced to meet. I was okay for money, and with the insider trading investments probably always would be if I played it smart. I thought of calling Brick, but didn't. Then one night I did. Her phone was disconnected. If I were a betting man, I'd say she had left the country. And I had bet the farm.

After the calming came ennui. I don't know how else to describe it. I would think about Elle, and Rose, and Ronnie, and everything that happened. I never did go overseas like Red had suggested. Whatever I had to let go to get my life back I had to do in the same terrain in which it had become lost. I think that is the story of the South. It's why people stay. Or leave and return. But I didn't know if that meant staying in New Orleans.

AND THEN SHE WAS dead.

It was just after dusk and I was walking down Decatur, trying to decide where to eat. My cell was in my pocket. It rang. I pressed the button to answer. I put it to my ear. I said my name. I listened to a silence, and then a voice.

"It's Lenora, Jack. I'm just calling to tell you Elle is gone."

I said something like, "What?"

The voice said, "I'm just calling to tell you because she said so in the note. It said, 'Call Jack, tell him I'm sorry. I love him. But I can't anymore.' That's what the note said, so I'm calling you. Jack?"

"Yes."

"We found her this afternoon. I did. When I went over. Oh. Oh my god. You know she'd tried a month ago, with pills, but it didn't work and I thought she was going to make it. I prayed for her, I did sacrifices for her, talked to her through the spirit but then . . . well."

"How?"

"She had a gun, a .38 revolver. For protection, she said, because of the crime going on around the neighborhood and some of the places she had to go. You know, she'd never have wanted a gun before."

"I know."

"My God. That's the other thing on the note. It said, 'I want to know how Rose felt.'"

"Damn."

"She wanted me to tell you."

"I don't have words. I am so sorry. I tried to do everything I could—"

"Did you? I hope saying that makes you feel better."

"Lenora—"

"And now my beautiful niece is gone, and her daughter, and her brother, and her mother and father, even her half-brother. You remember Trey, right?"

"I know you're angry. I'm sorry. I don't know what to say."

"Doesn't matter. I'm just telling you because she wanted me to."

"Are there services? I mean do you know yet?"

"Don't come."

"Who will?"

"Not your problem. Everyone loved her. Her friends will be there. Family. A few others. Artula. You remember her, with HIV and the kids? Right. Also, Elle's leaving a lot of money to her."

"Of course I remember her. How is she?"

"Fine. The rest of Elle's inheritance will likely to go me. I mean without Rose or anyone else."

"Sure."

"I'm not going to spend it on myself. I just wanted you to know. Elle had things she believed in. I can help with that."

"It's none of my business."

"Right again. Just telling you so there won't ever be anything to talk about down the road. So it'll all be clear. Okay?"

"I'm so sorry."

"You and Red, you gave him that money, right?"

"I did."

"So we're clear with that, too. No bills to pay."

"He's giving it to those girls who'd gotten into the same mess as Rose, so they could get their lives back. Elle probably told you about them."

"Elle told me everything."

"I'll be helping them, too."

I could hear her mind trying to work that out.

"I see. Well, good then. Good from bad."

"William says that."

"I can hear noise around you. You in the street somewhere?"

"In the Quarter. I was walking."

"Well, keep walking. I'll get off the phone now. It was her last wish in that note."

I could hear something in her voice that wanted to cry but would never, in my presence. I didn't think it fair that she hated me, but I knew it was justified.

"Goodbye, Jack Prine."

"Goodbye. I'm so very—"

She hung up.

I was only a few blocks from Napoleon's. No longer any desire to eat, but I did need a bar and that's where I went. I ordered a Pimm's Cup. I sat at a table near the one where I'd first seen her that afternoon when she walked into my life with an aura and beauty so powerful I knew I was changed forever. Just not like this.

I HAD MY OWN wake, and it went on for another day and then I just stopped. To revive myself, I ran along the river until I should have collapsed from overheating. When I got home, I knew that it no longer mattered where I was, what I did, when I did it. I couldn't tell if time started when I met Elle, or found her brother in the street, or if it started when I met Annalisa or when Ronnie was born or when I was born, or when Topper or Brick or Rose or Elle or their parents were born or died or toiled and careened into others who careened into others.

I couldn't pick a time when Red had to turn in the girls to the cartel or when I had to shoot Rose or why any of that had happened because as the Buddha said there is no beginning or end, just the thread of karma, and it connects everything, the hottest of pursuits and the coldest of trails. And it connects nothing, because if one step always leads to another and all matter is energy and nothing can be created nor destroyed then there is really no one separate thing.

And so every thing is also no thing, which is the dharma. You can't get to it by reason or rationality. Certainly not righteous intent. Karma is no fool. You can only hew to the path as you walk it, aware of each step. It will take you where it must, and only when you let go of what you think you are and find out who you really are. That's not exactly what Red meant when he told me to "let it go," but it was close enough. I guess he could be a teacher, too.

I slept like the dead that night and when I woke the next morning I called AK and told him I was bringing something to him. He asked when and I said in a few days. He said good, he wanted to see me. I said I might like to hang out awhile.

Elle's money was untouched in the pillowcases behind a loose board in my closet, and overdue for its rightful home. First I would take some to Chief William. An offering, a gesture—hardly a paid-in-full. That I could never do. If he hadn't saved me, almost none of this would have happened. Meaning that he, too, was in the karma that led to the bullet I put in Rose's arm, the ones that Red put in her chest, that Elle put in her wrist. We all were.

In the end, all that I had learned after a fortnight of killing in the name of a mother's love and righteous vengeance was that William's rule applied there, too. Good can come from bad. And the reverse. The trick is in the balance. I would never know where that lay amid what I had witnessed and wrought. But I did know one thing. Death and life are relentless. In their paths, people break. Hell, they disintegrate.

Don't miss the first installment of the Jack Prine series!

South, America

A Jack Prine Novel

ROD DAVIS

Author of Corina's Way, winner of the 2005 PEN/Southwest Fiction Award

Winner of the Inaugural
2000–2005 PEN/Southwest Fiction Award

Rod Davis's first work of literary fiction contains all the Creole spice, Southern spirit, and supernatural surprises of the Jack Prine series while focusing on a fascinating character: Reverend Corina Youngblood, a New Orleans minister and proprietor of a spiritual corner store. Trouble ensues when her ex-lover's plans to open a rival store are revealed and the chaplain of a local girl's school begins sending his troubled students Corina's way. Davis combines religion, voodoo, New Age philosophy, and good old-fashioned capitalism, greed, envy and a host of other unsavory motives in his entertaining first novel.

A spicy bouillabaisse, New Orleans-set. In the tradition of Flannery O' Connor or John Kennedy Toole: a welcome romp, told with traditional Southern charm. — KIRKUS REVIEWS

Davis captures the essence of New Orleans and nails the complicated racial and religious stew that makes up bayou culture. His witty, fast style perfectly complements the clever premise. — PUBLISHERS WEEKLY

Paperback • 268 pages • $24.95
978-1-60306-373-9

About NewSouth Books

Our company—founded by New York publisher Suzanne La Rosa and Alabama journalist Randall Williams—started in 2000 with a simple mission: to foster cultural change through the publication of socially conscious and impactful literature. Since then we have published hundreds of quality works of fiction, nonfiction, and poetry for both children and adults in the belief that good books can make a difference.

Enjoy this book?
Follow us online!

 facebook.com/newsouthbooks

 twitter.com/newsouthbooks

 instagram.com/newsouthbooksus

Sign up for our email newsletter to get news about our latest releases and events delivered straight to your inbox. Visit www.bit.ly/nsbinbox to sign up!